Books should be returned or renewed by the last date above. Renew by phone **03000 41 31 31** or online *www.kent.gov.uk/libs*

Libraries Registration & Archives

CUSTOMER SERVICE EXCELLENCE

Kent
County
Council
kent.gov.uk

First published in the UK in 2010 by Monarch Books
(a publishing imprint of Lion Hudson plc)
Wilkinson House, Jordan Hill Road, Oxford OX2 8DR, England
Tel: +44 (0)1865 302750 Fax: +44 (0)1865 302757
Email: monarch@lionhudson.com
www.lionhudson.com

Reprinted 2010.

ISBN 978 1 85424 968 5

Distributed by:
UK: Marston Book Services, PO Box 269, Abingdon, Oxon, OX14 4YN
USA: Kregel Publications, PO Box 2607, Grand Rapids, Michigan 49501

British Library Cataloguing Data
A catalogue record for this book is available from the British Library.

Printed and bound in the USA.

For this corruptible must put on incorruption,
and this mortal must put on immortality.
So when this corruptible shall have put on incorruption,
and this mortal shall have put on immortality,
then shall be brought to pass the saying that is written,
Death is swallowed up in victory.
O death, where is thy sting? O grave, where is thy victory?

1 CORINTHIANS 15:53–55

For the real life Father Dominic
and
For our own Dominic Ambrose

Every book is a team effort and I am so grateful to my team:
Father Lee Kenyon, for his research help;
Janet Benrey, my agent, for her faith in this work;
Tony Collins of Monarch Books for his vision;
Jan Greenough, editor extraordinaire, for her care and patience.

TIME LINE

AD

633   Oswald becomes king of Northumbria

635   Aidan establishes monastery on Lindisfarne

636   Cuthbert born

651   Cuthbert enters Melrose Monastery

654   Benedict Biscop's first journey to Rome

664   Synod of Whitby

673   Bede Born

687   Cuthbert dies

700   Lindisfarne Gospels produced

793   Danes sack Lindesfarne

797   Cuthbert's Folk begin journey with his body

883   Cuthbert's body rests in Chester-le-Street

925   Aethelstan crowned king over all England

995   Cuthbert's body taken to Durham

1083 Medieval cell re-established on Lindisfarne

1104 Cuthbert relics translated to new cathedral

1538 Durham Monastery dissolved by Henry VIII

1827 Cuthbert relics re-examined

Prologue

20 March, the year of our Lord 698
The Holy Isle of Lindisfarne

Hands folded, heads bowed, the black-robed brothers gathered in the front of their monastery church. The candles glowed beside the rough stone altar, casting flickering shadows on the hard-tamped earthen floor, marking the spot where their beloved Cuthbert had lain for eleven years.

Now the brothers must perform their solemn task. Eleven years was the prescribed period. Eleven years buried in the earth. Plenty of time for worms, rot and decay to have done their work. Plenty of time for the body of the holy Cuthbert to achieve the end of all mortal flesh. The prior, presiding in the absence of the abbot, who was on retreat, read out the solemn words, "Thou hast brought me into the dust of death."

And the brothers replied, "All flesh shall perish together, and man shall turn again unto dust."

The prior strengthened his voice, "The Lord knoweth our frame; he remembereth that we are dust."

Again the reply, "All flesh shall perish together, and man shall turn again unto dust."

"All are of the dust, and all turn to dust again. The dust shall return to the earth as it was: and the spirit shall return unto God who gave it."

"All flesh shall perish together, and man shall turn again unto dust."

Their brief litany ended, the brothers set about their task, digging in the consecrated ground. A few feet down their shovels hit the lid of the stone sarcophagus. They dropped to their knees and did the rest of the digging with their hands, brushing the dirt from the stone until they could grasp the handles on each end and lift the hewn stone box from the soil. Now the precious bones could be washed clean and enshrined above ground in order to be more accessible to the steady stream of pilgrims who made their way to Lindisfarne to pray at the holy man's grave.

The brothers knelt around the coffin while the prior led in a prayer of petition for rest to attend the soul of their dear departed. "May light perpetual shine upon him."

"And may he rise in Glory," the brotherhood replied. The prior sprinkled the coffin with holy water and blessed it with incense. Then, the two strongest brothers lifted the heavy stone lid.

All held their breath as stone grated on stone. The cloud of incense cleared, and the brotherhood crept forward to view the remains.

One brother fainted. Another shrieked. Several fell back, crossing themselves. The prior began babbling.

There before them was not the skeleton they had expected. The casket which had been buried in the earth, untouched, beside their own altar for eleven years held a fresh, fully intact body. Cuthbert looked more like a man who had been asleep for eleven hours than one who had been buried for eleven years. Even his vestments were clean and fresh, unstained by water, mud or worms.

One brother kilted his robe to enable him to run to the shore. The tide was in, so he was obliged to shout across the neck of water to the abbot, who was making retreat on tiny Hobthrush Island, just beyond the Holy Isle of Lindisfarne. The abbot paddled over in his tiny coracle and brought order to his astonished, agitated community.

He gave precise orders: dress the uncorrupted body in fresh vestments; place it, along with Cuthbert's portable altar and other holy objects, in the wooden coffin already prepared, and proceed with the elevation ceremony. God had spoken clearly.

Cuthbert was a saint.

Chapter 1

Felicity flung her history book against the wall. She wasn't studying for the priesthood to learn about ancient saints. She wanted to bring justice to this screwed up world. Children were starving in Africa, war was ravaging the Middle East, women everywhere were treated as inferiors. Even here in England—

She stopped her internal rant when she realized the crash of her book had obscured the knock at her door. Reluctantly she picked up the book, noting with satisfaction the smudge it had left on the wall, and went into the hall. Her groan wasn't entirely internal when she made out the black cassock and gray scapular of her caller through the glass panel of the door. She couldn't have been in less of a mood to see one of the long-faced monks who ran the College of the Transfiguration which she had chosen to attend in a moment of temporary insanity. She jerked the door open with a bang.

"Father Dominic!" Felicity was immediately sorry for her surly mood. Father Dominic was an entirely different matter. She was always happy to see him. "I didn't realize you were back from your pilgrimage." She held the door wide for him as he limped down the hall to her living room.

"Just returned, my dear. Just returned." As he spoke, he smiled with a twinkle in his eyes that belied his eighty-five years, but he couldn't quite suppress a small sigh as he lowered himself stiffly onto her sofa.

"I'll put the kettle on." Felicity turned toward her small kitchen. "I'm so sorry I don't have any scones."

"No, no. Just tea today—black."

She looked at him, puzzled for a moment, then remembered.

Oh, yes—today was Ash Wednesday. Solemn fast and all that. Felicity mentally rolled her eyes as she filled the kettle with water and clicked it on.

A few minutes later she filled his cup with a steaming, amber stream of his favorite Yorkshire Gold tea. A year or two ago, the Community had started serving a cheaper blend of tea, and donating the money saved to the African Children's Fund Father Dominic chaired—a worthy cause, but the tea was dreadful.

He raised his cup. "Oh, who could ask for more? The nectar of the gods." Still, she knew he was missing her scones, for which he sometimes provided little jars of quince jam from the Community kitchen. And at Christmas he had brought her favorite—slices of dark, rich fruit cake encased in marzipan an inch thick.

And yet today she wondered if he noticed what he was or wasn't eating at all, he was so animated with his plans for the major funding drive the Children's Fund was set to launch. "If one puts together abortion, infant mortality, AIDS and traumatic deaths, South Africa's daily death toll is appalling. Thousands die in a matter of months. If this were a war, such troop casualties would not be acceptable. The entire future of that nation—the whole continent, really—is at stake. They simply cannot afford to lose so many of their people—especially the children who are the future. If you don't maintain health and keep order, instability, violence and poverty tear a country apart."

Felicity nodded vigorously. *Yes, this was more like it. This was what she wanted to hear about, not some useless church history nonsense.* Father Dominic had spent his life working in South Africa, and today his passion made every word strike her heart. "And it isn't just South Africa, the rest of the continent looks to them—to us—for stability. If South Africa fails, millions of Africans will curse us—we who stand by and let it happen."

Still, there was hope; Dominic had talked to key people while on pilgrimage and had secured a source for a vast amount for the fund, although he didn't say what that source was. "This will be enough to build a first-rate hospital for AIDS babies in

Africa and fund a research wing for prevention and cure. There are good leaders in the government. There are people working for justice. If we can just give the people hope to hold on—" His eyes took on a dreamy look and a little smile played around his mouth. "Hope. That's what it's always been about. Through the centuries... At last, the treasure to be put to a truly worthy use..." He ducked his head and took a quick sip of tea. "Forgive me, I've said too much." He became suddenly thoughtful and lapsed into a most uncharacteristic silence. All Felicity's best efforts couldn't coax any more stories from him. Perhaps it was just the solemnity of the day, but Felicity did miss his stories—even the ones she had heard multiple times.

He drained his cup and set it down. "Ah, thank you my dear. Always a pleasure to be in your bright company. But now I must be getting back up the hill. Father Superior has asked me to do the ashing at mass, so I must prepare." He struggled to his feet, his broad-shouldered, once-muscular frame revealing gauntness under the weight of his black woolen cassock, as did the folds of flesh that hung beneath his square jaw.

"Oh, I almost forgot." He patted the canvas scrip which hung at his side from a strap slung across his chest. "I thought this might interest you." He held out a small parcel wrapped in brown paper and tied up with old-fashioned string. His hand shook ever so slightly as Felicity took it from him. The gesture was so endearing; his shyness charming; his eagerness humbling. If the circumstances had been vastly different, he could have been a suitor offering jewels to his beloved, or perhaps in an earlier age a troubadour bestowing an ode to his lady. And, oddly enough, Felicity had the distinct impression that he hadn't at all forgotten, but rather that delivering this small package had been the sole object of his visit. One might almost say his mission.

Felicity couldn't help herself. She stepped forward and kissed him on his cheek. "Thank you, Father."

Unexpectedly he placed his hands on each side of her forehead. "The grace of our Lord Jesus Christ, the love of God, and the fellowship of the Holy Spirit be with you always." She felt a warmth from his hands that infused her whole head and radiated toward her body, as if she were being bathed in warm oil. She almost fancied a faint scent of spice as he made the sign of the cross over her.

Moving inside a bubble of hushed awe, she held the door for him and he walked out slowly, as if reluctant to leave, stepping carefully to avoid limping. "I'll see you at mass, Father."

She shut the door behind him and turned to the window to watch his slow progress down the uneven sidewalk, his gray scapular blowing in the wind. Somehow she wanted to call out to him, to cling to the moment, but already it was passing, the normality of the day moving in on a holy moment. Yet even as she turned away from the window, the warmth of his touch remained on her head. She turned back one last time, holding her hand out instinctively – but he'd gone. Only a fleeting shadow brushed the corner of her eye. She shivered.

"Right. Back to the real world." Felicity spoke aloud to make herself focus. She looked longingly at the small brown package in her hand. It felt like a book. A very slim volume. Had Father D found a publisher for his poetry? Her fingers plucked at the string. No. If this was a collection of her friend's poetry, perusing it must not be rushed. Reading it would be her treat when she finished the work she had set for herself for the day. Lectures had been cancelled to mark the solemnity, but essays would still be due when they were due. With a sigh she slipped the gift into one of the copious patch pockets of her skirt, and returned to the tome on the Anglo-Saxon church Father Antony had assigned, forcing herself to concentrate on its obscure irrelevancies.

That had been the hardest thing she had found about adjusting to her first year at theological college—the constant pressure of work, the lack of time to pursue her own interests—and that in a monastery, even. You really would think, living with a bunch of monks and future priests, you'd have all the time in the world. Felicity shook her head.

And besides that, there was no margin for error on her part. As one of only four women among the student body of forty-some—and the only American—Felicity felt a double burden to reach the highest standard possible. This was the first year the Anglo-Catholic College of the Transfiguration had accepted women as ordinands, although they were still housed off campus, awaiting alterations to the dormitories. Before "the Great Change" a few women enrolled as students, but were not allowed equal status with the male ordinands. Last year, however, the college had submitted to the winds of change and the powers that be, so now the women had full status—and double pressure.

Felicity, however, was never one to let such obstacles discourage her. She could rise to any challenge, and her determination to succeed in this male-dominated world knew no limits. Anyway, she had few complaints. She had been warmly welcomed—by most. A handful of ordinands, and perhaps two or three of the monks or lay teachers, were less warm—because she was female or because she was American, she wasn't sure.

Two hours later, the insistent ringing of the Community bell called her back from her reading just in time to fling a long black cassock over her Shetland sweater and dash across the street and up the hill to the Community grounds. Her long legs carried her the distance in under three minutes—she had timed herself. Once inside the high stone wall enclosing the Community, she slowed her pace. It never failed. No matter how irritated she became with all the ancient ritual and nonsense of the place, there *was* something about the storybook quality of it all that got through to her in her quieter moments.

The spicy scent of incense met her at the door of the church. She dipped her finger in the bowl of holy water and turned to share it with the brother just behind her. Shy Brother Matthew extended a plump finger without meeting her eyes. They each crossed themselves and slipped into their seats in the choir.

"Miserere mei, Deus…" The choir and cantors had practiced for weeks to be able to sing Psalm 51 to the haunting melody

composed by Allegri. The words ascended to the vaulted ceiling; the echoes reverberated. Candles flickered in the shadowed corners. She had been here for six months—long enough for the uniqueness of it all to have palled to boredom—but somehow there was a fascination she couldn't define. "Mystery," the monks would tell her. And she could do no better.

What was the right term to describe how she was living? Counter-cultural existence? Alternate lifestyle? She pondered for a moment, then smiled. Parallel universe. That was it. She was definitely living in a parallel universe. The rest of the world was out there, going about its everyday life, with no idea that this world existed alongside it.

It was a wonderful, cozy, secretive feeling as she thought of bankers and shopkeepers rushing home after a busy day, mothers preparing dinner for hungry schoolchildren, farmers milking their cows—all over this little green island, the workaday world hummed along to the pace of modern life. And here she was on a verdant hillside in Yorkshire, living a life hardly anyone knew even existed. It was a very "Harry Potter" experience.

She forced her attention back to the penitential service with its weighty readings, somber plainchant responses and minor key music, set against purple vestments. Only when they came to the blessing of the ashes did she realize Father Dominic wasn't in his usual place. Her disappointment was sharp. He had definitely said he was to do the imposition of the ashes and she had felt receiving the ashen cross on her forehead from that dear man would give the ancient ritual added meaning. Instead, Father Antony, one of the secular priests who lectured at the college, not even one of the monastic Community, stood to hold the small pot of palm ashes while Father Anselm, the Superior of the Community, blessed them with holy water and incense.

Felicity knelt at the altar rail. "Remember that you are dust, and to dust you shall return." The ashes were cold, a sooty mark of grief, gritty on her forehead.

"Amen," she responded automatically.

She was back in her seat, turning ahead to the final hymn, "Forty Days and Forty Nights" when she heard the soft slapping of sandals on the stone floor. *Oh, there's Father Dominic!* She relaxed at the thought, putting away her worries that he had suddenly been taken ill. But her relief was short-lived when Father Clement, the principal of the college, and Jonathan Breen, a scholar making a retreat at the monastery, slipped to the altar for their ashes.

The final notes of the postlude were still echoing high overhead when Felicity rose from her seat and hurried outside. Dinner, a vegetarian Lenten meal, would start in the refectory almost immediately and it wouldn't do to be late. If she hurried, though, she could just dash back to her flat and pick up a book of Latin poetry for Father Dominic. She had a new volume of Horace, and she knew Father D loved the Roman's half-Stoic, half-Epicurean philosophy. He would have time to enjoy what he called his "guilty pleasure" while he recuperated from his indisposition.

She bounded up the single flight of stairs, flung open her door and came to a sudden halt. "Oh!" The cry was knocked from her like a punch in the stomach. She couldn't believe it. She backed against the wall, closing her eyes in the hope that all would right itself when she opened them. It didn't. The entire flat had been turned upside down.

Felicity stood frozen for perhaps a full minute, trying to take it all in: books pulled from shelves, drawers pulled from her desk, cushions flung from chairs. Hardly breathing, she rushed into her kitchen, bath, bedroom—all chaos—sheets and duvet ripped from her bed, clothes pulled from her wardrobe. She picked her way through scattered papers, dumped files, ripped letters. Dimly she registered that her computer and CD player were still there. Oh, and there was the Horace book still by her bed. She pulled her purse from under a pile of clothes. Empty. But its contents lay nearby. Credit cards and money still there.

Not robbery. So then, what? Why?

Was this an anti-women-clergy thing? Had she underestimated the extent of the resentment? Or was it an anti-American thing? The American president was widely unpopular in England. Had he done something to trigger an anti-American demonstration? Felicity would be the last to know. She never turned on the news.

Well, whatever it was, she would show them. If someone in the college thought they could scare her off by flinging a few books around, she'd give them something new to think about. She stormed out, slamming her door hard enough to rattle the glass pane, and strode up the hill at twice the speed she had run down it. Not for nothing her years of rigorous exercise at the ballet barre. When she reached the monastery grounds, she keyed in the numbers on the security lock with angry jabs and barely waited for the high, black iron gates to swing open before she was speeding up the graveled walk.

Felicity's long blonde braid thumped against her back as she charged onward, her mind seething. If those self-righteous prigs who posed as her fellow students thought they could put her off with some sophomoric trick—

She approached the college building, practicing the speech she would deliver to all assembled for dinner in the refectory: *"Now listen up, you lot! If you think you can push me around just because your skirts are longer than mine…"*

She punched a clenched-fist gesture toward her imaginary cassock-clad audience, then saw the Horace book still clutched in her hand. Oh, yes. First things first. She would have missed the opening prayer anyway. She would just stop by Father D's room—then she would tell them.

She hurried on up the path beyond the college to the monastery, ran her swipe card through the lock, and was halfway down the hall before the door clicked shut behind her. She had only been to Dominic's room once before, to collect a poetry book he was anxious to share with her, but she would have had no trouble locating it, even had the door not been standing ajar.

She pushed it wider, preparing to step in. "Father D——" she stopped at the sight of a man in a black cassock standing there, praying. He jerked around at the sound of her voice and she recognized Father Antony, her church history lecturer.

She took a step backward when she saw the look of horror on his sheet-white face. "Felicity! Don't come in." He held up a hand to stop her and she saw it was covered with blood.

"Father D! Is he hemorrhaging?" She lunged forward, then stopped at the sight before her.

The whole room seemed covered in blood. Bright red splotches on the pristine white walls and bedding, on the open pages of a prayer book, on the statue of our Lord, forming lurid stigmata on His hands extended in mercy...

And in the center of the floor, in a pool of red, his battered head all but unrecognizable— her beloved Father Dominic. The smell of fresh blood clogged her nostrils. Gorge rose in her throat.

"Felicity—" Father Antony extended his reddened hands to her in a pleading gesture.

"No!" She screamed, wielding her Latin book as a shield against the blood, a red haze of shock and horror clouding her vision.

She couldn't believe Antony's face could get even whiter. "Felicity, wait. Listen—"

She dimly registered his words, but the voice in her head shouted with far greater force. *No! It can't be. It's a mistake. I'm in the wrong room. Must be.* She shook her head against the nightmare she had seen yet couldn't accept that she had seen. Blackness rolled toward her.

She staggered backward into the hall and slumped to the floor as the room spun before her. She closed her eyes against the darkness as her mind reeled, groping for a coherent thought. *How could this be?*

Only a short time ago she had been revelling in the peace of this remote holy place. Where could such violence have come from? How was it possible here? In a place of prayer? To a holy man. *Why?*

If Father Dominic wasn't safe, who could be?

And even as the questions tumbled, half-formed through her head, even as her mind denied the act her eyes had seen, she knew she had to find an explanation. How could she continue studying—believing in—purpose and justice, if such senseless irrationality reigned free?

Focusing on the questions gave her strength to get to her feet again.

Antony was still standing dazed in the gore-splattered room, looking as though he could collapse in the middle of the pool of blood. Felicity grabbed his arm, jerked him into the corridor, and shoved him against the wall, where he stayed, leaning heavily. He held his hands before his face as if unbelieving they were his own. "When he missed mass I came to check on him… I felt for a pulse—"

"We must get help!" Felicity looked wildly around.

"Yes, of course." Her energy seemed to galvanize Antony. He pushed himself forward unsteadily. "Forgive me, I feel so stupid. It was the horror. I—we must tell the superior. He'll call the police."

"Police? You mean an ambulance." Felicity started toward the room again. Yes, that was it—how could she have dithered so when they must get help? "He's lost so much blood, but maybe—"

"No!" Antony gripped her shoulder with more strength than she realized he was capable of. "Don't go in there again, Felicity. It's useless."

She knew. She had seen the blood.

Chapter 2

The bell chiming for Compline told Felicity that four hours had passed, and yet she had no sense of time or place. The police had asked a few of them to remain in the common room after their initial questioning. Felicity had chosen a deep, overstuffed chair in a dark corner of the room, and managed to remain largely unnoticed. A woman police constable pressed a beaker of strong, sweet tea into her hands, and she realized she hadn't eaten since lunch. Still, she only sipped at it. The mug was far more valuable for its warmth as she cupped her hands around it.

To her surprise, Antony, who had changed out of his blood-smeared cassock, noticed her shiver and slipped his black suit jacket around her shoulders. "Thanks. Normally my cassock is warm enough— I…" She realized she was babbling and fell into silence.

Antony just smiled before he turned back to his discussion of medieval church history with Dr. Breen, who was using his retreat time to study the Community's collection of manuscripts. The athletic-looking, blond American was explaining the importance of one of the manuscripts Benedict Biscop brought back from Rome in the seventh century, and questioning whether or not Bede had interpreted it correctly. History. Irrelevancies. Felicity was furious. She wanted to fling herself at them and shake them both. *Father Dominic is dead! Some horrible, violent madman is stalking the cloisters of this monastery and there you sit engaging in sterile academic discussion!*

But Felicity did not scream, and gradually the discussion, which she vaguely realized was their means of clinging to rationality—a way of keeping chaos and insanity at bay until a glimpse of order could be grasped—drew her in and she became fascinated by the depth of the American's knowledge. It sounded as if Breen had made his own translations of some of the documents. What an unusual man—not many Harvard literature professors chose to become lay supporters of monastic communities. She might even enjoy discussing his interpretation with him. But later—when her head was clearer, when the world returned to its orbit—if it ever did.

The door to the side room opened and Inspector Nosterfeld strode in like a bulldozer. "Father Clement, I realize it's getting late." His broad northern accent made him sound like a character from *All Creatures Great and Small* which had so captivated Felicity in her growing-up years. "But if you would be so kind as to clear up just a couple of questions for us, we'll try to let you all go in a few more minutes." His intimidating attitude made a mockery of his polite phrases. The room lapsed into silence when the head of college left with the police officer.

Some time later Felicity startled awake, sloshing her cooled tea on Antony's jacket, as the inspector returned to apologize once again for keeping them so long, and to tell them they could go for the night. Breen jerked to his feet and strode to the door, barely pausing to bid a general "Goodnight" to the room. The door banged behind him, leaving them in an echoing silence.

Antony started to rise, but an ashen-faced Father Clement put a restraining hand on his shoulder. "If I could have a quick word—" The principal's voice came out in a harsh whisper, as if he had a sore throat.

Rotund Father Anselm pushed himself from the deep cushions of the sofa and smoothed his rumpled gray scapular over his black cassock. "I'll be getting along, then." He glanced at the clock on the wall. "Compline just over, pity." The Father Superior had spent the entire time with his head bowed over his prayer book, whether sleeping or praying, Felicity wasn't sure.

"And you, Father, please. If you could spare me a moment…" Father Clement's voice wavered on the last word, causing Felicity to look at the principal of the college more closely. His tall, usually vigorous form was slumped inside his cassock. He appeared to have aged a decade. His ashen gray hue was exactly the color a friend of her father had turned just before he suffered a fatal coronary. She wondered if she should go, but as no one seemed aware of her presence, she simply leaned deeper into her cushions and closed her eyes, not to feign sleep, but to make herself invisible. If only shutting her eyes could shut out the horrors of Father Dominic's room that were burned on the back of her eyelids. It was as if the whole world had changed in that one glimpse of the bleeding monk. Goodness, peace, sanity washed out with his lifeblood.

She heard the plump of the cushion as the principal more collapsed into a chair than sat in it. "I don't know what to do— what to say... They seem to think that I— I *was* late to mass—I explained over and over, I had been meditating in the oratory, so I set out late—then our guest..." He glanced at the door from which Breen had departed. "... waylaid me outside the church on some point of scholarship—he seems to have little concept of our rules and our hours—I didn't want to be rude— I did my best..." A long sigh interrupted his broken narrative. "I know they didn't believe me. In all the college and Community, I seem to have been the only person absent at the precise time. 'Don't leave Kirkthorpe,' they said. That's the same as an accusation."

Felicity jolted up, forgetting she was trying not to be seen, the steel blade of logic incising the chaos in her mind. "How do they know the exact time? He left me just after 4:00. Anyone could have gone to his room and not have been late for mass. *I* could have followed him. Any of us in this room—" she stopped abruptly, remembering the blood on Antony's hands. "Sorry, forgive me. That was stupid." She sank back in her chair, realizing they were all staring at her.

Father Anselm spoke first in his gentle, yet authoritative voice. "What do you mean, he left you? You mean you saw him this afternoon?"

"Yes, he dropped by my flat quite unexpectedly. I gave him tea. I told the police. I assumed that was why they asked me to wait. Isn't the last person to see the victim alive always supposed to be a prime suspect?"

"I don't understand. Why would he break silence?"

"He said he wanted to give me a book of poetry—at least, I think that's what it is. He often shared his poems with me. I had no idea it was forbidden—I…" Felicity floundered to a halt. Why was she making excuses? She would have welcomed Father Dominic under any circumstance.

"Most interesting. Did you tell the police?" The superior's calm questioning continued.

"No. I didn't think it was important." Felicity reached into her skirt pocket through the slit in her cassock. She handed it to Father Clement. He looked at her questioningly and she nodded. He carefully undid the wrapping. He was shaking so, Felicity was afraid he would drop it. It was, as it had felt through the wrapping paper, a small hardback book. The cover bore no title, just a pattern of green and gold antique marbling. It was very old. Or simply an imitation.

Father Clement turned several pages, his frown deepening as he scanned them. "What do you make of this?" He thrust it toward Antony. "Read it out so we can all hear."

Antony glanced at a few pages, frowning as Clement had. "Well, there's nothing very coherent here." He cleared his throat. "'I will bless the Lord, who has given me guidance. He has shown me the way. My heart is glad, and my glory—' No, he crossed that out. Hard to make out what he's written over it. Hm, 'soul', I think. Yes, 'my soul rejoices.'" He turned a page and his brow furrowed deeper. "Well, here we have a jotting of numbers. Prices, perhaps."

Clement looked over his shoulder. "Expenses, I should think. This entry with an 'r' after it," he pointed, "could be the price of a rail ticket."

"And those marked f would be food. He didn't eat a lot, did

he?" Antony flipped a few pages ahead. "Yes, here are some place names: Lindisfarne, Durham, Whitby…" He turned to Father Anselm. "Are these places he went on his pilgrimage?"

"I believe so, yes."

Antony nodded and returned to reading. "He did not suffer his Holy One to see corruption… grave can praise… death doth celebrate." He turned a page. "Neither will you suffer your beloved saint to see corruption." He closed the book, his finger keeping his place. "Do you want me to go on, Father? There's quite a bit more of these sorts of scattered jottings, interspersed with more place names and a bit of accounting."

"I think we have the idea. Thank you, Antony."

Antony started to close the volume when one last jotting caught his eye. "'Triumph in death, Death over death, Life over death.'"

The room was silent for the space of ten heartbeats. Antony handed the slim volume back to Felicity. She opened it at a random page and looked at the familiar handwriting. "Oh, look. This passage has a little triangle by it. I wonder if that means anything." She read, "'Cuthbert the beloved lies dead and buried, his sepulcher with us unto this day. As in the resurrection of Christ, his soul was not left in hell, neither did his flesh decay, no more to return to corruption.'"

Threatened tears made her blink and fight for breath. "It's so like him." She forced a ragged breath past the constriction in her throat. "And odd. He seems to have been gathering thoughts for a poem. But how strange that he would have wanted to share it with me when it's in such a rough state! And yet, even as it is, it's so—so comforting. He was so—" She gulped and forced herself to go on. "So gentle when he gave it to me—as if he knew I would need it. He was my best friend here." She thought for a moment. Her only friend, really. A wave of desolation and despair washed over her as she glimpsed how much she would miss him. Could she stay here after this? But where would she go? To turn her back on all that Father Dominic lived for seemed almost as brutal a betrayal as that of his killer.

"Yes," Antony drawled the word on a slow breath, his brow furrowed. "It is very comforting—applied to death in general. But also very confusing in trying to figure out what he's talking about. Does he mean his own death, or the death and resurrection of Christ? Did he have a foreshadowing of his own death?"

Felicity forced her thoughts back to the present and nodded. "And the bit about Cuthbert—what's all that? If he had a premonition, he could be using the saint's death as a symbol of his own." She covered her eyes with her hands as if to block out visions of her beloved friend covered in his own blood. Surely Dominic could not have had any inkling...

Antony frowned and pressed on. "Whatever it is, it *has* to be significant."

"I agree," Felicity said. "I suppose I should show it to the police, but they'll probably dismiss it as religious mumbo-jumbo."

"Sadly, most religious things are meaningless to the secular world. It's clear that it needs a religious person to sort out the meaning." Clement looked grayer than ever. It was frightening. The principal was always so dynamic, leading the college with such force. In the long silence of the room, everyone shook their heads.

Antony spoke into the void. "What could Dominic have recorded here that would be important enough to make him break silence?"

Father Clement cleared his throat and straightened his shoulders a fraction, as if he had come to a decision through all the fog surrounding them. "You're quite right, Antony. The key is there. And you're the man to unlock it."

Antony ran his hand upward through his thick, dark hair, then back down to flatten it, a nervous gesture Felicity had often seen him do while lecturing. It left his ashen symbol of mortality smeared across the ivory skin of his wide forehead. What irony: that the most Christ-like man she had ever known—could ever imagine—had been killed on Ash Wednesday, a precursor of Good Friday.

"Father, with respect," Antony's words recalled her attention. "I'm honored. But I don't think I'd be capable. I'm a plodding historian. I deal in facts. Obscure poetry fragments... If that's what they are—." He shook his head. "I'm afraid they escape me."

The principal cleared his throat a second time and his voice took on some of the authority it had lost. "Facts are exactly what we need. What I need. That the police could think that I could commit such an act of violence..."

"If there's a lead to Dominic's murder here, I don't see it," Antony protested.

Felicity gasped and pushed forward from her deep cushions as the thought struck her. "But what if there is? And the murderer knew? Maybe that's what the vandals in my flat were looking for."

"What about your flat?" Father Clement demanded.

She explained in a few words that it had been turned upside down, but apparently nothing stolen. "That's why I thought it was some sort of prank or protest." Now she realized how wrong she had been.

"Did you tell the police?" Antony asked.

"Yes. They said something about dusting it for fingerprints, and that they would keep an eye on it. I suppose they're watching the whole monastery."

"Right, then." Father Clement appeared to be rapidly getting a grip on his authority. "This must be solved. Dominic was definitely trying to tell us something. And someone seems to know more about it than we do." The principal looked steadily at Antony.

The room fell silent, all attention focused on Antony. He held his hands up in a gesture of rejection, shaking his head. "Really, I don't think—" He took a step backward.

Felicity gritted her teeth in impatience. The whole thing was so unfair. One more example of the injustice she had determined to fight. It was intolerable that such gross injustice had happened before her own eyes, and these dithering males were ignoring her. Of course deciphering Dominic's scribbled thoughts was the thing to do.

"Excuse me, Principal, but Father Dominic did give his journal to me. I rather think that if anyone is to follow it up, it should be me." They turned and looked at her as if the lamp had spoken. Well, everyone expected Americans to be pushy. Normally she worked hard to curb her outspoken instincts so as to avoid living up to the stereotype. But sometimes one just couldn't let natural talent go to waste.

Father Anselm's gentle voice broke the silence. "That's very generous of you, Miss Howard." He smiled at her with just a hint of a nod. Clement's nod was more of a jerk, but it signified agreement.

"But surely—" Antony began.

The superior quelled him with a look. "It strikes me that Miss Howard does have a point. It seems clear that, whatever his reasons, Dominic wanted to get this into the hands of someone he trusted. Someone who understood his cryptic writing." Felicity felt them all looking at her. "If you would be so good as to assist Father Antony in his labors, Miss Howard. I'm certain you are anxious to help in any way you can to see justice done."

"Yes, of course." But in spite of the alacrity of her words, she felt the hollowness of the goal. Nothing they did would bring Dominic back. She believed fervently in the importance of justice. But at the moment, such an abstract virtue seemed a cold compensation.

She paled as a ray of reality shot through her earlier impetuosity. What had she gotten herself into by her rash outburst? "But I don't really know…" Her voice trailed off.

Father Anselm rose. "Well, that's settled then." He cut through her floundering. "Miss Howard, will you be all right? Do you have a place to sleep?"

"Oh, I hadn't given it a thought. Yes, Kate. Upstairs. She has a couch." She held out Antony's jacket to him.

He stepped forward. "I'll walk you home."

"Don't be silly. I'll be fine." Felicity heard her own words and had the grace to blush. "Oh, I'm sorry. That sounded rude." She forced a smile. "Thank you. That would be very kind."

When they stepped out into the silent dark, Felicity was very glad to have Antony's escort. She looked to one side, then the other, wondering what the shadows held. A small creature rustled in the hedgerow, and she jumped. What a fraud she was. The gravel of the path crunched under their feet, sounding as loud as a shotgun.

Felicity's thoughts raced and lurched, entirely out of synch with their measured footsteps. How like her this was, she berated herself. All her life she had leapt before she looked, but she couldn't remember ever feeling so foolishly rash before. She slowed her pace to walk closer to her companion. "This doesn't make any sense. Why me?"

"What do you mean?"

"I mean that if there is some kind of hidden message in the journal, why would Dominic confide in me? In his lifetime of work here he must have had lots of close friends he trusted. Men with wisdom and knowledge and experience. I'm none of that. I'm not even English." It was a desperate cry for reassurance, for courage to go on—or to be let off the hook. Maybe Antony would see that she was incapable, and step up to the plate himself.

"Which means that you're probably a lot better at thinking outside the box than men who have lived enclosed, obedient lives for decades." In the dark she could only sense his grin, but it did a lot to lighten the atmosphere. "Which obedience means that no one in the monastery would have readily welcomed having him break the Greater Silence. For a clear emergency, yes; for a vague uneasiness, no. And apparently that's all he had. Also, remember, Dominic's life work was in South Africa. He spent most of his time going back and forth, working in Kirkthorpe's sister house in

South Africa more than half his life. He had only been back here a few months this time, perhaps not long enough to form really close friendships. But I think the key thing was your instinctive grasp of his poetry. I doubt that he connected with anyone else here as well on that point."

She nodded slowly, thinking over Antony's words as he opened the gate. With understanding came the weight of it all, and once again the desolation of loss. "Yes, I see. It's a huge honor. And a huge responsibility." She paused. "But what if I get it wrong? I mean, why couldn't he just have told me what he suspected was going on, and told me not to tell anyone unless I needed to? Why just bless me and give me those… those random scribbles—which I *don't* understand!" She ended on a note of desperation that rose to near-hysteria. She was suddenly taken with irrational anger toward Dominic.

It was his fault. If it hadn't been for his enigmatic ways… If he suspected anything—so much as a glimmer—why did he go ahead? Why did he let this happen? Why did he take a chance on landing them all in this mess?

He was so holy. He was so wise. How could he? With horror, she realized she had screamed the words she meant only to give thought to. And she had accompanied each word with blows of her clenched fists on Antony's chest.

"Felicity, Felicity." His hands on her shoulders held her firmly, pushing at her in a gesture that was more of a rocking than a shaking as tears drowned her angry words and she collapsed in his arms as the gate swung shut behind them.

Still the doubts continued to mount, looming in the darkness, when she was tucked up on Kate's couch with a large mug of hot chocolate. What had she volunteered for? To uphold justice, to avenge Father Dominic, to solve the riddle of his murder—yes, yes; high-sounding goals… truth, justice and mercy—all that— but what on earth did she think she could actually *do*?

Her rash speech would make her look more foolish than ever in the morning when she had to admit she literally didn't have a clue. But that's what she would have to do. After all, she couldn't go around making promises that she had no hope of fulfilling to the Superior of the Community and Principal of the College.

But if she didn't, who would? The dithering Father Antony—all brains and no action? The bullish Inspector Nosterfield—all action and no brains?

The image of Father Dominic at tea returned to her—the eyes sparkling with excitement in the lined face, the voice animated with hope for the future. A future he no longer had. But she did. She had a future and she would do everything she could to see that those African children Father D loved so much had a future, too.

She would think of something. Somehow she would carry on for him. She would make good on her promise.

Chapter 3

"O Lord, our heavenly Father, Almighty and everlasting God, who hast safely brought us to the beginning of this day…" The weight sat heavy on Antony's chest and sent its cold tentacles upward to close his throat, making it almost impossible for him to chant the morning prayers. Father Anselm had requested to see him in his office after Matins. He knew the superior would renew Father Clement's request for Antony to undertake this investigation. Although Clement, not Anselm, was his boss, the Father Superior bore great moral weight. What Father Anselm requested, Father Anselm got.

And Antony would have to face his demons. Most of the time they stayed conveniently out of sight, stuffed down by the rigorous demands of a combined monastic and secular routine. But now…

"Now is the healing time decreed/For sins of heart and word and deed … That we from this our abstinence/May reap the fruits of penitence." He filed out slowly behind the rest of the college and Community with the words of the closing Lenten hymn still echoing around him. He paused briefly to reverence the seventeenth century Russian icon of Our Lady of the Transfiguration in the side chapel, then made his way on down the corridor.

Everything around him was so orderly, so serene, so peaceful, he hardly remembered what the world beyond was like, even the world of a parish ministry, let alone some wholly secular lifestyle. Could he go out and face the world—as surely undertaking such an investigation would entail?

Could he do it? What if he learned, not just more about Father Dominic and his poetry, but more about himself? What if others learned more about him? What if this caused cracks in the careful shell he had spent so many years building around himself? The tightness in his chest threatened to choke him. He looked wildly around for an open room to bolt into, but there was none. Father Anselm's ample form loomed just ahead of him. Why hadn't he lingered longer before the icon? He took a deep, steadying breath. What must be, must be faced.

"Ah, Antony, thank you for coming." Anselm turned just as he reached his office door. "I was hoping you had slept somewhat better than the rest of us, but I can see you didn't. Terrible thing, this. Terrible." He indicated for Antony to take a chair on one side of the fireplace and took the other himself. "One advantage of spending the night awake is that it gives one plenty of time to pray and think. Have you had any insights on this matter?"

"Well, obviously, besides the entries which apparently apply to his travels, the more enigmatic entries were mostly Scripture— paraphrases of psalms and the writings of St. Paul." There could be no more dithering in front of Father Superior. He must focus and do his best to give intelligent answers.

"And what do you make of the Cuthbert reference?" the superior continued. "Is it only an analogy, or the central image? I can't decide."

Before Antony was required to answer they were interrupted by a soft knock. The superior smiled. "Ah, that will be Miss Howard. I asked her to join us." He raised his voice to carry through the door. "Yes, come in."

Felicity entered with her accustomed energy, as if propelled by a gust of fresh air, her long blond hair swirling loosely around her shoulders. "Sorry I'm late, Father. Jonathan Breen rather cornered me. He wanted to talk about the morning's Latin canticle—about it being a corrupted form. Of course, to one way of thinking all ecclesiastical Latin is corrupted." She took the chair Anselm indicated and looked around. "Sorry," she repeated. "I'm interrupting."

"No, no. We were just getting started. I had hoped the

principal could join us as well, but it seems the police are in further need of his help in their inquiry."

"They can't be serious about suspecting Father Clement!" Anger made Felicity's voice rise and her cheeks flush. "That's utter nonsense."

"Of course it is. But it seems they are less than happy about his being the only one in the Community to be late for mass."

"And Breen," Antony reminded them.

"It seems that his presence in the kitchen is well substantiated by all three cooks from whom he was begging a snack."

"Ah," Felicity took up the thought. "What about the staff? There must have been other people around. The main gates were locked, but the groundsmen might have left something open—"

Anselm nodded. "I'm sure the police will cover all that most thoroughly. As well as all the relationships inside the Community, of course."

"Inside? You mean the brethren? Surely, no one could think…"

The superior's ironic laugh cut her off. "My dear, no one could be so naive as to believe that some thirty men could live enclosed, even in consecrated space, and not rub each other the wrong way more than occasionally. Holiness can be a very irritating quality. But I want to know what new thoughts you have had on the journal entries."

Felicity jumped right in. Antony was more than happy to let her take the lead. The stark contrast of her spirit and energy to his reticence making him feel even more reticent. "Well, Dominic seems to have been excited about something. If the jotted thoughts were to be crafted into a poem, it's theme would most certainly be about death, but the tone is very upbeat—exuberant, even. I don't understand the references to Cuthbert, though."

"We were just mentioning that when you came in. It's what puzzles me most." Antony was happy to enter in here. He was on good ground on matters of church history. "It's a superb analogy, if that's all it is. Cuthbert's body remained uncorrupted for hundreds of years, which was taken as evidence of his special holiness. So all the references to incorruption could apply to Cuthbert—"

"So Cuthbert could just be a symbol of incorruption and not a real clue to the meaning at all?" Felicity asked.

"Yes, but that's the problem. Dominic was an expert on Cuthbert, so he would have known that the last time the tomb was opened, in the late nineteenth century, the flesh had completely decayed. Bare bones were reinterred behind the high altar in Cuthbert's shrine at Durham Cathedral—not the fully fleshed body the reference in the journal seems to imply."

Felicity leaned back and crossed her long legs, tangling in the folds of her cassock. Antony watched as she impatiently undid all thirty-nine of its buttons and freed herself. "But aren't we forcing this? Isn't the idea of this being some sort of message silly? If Father Dominic did suspect he might be in danger, why not just say so—or write it clearly in a letter? If I were in danger, that's what I would do."

"I agree." Antony nodded, his thoughts becoming clearer as he spoke. The vague feelings fuzzing his mind had begun to form a meaningful pattern. "His sense of excitement, joy even— I think they refer to something Dominic found or learned or accomplished on his pilgrimage. I don't think the poem he was working on was to convey any sense of doom, but more of spiritual ecstasy. I think the threat showed up suddenly and unexpectedly—so suddenly, he chose to break silence to get the message of his discovery to someone he hoped would understand, just in case the worst happened. And if it didn't, then all he would have done was share some thoughts with a friend."

"Quite right. Quite right." Father Superior slapped the arm of his chair. "And so you'll undertake the investigation. Excellent!" Anselm's bald head was as pink as his cheeks, making his gray fringe of hair look like a tonsure.

Antony held up a hand and pushed into the back of his chair. "With all respect, superior, that's not what I meant to be saying. And besides—" another thought, quite unconnected to the events of the past day, flashed into his mind. Here was the out he had been looking for. "Forgive me, but it's less than two weeks until I assume chairmanship of the Ecumenical Commission, and I'm afraid I'm woefully unprepared."

"As you are quite aware, Father Antony, I can't command you. Since you aren't a monk, you're under no vows of obedience to me. But I can beg you. I'm certain there are things here the police wouldn't understand. Things that could be of great importance."

Antony bowed his head in a gesture of acquiescence. He had made his best argument. There was no way he could refuse. And yet the fear that had dogged him all his life gripped him. The fear of failure. And always, at the back of his mind the little voice saying, *Maybe they're right. Maybe you aren't good enough. Maybe this is the time everyone finds out.* Aunt Beryl had always said he was useless. He had struggled all his life to prove her wrong. *But maybe she was right.*

"Excellent." Father Anselm's voice cut through Antony's abstraction. "You and Miss Howard will make a most efficient team, I'm sure." He crossed the room and sat at his desk, his gray scapular billowing out as he bent to open a bottom drawer. He pulled out a sheet of paper bearing a few lines of Dominic's distinctive handwriting.

Antony groaned. "Another poem fragment."

"Perhaps a bit more straightforward." Father Anselm smiled. "I requested an itinerary from Dominic before he left on his pilgrimage. Nothing detailed, just wanted to be informed as to where he would be."

Antony took the paper and read aloud:

> *"The talisman of Ninian;*
> *The knowledge of Bede;*
> *The treasure of Aethelstan;*
> *The energy of Hilda,*
> *The secret of Cuthbert:*
> *Lindisfarne, Jarrow, Whithorn, Chester-le-street, Whitby,*
> *Durham."*

He looked up, nodding. "Yes. Excellent itinerary, although rather a lot to cram into two weeks."

"It was a pilgrimage, not a retreat," Anselm said.

"Quite so." Antony returned to the paper. "Interesting couplet he ends with. Do you know what it means?"

Anselm shook his head. "I was hoping you might have some ideas on that."

Felicity held out her hand for the paper.

> *Three from the See, Shield-Bearers protecting;*
> *Three from the sea, Spear-Danes destructing.*

She laughed. "How like Dominic to attach a fragment of a poem to a travel schedule. He probably wrote laundry lists in Iambic Pentameter."

"The pilgrimage has to be the key, doesn't it?" Antony said slowly. "What did he do or see or find? What did he say to you, Felicity?"

"He talked mostly about his African Children's Fund. About how now they would be able to build a hospital. I think he said something about AIDS babies, I know he was terribly concerned about them from his work in Africa." She thought for a moment, then gasped. "Do you mean maybe he found *treasure*? Something to build his hospital?"

"Well, his journal notes do refer to treasure, but surely the idea of buried treasure or something like that today is just nonsense." Antony attempted to sound sternly no-nonsense. "And if he did discover something in that line, he couldn't legally keep it. It would be the property of the Crown."

"Oh," Felicity's excitement deflated. "Well, it was just a thought." She looked at the paper in her hand again. "What's this about the Three? Three what? And the triangle doodles—could they be references to the Holy Trinity?"

"Yes, I suppose that could be it—but..." Antony's voice trailed off, the thought almost too vague to grasp at.

"But what, Father Antony?" Anselm asked. "We need all

ideas on the table."

"Well, it sounds silly," still he hesitated. "But there is an old legend about some secret brotherhood in connection with St. Cuthbert." Antony shrugged dismissively. "Butler mentions it in passing in his *Lives of Saints*, but it's a myth. I never indulge in extravagant embellishments in my lectures. The lives of the saints are far too clouded with such embroidery, when their real value to us lies not in their superhuman powers, but in the fact that they were very ordinary men and women who triumphed by relying on God in their weakness." He stopped abruptly and ran his hand through his hair. "Sorry. Didn't mean to lecture."

Felicity just smiled as if she'd heard it all before. She was focusing on the list of place names. "I've never heard of most these: Jarrow? Whithorn? Chester-le-street? What's their significance?"

"Places connected with Cuthbert," Antony said.

Felicity twiddled her hair, thinking. "So… If you put this with the journal, the reference to Cuthbert must be more than a literary device."

Father Anselm glanced at his watch and levered his impressive bulk to his feet. "Do carry on. I'm delighted that you seem to be making headway. Unfortunately, our good Inspector has asked to interview me again. But please use my office for as long as you need." He left the room with a satisfied smile and a backward glance at the two heads bent over their work.

After a few moments of silence, Antony nodded. No matter how hard he tried to resist, how much he protested, he felt himself being drawn into the riddle. Especially now that there seemed to be so much church history involved. One of the things he had so loved about his subject was that it was safe. History was there for us to learn from—choose models to emulate, see mistakes to be avoided; but, unlike occurrences in today's newspaper, one was insulated from the events by the perspective of time. Now was history pressing on the present? On his life in a way that demanded he take action? He sighed as he mentally resigned himself to it.

Perhaps this was being thrust upon him as penance. A way to make amends for all the times he had shirked his duty? He must try. "It does all seem to revolve around Cuthbert. I suppose that's hardly surprising since Dominic was as devoted to Cuthbert as he was to Africa. I think he rather identified with him in a personal way."

"I was wondering about that," Felicity interrupted. "Was Cuthbert known as an outstanding preacher? Father Dominic once told me he took the name of Dominic at ordination because St. Dominic was such a passionate preacher, and more than anything in the world he wanted to preach the Word of God with passion."

"Yes, Cuthbert was a great preacher, but I think he is most remembered for his gentle, loving spirit."

"Like Dominic." Felicity's voice caught on a sob. "How could this have happened?"

Antony shook his head helplessly. He had no answers he could give her. *What's wrong with what we've taught—or haven't taught? With our worship? With our belief? Hundreds, thousands of hours of reading the Scripture, of praying, of singing hymns—and then this! How can it be? Is it all dust and ashes?*

The questions left him feeling overwhelmed with the futility of it all. Helpless and angry. Angry at Dominic who chose to be so obscure. Angry at Father Anselm who had maneuvered him into this impossible situation. Angry at God, who had allowed it to happen. God was all-powerful and all-knowing and all-present. Was it too much to think he could have prevented the evil that caused the violent, ugly death of one good man?

Antony pulled himself up short. That was a dead end, giving in to anger and despair. What ifs and why fors did no one any good at this moment. Action was called for. He must take action to atone for his own failures. Only God knew his sin. God and himself in the middle of the night. Sins of omission and sins of commission. *We have left undone those things which we ought to have done; and we have done those things which we ought not to have done; and there is no health in us.*

He pulled himself up sharply, picked up the itinerary which Felicity had laid on the table, and strode to Father Anselm's computer. Perhaps he should just check…

Felicity blew her nose loudly, then returned to Dominic's journal. After a few moments she began muttering the words half out loud. "Mmm, 'neither did his flesh decay…'" She paused. "I suppose he means in heaven."

Felicity's voice broke Antony's troubled concentration. "What?"

"Dominic's reference to Cuthbert's incorruption—you said his body did decay, but Dominic could mean in heaven; that would make sense after his reference to the resurrection of Christ."

It was a mere musing to Felicity—picking one phrase to read aloud—but the words echoed and re-echoed in Antony's mind. He held out his hands and looked at them in the cold light of the computer screen. Dominic's blood had been on his hands yesterday. He had washed it off sometime in the course of the evening. But he had not been any more successful in cleansing the deeper stain than Pilate had been.

He closed his eyes against the memory of all that blood. And if he didn't take up the cross of this investigation, he would be guilty of far more than merely shirking his duty. He would be guilty of acquiescing in Father Dominic's death. He would be guilty of murder.

Was the choice that clear? If one didn't champion the victim was one siding with the perpetrator? He looked at his hands again, half-expecting to see the incriminating stains still there. *How far did his own accountability go? If he had done things differently—if only…* He had an almost overwhelming impulse to attempt rubbing the spots out, like Lady Macbeth, but forced his hands back to the keyboard instead.

Felicity's musings continued in the background until she looked up at the clicking of computer keys. "What are you doing?"

"Checking train schedules. It seems to me the only way to

get to the bottom of this is to retrace Dominic's footsteps and see
if we can sort out just what he discovered that he was so excited
about. When we know why he was killed, we'll probably know
who."

"So you *do* think he might have found treasure!"

Felicity jumped as the office door swung open with a crash.
"Brother Matthew—" Her voice showed the astonishment she
felt at being burst in upon by the quiet, slow-moving lay brother
who served the Community as treasurer.

"F-f-Father Superior sent me." He pulled the door tightly
shut behind him. "You must g-go now, he said."

Both Felicity and Antony gaped at him, unmoving. "He
what?" Felicity asked.

"F-father S-s-s—Anselm says you must get out of the
monastery now. The police are asking for you."

Brother Matthew pushed his limp, pale hair back from his
forehead, and looked wildly around the room from behind his
dark-rimmed spectacles. "H-hurry," he said. "The inspector told
him. They found evidence. They're going to charge you."

It took Antony a moment to figure out who he was referring
to. "You mean Clement—that's who they suspected."

"No." Matthew pushed his spectacles back up his face in an
oddly stubborn gesture, then pointed. "You. Fingerprints on the
w-weapon."

"Me? They're going to charge *me*?" Antony had just been
contemplating his own guilt. Suddenly the nightmare had become
true. "No!" Fingerprints? What *had* he touched in Dominic's
room? Oh, the statue of our Lord. He had set it upright. Had *that*
been the murder weapon?

Matthew was insistent. "I was in the next room—d-doing
my accounts. The l-library expansion fund, you know? F-father
told them you had gone—on spiritual retreat, he said. Nosterfield
was m-most upset. S-S-Stormed out of the room. F-father knew
I was next door, he told me to run. To warn you." As he spoke he
crossed the room, opened the door onto the cloister and pointed

to the woods at the back of the monastery property. "Go on. Now!"

Antony sat frozen for a long moment, looking at his hands as if they were still covered with blood. *Lord, have mercy. Should I surrender?* It would almost be a relief. He'd been running all his life. Hoping to atone. And once again it was all shambles.

"Well, come on then. You heard the man. I don't fancy doing this alone." Felicity's firm yank on his arm jerked him to his feet. "Look. If there is treasure out there, Father D's murderer knows about it. That has to be what he was murdered for. That means the murderer will get it. Unless we get it first, of course."

"Yes, but if I just explain it to the police—"

"They'll lock you up and spend all their time looking for evidence against you while the guilty person makes off with the treasure."

"But there's no way I can escape from the police. And running will just make me look guilty."

"Fine. I hope you're very cozy in your cell." She turned with a flip of her head and marched toward the open door still held by Brother Matthew.

"No, wait—" Antony wasn't sure whether he was agreeing to help her, or darting out to try to stop her. But one thing was clear: he couldn't let Felicity tackle this alone. He couldn't live with another death on his conscience.

Yet even as they fled through the monk's garden, Antony knew he had made his decision. Surrendering to the police would be the easy route. The choice he had always made—to turn from challenge and danger of any kind. Running would mean facing his fears. This time he would run toward the challenge, not away from it.

And with each stride it became easier to run with the baton he realized he had accepted. He was not running because Father Anselm had sent a frantic message, but because he chose to.

Chapter 4

The back side of the Community grounds beyond the college cricket field was thickly wooded. The damp leaf mold on the seldom-used path was slick underfoot, especially when the trail cut steeply downward past the old quarry which had provided the stone for most of the monastery buildings in the mid-ninteenth century, when Anglican religious orders were being refounded in response to the Oxford Movement.

"Oh!" Felicity attempted to stifle her cry as her feet slipped under her. Had Antony not grabbed her arm she would have slid into the sludge; wallowing in mud would be an inauspicious way to begin a journey without luggage. "I don't suppose we dare go back to our rooms to pack? Not that I'm sure I'd be able to find much in mine."

They stopped by the side of the path to catch their breath. They hadn't exactly been running hard, but their abrupt departure had sharply elevated Felicity's heart rate, and from Antony's quick breathing it seemed to have done the same for him. He shook his head, his black hair wiping his forehead like a mop. "Father Superior must have been awfully insistent." He grinned. "Who would have thought Brother Matt could be energized to such forceful action?"

Felicity giggled. "And imagine Father A fibbing to the police that you had gone!"

Antony shook his head. "He didn't exactly lie—more predict that I would be following up on Dominic's pilgrimage, I suppose. Still, it does surprise me he would cut such a fine line. I've never known him to be Jesuitical."

"Isn't there something about that in the Scripture—something about being innocent as babes and wise as serpents?"

"I suppose," Antony nodded, but he still looked troubled by the hair-splitting. "Perhaps it applies. You may be thinking of 'be ye… wise as serpents, and harmless as doves. But beware of men: for they will deliver you up to the councils, and they will scourge you in their synagogues'."

"Oh, dear. That's not very comforting. Sorry I brought it up."

"Maybe not very comforting, but pretty good advice in the circumstances, I should think. I would say it's best to give our rooms a miss—police may be watching them. Probably shouldn't go directly to the train station, either."

"Right. So where are we going?"

Antony pulled Dominic's itinerary from the pocket of his black suit jacket where he had stuck it when Brother Matt had burst in on them. "Looks like Dominic started at Lindisfarne. I can't think of anything better." Then he looked at the light blazer Felicity wore over a ribbed turtleneck. "But will you be all right? It will be colder on a little island in the North Sea than it is here."

Felicity grinned. His tone of voice had indicated that it was really quite balmy where they stood in the dripping March morning. "I thought all of England was a little island in the North Sea. The critical fact is that I have my wallet. Not much cash, but I've got plastic. I hope Father Anselm thinks to ditch the cassock I left on my chair when I made that undignified dash out the door."

"Oh, I don't think you have to worry about Father Anselm. The superior doesn't miss much."

"He looks harmless as a dove, but he's as wise as a serpent?"

Antony grinned and glanced at his watch. "Now, if we can catch the 8:23 Leeds bus, it should be all right to switch to a train north from there." He thought for a moment. "Tricky getting to Holy Isle. Probably need to catch a train to Chathill in Newcastle. I think there's one at something like 11:48—I only glanced at the schedule, I don't remember the exact details."

Felicity shook her head, grinning. The English seemed to have a special compartment in their brains for train schedules. She turned toward the path, hoping they would be able to get out through the rusty, little-used gate at the bottom of the hill.

It wasn't until she was settled on the seat of a bus lumbering northward through the gray weather of a gray countryside that Felicity had time to really consider what she was doing. It had all been a matter of instinctive flight since Father Anselm's alarming message. Instinctive flight and reliance on Antony's leading. But now, she wondered what *had* she gotten herself into?

I'm traveling across England with a man accused of murder. A man on whose hands I saw the victim's blood. The police said they had evidence. Fingerprints. What if—She cut off the thought with a shudder at her own gullibility. She felt guilty that she could even entertain such a thought.

And yet it did make her ask what *did* she know about this man she would be working so closely with? He had already seemed so different from the man in black clerical attire who lectured rather stiffly but with such depth of knowledge on medieval history. The man whose classes she always left with such a bad case of finger cramp from attempting to keep her note-taking up to his delivery speed. Was it possible he was more than an encyclopedia? Perhaps she would have the opportunity to explore more than Father Dominic's pilgrimage poetry on this trip.

Even before she could think it, she dismissed the thought that she should also keep her eyes open just in case the police were right.

Felicity didn't know how many hours later the coach let them off at Beal, a tiny village on the Northumbrian coast, in driving rain. All the way north the sky had been getting darker, and what had been merely a threatening drizzle at Kirkthorpe was now bucketing. From Newcastle they had missed the train to Chathill, so had to wait for one to Berwick-upon-Tweed, just below the Scottish border. At least their wait at the Newcastle station had offered a chance to eat—having by that time missed two meals, not counting the dinner they had missed the night before. Felicity had fallen hungrily on a steaming steak and potato pasty, but Antony had stuck to his Lenten fare with carrot and coriander soup and an egg salad sandwich.

Felicity had wished she had tucked a second pasty in her pocket by the time they were in a coach twisting through the streets of Berwick lined with red brick buildings, tactfully flying, instead of a single Union Jack, the crossed flags of the English St. George and the Scottish St. Andrew. As the coach lumbered slowly back down the Northumbrian coast, Antony had explained to Felicity that the essential thing about getting to the Holy Isle of Lindisfarne was all a matter of catching the tides right. It seemed that they came in very rapidly and at a tricky angle. He said he hadn't had a chance to look up a tide schedule on the Internet before their precipitous departure, so all they could do was hope for the best. Then he had proceeded to take out his prayer book and read belatedly the midday office, while Felicity gazed out on the dreich weather, heartily missing the P. D. James novel that was somewhere in her still-jumbled room.

Had there been any sun that day, it would have been hanging low in the sky by the time they made a dash to the little kiosk to catch a bus to take them across the five-mile causeway to the island. Unless the tide was in. In which case, they would have a cold, wet wait.

Antony checked the tattered, weather-stained bus schedule and tide chart tacked above the single bench in the wooden shelter, then glanced at his watch. "Looks like we're in luck. The causeway will be crossable for another two hours, and there should be a bus along in about forty-five minutes."

Lucky? Forty-five minutes in this? Felicity wrapped her arms around herself for warmth, and huddled on the bench in the corner of the hut. It seemed psychologically warmer that way, at least. The roof of the kiosk wasn't leaking at that precise spot, but the pounding of the rain on the roof made it feel as if it could start any minute. She pulled her knees up to her chest and sat in a disheartened lump, trying to shut out the sound of the rain and thoughts of the brutal murder they had left behind them. There had been no time yet to grieve for her friend.

She could almost touch the sore spot around her heart, as if she had fallen and bruised herself deeply. At other moments it would take her completely unawares—the aching clampdown of her throat, the tingling behind her eyes. She hated to cry. And yet she longed for the release. A great, washing flood, far more than the rain pounding on the roof of their shelter, it would feel so good, so freeing; it would go on and on, cleansing out the anger, the pain, the loneliness, the fear, the blood.

But this was neither the time nor the place. And if she wasn't to give in to it, she needed a distraction. The threshold was very low, anything would do. Perhaps this was as good a time as any to get to know her companion better, although at the moment she didn't feel particularly interested. She just knew that if something didn't drown out the sound of the rain, she would start screaming. "So, tell me about your family."

"What! My family?" He sounded as shocked as if she had made an indecent suggestion.

She shrugged. Surely he needed something else to think about, too? But then, he was probably satisfied just praying or meditating or engaged in some other holy act they were always on about at the monastery. "I just thought we ought to get acquainted. If we're going to be working together for days— maybe even weeks—we might as well know something about each other."

The silence that followed her suggestion was not encouraging. "Sorry. I didn't mean to pry." Where did this man come from? He'd be dynamite at a cocktail party with a line in chat like his.

"I have an older sister. Gwendolyn and I were orphaned when I was ten." He was standing, facing forward, his back almost squarely toward her. His voice was even and colorless. "Gwena was fourteen. Our parents were sailing off the Scillies. Off the coast of Cornwall, you know? Storm blew up out of nowhere."

Felicity nodded. She had heard of the Scillies. Well, at least she'd heard of Cornwall. Someplace to the southwest.

"An aunt and uncle in Blackpool took us in—Beryl and Edward, my father's older brother and his wife. They didn't have any children of their own, didn't want any, and really didn't know what to do with us. They did their duty, though. We had all the necessities: healthy food, fresh air, regular exercise, precise schedules, lots of books, excellent schools."

Felicity shivered. "It sounds—" she groped for the word, "sterile."

He shrugged, his dark form silhouetted by the dim, gray light beyond the door of the kiosk. "Well, there wasn't much emotion, if that's what you mean. I suppose it suited me better than it did Gwena. I had my books, after all. Gwena took refuge in her friends. Mostly men friends, to be honest. She's on her third or fourth partner—I've lost track. But that's rather par for the course in the theatre world, I suppose." He didn't sound judgmental, just resigned.

Felicity racked her brain. Before coming to the monastery she had seen lots of British movies and television shows. "She's an actress? Gwendolyn Sherwood? I don't think I've heard of her."

"You wouldn't have. Although she's had some rather good parts. She specializes in farce."

Felicity clapped her hands, "Oh! I love them. Good old *Box and Cox* stuff. *Bedrooms and Hallways, Noises Off*, a lot of them make it over the pond."

"Yup. Good fun, as they say. I saw her in *Lend Me a Tenor* in Leeds when it toured the north." He went quiet as suddenly as if she had turned off a radio.

Felicity wanted to ask more. Were they close—ever? Those two orphaned children? Or had they gone their widely separate ways early on? How did he feel about that? Did he miss her? Did they write? At least he had gone to one of her plays. But it seemed that from his standpoint, the subject was exhausted. The wind picked up outside and the rain lashed the kiosk in gusts.

Felicity certainly hoped conversation wasn't going to prove this much work for the duration. Having slept little the night before, they had both dozed intermittently on the train and coach, so this was her first sustained effort. And it *was* an effort. "So what about you?" she tried again.

"What about me?" He turned and looked at her blankly through the thick gloom, as if he wasn't sure who she was talking about.

"Yeah, you in the dog collar. What did you do for emotional support?"

"Oh," he fingered his collar. "Isn't it obvious? The church."

"Mother, brother, sister, father, is it?" When he didn't reply she wondered if she could go further. Didn't seem like she had much to lose. "And girlfriend?"

To her surprise, a flash of white teeth in the gathering dark indicated a fleeting smile. "Well, there was one girl—a cellist— at Cambridge. But the friendship never went anywhere. Then I went off to the College of the Transfiguration for my MA, served my title in a small, rural parish." The pause was so long she thought the radio had been turned off again, but he continued after a while. "Then I went back to CT to lecture. As you might guess, living and working in a monastery doesn't offer much opportunity for—er, wider friendships."

He went on in phrases that struck Felicity as forced. "Of course, when I was in parish work I managed to excite a lot of interest amongst the female parishioners, as any single priest will—mostly middle-aged Barbara Pym heroine types—who made me casseroles and knitted me woolly jumpers." He shook his head. "I think I still have some of those tucked in the bottom of some drawer. There's a particularly heavy cable knit that would be most welcome at the moment."

Then suddenly his face shuttered, his body stiffened and the chill in the kiosk deepened by a good ten degrees.

Felicity waited for him to explain, but that, apparently, was the end of the sentence. Whatever he was recalling, he would not be sharing.

The wind shifted enough to blow rain into the kiosk, and the street light across the road came on. Felicity was determined to fill the silence. "Right. My turn then, is it?" She grinned; too bad she didn't have some really racy story. But then, if she was going to shock him she'd apparently have to top Gwendolyn, who had a huge head start on her. Best stick to the facts.

"Well, I guess you could say I had really good training for winding up in a monastery—two big brothers who brought home a constant supply of males. It was great practice for handling anything from snakes to karate." She smiled, remembering the biology field trip when she presented her teacher with a huge garter snake. "Who caught that for you?" he'd asked. "I caught him myself, I'll thank you to know!"

There had been a couple of serious boyfriends. Kevin was undoubtedly the most attractive of her brothers' friends: athletic, muscular, blond, good with kids, generous. She felt warmer just remembering that summer after her sophomore year at college. Kevin had just finished his Masters degree and was off to be a high school football coach. He had entertained visions of her as Mrs. Coach, complete with baking chocolate chip cookies in a ruffly apron and making chintz curtains—she could even use her dance skills training the cheerleaders. She gave Antony a brief sketch.

"His kid sister, Linda, was three years younger than me. She always followed me around, imitated my dress style—that sort of thing. I don't think Kevin was broken-hearted when I didn't accept his proposal, but Linda was.

"And then there was Michael at college in Michigan. A chemist. Nice enough fellow, but he went on to do research at Dartmouth, and I went to Oxford on that exchange program, then decided to stay in England. We still keep in touch sporadically."

It was hard to tell whether or not Antony was paying attention to her narrative, so she let her thoughts drift. At Oxford there had been great friends: punting parties, theatre parties, Scottish country dancing...

"What brought you to the College of the Transfiguration?"

In her mind Felicity had been revisiting a picnic on the banks of the Thames, complete with strawberries and Pimms, so Antony's question made her jump. She had discovered her love of the classics in a high school Latin class, and so from college had gone on to study at Oxford. After a year of teaching at a private school in London, she decided the church offered far more scope for applying her skills in Greek and Latin (and truth to tell, more scope for her stage skills). As a foreign student, she was allowed to register at the College of the Transfiguration without the usual rigmarole of the diocesan sponsorship and Selection Conference approval required of most students. She gave him the outline.

He still seemed perplexed. "But the priesthood—"

"Oh, I guess it sort of started in high school. We have this thing for seniors called Career Day. You sign up for something you'd like to do and then spend the day job-shadowing someone in that career. I didn't want anything ordinary like teaching or marketing, so I said I wanted to be a priest. It was really just a lark. The counselor loved it because no girl had ever signed up for that before—probably no guy, either.

"Anyway, I spent the day with an Episcopalian priest and it was really interesting. I'd already decided I wanted to study classics since shooting up to five foot ten made being a professional ballerina an impractical choice, and Latin was my favorite subject. Anyway, Father Edmund, the priest I was shadowing, said the priesthood would be a great way to use my Latin.

"I didn't take the idea seriously, though, until my first day at Mount Jefferson. My roommate and I were just getting acquainted. She asked me what I wanted to do. I didn't really have any idea, so I said, 'Be a priest'. It was as much a joke as anything, but Melody's response was classic. Her eyes got hugely round and she said, 'You can't be a priest. You're a girl!'" Felicity chuckled at the memory.

"I'm afraid my 'I'll show them' streak has gotten me into lots of trouble. The final straw, though, was my year of teaching in London." She shivered. "Teaching is definitely not my cup of English Breakfast."

Antony was thoughtful for a moment. Felicity might even have described his attitude as doubtful. "What was your church background?" he asked, finally.

"Oh, we were very devout! In all my growing up I can't remember ever missing a service."

"I'm impressed. That's quite a record."

"Yes, indeed. Never a single Christmas or Easter without going to church. CEO Christians, my parents."

"Huh?"

"Christmas and Easter Only."

Antony's furrowed brow relaxed and in the reflected light she could see the tiny lines crinkle at the corners of his eyes. "Ah, having me on, aren't you?"

"Well, yes and no. The point is, when we did go, I loved it. Sometimes I would even sneak off and go to church on my own. I'd say I was going to a movie or something so my brothers wouldn't tease me. Don't worry. I didn't just sign on to life in a monastery because I like men in skirts. I'd have gone for a bagpipe band if that was what I had in mind."

Their shared laughter was hardly more than a chuckle, but it was so good. Felicity suddenly realized it was the first time they had laughed since Father Dominic's murder. Probably the first they had ever really laughed together. His medieval church history lectures were seriously short of the comedic.

Suddenly the little kiosk felt less chill. She was warmed by her memories and she wanted to share them with her companion. She told him about Karen and Amy, her forever friends from childhood. The goofy, carefree things they did together in grade school; the blazing spats they had over absolutely nothing in junior high; the whispered confidences during high school sleepovers.

They had gone on to separate colleges and then to different parts of the world: Amy to teach English as a second language and study guitar in Mexico, Karen to work in an orphanage in

Russia. But they still kept in touch with sporadic, long, stream-of-consciousness e-mails.

Antony listened to her account with a small smile. "It sounds so warm. So, well, friendly." The tiny note of longing in his voice told her he had always been a loner.

He cleared his throat and manoeuvered to get his wristwatch into the light. "That bus is awfully late." He looked again at the schedule to confirm that he had read it correctly.

Felicity peered over his shoulder, squinting to read in the dim light. "Something is definitely wrong. And I'm freezing. That causeway will close in just over half an hour, and I have no intention of spending the night here." With that, she strode to the petrol station behind the bus stop. "This *is* where we catch the bus to Holy Island, isn't it?"

The plump man behind the display counter chock-a-block with sweets looked up. "No buses to Holy Isle, luv. Only on Saturday." He returned to his newspaper.

"But—" Her protest was interrupted by the sound of a car pulling up to a fuel tank outside. She ran to the window on the driver's side. "Would you perhaps be going to the island?"

"I certainly am."

She started at the familiar voice. "Jonathan Breen! What are you doing here?"

"Father Anselm's idea. He thought I might be able to give you a hand. Thought you'd already be on the island by now, though. I just stopped to top up the tank. Need a ride?"

"We sure do!" She ran to call Antony.

In a matter of minutes, they were whizzing over the seaweed-strewn causeway, past the tower provided as refuge for unwary travelers cut off by the rising tides. Felicity shivered. Had they been foolish enough to try walking, that could easily have been their perch for the night. To her right she could just make out the row of stakes marking the mile-and-a-half pilgrim route across the sand.

"How clever of Father Anselm to send you to help us. And

amazing we happened to meet up. You could so easily just have driven right past that bus stop." The heater was cranked up to high and Felicity held her hands gratefully over the vent.

"Just luck really. I wasn't even that low on gas—er, petrol. Oh, and at the Super's suggestion I stopped by your flat. Kate put a few things in a bag for you. You don't waste a lot of time on housekeeping do you?" His teasing was accompanied by a smile which also had a certain warming effect. She could definitely enjoy some extended conversations with this man.

"I'm amazed Father Anselm told you what we were about." Antony sounded curtly skeptical. "I wonder what sort of help he thought you'd be able to offer?"

"He didn't specify—but obviously transportation comes to mind." Jonathan flashed his easy smile. "Or perhaps just more intellectual energy directed at solving the riddle."

"Riddle?" Felicity wished Antony hadn't barked quite so sharply at their rescuer.

"Well, obviously, the riddle of why Dominic was killed—isn't that what we all want to know?"

Felicity was relieved when Antony subsided into silence. She could easily imagine him demanding, "Why you?" in his most caustic voice. And, really, it did make sense—Jonathan Breen was an oblate of the Fraternity of the Transfiguration—an order of lay people who took vows similar to those of the Community members, but committed to live in the secular world and work to support the Community. Undoubtedly Father Anselm saw this as a way Jonathan could lend his support.

And then—she all but blushed to think of it—there was perhaps the matter of chaperonage. Not that she and Antony were likely to need such a thing, but perhaps Father A had had second thoughts about the appearance of what he had rushed them into in the heat of the moment. If Jonathan had offered his services, the superior might have seen sending his oblate on this mission as a way of preserving the proprieties without asking one of the Kirkthorpe Fathers to leave their post.

Once on the island, Antony tersely directed them to the House of St. Aidan in the center of the tiny village. It was a sturdy gray stone structure like the other buildings around it, with a green picket fence surrounding a small, forlorn garden. The gate was locked, but Antony's ring quickly produced a tall, gangly man that instantly made Felicity think of Roald Dahl's Big Friendly Giant. "I'm Willibrord St. John. Welcome to St. Aidan's." He swung the squeaky gate open and ushered them into the fortressed haven decorated in floral chintz and lace. "I'll just go tell my wife to prepare for three guests. Lucky we're not booked at the moment."

"What kind of name is Willibrord?" Felicity asked, sotto voce.

"Saint's name," Antony replied.

Felicity rolled her eyes. "I might have guessed."

"A Northumbrian saint who went to Germany as a missionary in the eighth century. He's the patron saint of Holland," Jonathan added.

St Willibrord, with his lank sandy hair, huge nose, oversized hands and feet, and pale blue eyes returned on his long, thin legs. "My wife apologizes that she doesn't have a hot meal ready, but she can do sandwiches and tea."

"That would be wonderful!" Felicity tried to remember when she had eaten last. A Kit-Kat bar and cup of tea on the train—how many hours ago was that? Oh, yes, before that, a long-gone pasty in Newcastle.

While they ate, Willibrord explained the schedule observed at the retreat house which was sponsored by the Order of St. Aidan: "Compline at eight o'clock in the chapel downstairs. We observe silence after that. Holy Communion in the morning at the parish church just down the street."

Willibrord rose as if to lead the way to the chapel, but Antony stopped him. "First, I'm afraid I have some dreadful news." Willibrord refolded himself into his chair, all attention on Antony. "One of your recent retreatants, Father Dominic. He was found dead in his cell last night." There was no easy way to say it. "I knew you would want to know," he fumbled to a stop.

Willibrord paled. "Oh, that's terrible. But there must be a mistake. He was just here. He was so lively—given his age." He bowed his head for a moment, then looked up. "Heart attack, was it?"

Antony shook his head. "I'm afraid it was murder. He had been hit over the head."

Willibrord sat in stunned silence. Antony continued, "I'm so sorry, but I wanted you to know before prayers."

Felicity saw the shock on Willibrord's face. He seemed frozen for a moment, then folded his hands and headed for the chapel as if hurrying toward its sanctuary. She herself was so tired she was light-headed. Couldn't she just eat a sandwich and fall into bed? Didn't they ever do anything but say prayers around here? But Jonathan's hand was warm on her elbow, guiding her forward, so she went with the program. The chapel, fashioned from a basement storeroom, glowed warmly with indirect lighting and flickering candles. The service was a combination of the monastic end-of-day office blended with Celtic prayers. "I place our brother Dominic's soul under your guiding this night, O God. Flight him to repose in your bosom, O Father of help to frail pilgrims, Protector of heaven and earth."

An hour later, Felicity flung herself on her bed tucked under the eaves, almost too tired to crawl under the floral duvet, and listened to the wind howl around her dormer. She thought she would fall asleep immediately, but her mind swirled with questions as pounding as the elements outside. Their flight northward had been almost instinctive, feeling the long arm of the law grasping for them—or at least for Antony—without ever so much as even seeing a police officer. The feeling that somehow retracing Dominic's footsteps would lead them to his murderer now seemed impossibly vague. What impulse had made her put herself forward for this task? How could knowing the story of some 1,400-year-old saint have any application for today? It had seemed to make sense once, but now everything seemed as black, wet and wild as the pounding storm outside.

Somewhere in the blackness beyond her window, a winter-bare branch was banging against the stone wall, each whack driving home a single question: Incorruption? Immortality? Treasure? And then the thwacks were no longer questions, but deadly blows battering her beloved Dominic.

Was this total insanity? Should she insist on going back tomorrow and looking for clues closer to the scene of the crime? How could traveling 150 miles away from the action help them find clues? After all, it had to have been done by someone who was *there*. Someone who looked and acted perfectly normal, just like everyone else, and yet was raving mad. She shivered and rolled the duvet tightly around her as much for protection as for warmth.

And then her thoughts took quite another direction. She hated history and she had a feeling she could have let herself in for a heavy dose of it. Yes. This was definitely ridiculous. Her mind was made up. She would tell Antony in the morning. He and Jonathan Breen could stay here and commune with the past. She would return to the real world.

And then the memory of Jonathan's smile flashed at her through the dark. Well, OK. Maybe she would stay for one more day.

Chapter 5

The bells called to her as, pushing against the wind the next morning, Felicity shivered her way down the deserted village street to the parish church in the grounds of the ancient priory. She had no idea where Antony and Jonathan were, but she had no intention of looking like a slacker by staying in bed, no matter how her head pounded.

It was odd, really, this love/hate relationship she had with the daily office. Love/hate was probably too strong a term; it was more attraction/repulsion, but however she described it, it amounted to an ongoing battle inside her: this drawing to peace and beauty, while at the same time resisting submission to rigid discipline. Freedom versus order. Well, she wouldn't have to take any vows of holy orders for two years yet—three, if she decided to do an MA—so she had time to work it out, but she knew that ultimately these were issues she had to face, or her life would continue to be a series of internal conflicts.

A jaunty man greeted her at the village square. "Good morning." He waved, then grinned. "'Tisn't really, of course. But then, one can't say 'Bad morning', can one?"

Inside the old stone church the attraction-to-peace side of her struggle won for the moment as she knelt in silence, listening to the raging wind outside the thick, embattled walls. *What a metaphor*, she thought. It was the feast day of some obscure Northumbrian saint so the paraments lit the dim, gray stone interior with glowing red and gold, richly embroidered with designs that she guessed were from the Lindisfarne Gospels. Where had she seen reproductions? Note cards, maybe. Or was that the *Book of Kells*? Somehow, the artwork seemed familiar. Actually, the whole atmosphere was like worshiping inside an ancient manuscript as its intricate, swirling Celtic designs had served as inspiration for all the adornment of the church: The vicar's red and gold vestments, exquisitely embroidered; the rug before the altar, a lovingly handmade reproduction of—what was it called?—a carpet page from the Gospel book, maybe; stained glass, paintings and calligraphy around the church—all intricately interlaced patterns of glowingly rich colors.

As Felicity relaxed in the peace and silence, her mind returned to the questions of the night before; but now she managed to achieve more order to her thoughts. They had come here looking for something—for some clue to Dominic's murder, to Dominic's secret, but it all had such a sense of unreality to it. She kept expecting to wake up and find that Dominic hadn't been murdered, her room hadn't been tumbled, she hadn't made a mad dash to a remote island in the North Sea with a priest. But she had. And she was here.

Was it only yesterday they had left their sheltered world of the monastery for this tiny, wind-battered rock? How could so much distance have been traveled—both physically and emotionally—in such a short time?

Without thinking, she put her hand to her chest. Was she the same young woman who had known all the answers forty-eight hours ago—and had been so ready to share them with the rest of the world? She blushed at her own rashness, her vaunted certainty.

Her only thoughts had been for proving herself and bringing about justice in the world. She had never looked beyond her own ideas about inequality, poverty, abuse. She had never thought about the root cause of such wrongs. Just feed people properly and show them how to behave—she could certainly handle that—and they would. But if someone from the polite, well-fed world of Kirkthorpe could be driven to such an act of evil, there was far more wrong with the world than simple injustice. Not that injustice was ever really simple, of course.

In one violent act, she had glimpsed the face of evil. Suddenly that vague concept which she had always brushed off as a fancy word for bad behaviour caused by social deprivation took on a horrible reality.

How could she possibly face dealing with something of which she hadn't the least understanding? She blinked as a forgotten line came to her. "We seek understanding of the past to find understanding of the present." *Oh, groan. Was history the answer? Could Antony actually be right?* She had had her fill of the ancient world as a classicist. She put up with the required classes, but it was the language and the literature that drew her. Not the grotty everyday life or the endless wars.

It all seemed agonisingly vague, but she supposed the first order of business just might be to grant the possibility that Antony had a point, do her best to curb her impatience with events of the misty past, and attempt to learn all she could about St. Cuthbert. Unlikely as it seemed, perhaps in doing so they actually would learn something about Dominic's journey that would lead them to his murderer. Renewing her vow of the night before, she gritted her teeth and determined to give it a try. Although at the moment she couldn't quite remember what had prompted that decision.

Her thoughts came back to the service just in time to join in a fervent, "Lamb of God who takes away the sin of the world, have mercy on us. Lamb of God who takes away the sin of the world, grant us peace," a prayer she was always able to say a hearty *amen* to.

The words were still repeating in her head as she went forward and knelt at the altar rail on the edge of the Lindisfarne Gospel carpet. *Peace and Patience*, she prayed. Perhaps learning patience would bring the peace. As she extended her cupped hands to receive the host, Jonathan knelt beside her, increasing the warmth that, to her unending amazement, she never failed to experience when she received communion. Antony, Willibrord and a few elderly villagers completed the congregation.

Anna St. John greeted their return to the guest house with

a full cooked breakfast: eggs, fried bread, grilled tomatoes, bacon, sausage. Glad that she had no scruples about eating meat on Fridays, Felicity helped herself to Antony's portion as well. They were on their third rack of toast and fourth pot of tea when Felicity finally felt her appetite slowing.

"And are you sure you wouldn't like just another bite?" Anna was as normal-looking as her husband was odd. Short, slightly plump with brown hair curving around her soft face, she seemed born to her job of mothering pilgrims who came to Holy Island seeking solace.

Once Anna was assured they all had more than ample toast, she joined them, pulling a side chair closer to the table and picking up her knitting from a basket.

"Oh, what a beautiful sweater," Felicity said. "It's an Arran pattern, isn't it?"

"Yes." Anna smiled. "That's all I seem to make. They are the warmest."

"And I love that yarn," Felicity added.

Anna held it out to admire her own work. "Yes, it is wonderful, isn't it? The oatmeal texture is my favorite. It's hand spun by a lady in Newfoundland."

"In Canada?"

"Yes, she came here on retreat once. I've ordered all my yarns from her ever since."

"How long have you lived on Holy Island?" Felicity asked.

"About seven years, now, isn't it?" Anna looked at her husband for confirmation.

"Do you ever feel claustrophobic here?" Felicity thought that she certainly would.

"Not really," Anna said, with a slow smile. "I was the one who actually started coming here first—for classes in Celtic art and spirituality run by the Order of St. Aidan." She chuckled. "We never thought then we'd wind up here, did we, Will?"

Willibrord returned a half-eaten triangle of toast to his plate. "I suppose I thought I'd spend the rest of my life as a Newcastle schoolmaster, trying to drum maths into restless sixth-formers. I came to spiritual things late in life. Anna was the one who saw more to that side of things with the children."

"Oh, tell me about your family," Felicity urged.

"Two sons and a daughter. Frank is a banker and Brian a university lecturer. They both live in London. Susie is a nurse. She lives with her husband and two children in Scarborough." Anna reached for a framed picture on the sideboard as she spoke. She handed the family photo to Felicity. "That's our Jennie-bug." She pointed to a tiny blonde girl being held by an equally blonde, pregnant woman. "It was just before Tommy was born. The last time we were all together—at Will's induction."

Felicity had been surprised to see Willibrord in a black cassock similar to the ones worn at Kirkthorpe. "But you aren't a monk?"

Willibrord's Adams apple bobbed up and down as he laughed. "No, no, certainly not. Being a Warden in the Order of St. Aidan is quite enough for me, thank you."

"So what sort of vows does your order take?" Antony asked.

"Bede praised Aidan eloquently for his love of prayer, study, peace, purity and humility, as well as his care of the sick and poor. We try to follow his example while still living in the world."

Felicity smiled, wondering how much one was "living in the world" on Holy Island.

"Are you Benedictine?" Antony probed.

Willibrord shrugged. "All orders are Benedictine to some extent, it seems. Work. Study. Prayer. That just about sums up a meaningful lifestyle, doesn't it?"

Felicity was wondering if it did when Anna laughed. "Poverty. Chastity. Obedience. I could do with a bit less of the poverty— although I'm all for the obedience. As long as it's Will that's doing the obeying." She rose and began clearing the breakfast things they had all finished with.

Willibrord opened a drawer in the sideboard and brought

out a handful of colorful brochures. "We've had the pleasure of Father Antony's company before, but since you two are new to Holy Isle, I thought you might find these helpful." He handed the leaflets to Felicity and Jonathan. "Be sure you let me know if there's anything I can help you with to make your stay more pleasant."

Felicity glanced through the brochures about the Heritage Centre featuring an electronic reproduction of the Lindisfarne Gospels; the winery offering free samples of Lindisfarne Mead; Lindisfarne Castle, a sixteenth-century fort converted into a private house by Sir Edwin Lutyens with a walled garden by Gertrude Jekyll; the medieval priory ruins, founded in 1083, where "despite erosion by nine centuries of sea weather, the red sandstone church remains a superb example of Norman work…"

Then Felicity realized she needed to be paying attention to the questions Antony was asking Willibrord. Their host still seemed shaken by the news of Dominic's death, but was more than happy to reminisce about the monk's time with them. "Yes, indeed. Father Dominic was here several times. Even when his work was based in Africa, he got back to England occasionally. I like to think we were a true sanctuary for him." Their host stopped and shook his head, making it wobble atop his long, thin neck. "Dead." He gave it two syllables. "Murdered?" He made it a question as if hoping to be contradicted. "I still can't take it in." He removed his wire-rimmed glasses and wiped his eyes with a bony finger.

"Did you notice anything unusual about his visit this time? Did he have any visitors or seem unusually interested in anything on the island?"

Like buried treasure, maybe? Felicity wanted to ask. *For example, did he have a metal detector?*

"No, no. Nothing the least bit unusual."

"Did he seem nervous? Or worried?"

"Not at all. Of course, his gracious calm was one of his

outstanding qualities, wasn't it?" Willibrord took out a large square of white linen and blew his nose loudly. "It's so hard to realize that's gone from the earth. Somehow, one just felt better knowing that such holiness existed."

"How did he spend his time here?"

"Well, I don't really know. Just the usual for a retreatant, I expect. He always kept the office, of course. I think he spent time in the priory grounds, meditating. You understand," he turned to Felicity, "The original monastery is gone, but we believe the medieval priory was built on the very foundations built by St. Aidan, and hallowed by the life and death of Cuthbert. This little island was the most shining center of Christianity in the land in its day."

Antony cleared his throat as if to remind Willibrord that they hadn't come for a tourism lecture.

"Yes, where was I? Oh, yes, how Dominic spent his time here. Of course, I didn't follow him around or quiz him. But I know he spent time in the priory grounds because he mentioned more than once how much he admired the statue of Aidan and how disappointing—insulting, I think his word was—the statue of St. Cuthbert is. But I'm sure you'll want to judge for yourself. Everyone has an opinion. And he spent considerable time on Cuthbert's Island—he liked to meditate there just like the saint did. Stayed too late one evening, had to wade ashore. Turned up at the church for Evensong with his cassock wet to the knees. I worried about his arthritis—kneeling on that stone floor in a wet cassock, but he didn't seem bothered."

"Did he get any letters or phone calls while he was here? Or make any?"

"I wasn't aware of any. But I wouldn't necessarily know. The phone in my office is always available to our guests, even people who just drop in to pray in the chapel. And then, of course, there's the one in the shop in the village. Mobile reception is unreliable out here though."

"Did Dominic talk to you about funding his African children's hospital?" Felicity asked on sudden inspiration. Maybe they could get the conversation onto the topic of treasure.

Their host laughed. "If you mean, did he ramble on about his dream? He hardly did anything else. 'Twenty million Africans have already died from HIV/AIDS, and it is going to get much worse. In some countries, four out of ten people are infected. Life expectancy is falling, and will soon be down to just thirty years. One in six African children still die before their fifth birthday.'" His voice even took on an inflection reminiscent of Dominic's gentle, educated northern cadences. Felicity's throat closed, realizing she would never hear that beloved voice again.

"However, if you mean," Willibrord continued. "Did he ask me for money—I can't think of anything more far-fetched. Paying next month's electric bill is my idea of a miracle." He laughed again, although his eyes didn't look amused and there was an uneasy edge to his voice.

Felicity found the lack of information discouraging, but what had she expected? To learn that Dominic was visited by thugs carrying bludgeons?

The wind had subsided to a brisk breeze by the time they set out for the priory ruin behind the parish church. Antony led the way, with Jonathan and Felicity following behind. Felicity noticed that Antony was surprised, even displeased, when Jonathan indicated his plans to join them, but it seemed very natural and friendly to her. After all, if Father Anselm had sent him to help, surely he had intended more than that Jonathan should deliver her toothbrush and nightshirt.

"So, how did a Harvard professor wind up in such an unexpected place?" she asked, as her steps slowed and fell into place beside Jonathan.

"I'm on sabbatical this term." He answered lightly, treating her to his sun-coming-over-the-mountains smile. "But I expect you were asking for something a bit more existential than that."

She cocked her head and raised one eyebrow, waiting for more and slowing her steps almost to a standstill, widening the gap between them and Antony.

"The whole love of England thing, it's hard to explain, isn't it?" Jonathan said at last. "I expect you get asked the same thing a lot."

Felicity grinned. "Yes. The short answer is that I'm studying here. But that doesn't really do it, does it? There are some excellent—well, pretty good—Anglican seminaries in the States, but I never felt drawn to them, no matter how much my college chaplain pushed his alma mater in Wisconsin. But then I wasn't confirmed Anglican until I came to Oxford, so my spiritual journey has really been English." Now she came to a full stop, waiting for him to continue. Antony, stiff-backed, disappeared into the priory grounds.

"Yes. I understand that. It's a roots thing, isn't it? Of course, that's easier for me to explain because my grandmother is English, my mother an English lit teacher. That certainly influenced my subject field. I didn't know there *was* literature other than English until I got into high school. There certainly wasn't in our home."

"Yes, but surely not many of your colleagues become oblates of Benedictine orders."

He laughed. "I think more college profs live like monks than you'd suspect. Not many of us come up to the celebrity lifestyle of the few who make it into the media. But really, it was my love of medieval literature. The more I studied Bede and William of Malmesbury, even good old Geoffrey of Monmouth with his vivid imagination, I so admired the lifestyle—the whole monastic culture—that saved so much learning for civilization. I guess I just wanted to be a part of that."

"That makes sense. But what about the deeper stuff? Don't oblates take the same vows as the monks?"

Jonathan shrugged. "Like poverty? Even Harvard professors— untenured ones, at least— aren't paid enough for that to be much of a problem." He laughed, then shrugged again. "No, seriously, we're allowed to interpret the Rule in our own way. It's a pretty individual thing."

"Why the Community of the Transfiguration? Why not something closer to home?"

He grinned at her. "You already answered that—why not a seminary closer to home?"

"Touché."

"Actually, it's a better question than you realize." He was silent for some time, as if deciding whether or not to continue. Felicity smiled, willing him to go on. The warm sun, the soft breeze seemed to draw them together in intimacy.

Jonathan took a deep breath, apparently steeling himself for what he was to say. "My father left home when I was seven." Again, a long, deep pause, followed by a shuddering sigh that drew Felicity to lean closer. "OK, the truth is, he shot his father. Died in prison. I don't know why I'm telling you this. I knew I was attracted to you, but this is ridiculous." He ran both hands across his face, then turned abruptly as if he would head back to the retreat house.

Felicity was sure her face registered the shock his words gave her, but she controlled her features and put a hand on his arm to stop him. "No, wait. That is—if you want to talk I'm here, Jonathan." She spoke his name softly, picturing the blond, curly haired little boy he must have been.

Jonathan pulled aside from the path and leaned against the outside of the crumbling wall surrounding the medieval priory grounds, his head still in his hands. "I haven't talked about this to anyone but my confessor for years."

Felicity wasn't sure whether he was speaking to her, or praying. She held her breath.

At last Jonathan looked up, drew a breath and continued in a controlled voice. "What I was trying to say before that outburst— which I will appreciate your overlooking—was that my uncle, my mother's older brother, then became the father figure in my life. Coincidentally, he was a monk, a Vincent Brother. Do you know them?"

"I've seen the name on books. They do a lot of publishing,

don't they?"

"That's right. And their monastery is just off Harvard Square, along the Charles River. That was really why I chose to teach at Harvard rather than staying at Columbia where I took my degree." Again one of his abrupt silences. "How did I get to all of that? You didn't ask for my autobiography."

"Didn't I? I don't remember what I did ask. But thank you for telling me." She wanted to reach out and take his hand. Such long, strong fingers. So tanned. Such well-groomed nails.

"One last irony. My uncle's religious name was Cuthbert." He offered the information almost defiantly.

Felicity's laugh came out like a sneeze. "Amazing! It all sounds foreordained!"

Jonathan didn't reply.

"You said *was*. Is he dead?"

Jonathan nodded. "Three years ago."

"And that's when you became an oblate of CT?" Her companion had become suddenly withdrawn. His only reply was a curt nod. Had she intruded somehow? "You must miss him," she said at last. It would have been like losing his father twice. She couldn't imagine.

"Yeah." Jonathan pushed away from the wall and turned toward the turnstile into the priory grounds.

Felicity followed, her thoughts in turmoil. She felt so drawn to this intriguing, charismatic man. And—she caught her breath afresh at the thought—he had said he was attracted to her. She blinked at the memory of his words, spoken almost as an afterthought. And yet it seemed that approaching him was a minefield. An apparently mundane observation could cause his vibrant smile to evaporate, leaving her feeling as cold as if the sun had gone out.

And then there was Antony's inexplicably unwelcoming attitude toward this man who had been sent by the superior to help them. Why did Antony barely tolerate someone he should have welcomed as a colleague?

Well, at least she had no problem in that department. She could make up for Antony's unfriendliness by letting Jonathan know she welcomed his help and expertise.

Chapter 6

I nside the priory walls, they joined Antony standing in front of the statue of St. Aidan. Antony gave the latecomers a long, level look, then turned back to the statue. Felicity stood behind him and gazed upward. It was a remarkable piece of work. Perhaps nine feet tall and slim, the figure managed to suggest asceticism and yet great strength at the same time. The red sandstone image looked perfectly at home, standing where the man himself might have stood when he came to establish a monastery here in the very year Cuthbert was born. "Lightbringer to the North," he still held his torch aloft.

"The story really begins here." Antony turned abruptly, taking command at the foot of the statue. In spite of the stiffness in his demeanour, due, Felicity was certain, to his antipathy to Jonathan, he managed to look just as right there as he did in his classroom. Felicity was glad she had accepted learning about Cuthbert as a goal for the day, because she could tell she was going to hear the story whether she wanted to or not. The college lecturer stance was all too familiar to her. And, if she were honest, it made a welcome relief from thinking about Jonathan, who was a disturbingly warm presence just behind her right shoulder.

"We really have to go back to 616 when Oswald, in refuge on Iona, became a Christian under the tutelage of the Celtic monks there."

Felicity sighed. She was only in her first term of church history so she had to flip mentally through her lecture notes. Oh, yes, Iona—off the western coast of Scotland—Cradle of Scottish Christianity, founded by St. Columba; what were his dates? 560-something? But the story was racing ahead of her. She jerked her thoughts forward three quarters of a century.

War raged in the kingdom of Northumbria. The barbarian Welsh prince Caedwalla, self-proclaimed king of the Britons, led his savage troops of warriors, ravaging the land, slaughtering men, women and children, and finally, killing Edwin, King of the Northumbrians.

Oswald, Edwin's nephew, was now king. Oswald, who had spent his many years in refuge on the Island of Iona under the nurture of the Columban monks, learning the admonitions of their Christian God, returned to his kingdom and gathered his small, ragtag army.

Oswald's men were few. They were battle-weary and weakened by defeat. But Oswald knew a greater power. Before the battle, Oswald ordered a large cross to be made of hewn timbers lashed with leather thongs.

His troops assembled and waiting, King Oswald strode onto the field before them. He seized the cross and thrust it into the prepared hole with his own hands. The first cross to be erected in the kingdom.

The earth shook as the heavy, timbered cross thudded into place, sending a tingling shiver through the troops. Oswald cried out to his army: "Let us all kneel together and pray the all-powerful, everliving, and true God, the King of heaven, to defend us in his mercy from this proud and fierce enemy. He, the Almighty, knows that we are fighting in a just cause for the preservation of our whole race."

Oswald paused to let the power of his words sink in as a breeze rippled the air. Then the king and all his army fell to their knees before the cross and called on the Christian God to send heavenly aid to his people in their dire need.

Just as dawn was breaking, they advanced against the enemy. Oswald's victory was sure and swift. Peace was secured for all the kingdom.

In gratitude to God who gave the victory, Oswald sent speedy messengers to Iona, beseeching spiritual help for his kingdom. "My people live in darkness. Send us a teacher. Send one who will bring

the light of the gospel to shine forth across our land."
Iona sent Aidan. Abjuring life in the royal enclosure at
Bamburgh, Aiden and his small group of missionary monks settled
at Lindisfarne, so like their island home on Iona. Aidan and his
band lived an austere and ascetic life in primitive huts with only a
small oratory for their own worship, but from that foundation they
Christianized all of Northumbria.

Gazing up at the face of the statue, Felicity nodded. Skepticism aside, one could believe this was a man of vigor and devotion who could evangelize a whole kingdom.

They walked on over the thick green grass carpeting the former monastery floor, gazing up at the rough, red, ruined sandstone walls and broken arches. "Aidan was buried in this very cemetery and later translated into the church he himself had built here—not the one you see now, of course—the medieval priory came some 450 years later." Felicity followed the sweep of Antony's arm that carried her visually forward through the centuries.

"Even in its broken state, one gets a sense of it's fortified character—heavy, very Norman. Not hard to recognize the inspiration carried over from Durham by the monks who founded the medieval cell on the island in 1083." Antony pointed out the incised decoration of the nave pillars and the diagonal rib vault still standing between the crossing piers.

Jonathan gave it all a cursory glance, but seemed to be concentrating far more on Felicity herself than on the ancient architecture around them. Felicity was flattered, but somewhat surprised. She had assumed that, as a scholar, Jonathan would be as riveted by all this minutiae as Antony was. A compliment though it was, Jonathan's detachment helped her understand why Antony questioned what help he could be. But for that matter, what help did she think she was being? Other than as an audience for Antony to display his knowledge, of course. What did any of this have to say about the great clash of good and evil she had explored so tenuously in church this morning? Well, Oswald saw his victory as a triumph of good over evil, and perhaps it was more than a simple military victory. Certainly the result had been a triumph of good, as it paved the way for Aiden to carry his torch of truth and light to this remote area.

So long ago—and yet the results were still evident around them. And did it all make a difference to the way people believed and lived today? Surely, it must. Each generation had to renew its own faith, ideals, morality; claim it anew and pass it on to the next generation, or it would be lost. And so the sites must be cherished. The stories told. The values lived.

OK, it was important. With effort, she renewed her determination to be more patient with Antony.

"Now, the domestic buildings of the priory are thirteenth and fourteenth century." Antony waved an arm vaguely southward, bringing Felicity's attention back to the story she was determined to learn. "And down here is the controversial statue of St. Cuthbert."

"Oh." Felicity had made up her mind to like it no matter what. It was so appropriate for Cuthbert to be here in some physical form that she felt prepared to applaud any effort. But the green oxidized lump in a vaguely humanoid form defeated her. "Was he short?" Was all she could think to say.

To her surprise, Jonathan burst out laughing. "Caught him to a tee! I can't believe it. It's Uncle Cuthbert in the flesh."

At Antony's puzzled look Felicity explained about Jonathan having a religious uncle who had taken the name Cuthbert.

Then Jonathan turned to Felicity. "Sorry for that outburst, but it gave me quite a start. Actually, to answer your question, the saint probably would have been short to our eyes. People were then." His speech took on a rhythm that reminded Felicity she was in the company of not one, but two college lecturers. "I think the artist is trying to convey Cuthbert's oneness to the island by keeping him close to it. And notice how he chose to work with round, curving shapes which feel warmer and more welcoming than the stiff angularity of Aidan. The artist is trying to convey a spirit, not a replica. As a work of art I find this much more evocative than the more representational depiction of Aidan."

"Hmmm." Felicity nodded. She could see his point. She couldn't imagine anyone putting forth a better defense. Maybe Father Anselm was right. Jonathan's unique vision might be helpful after all; although Antony's withdrawn attitude didn't indicate that he would agree with her. Ignoring Antony, she flipped her long, thick braid over her shoulder and gave Jonathan her warmest smile.

Antony continued as if none of the side play had happened— or as if they were unruly students. Remembering her frustration over the inattention of her pupils during her exasperating year of teaching in London, Felicity blushed and vowed to focus on the task at hand. No matter how hard Jonathan's disturbing presence made it.

"Cuthbert's story really begins when he was only sixteen years old, and had already served for a short while in Oswald's army. He was home again, tending the sheep on his beloved Lammermuir hills and searching for his next step." Antony settled into his story, taking on more the quality of a Celtic bard than the academic he was. Felicity held her breath. She had never heard Antony lecture so poetically. He always gave all the facts with great precision, but now he painted a picture that put his hearers physically in the scene.

What should he do with his life? Cuthbert wondered as the bright August day turned to dark, starless night. Cuthbert sat alone on the bare hillside tending the drowsing sheep. His fellow shepherds were sleeping too, but Cuthbert would never choose to waste these hours in sleep. These were the best, the most valuable hours of the day. In the still and darkness of night he had what he most cherished: peace, quiet, time to be alone with creation and its Maker.

That night, though, was different. The air seemed to vibrate. Clouds moved across the sky, changing the shape of the dark. And then it happened. The still peace of the covering sky ripped apart. A beam of dazzling light emblazoned the blackness. A pool of light seemed to form around Cuthbert. As he stared, transfixed, a host of angels carried a soul of surpassing brightness to heaven in a globe of fire.

The next morning word reached them that the holy Aidan, the Light-bearer, Bishop of Lindisfarne, had died. Now Cuthbert knew. This was what he had been waiting for. Here was his call to arms, the sign to take action he had been waiting for without realizing it.

On horseback and armed with a spear, Cuthbert appeared at the gate of Melrose Abbey and asked to be admitted as a monk. "Behold a servant of the Lord!" The prior exclaimed and welcomed him in.

Felicity felt her resistance ebbing. She usually scoffed at saints' stories but here, on the site of these ancient events, with the sound of the sea lapping the island shore just over the hillock beside them, it was easy to believe such things could actually have happened. Especially when infused with Antony's vibrancy. Now she smiled, looking at the egg-shaped statue, trying to picture that striking a valiant pose on horseback. And yet—somehow there was a strength there. Almost primordial, as Jonathan had suggested.

At Melrose, Cuthbert took the tonsure—the Celtic half-moon shaving of the forehead from ear to ear—and, after undergoing a period of training and helping found another abbey at Ripon, he began a strenuous missionary effort that took him the length and breadth of Northumbria, teaching and healing the people— spreading the fire of his faith.

After the Synod of Whitby, Cuthbert was sent by the Abbot of Melrose to establish order at Lindisfarne in the wake of the chaos left by the decree that all their practice must change. In his gentle yet firm way, Cuthbert oversaw the change from the Celtic church to the Roman that the Synod dictated. This was the fulfillment of

*Cuthbert's fiery vision of Aidan's soul leaving Holy Island. Now
Cuthbert was to bear the torch of faith.*

*But it was a torch that would often scorch its own bearer.
Keeping the flickering flame of truth alight was not easy in those
early days of division and dissension. The thirteen years Cuthbert
had spent at Melrose in quiet prayer, disciplining his mind, focusing
his heart on God alone, prepared him for this monumental task.
Now all his resources were called upon.*

*Cuthbert knew that the church could bring no peace to its
people until it was at peace with itself. And so whenever discord
and controversy arose in his ranks, Cuthbert chose nonviolent
resistance. The monks met in chapter every day to discuss the
business of the monastery. Whenever arguments among the monks
became too heated—and they regularly did—Cuthbert would
calmly rise and walk from the room. Chapter was dissolved for the
day. The next day, the abbot would return as if nothing untoward
had occurred. Sometimes the brothers could then proceed to work
out their differences peaceably. But often not. Cuthbert would
rise again and leave. This continued until the monks could work
together as brothers in the Lord. Through it all, Cuthbert remained
calm and cheerful. Throughout his rigorous life, he never lost his
sense of humor or the twinkle in his eye.*

In spite of her best intentions, Felicity began fidgeting. OK, so
she *was* getting a feel for the man and the place—maybe even an
inkling of what attracted Dominic—but she was irritated by their
inaction; the sense that they were wasting time was driving her
crazy. "Can't we *do* something? Now?"

Her outburst came out much louder than she had intended,
but Antony turned to her calmly. "Such as?"

"Well, what I mean is history is—history. It's past. You can't
change it. The future is what matters. *That* we can change."

"And you intend to."

"Exactly."

"I agree."

"You do?" Her eyebrows shot upward to demonstrate her surprise.

"Of course you can't change the past and the future is what matters, but the past impinges on the future. We have a better chance of controlling the future if we understand the past." Right. She'd heard that before. But his next words made her blink. "'That which hath been is now; and that which is to be hath already been; and God requireth that which is past.'"

"Huh?"

"It's in the Bible. Ecclesiastes."

"Oh, sorry. Suppose I should have known. But do you mean we might have prevented Dominic's murder if we had paid more attention to history?" She didn't try to keep the skepticism out of her voice.

"It's possible, perhaps even certain, that if we all lived by the ideals Cuthbert and Dominic gave their lives to, the world would be a much better place." With that, Antony gave a nod of his head that indicated class was dismissed. He turned and led the way out of the grounds of the ruined monastery, walking along a grassy path toward the edge of the island. Felicity stifled her impulse to inquire if they would be quizzed on the morning's lecture. She knew that even at college they wouldn't—the English system was all based on essay writing. No quizzes.

The real quiz was the one Felicity was giving herself. She had to admit that, in spite of her restlessness, she had been enthralled by Antony's story. So why did she feel such irritation toward the storyteller? And why did he seem so disapproving of her? And why did she care whether he approved of her or not? They were here to do a job. It was nothing personal.

The sun was now shining strongly, dazzling in the almost cloudless blue sky. The wind, which was much stronger since they left the shelter of the priory grounds, ruffled the long strands of golden hair that had escaped from her braid. As she strode along over the uneven ground, a glorious sense of freedom suddenly infused her. She turned to Jonathan with a smile. "Thanks for having the forethought to bring my jeans."

"I'd like to take credit, but it was Kate. She said you would probably be wearing one of your long skirts and she thought you might welcome something more practical."

"Right on." Felicity gave her distant classmate a thumbs-up, then stopped abruptly when the path ended at the edge of a bank above the rocky beach. "Oh, another island. It's lovely." Perhaps a hundred feet offshore (Felicity was never a good judge of distances), a small round island appeared to float like a green-gold meadow in the sea. It seemed to be entirely smooth, except for a large wooden cross standing in the center.

"St. Cuthbert's Island we call it today. In his day it was called Hobthrush—"

"What's that, a bird?" Felicity asked.

Antony's eyes crinkled in one of his rare smiles. "Nothing so poetic, I'm afraid. It's a woodlouse, actually. Apparently the island is louse-shaped."

Felicity laughed. "And why the cross?"

"To mark its significance as Cuthbert's retreat." Antony clasped his hands behind his back and turned to Felicity and Jonathan in a manner that told her that, contrary to her earlier impression, lectures had not finished for the day. "Monastic life was far too bustling for Cuthbert to maintain his centered calm without frequent restocking. He regularly withdrew here for private retreats. It was convenient because he could walk to it when the tide was out, yet it was cut off from the main island for six hours every day."

"Oh," Felicity suddenly remembered. "Willibrord Dominic spent time there. That's where he was when he had to wade ashore." It made sense to her now.

Antony nodded. "That's right. And it proved a likewise problematic retreat for Cuthbert. The trouble was, it was too convenient. Too many interruptions. Monks could simply stand on the shore and shout questions across the narrow strip of water. There was too much coming and going. Life was too busy."

Jonathan shook his head, making the sun glint on his wind-tossed blond hair. "Can you believe that? Who would think that a seventh-century monk could have such a modern problem? He might as well have had a cell phone."

Felicity looked up and shot Jonathan a companionable grin. His use of the American term gave her a warm fellow-feeling.

"So, Cuthbert sought greater solitude," Antony continued. He turned from the water's edge and led the way up the spine of the little hillock above the beach. At the highest spot he pointed southwestward. "About six miles out there is the island of Inner Farne. It's quite famous now as a bird refuge, but once it was Cuthbert's refuge from the world." Antony squinted seaward. "You can almost see it, with a little imagination."

Felicity, balancing on the edge of the drop-off, squinched up her eyes and peered. *Was she supposed to see an island out there?* "Sorry. Not enough imagination, I guess." She continued gazing, surveying the land on either side of the ocean view before her. At last she pointed with both hands. "But what are those? Castles on both sides of the channel?"

Antony put his hand up to shade his eyes and turned toward the mainland. "Yes, that's Bamburgh Castle. You remember, Bamburgh was the capital of Northumbria? King Oswald had his fortress there." Felicity nodded obediently.

Then he turned to the left, the small castle perched atop a high round rock. "Lindisfarne Castle."

"Oh, yes, Willibrord gave us a brochure," Felicity said. "It looks charming."

"Want to see it? I'll walk down with you this afternoon," Jonathan offered.

Felicity was about to accept, when Antony cut in. "That won't be necessary. The castle wasn't on Dominic's agenda."

Felicity opened her mouth to protest. She would love to see the castle. But Antony cut her off. "We're not on a sightseeing tour."

Seething, but recognizing the accuracy of the statement,

she tried to focus where Antony was pointing—a little spot somewhere in the water between the two castles. Cuthbert's retreat in the sea, on a barren, rocky island just offshore from Bamburgh.

She continued to stare as Antony talked, stepping up onto a rocky mound for a better view. Maybe she could just make out a dark lump somewhere out there. Or maybe not. At least her imagination was improving.

"Cuthbert loved his little island. He spent his time communing with God and the birds and animals he loved. As well as ministering to the steady stream of humanity that sought him over the wind-tossed sea."

The sun was beginning to warm the sea breeze. The noontime light danced on the waves and on Jonathan's head above her. Felicity could no longer keep her mind on events that occurred a millennium and a half ago. Antony's voice tossed around her head, mingled with the splash of waves, rustle of grasses and buzz of insects. The story continued about Cuthbert leaving his refuge to accept a bishopric at the insistence of some ancient king.

How dare Antony forbid her going to the castle? He could carry on with his dusty research. She would simply tell him. She turned to Jonathan with a wink and a smile that let him know what she was planning. But there was no stopping the vigor of Antony's account as he ranged the length and breadth of Northumbria with the saint.

Tramping the high hill country and wild, windswept moors, Cuthbert taught the people who flocked to him, laid his hands on them, prayed for them. When there were no dwellings for him to stay in, people would collect branches and build a temporary hut so he could minister in the area for several days.

As a bishop, Cuthbert never told his clergy how they were to represent God to the people, he showed them by feeding the poor and healing the sick. His work as a healer earned him the name, "Wonderworker of Britain." And always, Cuthbert, who had served in the army as a young lad, continued to fight the spiritual war. Always he surrounded his people with constant prayer. The harder he worked, the harder he prayed. Days spent in physical labor were followed by nights of spiritual work.

On one such occasion, some women carried a young man with a grievous illness to Cuthbert on a pallet. The bishop asked to be left alone with the boy. Cuthbert prayed, signed him with the cross, and pronounced a blessing. Just as in similar stories in the New Testament, the lad got up, praised God, and asked for something to eat—"

"Well, thank you, Antony, well told. Very interesting indeed." Jonathan's forceful voice broke into the narrative. "Afraid I'm feeling a bit like that lad on the pallet, though. This sea air does stimulate the appetite, and we wouldn't want to keep our good hostess waiting."

"Oh, yes, I'm starv—" Forgetting she was standing on a narrow ridge, Felicity turned too quickly and stumbled against Antony, knocking him backward several steps.

At the same moment, a long, slim missile hissed through the air inches from Felicity's ear, just where she had stood seconds before.

A shriek tore from her before it was cut off by her heart leaping into her throat. Her temples pounded. For a moment she thought she would black out. Slowly the world steadied.

"An arrow!" She started to pull away from Antony, then was seized with violent shaking at her next thought. "We were almost shot. We could have been killed!"

"Get down!" Jonathan shouted, and took off at a run toward the abbey ruin from which the shot had come.

"Jonathan, be careful!" Her voice caught on a sob and the wind flung her words back at her. Antony pulled her into the long grasses lining the hillock, but as soon as he released his grasp she rolled away and began searching the grass. She found the projectile some yards beyond where they had stood.

Antony followed her. "What on earth? Who would shoot

an arrow at us?" He frowned and looked around at the empty landscape. "Must be some kid being careless with something they picked up at a museum gift shop."

"No." Felicity examined the steel-tipped shaft in her hand. "This isn't a child's toy. It's a serious weapon. And it isn't an arrow."

Antony's broad brow furrowed more deeply, his dark eyebrows almost meeting.

"It's a crossbow bolt."

"Crossbow? How can you tell?"

"Too short to be an arrow. And only two feathers; an arrow would have three. And there's no nock on the end to fit into the string of a bow." She ran her finger over the smooth end. "See, the string rests flat against the wood."

Antony scrutinized the bolt. "Amazing. How did you know that?"

"My brother shoots a crossbow in the SCA."

"Huh?"

"Society for Creative Anachronism. People who like living in the Middle Ages in their spare time. You'd love it. Makes a change for Jeff from being a computer engineer."

Antony shook his head. "Your brother is a hobby medievalist? You were set up to live in a monastery, weren't you?"

Jonathan appeared back at the top of the rise, panting for breath. "No sign of anyone. A couple of kids in the abbey grounds. I gave them an earful, but they protested innocence."

"Are you all right to go back now?" Antony placed his hand briefly on Felicity's arm.

"Of course." She dusted the sand off her jeans and strode off with a show of bravado that she was far from feeling.

That couldn't have been a random accident. Someone had just tried to kill one of them.

As her mind cleared, her focus sharpened. That crossbow bolt changed everything. Suddenly their time on Holy Isle was proven sharply relevant. Delving into the past as they had been doing had to be important, or someone wouldn't be trying so desperately to stop them.

She let her breath out as an exploratory token of submission. Maybe she wouldn't rebel. She would tell Jonathan she couldn't go to the castle with him this afternoon. It was a necessary decision. She dithered between her head and her heart.

Chapter 7

Antony's mind whirled as he made his dazed way back to St. Aidan's. Felicity could have been killed. He could have been killed. Was someone trying to get them to abandon their search? But how could that be? No one but Father Anselm knew they were here. And Willibrord and the handful of people at church this morning, of course. But why would anyone want to kill them? Were they closer to finding the secret than they knew? He didn't think they had discovered anything yet.

What should he do? Call the police? Where were the nearest authorities? Bamburgh? Seahouses? Beal looked too small. But the police were looking for *him*. To call the authorities would be to abandon hope.

And on a deeper level, one he tried to suppress as irrelevant, he berated himself. What was the matter with him? He knew he had nattered on all morning, boring his listeners. It was information Felicity needed to know as background for their search, but she wasn't in a classroom. It was as if he couldn't stop himself. It had always been the same—taking refuge in his studies. The real world could swirl around him with violence and romance, but he stuck to his history lecture.

What if that crossbow bolt had struck Felicity because he insisted that she stand there and listen to him, while all the time it had been obvious that what she really wanted to do was stroll up the beach with the abominable Breen? What was a breen—a kind of fish, wasn't it?—cold-eyed and squirmy. Oh, no, that was bream, a yellowish carp. Oh, well, close enough.

All right, he was being unfair. He would tell her after lunch to go on to the castle. He could peruse manuscripts at the Heritage Centre on his own. He was always best on his own anyway. Time he quit dithering and took vows. This feet-in-both-worlds life of being a secular priest working in a religious community was unsustainable. It was no wonder he felt so torn. Take vows of celibacy and be done with the anguish of indecision.

He squared his shoulders. Just the thought made him feel better. Decisive. As if he had a grip. Pity monks no longer took the tonsure. He ran his fingers backward through his thick hair.

But back to the matter at hand. What about Felicity? His responsibility for her. His heart went cold thinking that that arrow—er, bolt—could have been aimed at her. He looked at her striding ahead of him, head up, long, golden braid swinging in the wind. She was splendid. A long-suppressed memory pushed itself forward of another young woman, wide-eyed and innocent... No. He would not go there. *Think about Felicity.* He couldn't put Felicity at risk, even if it meant his own imprisonment. He jogged ahead to catch up with her.

"Felicity." She turned at his touch on her shoulder. "I'll check the tide schedules and call a taxi. I'm sending you back to Kirkthorpe."

She gaped at him. "Why?"

"You'll be safe there."

"Safe? Like Father Dominic was safe, you mean? And what do you mean you're *sending* me back? What about you?"

"I'll go with you, if that's what you want."

"*Want?* For you to go back and be arrested? Before we can prove who really did it?"

"Well, actually, I had thought of staying on and continuing the search on my own."

"Right. So next time there won't be anybody to knock you out of harm's way." She took a step backward and put her hands on her hips. "You do need me, you know."

"Hey, Fliss, are you coming?" Jonathan called from up the street. "We don't want to miss the afternoon opening."

She blinked, then smiled warmly. "Kevin was the only person who ever called me that." It was spoken almost under her

breath. Then she raised her voice. "Go on, Jon. I'll catch you up
in a minute."

Antony blinked. *Jon? Fliss?*

Felicity looked chagrined. "Yeah. OK, I'll admit that I did
think of taking the afternoon off. That castle really does look
awfully interesting. But then—that... that attack has to be
hopeful."

"Hopeful?"

"Sure, we must be on the right track. Nobody would bother
if we weren't."

"Felicity, I can't allow—" But she was already striding ahead
with her long, easy gait. His legs were almost as long as hers, but
too many years in the halls of academia and hallowed church
spaces had removed any tendency he might ever have had to
lope. How many years had it been? He did recall racing on
Morecombe beach with Gwena. And he would have won if she
hadn't cheated. Stuck her foot out in front of him and he landed
face downward, spitting sand. But he got her back later. Pulled
her into the water with her new white trousers on...

The creaking gate called him back to the present. Three
new guests had joined them at the retreat centre. Ms. Philomena
("Call me Philly") Johnson, exuding clouds of hyacinth scent,
was just coming down the stairs with her teenage son, Curtis, as
the latecomers dashed up to wash before lunch. Philly Johnson,
her professionally coifed blonde hair set off by a cerise sweatshirt
that matched her lipstick and fingernails, was explaining to
Willibrord her long-standing desire to see "The very ground that
had nurtured the glorious Lindisfarne Gospels."

When Antony returned to join the guests around the table,
she was holding forth on her success as an art teacher in Chicago.
"Would you believe that I have *nine* former students now studying
at the Chicago Institute of Art? Of course, it's their own talent
and passion for their craft that carries them onward, but I do
flatter myself that without good teaching in high school they
might have had a harder time."

She looked up and eyed Antony's clerical collar. "Oh, but then, *you* must know all about what it is to inspire people, vicar." Antony couldn't think how to reply to that.

Fortunately, the formidable Philly paused for a drink of water, so Willibrord could introduce the other newcomer, Stephen Bootham, who he said made frequent visits there whenever he could get away from his bookshop in York. Stephen, who appeared to be about forty, had clear blue eyes and a stubbly black beard matching the hair curling on his well-muscled arms as well as on his head. He explained that he was an enthusiastic birdwatcher and had found few better places to indulge his hobby than on the Farne Islands.

Felicity, apparently fully recovered from their recent encounter, turned to him with enthusiasm. "Oh, I have an aunt who is an avid birder. How many species have you logged?"

Bootham had been attacking a large bowl of steaming soup with considerable gusto, but he set his spoon aside at Felicity's question. "Almost 300. I've been at it for years."

"What are some of your rarest?"

"Well, you wouldn't call them rare, but the most unusual sea bird to nest in this area, from the standpoint of appearance and habit, is the puffin. It's often called the sea parrot because of its large triangular bill—a member of the auk family, but local fishermen call it Tommy Noddy. Puffins are better designed for swimming than for flying, really, and of course—"

"That's fascinating," Felicity cut in quickly. "Antony here," she waved a hand toward him, "mentioned the bird sanctuary on Inner Farne while we were on the beach just now. Perhaps you saw us there?"

"No, no. I just arrived."

Did he deny that too quickly? Antony wondered. But even more, he was amazed, flattered even, at Felicity's words. So she was listening to his rambles.

"Oh, yes? You a birder, too, are you, Father?" Bootham swallowed a spoonful of soup and went right on before Antony was obliged to answer. "Sanctuary's maintained by the National Trust. They estimate more than 70,000 pairs of birds breed there. Let me give you a little hint." He leaned forward and pointed his spoon in Felicity's direction. "If you visit in breeding season, be sure to wear a hat!" He ended with a deep guffaw.

"Have you been to all the Farne Islands?" Felicity continued, with polite interest.

Stephen Bootham laughed again whilst helping himself to a slice of Anna's excellent wholegrain bread. "I've probably come about as close as anyone, but no one can say for sure they've been to all of the Farne Islands. Official count is twenty-eight, but no one knows for certain. The tides cover different ones at different times, so it's impossible to keep track."

Anna cleared the bowls of carrot and coriander soup and set a platter of mixed salad greens on the table to accompany the slices of cold roast chicken. "Oh, I should have thought!" Anna jumped up from the table when she noticed Antony passing over the chicken. She returned with a bowl of hard-boiled eggs and a jar of salad cream. "This is what I always gave Father Dominic on Fridays; he did enjoy eggs mayonnaise."

Philly seized the opportunity of the interruption at the table to urge her son, Curtis, to finish his meal so they could get on to the Heritage Centre. Curtis, whose spiked black hair, tight black T-shirt and multiple piercings, hardly made the wearer look like the typical Lindisfarne pilgrim, merely nodded to his mother. There was, however a Celtic theme to his tattoos. "So you like Celtic art, do you, Curtis?" Antony asked.

"Yeah, it's cool."

Antony looked around the table. Where had these people been some twenty minutes ago? Had one of them been shooting a crossbow from the broken walls of the abbey garden? Stephen Bootham didn't get those muscles birdwatching. And what about Curtis? A Celtic culture enthusiast could be interested in medieval weaponry. At least it was clear Philomena hadn't had that hairdo out in the wind.

"Actually, Curtis is just being modest. He's a very knowledgeable collector. You probably recognize his torque as a zoomorphic dog from the Lindisfarne Gospels." Philly indicated the elongated animal-like tattoo circling her son's neck. "You know, at the center you'll be able to study the original in close-up electronically, Curtis."

Before the laconic Curtis could respond, had he wanted to, she went on to lecture the table in general as if informing a captive audience of art students. "I've read all about it, you know. With their touch screen electronic version, we actually turn the pages of the Lindisfarne Gospels. Of course, we've seen the original pristinely displayed under glass in the British Library, but here we can enlarge the tiniest detail on a page and revel in its full glory. Won't that be *thrilling*?"

She turned to her son who had managed somehow to sprawl even on his straight, wooden chair. "Sit up, Curtis." He moved fractionally, and Philly continued her monologue. "My fingers are just itching to get started." She wiggled her manicured, presumably tingling, nails. "The book is an absolute miracle, you know. Imagine the mechanics of producing it: 516 pages, which would have taken the hides of at least 129 calves. The text was copied from the Vulgate of St. Jerome, probably borrowed from the monastery at Jarrow. The script is Insular Majuscule, which originated in Ireland."

Antony sat amazed. Had the woman actually memorized all that?

"Imagine—one of the world's great art treasures—produced for ceremonial use for special church festivals." She leaned forward, one elbow on the table, her hand cupping her chin, as if flirting with him. "Wouldn't it be *thrilling*, Father Antony? I can just see you on a great feast day, processing down the aisle in full liturgical splendor, holding the precious book aloft, surrounded by candles and wafts of incense." Her half-closed eyelids fluttered. Antony squirmed and gritted his teeth. Had Felicity giggled?

Philomena recovered herself with a small shake of her head.

"Of course, the real interest is the fifteen pages of elaborate decoration. Perhaps you know—each Gospel has a page showing the Evangelist and his symbols, a carpet page of intricate Celtic knot work around a cross, and a major initial page—"

She was interrupted by the scraping of Curtis's chair as he left the table. Antony smiled. Was this how the formidable Ms. Johnson inspired her students to pursue careers in art? Perhaps her lectures drove them to their easels as an escape.

After lunch, Stephen Bootham gathered up his high-powered binoculars and made his getaway before he could be marshaled into visiting the Heritage Centre as Philly Johnson swept all before her.

Antony was anxious to return to their research. He could almost feel his neck crawl with the thought that they were being watched. Through Bootham's binoculars? Through Willibrord's wire-rimmed spectacles? Through Curtis's hooded, bored eyes? Through a window filled by an unseen occupant? Someone out there somewhere wanted to stop them before they had accomplished anything. Best to get Felicity filled in on the rest of the background quickly, and get on to hunting more current clues before something else happened.

Just so long as he didn't drag Felicity into new danger. Poor girl, wide-eyed American, he didn't want to be the one to quash her effervescence. Someone would sometime. It came to all I'm-off-to-change-the-world do-gooders, but he didn't want to be the one to quench the light in those wide, shining eyes.

Was the risk worth it? Could there possibly be anything here worth finding? Willibrord's lack of relevant information on Dominic's time here had been disheartening, as had his own careful reading of Dominic's journal pages last night. And now, return to their task was to be delayed as Willibrord asked him to lead the midday office. It was as natural a part of his life as breathing—the daily office. As a priest, he was sworn to keep morning and evening prayers, and at the monastery they kept a fivefold office. And yet today, he simply couldn't command the focus. He sensed Felicity's similar frustration at the delay—until Jonathan entered the chapel and the tension in her features relaxed into a brilliant smile.

But what really brought Antony up short was the realization that he had been thinking that praying amounted to a waste of time. What could possibly be less a waste in such a desperate situation? If he had prayed more instead of taking his own action, would he now be free of remorse?

It was a short office of psalm, reading and prayers. And as always, the appointed psalm was amazingly appropriate for their situation:

> *The Lord will not let your foot be moved and he who watches over you will not fall asleep.*
> *The Lord shall preserve you from all evil; it is he who shall keep you safe.*
> *The Lord shall watch over your going out and your coming in, from this time forth for evermore.*

By the time he came to the final collect, Antony's breathing was steadied, his mind focused. "O God, you will keep in perfect peace those whose minds are fixed on you; in quietness and trust shall be our strength." As always, Antony left the chapel more centered than he had entered it.

The short, picturesque walk with Felicity up the village lane to the museum was a pleasant respite past stone cottages with brave primroses struggling into bloom in their gardens. A respite that was shattered as soon as they entered the display room at the Heritage Centre.

Philly looked up instantly from her rapt contemplation at the computer screen and beckoned them over. "Look, look. Have you ever seen anything more *enthralling?*" Her bright red fingertip touched a corner on the page displayed, and the screen filled with a close-up detail of intense blue and gold. "Such intricate beauty. Just look at the spectacular elaboration, the creative flow of line, the intriguing geometric pattern, the glowing colors—"

Antony smiled. "Amazing, isn't it? And to think it was all produced by one man." He shook his head. "Think what it must have been like for the lone artist, working in his scriptorium, with only the most basic materials, to produce such a masterpiece in about two years."

Philomena looked decidedly crestfallen that someone else had detailed knowledge of her pet subject. "Yes. Quite."

But he had piqued Felicity's interest. "Surely he had help?"

"Undoubtedly, for basic tasks like sharpening his feather pens, mixing the soot and egg white for his black ink, and gathering plants and minerals for the colored paint, but all the illumination is by a single hand." Antony answered since Philly had fallen icily silent. "A monk named Eadfrith. He later became Bishop of Lindisfarne, but he is most important to us as the first English artist we know by name."

"Right." Jonathan, who had absented himself after noonday prayer, walked into the room just in time to hear the last sentence. "Most appropriate that he was such a near neighbor to Caedmon, who is the first English poet we know by name." Suddenly Antony felt a pulse of sympathy for Philly, whose soapbox had been pulled from under her. And he could hardly have missed the radiance of Felicity's smile when Jonathan strode into the small room, filling it with his presence.

Felicity, however, wasn't distracted for long. "Wait." She shook her head and held up a hand. "I'm confused. Who's Eadfrith? Didn't Cuthbert produce the Lindisfarne Gospels?"

Jonathan opened his mouth to answer, but Philly plucked at his sleeve. "Just let me show you this—"

Antony seized his opportunity to steer Felicity away with a hand firmly under her elbow. "Cuthbert was only indirectly responsible." Abandoning Jonathan to Philomena, Antony directed Felicity around the room to examine the murals covering the walls.

Felicity, though, wasn't so certain she wanted to be steered away. She had been wondering where Jonathan was, and now the minute he showed up, Antony pulled her away. Of course, the excuse was answering her question about Cuthbert—and she *had* asked—but she was still just a bit miffed with Antony for his attempts to order her about. She wasn't his student here.

As usual, though, it seemed she had little choice in the matter, for Antony was well-launched into his account. "Starting with the Gospel book is really telling the story backwards. I won't go into all the details here—"

"Right. Good." But she said it almost under her breath.

"—but these paintings do a good shorthand job of helping you get an idea of the story."

Felicity, who felt her head was about to explode with details, was glad to hear that she could get by simply looking at pictures.

"We left the story with Cuthbert in retreat on Inner Farne accepting a bishopric at the urging of King Egfrith." Antony pointed to a picture of a gray-robed, tonsured man standing in a small boat. "Cuthbert served his diocese energetically for two years before returning to his sanctuary."

Felicity nodded. Got it. Pictures were helpful.

Antony propelled her on to a panel showing three monks in a tiny coracle sailing a rough sea. The gray-robed brothers had huge, black, almond-shaped eyes. One was pointing ahead, presumably to Cuthbert's sanctuary. The other two were surveying the waves tossing as high as their shoulders. "When Cuthbert returned to his island retreat, the brothers from the monastery visited him regularly whenever the rough seas allowed. One day they found him gravely ill."

"Oh yes, I see." Wanting to hurry the narrative up—after all, if they finished early maybe she could still go to the castle with Jonathan—Felicity moved forward and read the plaque under the picture. "'At the end, Cuthbert, alone on Inner Farne, crawled to the guest house on the beach.'"

The picture showed the saint on his knees, dragging a little bag of onions. Antony pointed to the string bag through which one could see five amber globes. "His only food," he said. The saint's hand was thin as a bird's claw.

The next picture showed Cuthbert on a low cot covered by a rough blanket, five onions beside him, a paddling of ducks at his feet and a pair of ravens on the windowsill. His eyes were almost closed, his hands folded across his breast. "Cuthbert tried to pray. Can't you just hear it? His breath of prayer, the wind and the waves, accompanied only by bird calls?" Antony's voice indicated that he could hear the wind and the waves beyond the hut. Felicity could not.

Right, so Antony had a valid point about her desire for sightseeing, they were supposed to be solving Dominic's murder—and, incidentally, clearing Father Clement and Antony of wild charges—but what could all this have to do with it? Wasn't the truth of the matter that this was really just Antony's form of sightseeing?

"Yes, so the brothers arrived from Lindisfarne and found Cuthbert dying." Felicity's voice must have shown more impatience than she intended because Antony stopped and looked at her.

"I know it's a long story. Sorry. But just stay with me here. This is important for understanding what comes next."

Her attempt to repress a sigh wasn't wholly successful.

"I'm almost finished," he assured her. "Cuthbert wanted to be buried on Inner Farne, but his final words, which must have seemed strange to the brothers, turned out to be prophetic: 'If necessity compels you to choose one of two evils, I would much rather you took my bones from the tomb, carried them with you and, departing from this place, dwelt wherever God ordained.'"

"And so they took him back to Lindisfarne for burial, even though they knew it was against his wishes?" Felicity stood in front of the last painting in that row, picturing Cuthbert's grave inside the monastery church.

The painting gripped her, in spite of her impatience. Actually, the whole story *was* remarkable. "A beautiful ending."

Antony turned from the painting with a smile. "No, no—not the ending. That's the point, it's just the beginning. Actually—here's where the story gets good, because Cuthbert's most important work came after his death. Eleven years later, on 20 March, the anniversary of his death—which is still commemorated as Cuthbert's feast day—"

"Oh, how appropriate!" Felicity clapped her hands. "That's just ten days from now. Wouldn't it be wonderful if we could have this cleared up by then!"

Antony gave a rueful smile. "We'd certainly better have. I can't imagine how I'll manage to conduct the Ecumenical Commission meeting from jail."

Chapter 8

He had said it so lightly, he was amazed when Felicity gave his arm a quick squeeze. For a moment he thought he saw moisture in her eyes. It was hard for him to take the threat to his own freedom seriously. It had been enough to keep him from calling the authorities over the crossbow incident, but he couldn't really picture himself incarcerated. And yet, he knew he must face the all-too-real possibility. Father Anselm took it seriously, or he would never have abetted his escape. And even then, he could barely believe that it had happened; that he, a priest—thinking of becoming a monk—had traveled across half of England with a young woman, a student of his, no less, in a desperate attempt to show somehow that he wasn't a brutal murderer. What an impossible nightmare. How could something that began so innocently possibly have led to this? And yet it had all been so innocent all those years ago with Alice. That was the problem: innocence; stupidity. But no less guilt. He gave himself a mental shake. *Concentrate on the present.*

And now, to complicate matters, they were entangled with the odious Breen. What could Father Anselm possibly have been thinking? A man so renown for his careful thought processes.

Antony forced himself to focus on the task at hand; always, in his experience, the best way to deal with disturbing thoughts. "But let me finish my story. I apologize for its length, but here we come to the answer to your question about the making of the Lindisfarne Gospel Book."

He turned to the final set of panels along the wall to their right. The three pictures showed the monks digging up the casket that had lain buried for eleven years; then staring in confused amazement at Cuthbert's uncorrupted body; and finally, a single monk bent over a sheet of parchment with quill in hand while the brothers outside sang thanksgivings.

Antony cleared his throat. "And that's the answer to your question. The Lindisfarne Gospels were made as thanksgiving for the great miracle of Cuthbert's incorruption."

Felicity thought for a moment, frowning. "OK. But didn't the monks just make it all up—to encourage pilgrimages? I mean, it's well known that this saint business could be pretty lucrative."

Antony nodded, careful to suppress his smile. This was exactly what he enjoyed, and found all too rare in his college lectures—a bright but skeptical student ready to engage in debate. "Yes, that's a valid point. And it's really strange because that is exactly the charge that critics always leveled at Glastonbury—even to this day—that the monks' convenient finding of the body of King Arthur was a ploy to rebuild their monastery after it burned down."

"Right. I don't find that the least bit strange. That's the first thing I'd think, too."

"But you see—that's what's strange. As far as it's recorded, nobody—throughout history—has ever made that charge about the Lindisfarne monks. Certainly not forcefully enough to get into general scholarship."

Felicity shrugged. "Well, it's a gullible world."

"Maybe. But also there's the fact that they didn't really need the story—Lindisfarne already had more pilgrims than they could handle." He paused to allow his point to sink in. When she made no reply, he continued. "And look at the personal effort and risk the brotherhood went to."

"Risk? Making a Gospel book?"

"No, I mean later. If you were fleeing from rape and pillage, would you want to drag a stone sarcophagus with you? For 200 years?"

"Security. Tradition. Talisman." She ticked them off on her fingers. "Some people take strange things on airplane trips."

Now he smiled. "Well, yes, but the foibles of human nature

aside, there's the later record. But I really do think we should save that for another time."

He sighed inwardly. There was so much to tell—hundreds of years yet to cover before Felicity would really grasp what this was all about. If what he suspected was true. But what did he suspect? What could anyone suspect from the vague hints they had been given to work with? The merest suggestion of a scent, sketches of pictures, whispers at the corners of his mind. The thinnest of threads, really… but if there was any foundation to any of them, it must all be covered, all reconstructed, all sifted through. And, as Felicity had just pointed out, 20 March was a mere ten days away.

Still, that was enough for now. He turned to the curator of the museum who was sitting at a small table near the door. "I wonder if we could see your manuscripts."

The plump, bald man, whose name badge proclaimed for him the surname Higgins, blinked at him over his wire-rimmed glasses. "Manuscripts? You're welcome to use our workroom, certainly, Father. You understand, though, we have no originals here. Some interesting reproductions, and a small but rather good library. And then we have our bookshop, as well."

Antony's gaze followed the man's sweeping gesture toward the open door showing the small gift and bookshop in the next room. His attention was caught by the multi-pierced Curtis with his coal-black, spiked hair bent over a book. Antony was just wondering what was holding him in such rapt attention when Felicity, who was standing near enough the door to see the title, sprang forward.

"*Medieval Weaponry.*" She grabbed the book out of his hands. "A chapter on crossbows, just as I thought!" She brandished the book in his face and bent closer. "What did you think you were doing this morning, you jerk? We could have been killed!"

Curtis stepped back, surprised enough almost to open his eyes. "Huh?" He did look genuinely baffled.

Antony stepped forward and spoke slowly, distinctly. "Listen to me, Curtis. Just before lunch today, someone shot a crossbow bolt at us. Now we find you reading a book on the subject. You can see that the connection looks obvious."

Curtis took another step backward, shaking his head. "Huh? Nah, I just—" He shrugged. "That is—hey, this is cool stuff." He shifted his shoulders. "Chill, man."

Philly Johnson, lioness queen protecting her own, strode over from her computer. "How dare you?" She spat at them, eyes blazing. "What do you think you're accusing my son of?"

Antony held up a hand placatingly and tried to explain. He got less than two sentences out.

"What utter nonsense. We only arrived on the island just before lunch. Curtis was only out for the briefest of walks. Surely you aren't suggesting they let him bring a crossbow on the airplane?" She grabbed her son by one of his silver armbands and pulled him toward her while still glaring at Antony. "And you a priest! Whatever happened to justice and mercy?"

Antony stared, speechless, as Philomena Johnson marched away, prodding her son ahead of her. Somehow she managed to appear larger than life. At the door she stopped and turned to fling her parting shot at the still flabbergasted Antony. "You'll be sorry. I promise you. You'll regret this."

Silence echoed in the little shop after Philomena's departure. Only the scent of her strong perfume wavered on the air.

At last Antony shook his head to clear it. Whatever did she mean by that? She would report him to his bishop? Now she *would* come after him with a crossbow?

Well, nothing to do but get on with the matter at hand. He turned back to Higgins, who had followed them into the book shop and stood openmouthed through the entire confrontation. Antony forced a smile in an attempt to put the little man at ease. "I do apologize. But someone shot a crossbow at us this morning. You'll appreciate that it was a most alarming experience." It flashed through his mind that the confrontation with Philly had been almost as alarming as the actual shooting. Philly seemed to have that effect on people. "Now, as I was about to explain, originals aren't really necessary, we're interested in St. Cuthbert."

"If you could be a bit more specific, perhaps?"

That was the problem, wasn't it? If only they knew what they were looking for. "His work here and his subsequent, er— pilgrimage." That was the best he could do. "Perhaps you have some publications revealing information not generally known— archeology recently done where the body rested, theories on Cuthbert's incorruption, that sort of thing."

"Hmmm, yes. I see. Yes, there has been some recent archeology in the area, I believe, but nothing published that I'm aware of. Now…" Higgins turned to a shelf and ran his finger along the colorful spines. "We rather like to specialize in local authors. *Pilgrimage of Northumbrian Saints* by Cardinal Hume—he was Northumbrian himself, so wrote with excellent local color; *Fire in the North,* by David Adam—a good biography of Cuthbert by our local celebrity; A book of prayers inspired by the saint's life by—"

"Yes, yes." Antony's heart was sinking. Was it all going to be a waste of time? "I'm acquainted with these. I was looking for something less standard."

"Hmm. I see. Well, you might find this interesting, then. A bit far afield, perhaps. Rather controversial—" Higgins plucked a book from the shelf and handed it to Antony. "New book. Recently published by an American who has some bee in his bonnet that Cuthbert actually did speak at the Synod of Whitby, and that that helped propel him into the abbot's chair here."

Antony frowned. "But Bede records the debate in detail. He makes no mention of Cuthbert taking part."

Higgins shrugged. "Cuthbert was on the losing side, remember."

Antony was horrified. Surely the man didn't mean that as it sounded. "What nonsense! He can't be accusing the Venerable Bede, one of the most careful historians of all time, of being political?" He looked at the book in his hand. "Does the author have any documentation for this?"

"Unfortunately, it's a notoriously unscholarly work. Little footnoting and only the vaguest of bibliographies. I don't know how some of these things get published. Still, his theories are interesting. If Cuthbert had spoken, his arguments would likely have run in the vein Smith-Johnson suggests."

Antony started to return the book to the shelf, then looked again at the author's name on the spine and stopped: Ansel Smith-Johnson. Smith. Johnson. Philomena Johnson. Could there be a connection? Johnson was a common enough name. Still, both Americans. Worth a second look, surely.

"I don't suppose you have anything unpublished in your workroom?"

Higgins laughed. "Oh, everything in our workroom is unpublished. Other than the books needing their bindings repaired. Can't think what we might have that would be of interest, but come along and take a look." He led through a door behind the glass counter filled with Celtic crosses, bookmarks with Lindisfarne Gospel designs, and inexpensive jewelry. In the small, dim room, lit by a single light bulb and a small window, he turned to a large file of portfolios along one wall. "These are our facsimile manuscripts. You might find something of interest here."

Felicity, who had stood by in silence, now stepped forward. "Manuscripts? Good. There's something I might be able to help with." She turned and waved Jonathan in from the other room. "And you, too, Jon. Are you OK with medieval Latin?"

He shrugged as he stooped to clear the low doorway. "I prefer classical, of course, but I can cope."

Leaving the manuscripts to them, with only a brief, frowning, backward glance at their heads bent together, Antony sat at a small reading carrel near the window and opened the book Higgins had given him, *Whither from Whitby?* Silly title. The room was silent as Antony pondered the theory unfolded on the pages of the unarguably hastily written volume before him. What could it mean? What if the Smith-Johnson theory were correct? What would it mean to the life of the church today?

Did Dominic read this? Could there be a motive here for committing murder? What if Dominic had found something to prove the theory? To disprove it? Would someone really commit murder over disputed facts of a 400-year-old event? Could the royalties on a book like this amount to enough that someone would kill for them? Could an author be that jealous over his reputation?

Across the room, Breen was leaning over Felicity's shoulder as she sorted through the manuscript file. "Ah, *The Two Lives of Saint Cuthbert* by Colgrave. Yes, indeed, a classic. You won't find anything not already well known there, though."

"Here's the list from this file. Do you see anything I should work on?" Felicity held out an index.

"Hmm. Very interesting. Gotha, 1.81—unedited *Lives of Celtic Saints*—might just possibly be something of interest there." He scanned on down the list, "Oh, yes, B. M. Add. 39943. One of the greatest treasures of the British Museum, I'm surprised they allowed a copy to be taken. This is the source of the Cuthbert paintings on the stalls in Carlisle Cathedral. They're very fine, you know."

Antony bent deeper over his volume and resisted sticking his fingers in his ears. If Jonathan Breen had been looking for a forum for displaying his knowledge, he had found it. And Antony had to admit that even he was impressed by the man's scholarship. But being a good scholar didn't necessarily make one a good person. Or was that just his own sense of inadequacy speaking?

"No, actually, I didn't know," Felicity said. "Do you think any of that would be of help to us?"

"Doubtful. You never know, of course." He flipped to the next page. "Hmm. *Acta Sanctorum*, very careless transcription." He shook his head. "Very careless." He handed the index back to her. "Can't see that there's much worth wasting our time on here. Pity."

Felicity sighed. "Yes. I had hoped to be able to contribute

something to the search. I'm afraid reading manuscripts is about all I could hope to do that would be useful. Friends did warn me that a classics degree might not be the most practical thing in the world." She made a rueful face.

"I say," Higgins popped his shiny round head around the corner. "You do know about the archives in St. Mary's Church, don't you?"

Antony looked up. "The parish church maintains archives?"

"Very small collection. Don't know that it would be worth your time. Still, it's a thought if you're looking for something esoteric."

Antony took a small notebook out of his pocket and jotted a few notes from the book he was reading before handing it back to Higgins. "Thank you. Just as you say, interesting but unscholarly. Perhaps we will try the church, thank you for the hint."

In his present mood, one thing seemed as good as another. Had he been going on nothing but adrenaline stimulated by fear and excitement for the past two days? And had it finally drained away? Antony could think of no other explanation for the emptiness he felt. Now the futility of it all opened in front of him like a gaping black hole. All he had done was dig that hole deeper and get himself in more trouble by running away.

And yet the only alternative was to plod on. Giving up and going back seemed unthinkable. What had Macbeth said, something about being so far stepped in blood that returning would be as tedious as going on? Not a happy analogy.

How could he find the inner strength to go on yet again in the face of failure? Wasn't that what priests were supposed to be good at—helping people find the strength to endure, carrying on in faith when there was no sign of progress anywhere around? How could he hope to help others when he was so empty himself?

Lord, have mercy. He breathed the bottom-of-the-barrel prayer he always clung to when no other words would come.

Chapter 9

The vicar of St. Mary's was delighted to show them the church's small collection of documents which he kept in the sacristy. "Mr Higgins at the Heritage Centre just showed me a most curious book claiming to show that Bede got the Whitby debate wrong, that Cuthbert did participate. Don't suppose you have anything that might shed some light on that?" Antony asked as they walked to the small room off the north aisle. He must focus on the task at hand—no matter how hopeless. Surrender to failure wasn't an option. It was much easier to plod blindly onward than to contemplate what failure would mean to him. What it would mean to the Community. Perhaps worst of all, what it would mean to Felicity.

The Reverend Douglas shook his white head. "Wish I did. Cuthbert's silence at that pivotal point in church history has always seemed surprising to me, although I think it's easily explained by the fact that his focus was always firmly on prayer and pastoral work. Church politics probably bored him."

Antony nodded appreciatively. "Understandable. Lovely how some things never change, isn't it?"

"Yes, indeed. Still, your question does ring a bell. I got a fax... Months ago..." The Reverend Douglas mused for a moment. "Don't know if it would be of any interest; still... I'll just pop over to my office and see if I can unearth it. Feel free to have a good look round." He handed a small ring of keys to Antony. "Some interesting pieces in the cupboards. Should be in a museum, I suppose. I rather imagine the PCC will get around to giving them to the Durham Treasury someday. But I confess I hope they don't. Local treasures kept in situ and all that, you know." He turned to the door. "I'll be right back."

"Treasure?" Felicity asked, her eyebrows raised. She had headed straight to the low wooden filing cabinet in the corner, but turned back at the vicar's words. Jonathan, however, began sifting through the top drawer of dusty files.

Antony turned to the first cupboard, finding the right key on his third try. "Mmm, interesting, indeed, a collector of church artifacts would be in heaven." He took a pair of silver candlesticks from their felt bag and held them up.

"Those are beautiful," Felicity exclaimed.

Jonathan glanced up from a file. "Eighteenth century. No possible Cuthbert connection."

Antony felt that if he weren't wearing his collar he would be sorely tempted to swear under his breath. Or maybe not under his breath. Besides, he wasn't at all convinced that Breen was right. The candlesticks looked distinctly medieval to him.

Next was an ornate silver gilt chalice. "Victorian," Jonathan said dismissively.

"Looks valuable, though," Felicity said.

"Possibly. Victoriana isn't my area of expertise," Jonathan replied.

"Yes. Quite so." Surprised their invasive companion would admit there was anything he wasn't expert in, Antony returned the chalice to the cupboard and took out a beautifully embroidered burse, veil and pall set with a distinctive multicolored band that went unremarked by Breen. Was it possible ecclesiastical embroidery was not an area of expertise with him, either? "Wareham Guild, unless I am very much mistaken," Antony announced.

He replaced the items and turned to the next set of shelves: a heavily embossed ciborium lidded by a miniature spire that surely would have delighted the heart of Archbishop Laud before his untimely demise also escaped comment from Jonathan Breen, in spite of the appreciative murmurs it drew from Felicity. At the back were several more mundane vessels: crystal cruets of a smooth design; a rather soiled thurible, its charcoal smudges still giving a spicy aroma; an aspergillum and bucket with a broken handle.

Felicity turned her attention to the files as Jonathan opened the second drawer and Antony opened the last cupboard. It held only one item, a brass alms basin, much in need of a good polishing. The large round platter was scratched and dented, indicating a long, hard life. Antony hoped that meant it had served to collect a great many alms for the poor and tithes for the church. He was just putting it back in its bag when he realized that the scratches in the center were actually letters.

He carried the vessel over to the window. At first glance he thought the inscription was Greek, but on closer examination saw that the words appeared to be Old English. Could he actually be holding a vessel from the eleventh century or earlier? A copy, surely. But still, a rarity. "Er—do either of you read Old English? I'm afraid they didn't teach that at theological college."

Breen spun so quickly he almost knocked a pamphlet from Felicity's hand. "My specialty, as a matter of fact."

Oh, fine. Back to Breen's specialties. Antony started to bristle, then quickly repented his irritation. He had forgotten that the Fraternity of the Transfiguration oblate was actually a professor of Anglo-Saxon literature. Worse, he was chagrined by his lack of Christian humility in his own reluctance to relinquish the basin to him.

Breen held it in close scrutiny in the light. "Hmm. Interesting. I wonder if this is authentic. Not good style at all. It has the middle caesura, you see," he pointed to the break in the middle of the lines, "but the stresses are all wrong. Each half line should contain two feet with a single predominant stress in each foot—" He brandished the plate. "That would indicate this is a fake or of very late manufacture—not of the standard of Alfred the Great, certainly. There were, of course, pockets of Anglo-Saxon resistance long after the Norman Conquest, especially in remote areas like this, which would explain a low standard of scholarship—"

"Yes, yes. That's fine. But what does it *say*?" Felicity cut him off.

"Well, it's hard to make much sense of it. There is the required alliteration, in a way, but to be correct, one or two syllables in the first half line should be alliterated with the first stressed syllable of the second. I can't authenticate this at all. It must be some kind of elaborate hoax. I can't for the life of me see why anybody would bother, though."

"Jonathan!" Felicity appeared to stop just short of stamping her foot. "We aren't a class of undergraduates. Just read the—" She glanced at Antony. "Just read it."

"Yes, well, as I said, it doesn't make any sense. There's an attempt at kennings, but they don't sound authentic—"

Antony frowned. Was Breen stalling because he couldn't actually read it? Or was there some reason he didn't want to translate the inscription for them?

"Jonathan!"

"Oh well, all right then, but it really isn't worth our time. It says:

> 'Three from the See, Shield-Bearers protecting;
> Three from the sea, Spear-Danes destructing.'

"Really, it's gibberish. You see, the first line is all wrong, it shouldn't—"

Felicity's gasp was covered by Jonathan's continued lecture. Antony shook his head at her vigorously, but she didn't notice. "But that's—"

"Yes, indeed," Antony cut her off. "Total nonsense. Pity, thought we might have found something useful. Lucky you could explain it to us, Breen." He took the platter from the scholar and had it locked back in the cupboard before anyone could say another word.

"Oh, good, still here, are you?" The Reverend Douglas hustled back in, the disarray of his white locks showing the agitation of his search. "Good thing I keep every scrap of paper. Drives my housekeeper mad, but it's proven useful more than once." He held out a crumpled fax. "I did remember it correctly. A query from a Smith-Johnson fellow, wanting to know if we had

any unpublished documents on the Synod of Whitby. I told him I
didn't think so, but he was welcome to come look for himself."

"Did he come?"

"Possibly. About a year ago. I was away at the time, but Mrs.
Inman, my housekeeper, said someone was here for a day or two."
He turned to Felicity, standing by the open file. "I say, you didn't
find anything in that vein, did you?"

Felicity shook her head. "Sorry. Just parish records, that sort
of thing."

"Pity. Yes. I should be more on top of such things, I suppose.
Still, one does one's best."

"Yes, absolutely, Father. We appreciate your help." Antony
returned the keys and took his leave as quickly as he could,
leaving Felicity and Jonathan to follow at their leisure. Here at
last was something that seemed pertinent. He had no idea what
the Anglo-Saxon couplet meant, but it had to be confirmation
that they were on the right trail. Dominic had quoted the precise
lines. They had to mean something.

Willibrord seemed to have been watching the door for him
as he all but sprang forward on his long legs when Antony entered
the retreat house. "Ah, welcome. Welcome back. You had a good
afternoon, did you?"

"Yes. Very good, thank you."

"Ah, excellent. Excellent. So glad to hear it. You enjoyed the
Heritage Centre?"

"Yes, fine display. Very nicely presented."

"Go-o-od. Good. I think so. People always seem to enjoy it.
And did you find anything else? Anything of real interest?"

"Oh, well, you know—it's all interesting, really, isn't it?"
Antony made for the stairs. He felt desperate to be alone and
think. He escaped by taking the stairs two at a time. He certainly
wasn't going to discuss Dominic's writings and their newly
discovered Anglo-Saxon fragment with anyone but Felicity.

A few moments later there was a knock at his door. His sigh
turned to a smile when he saw that it was Felicity. Alone. She had

managed to escape the attentions of Jonathan Breen. His relief was purely for the sake of the investigation, of course.

"Hi. Look, did you get one of these, too?" She strode in, holding out a flat, rectangular bar in a green and white wrapper.

"Oh, Kendal mint cake." He looked at the windowsill where his electric kettle sat on a tray. "Yep, looks like I did." But their intriguing find had replaced any interest he might have had in food, even if he were eating sweets in Lent. "What do you make of the inscription? I wish we knew whether or not Dominic saw the alms basin." Antony began pacing his small room.

"He didn't."

"What?" He stopped mid-pace. "How do you know?"

"After you left, I asked Father Douglas. He knew Dominic well. He said he worshiped there regularly when on retreat here, but never asked to see their sacristy, and he has the only set of keys."

"Interesting." Antony resumed his pacing, accompanied by running his hand up and down through his hair. "Very interesting. That means Dominic knew the inscription from another source."

"Oh," Felicity sounded disappointed. "So the basin isn't a clue?"

"Only in the sense that it gives significance to the couplet. That's what makes it so interesting. It means it has a wider meaning than just something Dominic copied off a piece of church plate."

"Yes, I see." She thought for a moment then plopped down on the only chair in the room. "Besides, it was on his itinerary, not in his journal. That means he knew it before his trip. It's like that was the purpose of his pilgrimage."

"Let's take a look at Dominic's jottings again." Antony turned to open the drawer in the bedside table for paper and pencil, then stopped, frowning. "That's not right. My notes were under my prayer book. I'm sure of it."

"Someone's been going through your things?" Felicity

shivered. "Like they did mine back at college?"

"Someone has been in here." He gazed around the small room, feeling as if they might be hiding there yet. "My papers are out of order."

Felicity jerked upright. "That means someone wants to know what we know. They apparently don't have the answers yet, either. So we've got to beat them to it." She sighed and flopped back against her stiff chair. "Whatever it is."

Antony turned with Dominic's itinerary sheet in his hand. "Good thing I keep this in my pocket." He handed it to Felicity.

"'Three from the See,'" she read out. "The See—that's Rome, right? 'Three from the sea'—so three people sailed from Rome?"

Antony nodded slowly. "Perhaps."

"See, maybe this fits all that you were saying about the Synod of Whitby—that young abbot that led the debate for the Roman party what was his name?" She struggled to remember.

"Wilfrid," Antony supplied.

"Oh, yes. Well, Wilfrid had just returned from Rome before the Synod, hadn't he?" She held up one finger. "And that other guy who brought all the manuscripts." She held up another finger, then paused. "Sorry, I don't remember that lecture as well as I should."

"Benedict Biscop. Yes, but that makes two, not three. And at the Synod, there were two speakers for Rome, not three."

Felicity twisted the paper in her hands as if looking at it from another angle would shed new light. "Hmm, maybe it's not about missionaries from Rome at all. Maybe it's a warning of some kind. Spear-Danes were Vikings, weren't they? Marauders?" She paused and handed the journal back to Antony. An intense silence filled the room as if they could hear each other thinking.

"All this stuff about Three—that morning in Kirkthorpe... You said something about an apocryphal story about some brotherhood. What if it isn't apocryphal? What if Dominic found out some secret society or something was for real? Is still for real today? Is it possible?"

Antony felt a cold tingling at the back of his neck as he followed her thought. It was so improbable, and yet… It seemed the theme of three kept turning up, even in the doodled triangles in the journal. "I don't know. I wish I could recall Butler's exact wording—something about a secret known only to three English Benedictines who hand on the secret before they die." He shook his head.

Felicity's eyes were huge in her pale face.

"Maybe the Three killed Dominic because he found out about them. Maybe they're trying to kill us." Her voice was barely above a whisper. "But Benedictines are monks—sworn religious. They wouldn't kill. Would they?"

Antony looked at her, wanting to give the assurance she sought. "It's impossible to imagine. But the whole thing is impossible—to think that anyone could hold a heart so wicked they could be stirred to such violence." Impossible. And yet it happened every day. No one could know better than a priest the evil the human heart was capable of.

Chapter 10

Felicity woke with a start. She and Antony had sat long into the night analyzing Dominic's journal. The entries were sporadic and very sparing in the useable information they conveyed. It would be so helpful if he had given dates, recorded how he traveled, identified people he had talked to, if only by initials. Sometimes there would be a page or two recounting a worship service, describing a church, recording a prayer. And his observations of flora and fauna. Far more detail given to the natural landscape, like the hedgerows laden with bursting rose hips still red-orange after the winter, and the birds they attracted, than to any useful hints at hidden treasure.

Was the lack of clues a clue in itself? Did the omission of names mean he was protecting someone? Or investigating a society so secret he dare not name its members?

The more possible clues, or lack thereof, they found, the more confused they became. Was it possible that some legendary Brotherhood of Three had existed to protect Cuthbert's secret? *Still existed?* Or had some recent group stumbled across an ancient myth and taken on the mystique? Was that what Dominic was trying to reveal—some secret brotherhood sworn to work mayhem in the church? Or someone just using the whole idea for personal gain or power?

If so, how did one interpret the couplet they had found repeated on the alms basin? Were the Shield-Bearers and the Spear-Danes the same three? Or were there two groups—one from "Rome," surely meaning the church, and one "Viking," meaning, what? Those who would destroy? Or someone trying to protect? Protect or destroy what? They hadn't protected Dominic. And Felicity's circling thoughts repeated their circuit.

Until at last she spiraled down into a few hours of restless sleep where she tossed as if her bed were churned by waves. In her broken dreams, Viking raiders swarmed over the island, war horns bleating, black-skinned drums beating. Flames surrounded her, the dragon-head prow of a Viking warship sailed through the smoke, breathing more fire. As she sat up, gasping for air, the dragon warhead evolved into a zoomorphic creature from the Lindisfarne Gospel.

Then she realized the beating of the drums was actually a knock on her door. "Yes? Who is it?"

"It's Antony. Are you coming down to breakfast?"

"Oh. Yes. Five minutes." She stumbled toward her sink to splash water on her face. How could they be doing anything so normal as having breakfast in a retreat centre?

She was surprised to find that she and Antony were alone at the table. "Where is everyone?" she asked when Willibrord brought in the toast rack. She tried to keep her voice neutral. She didn't want to show her disappointment at Jonathan's absence.

"Stephen Bootham had an early breakfast and went to Seahouses to rent a boat for Inner Farne. Ms. Johnson left as soon as the tide was out last night." He shrugged. "Odd, she had booked for three days, but must have had a change of plans."

Felicity looked around. "And Jonathan?"

"Oh, I was under the impression he was with you."

Felicity wondered if she should be insulted, but Willibrord seemed too innocent to be implying anything. Anyway, she didn't want to admit that she had knocked on his door that morning, but got no answer.

Willibrord looked out the window. "His car isn't here. Might have driven up to the castle, I suppose."

Felicity was surprised at the sharpness of her disappointment—purely in the interest of their research, she told herself hurriedly. She had wanted to ask him more about Anglo-Saxon poetry in hope of learning something about the inscription. It would be helpful to know whether Anglo-Saxon poetry was purposefully repetitive like Hebrew poetry, with the second line echoing the meaning of the first in different words as the psalms do. That would be a big help in deciphering whether the fragment referred to one or two sets of three.

"What are your plans for the day?" their host asked as he refilled her teacup.

"I thought we'd walk around to the Viking beach," Antony answered.

"Oh, sorry." Willibrord wiped up the bit of tea he had sloshed. "Why would you do that? I thought you said you were following Dominic? He didn't go there at all, you know."

Antony looked confused for a moment, then swallowed his bite of toast. "Oh, well, it's a nice day for some fresh air. Might rain later, so we'll take our chance now. I'm sure you'll forgive us for not attending morning prayers. Thought we'd say the office by the sea."

"Ah, in true Cuthbert style. Pity I can't provide you with any otters."

Felicity wondered at Willibrord's obscure reference, but was even more disconcerted by Antony's reference: Viking beach? After her dreams last night, that sounded none too inviting... although fresh air and sunshine would be very welcome.

They stuffed Felicity's backpack with bottles of water and lemonade, snacks, notebook and other useful items, and set out through the village toward the back of the island. In only a few minutes they had crossed the cultivated fields and pastures and were into an open sweep of land with nothing but waving grasses on their right and an occasional glimpse of a sparkle of blue ocean on their left. The trail was rough, little more than a single footpath through the weeds.

Felicity flung her arms out, threw her head back and breathed deeply. After last night this was exactly what she needed. The persistent wind blew the smoke of the Viking fires of her dreams from her mind, and the sun was warm on her head. Clumps of tall grasses swished on either side of them and dried burrs stuck to Felicity's socks and jeans. Seabirds swooped overhead and wildfowl called from nests hidden in the grasses and bushes.

After the alarms of the previous day, Felicity was so absorbed in the peace and beauty around her it was a moment before she realized Antony had spoken. "What?" She turned back, as he was lingering several paces behind her.

"I said I don't understand why Willibrord would lie about that."

"Hmm? What? Willibrord lied?"

"Didn't you hear a word I said?"

Now she realized Antony had been keeping up a steady murmur of monologue ever since they left the village. "Sorry. Afraid I was rather exulting in all this." She gave a final spin with her arms out, then stood to give him her full attention. "What did Willibrord lie about?"

"He said Dominic didn't come out here, but he definitely mentions it in his journal."

"Perhaps Willibrord didn't know?"

"Possibly. But this is a serious undertaking for one of Dominic's age and frailty. I would think his host would have known."

"What could Dominic have been doing? And why wouldn't Wills have wanted us to know?" She looked at the emptiness around them. "What could be out here anyone would want to cover up?"

Antony shook his head. "I can't imagine. I only thought we should make time for the trek because Dominic did."

Felicity turned and strode ahead of Antony on the single, sandy path, but her pace slowed as her concentration returned. "Antony, you can't possibly think Willibrord—"

"Is a violent murderer who bludgeoned Dominic, ransacked your room at the college, rifled my room here and tried to shoot us with a crossbow?" Just saying the words out loud in the fresh, luminous air made them sound ridiculous enough to laugh at. But they didn't laugh. Someone had done just that.

The thought took the spring out of Felicity's step, and the next twenty minutes became a drudging march instead of the holiday outing it had been minutes before. They had cut across one side of the island and were now following a curving path with the blue ocean rolling against rocks and steep banks on their left, and the seeming endless waving grasses on their right. They rounded a wide curve in the coastline to the back of the island, and Felicity came to such an abrupt stop Antony almost stepped on her heels.

"Oh, it's beautiful!" Spread before them was a vast, white sand beach edged with black boulders. Felicity put her hand to her eyes and stood gazing out at the mesmerizing water.

"This is it," Antony said. "Hard to imagine in such peace and beauty, isn't it?"

"Viking Beach?"

"Yep. This is where the Vikings launched their first attack on England." He pointed. "Straight out there, as the gull flies, is Scandinavia. It was a natural progression for a seafaring people pushed by their own population demands."

Antony took the lead in descending the steep drop from the grassy clifftop to the curving expanse of white sand. It was only a drop of a few feet, but wind and surf had cut sheer walls. The bay was a gentle white crescent of perhaps 500 feet, bordered on the landward side with a few largish boulders and fringed with white-edged waves along the water.

Felicity would have liked to sink down on the white sand and relax after her restless night. But here, on the very spot where her nightmare had been a reality, the unease of the night before returned. She could almost hear the drumbeats, see the flaring torches.

Antony began a steady pacing along the full length of the crescent, examining every step. She fell in beside him. "Surely you aren't looking for footprints—or even anything someone might have dropped? Anything like that would have been washed away within hours."

Antony shook his head. "I don't have any idea what I'm looking for. I just know Willibrord didn't want us to come here, so there must be something we're not supposed to see."

At the far end of the crescent, the beach ended with a small grassy mound that extended to the water's edge. Antony walked to the top of the hillock and sat. Felicity stood behind him.

"Treasure," she mused. "Vikings were famous for plundering treasure. Perhaps someone has located a trove. Like the—what was that famous find last century?"

"Are you thinking of the Mildenhall Treasure? That was Roman."

"No. Sutton Hoo."

"Oh, yes. That was Saxon, but I take your meaning. There have been Viking finds. Of great archeological interest, of course."

"But not monetary?"

"There are very strict laws covering discovered treasure. If someone finds a hoard, they have something like two weeks to report it to the authorities, or stiff penalties ensue. In most cases, the find goes to the Crown."

"That doesn't seem fair."

"Actually, I think it is an attempt to be fair—to preserve valuable historical relics for the people as a whole, put them in museums and the like, rather than letting them be absconded with and sold off. And there's usually a reward for the finder, usually some portion of the value."

"Ah, ha! And would this finder's fee be worth killing for?"

Antony shrugged. "Is anything worth killing for? But I take your point. I think, though, the more appropriate question would be, how likely is it that someone who would commit murder would suddenly become law-abiding enough to report their find?"

"Right. They'd just steal it." Felicity returned to surveying the marvelous view. The sky was no longer the unbroken blue it had been. Fluffy white clouds, echoing the white waves below, hung low in the sky. She followed the soaring and swooping pattern of a large white seagull for several moments, smiling as it dove for food, then ascended steeply again. A low-throated quacking from the other side of the little hill caught her attention. "Oh, a duck."

Antony looked in the direction she was pointing. "Yes, that's an eider—St Cuddy's ducks they're called, because they were his favorite."

"Do you suppose it's nesting here?"

"Rather early in the season for nesting, but possible I suppose. They nest on all these islands."

Moving cautiously so as not to disturb the birds, she turned to search the tall tufts of weeds. At the bottom of the hillock where the sheltered land curved back from the sea, she stopped abruptly at the sight of a large duck with white and black plumage and a bright green patch on the nape of his neck. Looking closer, she saw that he was standing over a rather drab-looking female covered with brown feathers barred with black. She smiled. If the pair were thinking of nesting early they had chosen well, right below a mound of unusually short, bright green grass. Then she realized that was no grassy dune. She was looking at the bottom of an upturned boat half-hidden in the weeds.

Not wanting to disturb the ducks, she backed away. "There were two ducks," she reported. "Male and female. They are lovely."

"Hmmm." Antony gave an acknowledging nod.

"And someone has left a boat." She pointed.

Antony scrambled to his feet. "Hmm, that's interesting. I didn't know there was boating done on this side of the island." He started down the hillock.

"Careful, don't bother Cuddy's Ducks," Felicity called, following him. But the pair of Eiders were waddling unconcernedly away toward the water's edge.

Antony spent several minutes walking around the boat, examining it from every angle. "Give me a hand, let's turn it over."

The large wooden craft was heavier than Felicity had imagined. And entirely empty. Felicity even dropped to her knees and attempted digging in the sandy turf with her hands, but there was certainly no evidence of buried treasure underneath. She felt rather foolish for having allowed herself to follow so forlorn a hope.

"Nothing here. Let's put it back." Antony sounded disappointed.

Felicity reached to grip the side, prepared to shove with all her strength, when her finger touched something soft caught under the rim. "What's this?" She couldn't see, so hooked a long leg over the side of the boat and sprang in. A moment's prying produced a two- or three-inch long piece of yarn. She held it up and examined it. "Oatmeal textured wool."

Antony took it from her hand and examined it closely. "Do you recognize this?"

"Maybe. It looks a lot like the yarn Anna was knitting with. It could be from anywhere, but she did say she ordered hers from Newfoundland."

"It definitely could be Will's." Antony nodded. "The fact that he had a boat here could be what he was attempting to cover up."

"But why? It's an island. People must boat around here all the time. Why lie about it?"

"Why, indeed?" Antony asked.

"Well, what do people do in boats that's illegal?" Felicity took up the thought. "Smuggle. French wine? How close are we to Sweden? Don't they have really soft porn laws?"

Felicity couldn't have been more surprised by Antony's explosion of mirth at her ramblings. He laughed so hard it was several moments before he could speak, still holding his sides. "Besides the impossibility of imagining Wills involved in anything like that—" He stopped for breath and wiped his eyes. "I told you my sister did farce. Have you ever seen *No Sex Please, We're British?*"

Mystified at the reference, Felicity shook her head.

"That's the plot—porn smuggled into England in crates of Swedish crystal. All unawares by this very proper English lady who has her uncle the bishop visiting her. And then a hooker—which Gwena played—comes in just before the police, and the bishop jumps in the hedge… I'm sorry." He paused to chuckle again. "It's all totally irrelevant, but I did enjoy that play, and your comment brought it all back."

"Right. It sounds brilliant." Felicity felt ever so slightly miffed. She didn't enjoy the feeling that she was being laughed at in some obscure way. And then her irritation turned to amazement that her sedate, almost-monk companion was laughing until he cried over such a risqué plot. Maybe he was more human than she gave him credit for.

She turned her mind back to the question before them. "So then, if not smuggling, what about poaching? Maybe Wills is poaching. Or some of the locals are, and he's trying to cover up for them?"

Antony, still grinning broadly, nodded. "I don't know enough about local fishing laws. But that excellent sea trout Anna served last night does give one pause for thought."

Felicity was quiet.

"Felicity, I'm sorry. I wasn't laughing at you. Honestly—"

"No, no, of course not. I was just thinking about something else," she lied. "This boat—it seems absolutely mammoth when we're trying to turn it over. But it's really pretty small to be sailing the North Sea."

"Yes, certainly, for a voyage of any length. But at least as large as Grace Darling's."

"Huh?"

"Local heroine. Victorian lighthouse keeper's daughter who helped her father rescue the crew of a stranded Scottish steamer. Grace rowed through tremendous seas and gale force winds, so it can be done."

"Right, then. If a Victorian maiden could manage all that,

surely I can do my bit to get this one turned over again." Felicity and Antony grasped the rim of the hull and, with considerable huffing and puffing, they managed to return it to its upside down position.

Felicity straightened, rubbing her back. "So we found a boat. What did we expect to find in a bay? I suppose the real mystery is that there aren't more." She led the way back toward the beach where she had left her backpack. "I'm hungry."

They sat on the grassy knoll, and Antony opened the pack of sandwiches and fruit Anna had provided for their hike. Before passing out the packets, however, he reached in his breast pocket and drew out his prayer book. "A little late for morning prayers, I'm afraid." Antony opened the slim volume. "We'll do the midday office, I think."

Felicity sighed, eyeing the sandwiches with her stomach growling. She wished they could eat first and do the office later, but it probably wouldn't be the thing to do to ask since they had skipped morning prayers. She wasn't sure what the rules were.

"O God, make speed to save us," he began.

"O Lord, make haste to help us," her reply was more fervent than she expected.

"Responsive by half verse?" Antony pointed to a selection from Psalm 119. She nodded.

"I am deeply troubled," he read.

"Preserve my life, O Lord, according to your word," she responded.

Felicity's mind had wandered back to her lunch when the psalmist's words made her sit up with a shiver: "The wicked have set a trap for me…"

It made her final response of "Let our cry come unto you" entirely heartfelt.

And at last they could eat.

They were quiet for the space of several bites, savoring the fresh tang of their cheese and tomato sandwiches in the invigorating air. Finally Felicity asked, "What did Willibrord mean about being sorry he couldn't supply otters?"

Antony took a long swallow from his bottle of lemonade and smiled. "It's one of the most endearing stories about Cuthbert. As was his habit, he slept only one night in three or four. While others slept he slipped outside to pray, often on the beach to be near the sea he loved." Antony swept the coastline before them with an arc of his arm. Felicity nodded in resignation, sensing another story coming on. This had better be worth listening to. What she really wanted to do was take a nap.

The night was cold. Clear, crisp and cold. Brother Alphege would have preferred to stay on his pallet, rolled tightly in his woolen blanket, but he was determined. He must know. And this was his chance. Their beloved Bishop Cuthbert didn't visit the monastery of Coldingham above two times a year. He must seize the opportunity.

Shivering as his bare feet touched the pounded earthen floor of the monastery, he crept silently along the cloister, keeping to the shadows. Would the bishop be angry if he knew he was being followed? Brother Alphege didn't want to find out.

Outside the wooden enclosure of the monastery Cuthbert took a path leading directly to the seashore. Bending low, Brother Alphege darted to an outcropping of boulders and hid behind the largest of them. It was several minutes before he could gather the courage to peep around the side. Blinking to focus on the moonlit figure, Alphege saw Cuthbert standing at the edge of the water, his arms out-flung as if on a cross. The bishop began his prayers, chanting the psalms in rhythm to the rolling waves. The moon shone on his face, circling him with pools of light. The waves lapped at his feet, rolling shimmers of light onto the shore, washing it clean, bathing all smooth and pure.

Alphege caught his breath at the holiness of the scene he had had the audacity to spy out. At length, Cuthbert's arms seemed to waver. Slowly, in rhythm with the peace and gentleness around him, Cuthbert walked out into the water until, chest deep, it supported his arms in his cross vigil. "He gathereth the waters of the sea together, as it were upon an heap; and layeth up the deep, as in a treasure-house..." Cuthbert prayed and the brother hiding on the shore echoed the words in his heart.

Around Cuthbert the sea continued rolling, bearing his prayers to the land in waves of holiness and light. Through the night the chanting, praying and praising continued until the first streaks of sunlight fell across Cuthbert's face.

Cuthbert walked back to the shore and continued his prayers kneeling there. Now not invoking God's holiness and light on this land that he loved, but thanking the God that hears and answers.

And now Cuthbert was not alone in his devotions. Two sleek brown otters with luminous, round eyes followed him up the sand. As he prayed, the otters curled around him, rubbing his feet with their soft fur and warming him with their breath. When he finished his prayers, Cuthbert stood and, raising his right hand, blessed the creatures with the sign of the cross. Smiling, he then sent them back to their sea home.

Overcome by what he had seen and aghast at his own temerity, Brother Alphege confessed his guilt to Cuthbert. Cuthbert forgave him, but made him promise that he tell no one what he had seen as long as Cuthbert was alive. Alphege kept his promise, but told the story often after Cuthbert's death, until the otters have become Cuthbert's symbol.

Felicity frowned. She had listened carefully, in spite of her desire to nap. Surely there hadn't been a clue to a murder or to hidden treasure there. "Um, yeah. That's a really nice story. But what does it have to do with Dominic's murder?" And then she smiled in spite of herself, picturing the round black pools of the otter's eyes. "But I did like the otters."

"You'll often see otters in paintings of Cuthbert," Antony said. "As to the treasure, I realize it's tangential, but I wanted you to get a sense of why Cuthbert was so beloved. Why pilgrims through the centuries brought such an outpouring of treasure to his shrine."

Felicity finished her sandwich. "OK. I get it, although I think it's more likely to spur me to contribute to a save the otters fund. You know, though, I remember my biology teacher saying that otters are really obstreperous critters in spite of looking so cuddly. So, maybe it really does tell us something about Cuthbert." She picked an apple from the lunch sack.

"Yes, all that gentleness and beauty are a stark contrast to the next chapter in the story. And it happened right here."

Felicity looked out to sea, squinting against the brightness. In general terms she knew what came next. She scanned the horizon as if looking for the black shapes of warships. Instead, two RAF fighter jets roared overhead so suddenly she almost dropped her apple. Had so little changed from Viking times to now? Her mind flickered through the ages—the Hundred Years' War, Agincourt, the Crimea, World War One, World War Two, Iraq—and all the interminable conflicts between. The huge, blood-soaked conflagrations where thousands, even millions, died and the personal, sudden violence that left one person like Father Dominic dead. And it was all the same. All evil, hatred, greed flaring up to mar endlessly the peace and beauty that life could hold. The conflict in the world was a constant. Ashes to ashes. Dust to dust.

Antony made quick work of his sandwich, then leaned back and settled into his second story. "And this just might possibly have something important in it. If there's anything to the 'Three from the sea' allusion.

"Suddenly, everything changed. The peace, the beauty, the artistry, the devotion of life on Holy Isle were torn apart. In the year 793, the first Viking raid struck the British Isles— on Lindisfarne. Symeon of Durham, an early twelfth-century historian records: 'They came like stinging hornets, like ravening wolves, they made raids on all sides, slaying not only cattle but also priests and monks. They came to the church at Lindisfarne and laid all waste, trampled the Holy places with polluted feet, flung down the altars and bore away the treasures of the church. Some of the brethren they slew, some they carried away captive, some they drove out naked after mocking and vexing them. Some they drowned in the sea.'"

Felicity threw away the remainder of her apple. She couldn't swallow. It was last night's nightmare again, only more concrete. Now she could see the blood, hear the cries, smell the smoke.

Antony paused for a long breath. "The survivors rebuilt the church, and the monastery struggled on for another seventy-five years. Then a series of repeated attacks convinced the monks they must leave. Miraculously, the shrine of St. Cuthbert and the Lindisfarne Gospels had survived intact. The brothers lifted Cuthbert's carved, wooden coffin from its stone enclosure, and placed their most precious treasures in the coffin with Cuthbert: the relics of St. Aidan, the head of St. Oswald, the precious Gospel book. First carrying the coffin on their shoulders, and later drawing it on a cart, they began a saga of more than 200 years of wandering. A remnant of holy brothers and their successors guarding Cuthbert's body and the treasured Gospel."

"Hmm," Felicity mused. "A brotherhood. Guarding Cuthbert and the treasure." As she spoke, she rummaged in the bottom of the backpack, still feeling hungry. "The brotherhood thing," she repeated. "Perhaps it all began there."

"Perhaps so. If it began at all."

"Oh, how did this get here?" Felicity drew a candy bar from the pack.

"I put it in," Antony said. "You left it in my room, remember? Thought you might need an energy top-up. They're good for that."

"Kendal mint cake, you said?"

"The very same as eaten by Sir Edmund Hillary on the summit of Mount Everest. He gave his eye-crinkling grin and pointed to the green wrapper picturing the explorer and his mountain. "See, he recorded it in his journal."

Felicity read from the back of the wrapper: "'We sat on the snow and looked at the country far below us … we nibbled Kendal mint cake.' What fun." She pulled the wrapper off and held the bar out toward the waves. "Tradition! But at least we aren't sitting on snow." She took an enthusiastic bite. "Hmmm, like a hard peppermint patty."

"Yes. Some people say they taste like toothpaste, but I quite like them."

"Why aren't you…" eating yours, she started to ask around her second bite, then remembered: Lent. No sweets. She bit hard on another mouthful, then frowned. "Funny texture. What are the crunchy bits?"

Her teeth ground on another bite. "Ouch!" She spat. Red drops of blood gleamed on the white sand.

"What?" Antony grabbed the remaining bit of Felicity's bar and broke it apart in his hand. "Glass!"

Horrified, she dabbed at her tongue with a paper napkin and viewed the red smears.

Felicity's hand flew to her throat. The slight scratchiness was beginning to burn. Her mouth tasted salty. She spat again. More blood.

Antony's arm was around her, pulling her to her feet. "We've got to get you to a doctor. A hospital. How far down is the pain?" Then he held up his hand to silence her attempt at an answer. "No, don't talk. It might aggravate it."

He rummaged in the lunch sack then groaned. "No bread left. That might have helped." Already he was guiding her forward, down the hillock and along the path to the town.

Felicity was beginning to shiver, more from the thought of what she had done than from any weakness. She had swallowed shards of glass. What was going to happen to her? Would she bleed to death? Would they pierce her stomach? She didn't want to think about the inner workings of her digestive tract.

Antony's arm stayed strong and firm, keeping her on the path, moving unfalteringly forward without rushing. "Steady.

Breathe. Swallow."

She obeyed and felt herself relax. She hadn't realized she was holding her breath. But then her next thought brought a fierce shiver. Who had done this to them? Who had put those mint cakes in their rooms last night? Willibrord? One of the guests? Someone from the outside? Not even Jonathan could be immune from suspicion. Was it the same person who had shot at them the day before?

Well, if they thought she was going to mope around here and bleed to death, they had another think coming. She put a hand to her throat for warmth and comfort and strode forward.

Chapter 11

"But that's terrible!" Willibrord turned an ashen gray and his head seemed more in danger of bobbing off his spindly neck than ever. "No, I have no idea who put those bars in your room. Are you certain it was someone here? I mean someone here who tampered with them? Maybe at the shop, or even the factory—you know, some maniac, like the Tylenol tragedy in America a few years ago. Did the wrappers look like they had been tampered with?"

Antony realized his mistake. "I—I don't know. I didn't notice anything. I was so alarmed I didn't think to bring them along. I should have. Evidence..." He struck his forehead. "Stupid! I should have noticed—the wrapper was green. Those are the chocolate-covered bars. Plain, like this one was, should have been in a bright pink wrapper."

"Never mind about that. The important thing is to get Felicity to a doctor. The A and E in Berwick—"

"Accident and Emergency room," Antony translated for Felicity.

"Or the doctors in Seahouses. That's the best plan. Anna and I see Dr. Knowle there. Fine man. Very efficient. I'll jot down the number for you." As he spoke, Willibrord rummaged wildly through the stacks on his desk, tossing papers and files onto the floor. "She'll be all right. Has to be."

Anna rushed in, two slices of bread in her hand. "Here. Small bites. Chew them well, swallow carefully. We've never had anything like this before, but a guest once scratched his throat with a fish bone. I looked it up in my first aid manual." Felicity took the bread and began chewing obediently.

Antony saw with a wrench that the chewing motion was

difficult for her. "A drink of tea, do you think?"

Felicity shook her head emphatically.

"Ah, here it is. Knew I had it." Willibrord held out the tide table, ran his finger down the chart, then consulted his wristwatch. "Fifty-three minutes until the causeway closes. You've just time. Barely." He began slapping the pockets of his baggy trousers. The first ring of keys he produced, he tossed onto the desk. The second, he handed to Antony. "Take my car. The blue Escort by the gate. There's a map in the glove box. I'd drive you myself, but I promised the vicar I'd—but maybe I could change that. I'm not certain—"

"No problem. Thanks. We'll be fine." Antony clutched at the keys and began steering Felicity toward the door.

The ancient little car started obediently on the first try, and Antony eased it into gear. Fortunately he had his license, even though he had never owned a car; never seemed he needed one, really. Now he wished he was a more experienced driver. How long had it been since he had driven? Several months, at least. Last fall's student trek to Rievaulx Abbey must have been the last time, and that a leisurely outing—not a mad dash across a narrow causeway, racing the incoming tide to get an internally bleeding passenger to hospital.

What if he was too slow? What if he slipped on the causeway? He gripped the wheel until his knuckles whitened. At least there was only one road. No worry about losing his way.

They had barely started across the causeway when Felicity pointed at the waves rushing toward them, stopping only a few feet short of the roadway. How could they be that close already? Antony looked at his watch. "We should have thirty-five minutes yet—" He forced his voice to sound calm. "Plenty of time." *Please, God* he added under his breath. He drove on, forcing himself not to take risks with increased speed.

Felicity shook her head, her face white with strain.

"I agree, it doesn't look good." Almost before he could accelerate, water began washing over the causeway. "Felicity, I don't think we're going to make it." He couldn't believe how matter-of-fact his voice sounded. His hands gripping the steering wheel were wet with sweat, and his heart pounded. In another three or four minutes, he wouldn't be able to see where the causeway was. Would they have a better chance staying in a marooned car or trying to swim for it? How deep did the water get? Would they be swept away if they got on top of the car? How long would they be marooned? How could this be happening?

"Mmm!" Felicity's muffled squeal was accompanied by enthusiastic pointing ahead to the right.

"Yes! Thanks be to God. We're saved." The refuge tower gleamed whitely, maybe twenty meters ahead, its poles washed by waves. If he could just hold the car steady against the pull of the tide… Seaweed bumped and squished beneath the tires, it's slickness harder to hold against than simple ruts. Amazing how strong the pull of the water was; it looked like gentle lapping, but he could barely hold the wheel against it.

They were nearly there—perhaps another two or three car lengths—when he miscalculated and the front right wheel slipped off the causeway, sticking in the sand. There was a sickening thud and he felt them tilt sideways as one tire sank deeper. The little blue car sat firm, water washing against the bottom of the passenger door. "Out!" he cried. "Can you open your door?"

Felicity yanked at her door handle and threw her weight against it as he scrambled after her, grabbing her hand before she was out of the car. "Hold on tight. Don't let go!" he shouted over the sound of the waves, moving them forward, holding against the pull of the sea with all his strength.

His every instinct was to rush. The water was still below his knees, but it was coming in at breakneck speed, the undertow sucking hard. How could such gentle-looking waves be rolling so fast? But he didn't dare lunge forward. One misstep could drag them off the roadbed where the water would be over their heads. He was very uncertain of their ability to swim against that powerful current.

"Hang on! We'll make it. You're doing great!" He yelled above the sound of the surf, as much to build his own confidence as to encourage Felicity. She was strong and courageous, but light. The surf could carry her off with a single surge. He tightened his grip on her hand and stretched forward, battling the sea and his own rising terror.

It could only have been a matter of a few minutes until he felt his hand tighten around the rail of the wooden stairway, but it seemed like hours. He pulled Felicity forward and pushed her up the steps ahead of him. As they ducked under the roof of the tower, he looked back. The water was halfway up the windows of the Escort.

Gasping and shaking, they settled themselves on the wooden bench. Felicity shivered so hard he was afraid she might fall. They were soaking wet, the breeze was cool and would get colder when evening drew on. Antony struggled to remember how tides worked: twelve hours from high water to high water, so it would be six hours from high to low. It still had some way to rise, so it might not turn for three hours, and wouldn't be safe to cross for something like another three after that. Which all meant they had at least "Six hours to wait," he reported. Six shivering hours.

And what then? Would the car run when the water subsided? Unlikely. He was just wondering if he should put his arms around Felicity to warm her when he felt her hands firmly turning his shoulders. Grinning at him, she turned him around and let him know he was to stay turned away. A moment later he heard her removing her jeans and the splat of water as she wrung them dry. At least as dry as she could.

Next she was signaling for him to do the same. "Er—" She put her hands on her hips in an emphatic gesture. He grinned, filled with awe at her practical calm. "There's no arguing with you, is there, woman? Even when you can't talk." She turned away and he wrung as much water from his clothes as possible then climbed back into them, feeling even colder with the wet fabric against his skin. His black suit trousers were in a sad state.

Burrs still clung to them, along with bits of grass, sand and seaweed. Priestly clothing was not designed for the adventures he had experienced the last few days.

"Are you OK?" He jumped in surprise at the sound of Felicity's raspy voice.

"You can talk!"

She grinned and shrugged.

"How does it feel?"

"Like a bad sore throat," she croaked. "Very bad."

"Maybe you shouldn't talk."

"Need to—got to figure out what's going on." She spoke in a low, breathy whisper. They resettled themselves on the bench, sitting as close as they could to share what little body heat they had. Felicity attempted to speak again and Antony inclined his head toward hers to hear her better. "What happened? Was the table just wrong?"

Antony shook his head. "No, the Admiralty doesn't make those kinds of mistakes." He thought for a moment. "Tide tables are printed and published in little yellow books. Willibrord typed out the tides for each day on a separate sheet so it would be handy to give out to guests."

"So maybe he mistyped. Or in his hurry maybe he read it wrong. Or grabbed an old one by mistake."

"Or someone put a fake one on his desk. Someone who knew we'd be needing to get to medical help fast."

Felicity shivered. "Why is someone trying to kill us? We don't know anything."

"I suppose to keep us from learning something." That seemed the obvious answer. He hadn't really had time to analyze it all. But now he wasn't so sure. "On the other hand, I'm not convinced they *are* trying to kill us."

Felicity's eyebrows shot up. "Three times they almost have."

"Yes, frighteningly near misses, but pretty feeble attempts to kill compared to the brutal bludgeoning Dominic was dealt. I think someone is just trying to scare us off."

Felicity thought that through, then her head jerked up. "Well, then—they won't!"

Antony grinned at her. "Full marks for spunk. But we still need to know who's doing it and why. I take this as proof that there is something to find and that we're on the right track. I just wish I had more idea what we're looking for."

They sat in silence for several moments. Antony's comments brought into focus another thought that was niggling at Felicity's mind, but she was uncertain whether or not to voice it. Would it just confuse the issue more? In the end, she spoke, as much to fill the silence as anything. "That's been bothering me."

He looked at her, questioning. "Hm?"

"Why was the attack so brutal?"

"What do you mean?"

"Well, Dominic was an old man—a frail old man. Large frame, but gaunt. Surely one good blow with something heavy would have done for him. But there was blood all over that room." She closed her eyes at the memory. "There was something emotional, personal even, about the attack." The long speech made her throat burn, but she wanted to get the thought out.

"Something in his background, you mean? His family? His time in Africa?" Antony suggested. "I don't see how we could look into that. And the fact that we've been threatened seems to indicate we're on the right track. But we shouldn't let ourselves get too coldly academic. You're right that there's an emotional element to all this somewhere."

"A madman?" Felicity shivered.

Antony shook his head. "It seems anyone would have to be mad to do that to another human being. But that's really too easy an answer. There was a great deal of anger behind that attack, but it was coldly directed. Someone might have hated monks in general, or Dominic for a personal reason, but I don't think the attack was purposeless."

Felicity considered. "So if not insanity, what could make

a person capable of such an act?" she asked, holding her hand around her throat.

"Evil, certainly. As a priest, I have no trouble pointing at the root cause of all the world's problems, but that's so ubiquitous as to be a non-answer."

"So was someone capable of committing such an outrage born evil?" Felicity's voice rasped and strangled. It was questionable whether or not an abstract philosophical question would help find answers, but it would help pass the time. Antony had said they had six hours to wait. Besides, trying to understand the mind of a murderer was hardly abstract.

"You mean something twisted in his genetics beyond the original sin common to all human beings born into a fallen world? No, I couldn't accept that, because that would mean such a person had no choice, was predestined to commit an atrocity and had no free will. I can't conceive of such a God. I certainly couldn't worship him."

"So society was to blame?" She voiced the commonly heard, anodyne reason. "Someone so severely deprived they felt driven to a desperate act, you mean?"

Antony shook his head. "The idea that 'we were all to blame' for the poverty, ignorance, inequality in the world that leads to atrocities? That's a dead end. If we're all guilty, no one is guilty."

Felicity was silent for several minutes.

So was their murderer so deformed by some traumatic event in his life—it must be a man, surely—that he was set on such a path? Something that led him to choose violence or revenge? "It's terrible to contemplate, but it seems that knowing more about our suspect's childhood might help. The only problem is, we don't have any clear suspects."

Even as her words wafted on the chill air, Felicity refused to give in to debilitating thoughts that all their efforts might be a total waste of time.

In spite of the fact that her mind felt as sodden as her clothes, she clung to the fact that there *had* to be an answer. Somewhere.

She believed with all her heart that there was ultimate justice in the world. She had to hold on to that. She had to believe, or she would have nothing to hold to. She refused to give herself to the void of despair that would be colder and deeper than the waters surrounding their fragile refuge. Faith, the monks called it. Such a simple, comforting concept in church, but it seemed so coldly distant perched atop an open tower with dark waters swirling beneath and a possibly insane murderer stalking them somewhere beyond.

Chapter 12

Silence again. Antony attempted to factor in the incalculable. It was difficult enough, attempting to decipher some coldly rational motive, but understanding the psyche of a rage-driven maniac seemed impossible. At last, Felicity pointed to his breast pocket where he kept his pen and notebook. He took it out, thinking she wanted to write notes rather than talk, but she said, "Make a list. Suspects."

He opened the book, then paused. A page had been torn out. He had had notes on something. Oh, yes, he had jotted some information from that strange book in the Heritage Centre. But why would anyone be exercised over some theory of whether or not Cuthbert debated at the Synod of Whitby? Bothered enough to steal his notes, try to kill them with ground glass, and then send them onto the causeway with the tide coming in?

"I can't believe it, but it does look bad for Willibrord, doesn't it?" he said at last. Their host had access to their rooms, and he had rushed them out onto the causeway with the tide rolling in.

"If someone switched the schedule..." she began.

"That could have been anyone at the Retreat Centre. Anna and Willibrord, of course, and the other guests. My room wasn't locked. Was yours?"

She shook her head.

"Beyond that, it seems like about anyone on the island could have slipped in—said they wanted to pray in the chapel, maybe even use the telephone. The St. John's run a pretty open door policy from what I've seen."

"The mint bar—who could have made that?"

He was silent for a moment. "I've been thinking about that. The ingredients are simple: sugar, glucose syrup, oil of peppermint.

That's what makes it such a good energy source—"

"Ground glass—" Felicity added in an ironically flat voice.

Antony squeezed her hand in quick sympathy. "Hammer and an empty jam jar. The process might take a little practice in the kitchen, but it's not rocket science. Then buy a bar at the village shop. Reuse the wrapper…"

Antony peered over the edge of the tower. Impossible to tell which direction the swirling water was moving. How soon could he hope for it to recede? He had to get medical help for Felicity. But in the meantime, best to keep her mind busy.

"I think the wrapper being the wrong color is a really good clue," he continued. "Either our 'poisoner' was careless, or else not a native. He—"

"Or maybe it could have been a woman— I think I've read that poisoners are usually female," Felicity added.

"Right. He or she knew enough to be dangerous, but not enough to get the details right."

"Oh, good. Not Willibrord or Anna, then."

"I wouldn't think so. Although it could have been sheer carelessness, I suppose. And the kitchen is there…"

She nodded. "Put their names down."

He did. "One thing more. The mint cake seems like a very English thing—someone who would know they are traditionally taken on hikes and adventure outings."

"So not Philly?"

"It's hard to imagine her whipping up sweets in the kitchen. Although using ground glass seems exactly in character for her. I can't think where she would have had access to a kitchen unnoticed, though."

Then his thoughts went on in another direction. "However, an English person could have suggested it to her and, if she is related to the Smith-Johnson author of that book, there might be some motive there."

"Maybe pride."

"What?"

"If the book contains errors. Errors you—we—are likely to point out and refute; it could be embarrassing to the author. Even a setback to his academic career. If he's her husband, for example—"

Antony took up the thought. "Yes, I can just imagine our Philomena insisting her husband add her name to his while she just retained her maiden name. And his status would be important to her."

"If such a man even exists. It's all conjecture."

"Yes, but it could explain the missing notes from my book." He explained about the ripped-out pages as he wrote Philomena Johnson on his suspect list.

"And Stephen Bootham," Felicity said.

Antony paused before writing. "I can't imagine what the book dealer/birdwatcher would have to do with it." He scratched in his name. "But he was there. Maybe closer than we knew. Maybe he didn't really go off to other islands birding. And he would know about tides. Maybe he's handy in the kitchen—who knows?"

Suddenly a silence developed between them. Silence and chill. Antony knew what had to come next, but he dreaded it. He didn't want to upset Felicity, and he was determined not to let his personal dislike of Breen color his analysis. But it had to be said. "Breen's behavior is so erratic…"

He felt Felicity stiffen beside him. "Well, Philly Johnson is my favorite."

"Why?"

"Not just because I don't like her. Bootham was so detached; Willibrord runs a Christian centre; and Jonathan is practically a monk, isn't he?"

"Not exactly. Although oblates do take a form of vows… Actually, Breen's vows are precisely what's been bothering me."

"Why?"

"Well, maybe I'm nitpicking, but his excuse for being late to the ashing mass was that he was in the kitchen rustling up a snack."

"He was. The staff confirmed it."

"Yes. But, besides the fact that Ash Wednesday is one of the two most solemn and obligatory fasts of the year, if he were sincere about observing Community rules, he would regularly keep a Eucharist fast—not eat within at least two hours of receiving communion."

A look of stunned incredulity held her immobile for several seconds. Antony held his breath for the angry explosion to come.

Instead gasping laughter shook her body. "You can't be serious! 'Nitpicking' doesn't even come close. I thought the Eucharist was supposed to be a feast. A celebration."

"It is, but we prepare for it—"

She held up her hand. "Oh, spare me the theology."

The sound of the waves lashing the poles of their refuge emphasized their desolation, their complete cut-offness from outside help, and yet it created a coziness in their tiny shelter in spite of the cold and draft. They were together. Close together.

Felicity shrugged. "Right. Put his name down."

The silence deepened. Felicity spoke first. "What next?"

Antony had been wondering the same thing. He looked at his watch. "Well, first we wait for the water to go down. Could be three or four hours yet, I'd guess. It'll be pretty dark by then. I hope to goodness we can manage to get to help... Somehow. It's unlikely that car is going to run again without some serious mechanical work. How are you doing?"

"OK. Throat hurts. And I'm cold." She scooted even closer to him on the bench.

He pulled off his jacket and put it around her shoulders. Without thought, he left his arm there for added warmth. She leaned into it. And with that simple gesture, the questions he had been pushing to the back of his mind leapt to the forefront: was his concern for Felicity simply what any responsible person would feel for another under their care—never mind an attractive young woman? Was it an attempt to make up for his failure with

Alice? Or was his concern for her welfare—and his dislike of Jonathan Breen—rooted in a far deeper emotion?

And if it was, what would he do about it—beyond a good, long discussion with his confessor? At the bottom, of course, was the old, nagging question, frequently wrestled with, never resolved: was he called to celibacy?

Living and working in a monastery as he did, becoming a vowed member of the Community had seemed like a natural next step, and yet every time he had approached it, he drew back, although he couldn't define why. It wasn't women. Christina at Cambridge had been a pleasant enough flirtation. And then Alice. He startled at the unreality of saying, even mentally, the name he had so long suppressed. Alice Marie. Enough. He slammed the lid shut on that box. And truly, since then he had been busy and happy. Hadn't he? If tranquil routine could be equated with happiness, he had. He had thought that might be God's way of telling him celibacy was for him. But now he wondered.

And yet, in spite of his long-standing hesitations and newer questions, the drawing he felt to the monastic life was very real. The deep spiritual bond he had forged with many of the men, the peace of the way of life built around regular periods of daily work, study and prayer, the beauty of the worship, the silence— even, in an odd way, the security of taking vows of poverty. Putting aside the striving for worldly success... Yes, he could certainly understand why some chose that way, had hoped and prayed that it would be his way, and yet, he was never *sure*.

Father John, his spiritual director, had been through it with him so many times. He could see him now, sitting across from him in the small, bare room with the crucifix on the wall and the *prie-dieu* in the corner. The placid monk, about the age his own father would be now, sitting with his hands folded in his lap, nodding patiently with a hint of an encouraging smile while Antony poured out his struggles.

Always followed by instruction to meditate on certain passages of Scripture and the encouraging advice not to rush, not

to fret, God would make all known. Stay open to his guidance…
That beautifully tranquil life. All suddenly gone wrong. How was
it possible? So very, very wrong indeed.

Felicity shifted under his arm, bringing him back to the
present moment.

"I'm worried about you," he said. "Are you having any
pain?"

"Fire in my throat when I swallow."

"Stomach cramps?"

She grinned. "Just hunger. Wish I'd eaten more of Anna's
bread."

He picked up the notebook with his free hand and looked
at the names jotted there. There just didn't seem to be any pattern
to connect with the clues Dominic left them.

"Do you have the journal with you?"

Felicity patted the breast pocket of her shirt. "Never without
it." She pulled it out. "It got a bit damp; fortunately not soaked
through, though." She held it out.

"I just thought we should give it another look." Antony
opened the small volume. He turned the pages slowly, pausing to
read out the disconnected bits that appeared to be musings for a
poem—or maybe a prayer. Surely they would have made more
sense if Dominic had been granted time to form his scattered
thoughts into a cohesive whole.

> *You have made known to me the ways of life, The secrets*
> *of your treasure,*
> *You make me full of joy with your knowledge.*

Antony smiled at the contrast this bore to his own troubled
musings. Yes. Assurance one had found the way would, indeed,
be cause for rejoicing. And there was good general advice—seek
guidance, rest in hope. But anything more? He read the next
words aloud. "'I will bless the Lord, who has given me guidance.
He has shown me the way.' Does that suggest anything to you?
Anything specific?"

Felicity thought for a moment. "Mmm, could be his pilgrimage itinerary. Or the Children's Fund, I suppose. That's what he was so excited about. I think he even said something about seeing the way forward. But then, maybe I'm reading a reference to funding into that."

"Interesting. Yes, that could be the allusion." Three pages further on contained lines that showed the beginnings of stanza form:

> *For he did not suffer his Holy One to see corruption.*
> *Even the grave can praise thee, death doth celebrate thee.*

"For he did not suffer his Holy One to see corruption." Antony pointed to the line. "In the context of his pilgrimage that seems an obvious reference to Cuthbert."

"Or," Felicity took up the thought, "possibly the Lindisfarne Gospels, since they were produced in thanksgiving for Cuthbert's uncorrupted body. Could there be anything about the manuscript? Something hidden in the design? A second copy kept sealed away for 1,300 years?"

"Intriguing." Antony ran his hand up and down through his hair. "Seems like it could mean anything. Or everything. Which amounts to nothing."

They lapsed into another silence, the water still rushing beneath them in swirls, occasional seabirds dipping above. The day which had begun in such brilliant sunshine was now graying as clouds filled the late afternoon sky.

Felicity riffled the pages of the little book, turning back to an earlier line: The secrets of your treasure. "If only we knew what the treasure was."

Antony nodded. "I was hoping we might find a clue to that on Holy Isle."

"There was all that in the church."

"Yes. Some nice pieces. But I wouldn't think enough to build a hospital, even if they would sell them. And only the one piece seemed possibly related to Cuthbert."

The silence deepened, broken only by the sound of the waves washing against the poles of their eyrie and the call of seagulls swooping overhead. Felicity resumed turning pages until she came to the bit she especially liked. She had read it several times on her own. Now she held it out to Antony to read:

> *For this corruptible must put on incorruption,*
> *and this mortal must put on immortality.*
> *So when this corruptible shall have put on incorruption,*
> *and this mortal shall have put on immortality,*
> *then shall be brought to pass the saying that is written,*
> *Death is swallowed up in victory.*
> *O death, where is thy sting? O grave, where is thy*
> *victory?*

"That is so beautiful," she said.

"Yes, but not Dominic's, you know?"

She looked at him questioningly.

"It's St. Paul. Fifteenth chapter of First Corinthians."

"Oh, I suppose I should have known that. Still—Dominic *did* write it down, so it could be important. And it has one of those triangles doodled beside it. Maybe that meant Dominic especially liked it. I think the Children's Fund is a type of incorruption coming from corruption—a triumph of life over death."

Antony nodded. "A lovely way to express the hope of saving children from infant mortality and AIDS. And a neat double entendre on Cuthbert's uncorrupted body. It all seems to hang together in some vague, rather useless way." He smiled suddenly. "'About as useful as a chocolate teapot,' my Scottish friend would say."

After another pause, he continued. "So much speculation… Maybe we're just reading our own ideas into it all." He turned to the final lines, a kind of coda:

> *Triumph in death,*
> *Death over death;*
> *Life over death.*

"You are right." He turned toward Felicity, pointing to the words he had just read. "If something about Dominic's work will save the children as he envisioned, it certainly would be a triumph of 'Life over death.'"

Felicity's eyes misted; her whisper was barely audible. "It meant so much to him."

"It did," Antony agreed. "He loved Africa and its people, especially the children. He felt that saving the children could save the nation of South Africa and that, in turn, perhaps the whole continent. You've heard his story about Desmond Tutu?"

Felicity looked at him as if to indicate that she had, but couldn't quite recall it, so he continued, "It was one of his favorites. Tutu had tuberculosis as a young child. One of Father Dominic's duties as a young monk was visiting the children in hospital. He took some comic books to the young Desmond. After visiting for a while he said, 'I'll come again and bring you some more.'

"'No, Father,' the six-year-old said. 'Next time bring me proper books.' Dominic often said what bright, eager students the African children were. All they needed was to be given a chance."

The sun was setting, the sky between their perch and the mainland ribboned with red-gold streamers beneath dark gray clouds. The water below them took on an ominous black depth. The chill deepened with it. Surely the tide would turn soon, but there was no indication yet.

Felicity sighed and her body relaxed. Her head slumped against his shoulder. "Tell me more about Cuthbert. Just talk to me. I don't even care if it doesn't have any clues in it."

Yes. Antony would happily do that. A welcome escape from the depression that was settling over him like the chill, penetrating air. That was exactly what it was like—like trying to battle one's way through one of those heavy dark clouds hanging over them. And like everything else in his life, it came down to his own inability. All the disappointed people and failed causes in his life: his parents, Gwena, Aunt Beryl, Alice, the Ecumenical

Commission. Now he must add his inability to make any headway with whatever clues Dominic's journal might hold and his inability to get Felicity to medical aid to his list.

Yes. Do what he had always done. Take refuge in telling stories. He mentally flipped through his lecture notes for a story he hadn't yet told. In their present situation, the pictures of Cuthbert praying by or in the water were all too vivid. The image was almost physically visible:

> *Stars reflecting in the obsidian water washing over his feet, Cuthbert would stand for hours with his arms out-flung, voicing his deepest longing. In his retreat on Inner Farne, Cuthbert never lost sight of the fact that his most important work was that done in the solitude of the night and in those lonely days when high seas and winter storms left him in isolation. Cuthbert's deepest desire, his greatest passion, was for the spread of Christianity in his kingdom. He would gladly give his life for the salvation of his beloved land. And he knew that that was exactly what he was doing. He came to understand fully the double meaning of the word "passion"—which isn't really a double meaning at all—for to care so much is to suffer. His greatest burden was his greatest joy.*

At first he thought Felicity had drifted off to sleep. He hoped so; surely that would be healing for her. He couldn't bear to think about what those shards of glass might do when they reached her digestive system. He had no medical knowledge, but the concept was terrifying. He felt her stir and held her closer. He was surprised when she spoke. "Like Dominic's passion for Africa. It would be wonderful to have so clear a vision of what you were to do, wouldn't it?" She took a deep breath that was almost a sigh. "Do you? Have a passion?"

He was startled into silence by the arrow-like sharpness of her question. And the precision of its aim. He did. But he seldom spoke of his inmost desires. Occasionally to Father John, of course, that was what spiritual directors were for. But to a young woman? The silence lengthened.

"Sorry. Didn't mean to pry."

"No. That's all right. I suppose I do, really. Well, perhaps it's more of a dream." He fought his shyness. His desire to turn inward; to be silent. "Funny, isn't it, how much easier it is to talk about another's passion than one's own."

"It's a baring of one's soul. I shouldn't have asked."

"No, I think I'm glad you did. It's just… somehow I'm not much accustomed to talking about it—not as personal commitment. Academic debate is fine, of course. But I really feel much more deeply than that." How much did he dare reveal to her?

He took a breath; he didn't want to say too much, or to sound didactic or overly pious. "I have a great desire to see unity in the church. A real oneness. Not necessarily unity of government, which is what most ecumenical efforts aim at, but unity that would allow openness at the Communion Table."

Her blank look spoke her incredulity more clearly than any words could have. Bizarre was undoubtedly the most generous of her judgments. At least he was spared her laughing at him. "Mmm, interesting," she managed. And then, after a space of time, "Why?"

"Why do I care so much about that?" She nodded, and he thought, *Yes, why? Why can't I crave money or power or sex, or even food? Something "normal"?* Why should all his charged energies be focused on reforming the church? He shrugged. "Can anyone explain? Do we choose our passions, or do they choose us?

"But if you mean why is it important—why can't we just keep on with each group doing their own thing as we've been doing through the centuries?—I can answer that: because the church should reflect God—his holiness, his beauty, his love, faithfulness, glory, purity…"

"So?"

"So, also we should reflect his unity. His oneness."

She nodded slowly. "The Holy Trinity. Three in One. Like a triangle."

"One God in three Persons. We *say* it constantly, but we don't *do* it at the one place we are meant to come together."

"His table." Her whisper was as soft as the breeze.

"Did you ever think… what if you spent days—weeks— preparing a special dinner for your family—Christmas, perhaps— and then some refused to come to the table, and some came but squabbled because it wasn't served right, and some came but said others couldn't…" He stopped as his voice caught. "Sorry. I get carried away. But sometimes the thought is just so painful."

"I understand the theology—sort of. But why *personally*? Why does this mean so much to you? I mean—this is a great cause—but there are lots of really important causes. Why this one?"

All the time she had spoken in her rambling way he had looked at her with a totally blank face. Now the whipping of the wind was the only sound in the tower.

"I have no idea. Spiritual calling, maybe." He spoke slowly, followed by a long pause. "Lots of people know all this, give lip service to it, even, but why did it take hold in me?" His pause grew. "Perhaps because of my own experience of brokenness in my own family. That certainly taught me the pain of disunity, and gave me a longing for unity in the relationships of my life."

"What can you—we—anybody do?"

He shrugged. "Pray. I should be home right now preparing for that commission meeting. When I accepted the chairmanship I thought, 'Here's my chance to accomplish something—to make a real difference.' We're direly underfunded—quite desperate, actually—but the more important fact is that I don't have anything new to offer. It'll be the same tired arguments again." The same failure he had always been, a little voice in his head said. "If only I had something to get their attention—a new argument for unity that would actually move them toward progress." He paused. "Assuming I'm not under arrest by then, of course."

"You won't be!" Felicity's sureness was warming. He just hoped it wasn't unfounded.

"But has the commission accomplished anything?" she asked.

"Sometimes there are hopeful breakthroughs, but for the most part we just express good intentions and then go back to the old debates."

"How old?"

"Since the disciples said, 'I am of Paul. I am of Apollos,' since the Great Schism, since the Synod of Whitby, since the Reformation, since yesterday's Eucharist…"

"Oh!" Felicity jumped up and pointed.

In the twilight it was hard to tell, but as he looked, he became certain. "Yes, the tide has turned. Thank goodness!"

"How much longer?"

"I don't really know. Close to three hours, I expect." They resumed their huddled position. Hours yet to worry about what next. It was hardly worth trying to start Willibrord's car. It would be a long walk to Beal, the closest mainland village. The causeway would be slimy with water and seaweed. It would be dark. Felicity needed medical attention. She needed it hours ago. *Lord, have mercy. Don't let it be too late. Christ have mercy.*

Faith, he reminded himself. Hold on, just as he had admonished himself hours ago. Around the same circle again. But for how many more times?

Chapter 13

"You're a very lucky young lady, you know." Felicity nodded and tried to look lucky. The way Dr. Knowles's swab burned her throat she didn't feel especially lucky. "That glass could have perforated your stomach. Those cuts in your throat could have been much deeper." Right. So she did feel lucky. But he needn't lecture her. It wasn't as if she had eaten ground glass on purpose. "If you had got here sooner we could have pumped your stomach. Made certain it was all out." What? Did he think they had planned to get stranded by the tide?

"Still, the stomach will attempt to isolate the irritant, wrap it in mucous so it can pass on through your digestive system. Rest tomorrow. I want to see you Monday morning. Health Centre opens at 8:30. James Road. Just past the police station. If you're all right then you can go on your way." *What's this "If you're all right" business? English understatement for "If you survive"? This must be what Willibrord meant by "Very efficient".*

Felicity nodded and snuggled deeper in her duvet. Here on the Northumberland sea coast, they were probably expert at warming and drying half-drowned stragglers. And lecturing them with a stiff upper lip. Still, she had no desire to move from her makeshift bunk.

When the doctor left, Antony pushed her door open and peeked around speculatively. She gave him a weak smile. The swab still hurt too much to talk.

"He seemed to think you'll survive." He touched her hand briefly and gave her his eye-crinkling grin. She wobbled her hand up and down to indicate a 50/50 situation. "It was truly a Godsend that Bootham came along when he did."

Felicity nodded. Yes, indeed. Returned late from his Farne Island expedition, he'd said. Missed the tide, so had to wait in Beal for the causeway to open. Antony had seen the approaching car, climbed down from the tower and stopped him. The birdwatcher had been jovial about turning in the narrow space and making the return trip to Seahouses, although Antony did have to talk quickly, insisting that it was all a deplorable misadventure, when Bootham made rather insistent suggestions about going to the police.

When Bootham acquiesced, it was with his characteristic jauntiness. "No problem. No problem at all. Probably a closer medic somewhere around here, but I know Seahouses well. Just came from there, of course. Great day with the birds."

"What did you spot today?" Antony had asked, once they were speeding on across the causeway, trying to keep Bootham's mind off the idea of going to the police.

"Terns," Bootham had declared. "Best to observe them now. Can be mighty tetchy in the breeding season—dive right at you with those bright red bills of theirs. Five species of British Tern on the Farnes, you know. I've seen 'em all."

The Health Centre was long closed by the time they'd arrived, so Antony had directed their way to a hostel run by the local parish church. As a young curate, he had once brought a group of lively teenagers here on a weekend retreat. Nick Dawson, the warden, had studied at CT shortly after Antony began lecturing there. Fortunately, the retreat house was empty, so Nick had been more than willing to rustle up some thick blankets to cover the wooden bunks in two of the rooms for his marooned guests, while Antony rang the number Willibrord had given him for Dr. Knowles.

Felicity could feel the hard boards of the bunk under her, but it was blessedly warm. The throb in her throat began to relax into a dull ache.

"Bootham's gone back to Lindisfarne now." Felicity opened her eyes as Antony's voice called her back to consciousness. "Said he'd tell Willibrord everything and they'll see if anything can be done about the car. He'll check back with us before he leaves the area in a day or two, in case we need a ride anywhere, or anything. Obliging fellow."

Too obliging? Felicity wondered, but she wasn't about to quibble with her rescuer.

"He did happen to mention he was headed to Whithorn next. We'll see how you feel. I don't know—I haven't really decided where we should go next." Antony started to turn away, then stopped. "Oh, yes, I asked Bootham to bring our things when he comes back this way."

Felicity nodded, then frowned and raised one eyebrow, the best way she could think to communicate her question.

"Oh, I'm sure Anna will pack them for you."

She raised both eyebrows and rolled her eyes. Maidenly blushes over Stephen Bootham packing her knickers was the last thing on her mind.

She wanted to ask why they should go to Whithorn, but communicating the question wasn't worth the effort. She nodded and closed her eyes. She didn't remember Antony turning out the light.

Felicity was still lolling in delicious semi-consciousness when she was aware of her door being pushed gently ajar. She forced one eye open just a slit. Full sunlight was seeping into her room around cracks in the ill-fitting curtains. She opened the other eye and turned to look at Antony. "What time is it?"

"Just past noon. Fancy a bowl of Nick's chicken soup?"

The steaming bowl on the tray he held smelled delicious. Felicity propped herself up in her bunk and invited Antony to sit and talk to her while she ate. "What did you do this morning?"

She should have known. He had been to the Matins service the warden had conducted in the church next door. She concentrated on her soup. "Do you feel up to an outing this afternoon?" he asked. "It's a nice day—sunshine, even." He opened her curtains to demonstrate.

Felicity still felt a bit wobbly, but the promise of an outing in the sunshine got her out of bed readily enough. And the soup soothed her throat. At least her jeans were dry, if stiff from their saltwater dowsing.

Nick Dawson drove them up the Northumberland coast, green hills and fields on their left, rolling blue sea on the right, to the summit of a massive rock outcropping on the very edge of the North Sea. "Bamburgh Castle," Nick announced.

"Did Dominic come here?" Felicity asked.

Antony grinned at her. "Not that I know of, given the cryptic nature of his journal entries, that is. This is a day off—just a bit of pleasure since we need to wait until tomorrow to be sure you're fit to travel."

Ah, no sleuthing. Felicity felt herself relaxing. "Sunday as a day of rest and all that?"

"Right," Nick said as he drove under the archway of the gatehouse between a pair of round towers. "In these parts we like to claim Bamburgh as the finest castle in England. It's certainly one of the best. The original was already a century old when Oswald ruled Northumbria and sent for Aidan to come convert his kingdom to Christianity."

Felicity tried to imagine what it must have been like on that spot fifteen centuries earlier as Nick parked the car. They climbed the stairs and walked along the defensive stone wall that had been a wooden fence in Aidan's day.

"What an amazing view!" Felicity exclaimed, looking down the green hillside to the strip of white sand and the blue sea beyond.

"Just a mile out there to Inner Farne." Nick pointed. "It's said that Aidan was meditating there when he saw a heathen army attacking Bamburgh by setting a ring of fire around the castle. Aidan prayed, and the wind changed to blow the flames into the faces of the pagans."

The sun was beautiful, but the wind was sharp and Felicity was weaker at the knees than she had realized. She leaned against the parapet for support. "Unfortunately, the castle isn't open until April," Nick continued. "The Great Hall is magnificent. Of course, the dungeon is always the favorite of our young visitors."

"That's all right. I'm quite happy with just the view." Felicity was ready to suggest they might seek a more sheltered viewpoint, however, when she noticed a boat making for the beach. Leaning over the parapet, she watched intently as two figures got out and pulled the boat up on the sand, securing it well.

The figures were little more than sticks at this distance and yet, it was hard to tell, but surely the taller one, clad in something bulky and beige, moved with a distinctive wobble to his long-legged gait. And the shorter, stockier one—possibly Stephen Bootham? She frowned against the bright light. There was really no telling. It was just a matter of vague impressions.

She nudged Antony's arm and pointed to the boat, half hidden in the grasses at the edge of the wide, sandy beach. Surely that was the same shade of electric green as the boat they had seen on Viking Beach the day before?

Antony nodded. "Yes. It looks like the same one. I wonder what they're doing."

Nick watched the figures disappearing toward the green far below them, and shrugged. "Looks like they're making for the football match. Shall we go down there? We'll be out of the wind."

Felicity readily agreed. They drove down the steep hill from the castle and around toward the tiny, picturesque village of Bamburgh, which ambled along a single street running down from the north side of the castle. Between Castle Hill and the church, a broad village green was alive with the efforts of local football players.

They walked around the edge of the flat field toward the monumental stone cliff and the looming castle with its foundations clinging to the sides. Felicity thought she had never felt so dwarfed in her life. At the foot of the rock a cave sheltered a large white stone cross, and on up the side of the hill, raw gashes in the rocks and vegetation showed evidence of recent excavations. A bench at the foot of the castle rock offered shelter from the wind. They sat and watched for some time as the teams ran from one end of the field to the other. The men followed the game, quickly choosing the team in red jerseys to cheer for. Nick pointed out a particularly good player to Felicity, trying to draw her into the game, but she shook her head with a smile. "Too much effort. Just watching all that energy makes me tired. I just want to sit here with my eyes shut."

She had been looking out for the figures from the boat among the scattering of other spectators, mostly sitting comfortably in canvas lawn chairs, standing in groups or strolling about the edge of the field, but hadn't seen anyone that seemed to match her earlier impressions. Now she gave in to the luxury of letting the sun warm her closed eyes.

"Would you mind if we left you for just a bit, then?" their host asked. "I'd like to show Antony the archeological dig up here on the hill. We won't be long."

Felicity was too relaxed even to bother answering; she just nodded. A few observers of the match ambled by, chatting. The thwack of a player blocking a pass with his head, the occasional cheering of the fans, the riffling of breeze bearing the scent of spring grass lulled her into a sense of letting the world go by—a world she didn't have to participate in. Felicity continued to sit in her half-daydreaming state until a snatch of conversation nearby cut through her doziness. *Did she hear the word "treasure"?* Carefully, so as not to attract attention to herself, she turned her head and surveyed the people milling around her.

She glimpsed their backs as they walked on. Certainly Willibrord and Bootham. She scrambled from her seat and moved toward them as quietly as possible, praying they wouldn't turn around.

"So where do you think he got it?" She could just make out Willibrord's words whipped by the wind.

"That's what I'm trying to figure out. But I'm sure nothing

of *that* value came out of that hole."

A cheer broke from a group of supporters just to her left, but Felicity was almost certain that Willibrord asked, "So what about Father A?"

Felicity was desperate to hear more, but her quarry now turned away from the field, walking across a wide open space apparently toward the town. There was no way she could follow them without being discovered.

She returned slowly to her bench. What did that mean? Father A? A reference to Antony, surely? Her Antony. Who had gotten what of significant value out of what hole? At least she had positively identified the men from the boat. But answering that question only raised more.

The bells from the square Norman tower of the church on the other side of the green began ringing just as Nick and Antony returned. "Just in time for Evensong," Antony said.

"Yes, I wanted you to see St. Aidan's church anyway." Nick led the way. Felicity was bursting to tell Antony about her discovery, but their guide was leading several paces ahead to focus their attention on an ornate monument on the edge of the churchyard.

Inside a wrought iron fence was a large medieval-style sarcophagus with the stone figure of a woman resting under an elaborate Gothic-arched canopy. "The Grace Darling Memorial," Nick announced. "Do you know her story?"

"Oh, yes, I do." Felicity vividly recalled Antony's recounting it to her just before their picnic on Viking Beach—the brave lighthouse keeper's daughter who rescued the stranded seamen in a raging storm.

"And right there, opposite the churchyard," he pointed, "is the cottage in which she was born."

Felicity smiled appreciatively in memory of the young girl, but this was the briefest of diversions, because Nick continued his account of the church's history as he hurried them forward. "This is the very site of Aidan's mission church. It's also where he died. A wooden shelter was constructed at the west end of the church for him while he was ill. The buttress he rested against was considered to have miraculous powers and survived the church being burned down—twice."

They entered the fine stone church and Nick pointed to a beam in the roof of the baptistery. "And there it is."

Felicity nodded. The beam wasn't even smoke-damaged, apparently. Uncorrupted, like Cuthbert? Then she brought herself up short. Giving rein to the instinct to mock at stories of the miraculous was all too easy a reflex. Had a great deal of the beauty and mystery of life been lost by our modern insistence on scientific proof for everything? What was scientific about love or joy for example, and yet what would life be without them?

Still, science could be brought to bear on some mysteries. The whole thing of Cuthbert's body being uncorrupted, for example. Surely a spot of radiocarbon dating could answer a lot of questions. Wasn't dating archeological finds its most valuable use? If the bones in Cuthbert's shrine could be...

Antony ushered her to a seat in the first row of pews. The evening light coming through the stained-glass windows bathed the rich carved wood of the chancel in a golden glow. The front of the church was richly carved and filled with figures of Northumbrian and other saints. The altar was dressed in plain sackcloth for the first Sunday in Lent, but the golden light through the high, narrow windows turned the rough burlap to molten gold.

The service was a simple, said Evensong, conducted by the vicar in a black cassock and white surplice with a black scarf. The very pared-downness of the liturgy made the richness of the carving and glowing glass seem all the more sumptuous. But that was not the center of Felicity's attention.

The magnificent candlesticks on the altar, unlit for the evening office, yet aflame with sunset like the rest of the chancel, held her full attention. She was sure she was right. She tugged at Antony's arm and pointed. He blinked, then nodded. Yes, he saw it, too. The pair of tall, silver candlesticks on the altar *were* a match for the pair in St. Mary's sacristy. Of course, they would need to see them closer to be certain. But there could be little doubt.

The words of the Grace had barely faded when she nudged Antony. "Find out about them."

It was a simple matter of asking the vicar. "Oh, yes. Very fine, aren't they? They're from Inner Farne, you know."

Felicity expressed amazement that Cuthbert's small island retreat had possessed anything so ornate. "Well, not in Cuthbert's day, you understand. But the hermitage on Inner Farne became rather wealthy during the Middle Ages. Seal oil was highly valuable, and the monks profited from salvaging wrecked ships." The vicar paused to smile conspiratorially. "And apparently that wasn't all they profited from, because in 1443 the Master of Monks at Farne was dismissed for 'pawning the best chalice and divers silvers.' Our candlesticks are believed to be part of a set of six that the master turned to his own profit."

All the way back to Seahouses, puzzle pieces danced in Felicity's mind. Was it all just scraps of unconnected information? Or did the candlesticks and church silvers mean something? There had been six in the set—had the missing ones been found? Could they possibly constitute Dominic's treasure? Was Willibrord St. John emulating the medieval Master of Monks and selling off valuables? Would he commit murder to protect his enterprise?

Chapter 14

Monday morning was gray, damp, cold and windy without any vestige of the sunshine they had enjoyed the day before. Weather the locals seemed to be well prepared for. Felicity felt much better once she had managed to down a large bowl of porridge cooled with rich milk almost as thick as the porridge itself, and a cup of sweet, not-too-hot tea.

Better enough to attend morning prayers in St. Paul's Church, next door to the retreat house. When she stepped inside the sanctuary, the gray light suddenly became clear and luminescent in the long narrow room with pale blue walls and a high barrel ceiling. Leaded glass windows sparkled, illuminating the cross in the center roundel of each window. The crisp atmosphere of the whole room was warmed by a red curving expanse of apse beyond the open chancel screen.

Felicity also found Nick Dawson's prayer service warming and comforting—as was the navy blue woolen cap he gave her to pull tightly down over her ears before they set out to walk to the Health Centre. Dr. Knowles was as abrupt as on her first encounter with him, but his diagnosis was more encouraging. "No permanent harm. Stick to soft foods and avoid extremes of heat and cold for a few days." He scribbled the name of some throat lozenges on a pad of paper, ripped off the top sheet and handed it to her. "Suck on these, you'll find them soothing." That seemed to be it.

"Thank you," Felicity managed in her recovering-from-a-sore-throat voice, and started to get up.

"And be more careful next time."

Antony was joyful at her good report. "Excellent. Excellent. Just what I hoped and prayed for." He guided her past the high-backed, pink plastic benches lining the walls of the room where patients waited resignedly. A bouquet of orange plastic flowers on the windowsill was Felicity's last image as the door closed behind her, and she took a deep breath of the fresh air.

Antony steered their steps down the walk toward the small seaside village with the harbor beyond. "I don't know about this, the sea looks a lot heavier than it was yesterday," Antony said. "But let's see if we can catch a launch to Inner Farne. I'd like to show you the scenes of Cuthbert's last days before we go on tracing Dominic's pilgrimage."

They walked toward the harbor, glancing in the windows of the various small shops occupying the gray stone buildings. A few well-bundled people passed them with murmurs of, "Morning."

Felicity took a deep breath and smiled. With each step closer to the harbor it became stronger—that inimitable seaside smell of salt air and fish. She half-closed her eyes, recalling the same smell thousands of miles and tens of years away, when their family vacationed on the Oregon coast. It always rained. Her parents had booked a room in a motel that bordered the beach so they could keep an eye on Felicity and her brothers digging sandcastles, while her father relaxed in the room with a book and her mother worked. Even before the days of laptop computers and faxes, Cynthia Howard was never away from her work. When it was time to come in, their dad would hang a red beach towel in the window...

She realized they had reached the bottom of the street and Antony had come to a stop in front of the memorial for the 1914–18 war in the center of the roundabout. The plaque read: "This have I done for you." Such a small village. So many names. All in the Royal Navy, one would expect.

The pier was lined with tiny, colorful huts serving as booking offices for tours to the Farne Islands: John Mackay's Boat Trips, blue; Billy Shiel's Farne Islands, white; Farne Island Cruises on MVS *Cuthbert*, red. The next one was yellow. They made a welcome break in the world of gray stone, gray water, gray sky.

But all were tightly closed.

Further along, where the high stone sea wall blocked some of the wind's ferocity, two or three clusters of men stood around chatting dispiritedly, their hands thrust deep into the pockets of their pea jackets, heavy woolen caps pulled well down over their heads. Felicity wondered if they should approach the men for information, but Antony turned back up the harbor to a small, glass-fronted building marked Harbour Master. Just as they arrived, a small car pulled up and a tall, authoritative-looking man in a nautical cap got out. Antony approached him. "Might boats go out later in the day?"

The Harbor Master shook his head. "No chance of sailing. Sea's too heavy. If you could get out there, you couldn't land." His tanned skin, craggy features and entire bearing carried as much authority as his words. "We've had none out for a week now."

"What, no launches out last Saturday?" Felicity broke in. "Are you sure? It was so sunny."

"Not from my harbor. Heavy sea."

Felicity and Antony looked at each other, obviously thinking the same thing—didn't Bootham specifically say he'd taken a boat from Seahouses? If these rugged, professional seamen didn't go out, how likely was it that a birdwatching bookseller from York could? But what was the point in lying about it?

And what about the boat they watched beach at Bamburgh yesterday? Were Wills and Bootham intrepid seamen of the same stock as Grace Darling? There must have been some urgency behind their journey—no pleasure cruise, in spite of the sun that had sparkled on the waves.

Felicity had told Antony last night of the snatch of conversation she overheard between the two men, but they had come to no conclusion. They revisited it now, adding this new fact, but it all just seemed to make the matter more obscure.

Hands in pockets, heads against the wind, mimicking the dispirited air of the beached fishermen, they returned to the harbor edge and leaned against the sea wall, looking over it at the mossy rocks below, watching the heaving, white-crested sea roll in, listening to each crashing billow, an ostinato bass to the cries of the gulls circling above and dotting the rocks below.

Frustration overtook Felicity. Just there, beyond them, straight out, a gray hump rose in the mist. She pointed. "Inner Farne?"

Antony nodded.

"If we could just sail around it, even without landing. It's so awful to be so close…" The Harbor Master's "No chance" rang in her ears. She knew. And yet, to be so heartbreakingly near… She sighed. "OK. So tell me what we would have seen."

Antony grinned. "Gray rock. Birds. Water."

"Oh, thanks."

"Actually, there's a surprising lot to see: a lighthouse, the remains of the medieval monastery, a chapel marking the site of Cuthbert's hut, a cross marking the site of his death…"

"And birds."

"Definitely lots of birds."

Felicity turned her back to the crashing sea and leaned against the wall to face Antony. "Can you imagine—actually living there? And there must have been days much worse than this one—lots of them."

Antony leaned against the wall as well, looking out to sea— as if watching Cuthbert in his mind's eye. "St. Antony and the Desert Fathers had set the pattern centuries before in Egypt—go to a barren, desolate place—a *desart*— to commune with God."

Felicity shivered. "At least Saint Antony's desert was warmer."

"Yes, the Celtic and Anglo-Saxon saints set something of a new pattern in choosing lonely rocks in the sea for their *desart*s, but they served the same purpose. And like Antony and the Desert Fathers, before they could spend time in holy contemplation they had to clear the area of evil spirits."

Felicity blinked. Holy contemplation was one thing. Even on a dot of rock in the middle of a heaving ocean. But evil spirits?

She wasn't so sure what she thought about that.

"This was no withdrawal from spiritual battle, but an advance into enemy territory. Cuthbert had learned early in his career, when establishing the monastery at Ripon, that land, like people, doesn't become holy without a struggle. The devil doesn't easily abandon territory." He spoke matter-of-factly.

Felicity looked at him. She had reserved judgment on the uncorrupted body story. Now she was being asked to take the devil and evil spirits on board intellectually?

Either Antony didn't notice her skepticism or else he figured the best answer was simply to tell his story.

And so, like Christ in the wilderness, and as we do symbolically every year at Lent, Cuthbert spent forty days in prayer and fasting, preparing the rocky soil for spiritual growth as carefully as a farmer would prepare a new field to grow vegetables. Evil had to be banished in the name of Christ, peace and goodness had to fill the void, order overcome chaos, love subdue hate.

Now Felicity nodded. OK. She wasn't big on the idea of evil spirits, but peace and goodness—order over chaos—love over hate... now, that was more in line with her vision of making the world a better place. Yes, if you thought of evil spirits not as little beings in red suits with pointy tails, but as spirits of chaos, hatred, ugliness—oh, yes, she could believe in that.

Cuthbert's description of his battle with the powers of darkness is historical record: "Often they would throw me down headlong from a high rock. They have thrown stones at me as if to kill me. But though they have tried to frighten me, by one attack after another, and to drive me from my hermitage, they have not won the victory. In no way have they been able to injure my body or my mind... I know that God will never leave me nor forsake me, and my God is a mighty warrior." Here, Cuthbert had returned to his original profession, serving in the army. But now it was God's army, rather than Oswald's. For hermits were God's front-line soldiers in battling the forces of evil. The hermit's prayers fought on God's side, holding the powers of darkness from the land. And so, truly Cuthbert's hermitage on Inner Farne was a mightier fortress than the royal stronghold at Bamburgh.

Antony turned his gaze from the mesmerizing water and looked at her. Almost against her will, she nodded, not sure whether she meant to indicate agreement, or simply that she heard him. But he apparently found her response sufficient, because he continued.

Again, Cuthbert followed his practice of praying by the water, allowing the star-twinkled tide to wash over him. Pools of light, waves of holiness, rolling toward his island, light and holiness washing toward him in rolling tides. Cleaning, purifying, sucking out the darkness, the evil, carrying it out to sea in the undertow. Leaving the land free and bright, cleansing his island desert, then running on to the mainland, sucking the darkness and evil out. Pools of light, waves of light and holiness washing in.

Whether the prayer was one of Cuthbert's or Antony's own, Felicity wasn't certain, but out of habit she joined in the "Amen" at the end.

To her surprise, Antony suddenly pushed away from the wall and gave himself a shake. "Let's walk out to the end of the pier." He indicated the great stone structure extending several hundred feet into the ocean, providing protection for the north side of the harbor. In better weather it would have been full of parked tourist cars, but today it was deserted. Felicity recalled that wonderful scene in *The French Lieutenant's Woman* where the heroine—was it Meryl Streep?—in a dramatic black, hooded cloak, walked the length of a similar structure. She would have welcomed that hooded cloak now.

"This was built in the 1890s to protect the herring fleet," Antony said as he guided her forward. "They used to export over 20,000 barrels of salted herring a year. Today there are only four trawlers and five smaller fishing boats registered here."

She stopped and turned to him with her mouth open. "You are amazing. How do you know all that stuff?"

He grinned and pointed. "Read the sign, didn't I?"

"Smarty!" Suddenly she was back at Seaside with her brothers. She gave him a solid shove with both hands. "Race you to the end!" And she was off.

She had a fraction of a head start and fractionally longer legs, but it was a close call. Close enough that they continued to argue for some time over who won when they reached the end, both gasping for breath against the strong, wet, wind. Now she was glad she wasn't wearing anything so impractical as a Victorian cloak to slow her down. And she felt warmer, too. Warm enough to sit down on the end of the pier. If she squinted hard, could she really see the faint outline of the little stone church marking the spot of Cuthbert's hermit hut on the island? She couldn't be sure.

Antony sat beside her, on the upwind side, sheltering her. "You're feeling better."

She smiled and nodded.

"How's the throat?"

She held her hand to it as if to check. "Better. Still scratchy, but not burning."

"Great. Let me finish up this story, if you can stand any more, and then we'll go get some lunch."

She nodded vigorously. A hot lunch sounded great; her breakfast porridge seemed hours ago. But she surprised herself with the realization that she was also eager to hear the rest of the story. Not at all in a hurry to leave this cold, wet, gray stone perch with the sea crashing around her and seabirds crying forlornly overhead.

The spiritual foundations laid, Cuthbert could turn to the physical building. Brothers came from the monastery to help erect a small hut for the holy hermit and a chapel for his worship inside an enclosure, and a guest hut down by the beach. Lack of fresh water was a problem. At first, Cuthbert collected rain water in an animal skin, but he needed a well. He asked the brothers to dig in the center of his hut. Baffled by the instruction, they nevertheless obeyed, but the hole was dry. In the morning, however, it was full of water. And so it remained, never to run dry, nor to overflow.

"Is it still there?" She interrupted his narrative.

"Yes, certainly." He sounded surprised that she would question it. After a moment, he continued:

The rocky soil was shallow, the winds fierce, but Cuthbert wanted to live by his own labor, so he planted wheat. The wheat crop failed to sprout. Next he tried barley. It was now well into the summer months—late to be sowing. Yet Cuthbert planted and prayed. The seeds sprouted. When the crop began to ripen, however, a new problem arose. Birds came to eat it.

Cuthbert confronted the thieves: "Why do you eat that for which you did not labor? Is your need greater than mine? I will not survive here without this crop. Surely your area is larger than my small field. If you have been given permission by God, then stay, but if not, be off with you."

Felicity laughed. "That's wonderful! Did anyone ever reason more logically with birds?"

Antony returned her smile. "The best part is that it worked. The birds departed and didn't bother him again. This wasn't the last of Cuthbert's problems, though."

Next a pair of ravens began pulling the thatch from his roof to build their nest. This time he didn't try logic, he merely commanded. "In the name of Jesus Christ, depart and do not stay any longer in this place that you are damaging." As soon as they had flown away, Cuthbert regretted his hasty words. They weren't really taking much straw. He could share with God's creatures.

Three days later, one raven returned. Cuthbert greeted it with gentle words, but was disappointed when it left. A few hours later, however, it returned with its mate, carrying a large portion of pig's

*lard which it dropped at Cuthbert's feet. Cuthbert used the gift to
grease the brothers' shoes when next they visited him.*

Felicity laughed. "Logical and practical. I like this man better all
the time." And now, she recalled with a sense of chagrin how
she had shut Antony out when he had tried to tell her these
things earlier at the Heritage Centre. "I remember the birds in
the murals in the Centre."

"Oh, so you were paying attention, after all."

She looked down, hoping she wasn't blushing. "Consider it
an apology."

"No apology necessary. I know I do go on a bit—well, a lot,
actually. And I'm not really sure why, but I just do believe that it's
important to understand all of this to get to the bottom of what's
going on."

"I know. You're probably right, but it's so hard to see how
anything that happened that long ago…" Felicity let her voice
trail off on a gust of wind. "But do go on, I am listening. Now,"
she added.

He gave a single, sharp nod.

*Cuthbert's island retreat—which should more rightly be called
an island advance—became a spiritual center. People made their
way there from all parts of Britain to seek healing—spiritual or
physical—of the "Man of God," as he became known. And none
were disappointed. Cuthbert's gentle wisdom, his healing touch,
comforted and strengthened all who journeyed the rough sea mile
in a little boat from Bamburgh. And, of course, they would tell
their friends, and others would come, return refreshed, encouraged,
healed, to tell others, who would then make the journey themselves.
It was much the same as in the early days of his ministry, when
he traveled the length and breadth of Northumbria ministering
to tiny villages and outlying farmsteads. Only now they came to
him.*

*Cuthbert loved his little island where he could talk to his
companions the birds, pray in solitude, and serve the steady stream*

of humanity that sought him and always found him at home, at their service. It was his preferred way of life above all others. But he was not to have his own choice in the matter.

The end came sooner than he had thought to expect. And it came in the form of a royal messenger and the Archbishop of Canterbury. King Egfrith's personal envoy and Archbishop Theodore arrived on Farne to inform Cuthbert that he had been elected bishop. Cuthbert was dismayed. Could anything this counter to all his instincts and desires really be God's will? He had worked so hard to establish his hermitage. His ministry seemed so satisfying to himself and to those who came to him for help. Perhaps the council had got it wrong. He would pray.

Cuthbert remained on his island. More messengers came. Cuthbert remained. At last the day came when messengers arrived that could not be ignored. King Egfrith himself, Bishop Trumwine, and a whole retinue of clergy all in full regalia knelt before Cuthbert surrounded by his eider ducks on the rocky shore of Inner Farne.

Cuthbert looked at the august delegation with sadness in his eyes, knowing he had been defeated. "If God is determined to subject me to so great a burden, I believe that in a short time he will set me free. I am sure he will let me return to my island solitude." With this uneasy submission, Cuthbert accepted the Bishopric of Lindisfarne, the most venerable sanctuary in the north.

Antony turned to her. "You remember the painting?"

Felicity did, indeed. It was one of her favorites, because one of the most colorful, the king's red and gold robes, the bishop in purple…

At that moment, a sharp horn blast split the air. They both jumped and turned toward the signal tower of the lifeboat station behind them. "Oh! Is there danger?" Felicity's heart was racing in her throat.

"No, light's green— all safe." Antony pointed to the harbor signal light. "I think that just means it's lunch time."

"I couldn't disagree with that."

The Olde Ship Hotel sat on a rocky promontory overlooking the harbor, sturdy and stone, like all its surroundings, as if it had grown there. Inside was all natural wood and maritime memorabilia, bits of ships, fishing equipment, models, old black and white photos. Two men and a woman sat at the bar. Felicity and Antony chose a table looking out over the same ever-moving, ever-changing, mesmerizingly powerful scene they had stared at for the better part of two hours, but now they were warm and dry. Felicity gave her order—vegetable soup and a cheese toastie, and settled back for more story.

Cuthbert was consecrated Bishop at York on Easter Day in the year 685. Cuthbert, surely the most reluctant bishop in all of Christendom, must have also been one of the most vigorous. Once again he took the faith out to the people. Tramping the high hill country and wild windswept moors, teaching the people who flocked to him, laying his hands on them, praying for them. When there were no dwellings for him to stay in, people would collect branches and build a temporary hut so he could minister in the area for several days.

The soup arrived in steaming bowls, creamy thick and tasty. "Mmm," Felicity savored her first mouthful.

"Not too hot? The doctor said to avoid extremes."

"No, it's delicious."

Antony sampled his, then continued his narrative, as Felicity emptied her bowl.

After two arduous years serving God and his people throughout his diocese, Cuthbert again withdrew to his island desart. He knew that he was very ill and that he would not be required to leave his retirement this time. He went to Lindisfarne for the Feast of the Nativity. When he was leaving, a brother asked when they could hope for his return. "When you bring my body back here," Cuthbert replied.

For two months the brothers from the monastery made regular visits to Farne to minister to Cuthbert. One day they found him gravely ill. Cuthbert gave Herefrith, one of the brothers, instructions for his burial on Inner Farne. Herefrith begged to be allowed to remain and nurse him, but Cuthbert refused. "Go now and return at the proper time." Herefrith asked when that would be. "When God wills," he replied.

That night the sea rose with heavy, rolling waves, leaving Cuthbert isolated for five days.

Antony gestured seaward and Felicity nodded. Yes, it took no imagination to see what that must have been like. She longed to be on the actual site. She leaned closer to the window, imagining herself on that lump of windswept granite. Again Felicity recalled her brief introduction to this story with the pictures on Lindisfarne. Now she wished she had paid more attention to the details.

The island was tiny, but even so, the way from his enclosure to the guest lodge on the beach was long and arduous for Cuthbert. At one point he dropped to his knees to rest against a boulder. Too weak to stand, he crawled the final distance, dragging his little bag of five onions—his only food.

"Yes, I remember the onions in the picture." At that moment their toasties arrived, oozing melted cheddar cheese. Felicity really couldn't imagine biting into a cold, raw onion.

Lying on the pallet, Cuthbert tried to pray. It was as natural to him as breathing; his very heartbeat. He could hear the waves washing high on the beach outside the hut. He could hear the wind whipping at the thatch. Always he had prayed in rhythm with the wind and the waves. Bright images of beauty and purity, carried on water and on the dipping white wings of seabirds, filled his mind, but no words would form. The seabirds called, seals sang, eider ducks waddled close, but Cuthbert could not join his voice to theirs. They must do his praying now.

At last the seas stilled and the brothers rowed in a frenzy to reach Cuthbert. This time he allowed them to stay and minister to him. One final struggle remained to Cuthbert. He requested that he be buried on his island retreat. But even in death he was not to be granted the peace he sought. Herefrith persuaded him to accept a proper burial on Lindisfarne. In his final hours, the bishop instructed his brethren: "Always keep peace and godly love among yourselves. Always live in mutual agreement with the other servants of Christ. Do not cease to be hospitable to all who come."

Antony stopped to chew a bite of his sandwich. "And then Cuthbert's final words—his instruction that the brothers should take his bones with them if they had to leave Lindisfarne."

"Yes, I remember." Antony raised an eyebrow at her. "I was listening, you know. It sounded so odd—'carry them with you to wherever God ordains.'" She thought for a moment. "But maybe it makes sense; he didn't really want to be buried on Lindisfarne anyway. Maybe he hoped that would be his way of getting back to Inner Farne where he really wanted to be."

"Or prophetic vision? Who knows?"

At the appointed time of evening prayer, Cuthbert received Holy Communion, lifted his hand high in praise as the monks chanted their prayers… Then silence.

One of the monks lit two torches, ran to the highest ground on the island, and waved the flaring lights in signal to the community at Lindisfarne. Cuthbert had departed for his heavenly home.

When the sea was calm enough, they returned to Lindisfarne. The community washed Cuthbert's body, placed a communion wafer on his breast, dressed him in his priestly vestments, swathed all in waxed cloth and, to the accompaniment of chanted psalms, placed the body in a stone sarcophagus, and buried him in the ground on the right side of the altar.

"Right." Felicity smiled at the young waiter who brought their tea. She poured a cup and indulged herself with two scoops of sugar. "And then eleven years later they dug him up and he was uncorrupted and they made the Lindisfarne Gospels."

Antony ran his hand through his hair and laughed. "You do make it sound simple."

"The history of the world in a forty-five minute lecture? I think it can be done." She flipped her head; her hair was beginning to dry and it felt good against her shoulders. "And so all was peaceful for about a hundred years. Until the Danes came."

"Exactly. You really are a keen student, aren't you? Amazing those details stayed with you. As I recall, that was about the point where you developed a penchant for gulping ground glass."

Felicity put her hand to her throat. "Don't."

"I'm sorry."

"No, I'm fine. Rather appropriate, I guess, in retrospect, the attack of the Vikings and the brotherhood fleeing with Cuthbert's body and their treasures—we sort of re-enacted it. We were attacked and fled."

Fortunately, Nick had loaned Antony some money until their belongings caught up with them, so he was able to pay their bill. As they stepped out, the signal tower gave another blast, startling, alarming, chilling. Felicity, who had felt so warmed by the food, surroundings, and story, felt suddenly frozen and oddly fearful. For the time, concentrating on getting well and listening to Antony's story had served as a buffer to the harsh realities of their journey.

She had felt protected, coddled, even—but someone out there, somewhere in the cold mist, had done terrible violence to a gentle, loving man and would willingly do the same thing to them.

"Antony!" She grabbed his arm with both hands. "I've had enough of this. Let's move on. Quickly."

There had to be warmth and light—somewhere. The security she had taken so for granted until Dominic's murderer shattered her world—it had to exist yet—somewhere beyond the cold and the gray of violence and evil and suspicion. They had to find their way back to it.

Chapter 15

Back in the cold, spare parlor at the hostel they perched on uncomfortable furniture, surrounded with copies of tattered, outdated magazines. "Move on," Antony repeated her words and nodded. "I agree. And I think we should accept Bootham's offer of a ride to Whithorn."

There was an implied question in that statement, and Felicity felt gratified that her opinion was being consulted on their next move. So far she felt as if she had been hustled, shoved and dictated to—all in the most courteous possible way, of course. "Um, *Whithorn*?" It sounded familiar—listed on Dominic's itinerary— and had Antony mentioned it recently? "Er—remind me."

"St. Ninian, fifth century, first to Christianize Scotland, built his Candida Casa after he returned from studying in Rome and began his missionary efforts. Great place of pilgrimage in the Middle Ages." He ticked off the facts.

"And we want to go there because—"

"'The talisman of Ninian', remember? We don't really know why Dominic went there, but it must be because he was following the route of Cuthbert's body."

"Right. After the Vikings. Cuthbert's Folk carting the sarcophagus with his body and assorted treasure and relics, including the Lindisfarne Gospels." Felicity nodded with satisfaction. She was getting this down.

"That's right. Their journeys took them through Northumberland, Yorkshire and across most of northern England. In despair of finding a safe haven in England, they even decided to cross over to Ireland. At the mouth of the River Derwent they boarded a boat, but a fierce storm drove them back. In the ferocity of the gale the Lindisfarne Gospels were washed overboard, probably in a tight leather bag. Once on land, they began searching the shores of the Solway in hopes of finding where their precious book might have washed up. Their searches took them to Whithorn where, indeed, they did find their treasure, and St. Cuthbert's body was able to rest for a time in Ninian's Cave."

"Yes, I see." Vaguely she did. A map would have been helpful. Her geography of England was rather on the vague side, her idea of Scotland entirely misty. "That's why Cuthbert and his folk went there—to find the Lindisfarne Gospels. What do you—er, we—hope to find there?"

Antony shook his head. "Same as always—what did Dominic do? What did he find or know? Who did he talk to? If only I knew what we're looking for." He ran his hand up and down through his thick black hair with even more vigor than usual.

"But then the other issue is, should we accept a ride with Bootham? Do you trust him?"

"At this point I don't see how we can trust anybody. But I'm not sure what a lot of choice we have. This hasn't turned out to be a particularly safe area for us, and public transport around here being what it is, a ride with Bootham's our quickest route out. Besides, we can't go anywhere until we get our bits and pieces we left behind on Holy Isle, which he offered to bring."

"I just can't get my mind around the fact he said he was birdwatching on Inner Farne and we know no boats went out." She paused, frowning. "At least, I think he said he was on Inner Farne. He certainly gave that impression."

"He did, indeed. And to what purpose? As if we'd care where he was." Antony was quiet for a moment. "Which probably all adds up to say that we should get to know him better—try to find out what he's really been up to."

Felicity thought of the muscles rippling under a tight-stretched shirt and shivered. Did she really want to know? He was definitely strong enough to cudgel someone to death.

Bootham returned early the next morning, looking more

gypsy-like than ever in a dark jersey with a jaunty red kerchief tied around his neck. He shifted binoculars and bird book from the passenger seat to a side pocket to make way for Felicity, while Antony wedged in the back beside boxes of used books. "Sorry about that. Always try to combine business with pleasure. There's some good used bookshops around these parts. Found several things that should go down well with the punters in York."

"Why are you going to Whithorn?" Felicity's throat still hurt, but it was more like the tail end of a cold, not the raging soreness she had known earlier. Her voice was a bit breathy, but it was a joy to be able to talk freely again. A few extra hours of good sleep and a warm gargle had done wonders.

"Collector selling his library—or rather, his estate selling up. Sounded like good stock for the shop. Never know, though, until I look through them." He threw a glance over his shoulder toward Antony. "And you? Interested in archeology, are you, vicar?"

"Archeology? No, not particularly. This was supposed to be a Lenten retreat—a chance to meditate in the footsteps of the Northumbrian saints."

Bootham laughed. "So did you get plenty of time to meditate on the top of that refuge tower? Not exactly what you had in mind, I'd guess."

"Right. We're hoping Whithorn will be more peaceful."

"Oh, it should be that, all right. Out of the way place, Whithorn." He directed the next question to Felicity. "So, what's it like, then? Traveling with a priest? How about I take you to the pub for a change?"

Felicity couldn't decide whether he was being offensive or friendly. "I'm a student. Father Antony is my church history lecturer." She hoped that would settle the subject.

Bootham laughed as jovially as if she had returned a bit of witty banter, and proceeded with quizzing Antony. What did they do on Holy Island? Who did they talk to? What did they make of Willibrord—and that Ms. Johnson when it came to it? She was something else, wasn't she?

While Antony returned evasive answers, Felicity picked up Bootham's bird book and glanced through the listings: guillemot, razorbill, fulmar, herring gull, lesser black-backed gull... each followed by their Latin name, date and location of sighting. All on various Farne Islands and all within the past few days. And all entered in the same ink. Either birding was a recent passion with Bootham or he was just beginning a new book...

No, he said he had been at it for years—had logged hundreds, hadn't he? And no boats had gone out on the dates he recorded. Felicity didn't know much about birds, but she had the feeling these were entries one could find in any tourist guide to the Farne Islands—she had seen most of them listed in the brochures Willibrord had given her. And was it too much of a coincidence—Bootham going to Whithorn? Was he following Dominic's path as well? Was Stephen Bootham the one who had searched their rooms? And left Kendal glass cakes behind?

Felicity's head began to nod and the book slipped from her fingers as the little white car sped down the A1 and the rolling Northumbrian countryside flashed past her window. They stopped at a roadside turnout near Newcastle for a late lunch. Felicity found herself ravenous enough to disregard any discomfort to her throat as she devoured hamburger, chips (at home she would have called them French fries; potato chips would have been too crisply scratchy) and savored the cooling bubbles of a Coke. How she wished she could talk to Antony, sit in the back near him so there could be some kind of communication.

At least, once they were back in the car and they turned toward Carlisle, Antony was able to take over the quizzing role. Although he always maintained his jovial, energetic air, their host managed to give even more evasive answers than Antony had done to his questions. Any information they needed to gain about Stephen Bootham was not going to come from him. Which was certainly a good reason to be suspicious of him. Felicity racked her brain; had she ever seen anyone that looked the least bit like him around Kirkthorpe? What would he look like without the stubbly black beard? Could he have grown that in just a week? The thought startled her. Had they only been at this for a week? It seemed a lifetime.

Just beyond Carlisle they turned north into Scotland and drove along the Solway Firth. Evening was falling with long shadows across the gentle green Galloway farmland when Stephen Bootham let them out at a farmhouse B&B near Whithorn, promising to return when his work was done. Fortunately, this was off season. Almost any B&B hostess was likely to welcome paying guests in March. And this was within walking distance of the town.

Maeve Ayre, accustomed to having weary travelers turn up unannounced on her doorstep, made them comfortable with a tray of sandwiches and pot of tea served in the glassed sun porch between their rooms. "Breakfast's at 8:00. There's a bell if you need anything." She pointed. "All right, then?" They assured her they were, and she departed.

At last Felicity could turn to Antony. "So what did you make of Stephen? Why did he offer to bring us here? Do you think he really has business, or is he keeping an eye on us? I definitely don't buy his birdwatching story; his logbook looked like something filled in the night before a science project was due. I'd sure like to know where he was last Wednesday. But then, I can't see any motive he would have for killing Dominic, can you? And what do you think—did he bring us all the way up here to keep us from finding something on Lindisfarne? Or get us out of the way to kill us? I think he rummaged in your room and took your notes. But why? Or maybe—" She paused for breath. "Oh, I don't know! What do you think?"

Antony was laughing so hard he was sloshing his tea. "I think it's a wonderful thing you've got your voice back. I can't remember a single one of your questions, it was just so good to be hearing you asking them." He laid his hand briefly on her arm. "I was so worried about you, Felicity."

She grinned. "Yeah. I know. Thanks. But what *do* you think

about Stephen Bootham? I mean—I've been thinking. Nothing about him seems *right*. So what if we're right in guessing that the Three still exist, and what if he's one of them? The way he just shows up in all the right—or wrong—places, it's possible. Now, these Three, what if they aren't there to guard some secret, but to keep it hidden?"

Antony was still grinning broadly at her. "There might not be much difference. Go on."

"Well, what I mean is, I think we—I at least—have seen this brotherhood as noble, heroic, Guardians of the Good. But what if we've got it wrong? What if there's some secret they're sworn to keep hidden—something evil—something they're willing to kill to protect?"

"Like what?"

She sank back against the flowered cushions of her wicker chair with a sigh. "I don't have a clue. It was just an idea."

They ate their delicious cold beef with English mustard on brown bread in silence. At last Antony spoke. "Yes, I do see what you're getting at. If that were the case, then one of them could have killed Father Dominic if, say, he had uncovered their secret on his pilgrimage."

"That's right—just by accident—while talking to people about his Children's Fund, or about Cuthbert, for example. And then we wouldn't have one enemy—we'd have three."

"Of course, if they are English Benedictines like Butler says, that would eliminate Bootham, but—" He took a deep breath. "I hate to say this, but—Father Clement is an English Benedictine, and the police did suspect him."

Now it was Felicity's turn to slosh her tea. "That's ridiculous! All the Brothers of the Transfiguration are Benedictines. As was Dominic. You can't possibly think Father Clement killed Dominic. It would be as easy to think the superior did it or—" She came to a sudden halt.

"Or that I did?" His voice was soft with sadness.

"No! I—"

"We might as well talk about this, Felicity. I did have blood all over my hands. The police suspect me."

"Well, I don't!" Her voice was almost fierce. "Nor do I suspect Clement or Anselm or anyone else at the Community. And nor do I suspect Willibrord or Jonathan who are sort of quasi-Benedictines. If we let this make us paranoid we'll be too frozen with fear to accomplish anything." After a moment's thought she added, "But I do think there might be more than one enemy. So we need to be awfully careful."

Antony nodded. "I agree. And thanks for that vote of confidence. But that brings us back to Bootham, doesn't it? I agree he doesn't quite seem to add up. And I got a peek at some of the books he'd acquired for his shop. Not the ones on top, mind you—he'd taken care to put some innocuous nature walks and children's stories on top. Then a couple of art books and some history—things one would expect to sell well in a used book store. But when he stopped for petrol, I dug deeper. The bulk of them were very heavy, dry-looking volumes on archeology."

"Specialist stuff?"

"Definitely."

"So maybe he has a specialist client."

"It's possible, I suppose. Just another one of those things that doesn't add up." He thought for a moment. "Or maybe it does. He asked me if I was interested in archeology. And kept quizzing me about what Nick and I saw on our walk."

"As if there was something you weren't supposed to see?"

"Exactly."

"There were those digs below Bamburgh Castle that Nick showed you. Could Bootham and Wills be stealing treasures from archeological sites?'

The straw-grasping speculations hung unanswerable in the air. Later, however, back in her room, Felicity found herself facing the even more unimaginable question of Antony's guilt.

As earlier, her instinctive response was that it was impossible. And yet… Her denial had been a fiercely loyal reaction in the heat of the moment. And she had meant it. But now, alone in the cold and quiet of her room, she needed to think rationally.

He wouldn't—couldn't... But how did she know? How could anyone ever know what was in another's heart? Know what another was capable of? What their life had made them?

What if? What if the end of all their sleuthing were to lead to the totally impossible, totally unacceptable answer? What would she do? If she found evidence against Antony, could she betray him to the authorities? His tousled hair, furrowed brow and lopsided smile rose before her and her eyes filled with tears. She had been so rashly idealistic—so sure she could right the wrongs of the world. And now she knew nothing. Nothing was solid. It was all shifting ground. Dust and ashes.

She was several moments considering. But in the end there was only one answer. She had always seen her grand goal of pursuing justice as a lofty, mountain-top thing. Suddenly she saw the possibility of personal cost. The pain a noble goal could require. But her answer had to remain unswerving.

Besides, if the unthinkable proved true—if Antony *were* guilty—that would make her work all the more important... if more dangerous. Who would be better placed to discover such treachery?

As a boost to her own determination, she spoke aloud. "I'll do what it takes." The words echoed comfortlessly in the bare room.

Chapter 16

The next morning with Maeve's full cooked breakfast warming them from the inside, Felicity and Antony walked across a wide green, dew-damp pasture filled with red cows, then along the edge of an alfalfa field to arrive at the bottom of the main street of Whithorn, the transition from farm to town being only a matter of crossing a road. As they walked up the long street, Antony returned to his history lecturer mode to bring Felicity up to speed on St. Ninian, still Whithorn's most famous citizen.

In the year 380, the mighty Roman Empire was crumbling at the edges, but still it churned on, binding distant lands together with the strength of its armies, the prosperity of its traders and the passion of its missionaries. Not a bad time to be alive for a vigorous, aristocratic young man for whom Roman citizenship and membership in the Christian church opened all doors. Christianity had been the official religion of the empire for almost three quarters of a century now, since the great Constantine had so declared in 313, and Ninian, born of royal parentage, was raised in its traditions.

A serious, devout and scholarly youth, Ninian was the delight of his tutors. He readily devoted himself to the study of the sacred Scriptures and soon had learned all that was available from the local teachers. It was time for him to launch out. "What shall I do? I have sought in mine own land Him whom my soul loveth. I sought Him, but I have found Him not. I will arise now, and I will compass sea and land. I will seek the truth which my soul loveth." And Ninian set forth.

Seeking the faith of Peter, he went to the See of Peter. Turning his back on the pleasures and prosperity that life at the court of his noble father offered, Ninian set off on pilgrimage to Rome.

Felicity brushed strands of her long hair out of her face. If she'd realized it was so windy she would have braided it today rather than leaving it loose over her shoulders. "Hm, 'Three from the See'—could Ninian somehow be part of that reference?"

Antony considered, his brow furrowed. "Well, Ninian was a lot earlier than Cuthbert's story—about 200 years earlier—still, it might be worth looking for a connection."

"And Ninian was a pilgrim. We just can't get away from the pilgrimage theme, can we?"

Antony smiled at her, and for a moment she had the feeling he was admiring the sun shining on her hair. *Maybe leaving it loose wasn't such a bad idea.* Then she caught herself. What was she thinking? She didn't care what he thought about such things. He was almost a monk, after all.

He cleared his throat and returned to business. "Yes, it was prophetically appropriate that Ninian's career should begin with a pilgrimage, because throughout the Middle Ages Whithorn, called 'The Shining Place,' shone as the brightest place of pilgrimage in southern Scotland."

And Ninian's pilgrimage was a success. He flourished in Rome; visiting all the shrines of the apostles, praying before their relics, then going to see the pope himself. Pope Siricius was apparently impressed with the devotion of the noble youth, and treated him with the greatest affection as his son. The pope provided the best teachers Rome had to offer, and Ninian took to his studies with the diligence of a bee. It was said he formed for himself honeycombs of wisdom, gathering the arguments from the different doctors as of various kinds of flowers.

The rhythms of Antony's lecture-mode speaking put Felicity mentally back on Lindisfarne when he had been telling another story on a bright, breezy day. Only then she had been in the distracting company of Jonathan Breen. Where was Jonathan? Where had he been when they returned from the Viking Beach and departed in such a flurry? Did he know what had happened to her? Was he worried? Did he care? Why hadn't she thought to ask Stephen if he saw him at the retreat house? She curled her hand inside her pocket, thinking how companionable it would be to be holding Jonathan's hand strolling up the street of this quaint little town.

Suddenly she realized Antony had stopped and was looking at her. "Sorry. Boring you again, wasn't I?"

Felicity blinked. What was that expression in his eyes? Had she hurt his feelings by her wool-gathering? Surely he hadn't read her thoughts. "No, no. Sorry. It's just a lot to take in. I realize I need to know this if we're going to figure out what Dominic did here. Please go on."

Antony ducked his head and ran his hand through his hair. "I am almost done. Promise."

"Right. That's fine. What did Ninian do next?" Felicity felt Antony was due a bit of encouragement from her.

Ninian continued his friendship with Pope Siricius who was concerned that in some areas of western Britain the Christian faith had been little taught, or taught very poorly by men not themselves well-instructed. And so it was that the pope himself consecrated Ninian a bishop, blessed him, and sent him forth as an apostle to his own people.

On his return journey, Ninian turned aside for a time to visit the monastery of Martin of Tours. Martin's holiness of life and the order of his monastery had a great influence on Ninian, but most impressive of all was the building itself. There were no stone buildings in Ninian's homeland, so he asked Martin for stonemasons so that he could build a church like those he had seen in Rome and Gaul. Martin assented.

And so Ninian returned, bringing the fully burnished light of his faith to teach his own people, and to reach out to the untutored Picts living around them—even carrying the faith as far north as the Orkney Islands, some speculate. But his first priority was to build a firm foundation for his missionary efforts in his own home of Whithorn, Scotland's oldest town. Martin's stonemasons built perhaps the first stone church in Britain, and at Ninian's own direction they whitewashed the stones. And so Ninian's Church has come down to us in legendary fashion. Candida Casa. The White House. The Bright, Shining Place.

Antony concluded his narrative by flinging out his arm toward the structure before them. Felicity gasped as she looked at the white portal, shining with the rays of morning sun striking the red and gold emblem over the archway. "It can't be!"

Antony laughed. It seemed to her he was doing more of that lately, and more easily. It made her smile in return. "No, not Candida Casa, but you'll admit my timing was good, wasn't it? This is, however, the gateway to the medieval monastery that may well have been built on the site of Ninian's original foundation. The impressive entranceway was important as it symbolically and literally separated the worldly life of the town from the sacred space of the monastic enclosure. Through that gate and up the hill, we'll be following the path trodden by kings and pilgrims for hundreds of years. Thousands of feet have walked this way seeking healing, forgiveness, enlightenment." Felicity smiled at the thought. They were certainly seeking enlightenment. She hoped this was a good omen.

Their feet crunched on the gravel path and the wind, which had been a lively breeze when crossing the fields, increased its vigor. "Ninian's grave, first in the crypt of the medieval cathedral and later moved to the high altar, became the greatest pilgrimage site in southern Scotland." Antony pointed to the church on the hill ahead of them. "Robert the Bruce came here, as did David II, who had an arrow miraculously removed from his shoulder, and James IV who made annual pilgrimages to Whithorn." Felicity smiled, hearing in her mind the jangling harness, minstrel songs and cheering crowds that would have attended a royal pilgrimage.

But then she gave herself a mental shake. They weren't on a pilgrimage, royal or any other kind, and the image of King David with an arrow in his shoulder was too vivid a reminder of their narrow escape from a similar weapon. She looked around at the medieval ruins and more modern stone buildings surrounding them. Was someone lurking there waiting to drop a stone on their heads, or make another attempt with the crossbow? Where had Philly and her Neanderthal son gone when they left Lindisfarne?

Antony, apparently oblivious to her misgivings and thoroughly in his element in this historical site, turned to the left off the gravel path to ascend a grassy slope. "This is the area of the archeological digs. It's been worked extensively and a great deal of information has been recovered about the Middle Ages; less, of course about Roman times—"

Archeology. Those books hidden in Stephen's car. Was there treasure being uncovered here? Did Ninian bring more than faith back with him from Rome? Or what about those centuries of devout pilgrims? Didn't they always bring rich gifts, especially the royal pilgrims? What would David of Scotland have given as a reward for his miraculous recovery? And what—

"Can I be of help to you at all?" They spun around at the sound of a soft Scottish lilt behind them. Felicity stared at the young woman—hardly more than a girl: short, curvaceous in her khaki trousers and blue shirt, with a cloud of red hair, pouty scarlet lips and enormous blue eyes that blinked at them from under eyelashes long enough to knock off her gold-rimmed glasses. "I'm Fiona McBain, in charge of the dig. Well, sort of in charge at the moment. Professor Laird had to go back to university, so that leaves me. We mostly use volunteers."

Antony cleared his throat. "Um—thank you. We're interested in your archeological findings."

"Ah, right then. Come away into the museum. I'll show you our treasures."

Treasures? Felicity's eyebrows shot up. So she was right! They actually could be onto something. It had seemed such a wild goose chase, coming so far away from the scene of the crime they were supposed to be investigating. They crunched back across the gravel to a small stone building with a wooden sign that marked it as the museum, and Fiona led the way into a room filled with incised stones.

"This is our greatest find, the Latinus Stone, the earliest Christian monument in Scotland." Her fingertip just brushed the inscription, *TE DOMINUM LAUDAMUS.*

"'We praise thee, O Lord,'" Felicity translated. "'Latinus, aged 35, and his daughter, aged 4.'"

Fiona smiled appreciatively at her. "Well done. It's from the first half of the fifth century. First thought to be the grave marker of a chieftain and his daughter, now it's believed to be a memorial to the man who gave the ground or built the church by which it stood."

"That's amazing," Felicity said, working out that the stone would have been carved between the times of Ninian and Cuthbert. Disappointing that it was not old enough, or too old, to be of use to them.

"And over here," Fiona indicated more venerable standing stones, "several fifth century stones inscribed with the chi-rho—evidence carved in stone for Whithorn's claim to be the cradle of Christianity in Scotland."

"But do you have anything from Ninian's time?" Antony asked.

"Well, we found some fragments of whitewashed stone, which seem to indicate this is the site of the original Candida Casa, but we can't be certain." She hesitated. "And some think the original Candida Casa was down by the harbor where St. Ninian's Kirk is. You've been there?"

They both shook their heads.

"Beautiful location. Some say it's where Ninian landed when he returned from Rome. Anyway, a medieval chapel, to welcome sailors home from the sea." She shrugged. "Ruined now, of course. Too new to be of interest to us."

Antony nodded, wrinkling his forehead. "Aye, I was rather

hoping you might have something directly connected with Ninian."

And since when did Antony have a Scottish accent? Felicity wondered.

"Oh, but you must be meaning the papyrus casket?" Felicity almost gasped at Fiona's eager offering. It was that "little boy lost" look Antony pulled. Felicity bristled. She couldn't believe even Fiona would fall for that. And she couldn't believe Antony would use it.

"Oh, aye. The Ninian Papyrus." He gave Felicity a sidelong glance. Why did she have the feeling he had never heard of such a thing before, either?

"Of course, we can only speculate what was in the casket, but it's generally believed to have held manuscripts Ninian brought back from his time in Rome. Probably some he copied while he was with Pope Siricius."

"Er, could we see the casket?" Felicity could tell Antony was barely able to suppress his excitement.

"Oh, and if only you could. But didn't I explain? That's why Professor Laird went back to Edinburgh. A monk fellow was here just a few weeks ago. Very interested in the casket, had some theory about what the papyrus might have been. I don't think the professor much liked his theories. Anyway, as soon as the monk left, he packed up the casket and drove off."

"Do you have any idea what the monk's theories were?"

"I only got bits and pieces of it because he was talking mostly to the professor. I did like him so much, though, a right old darling, I thought." She smiled and batted her eyelashes at Antony. "Of course, they spent a lot of time in the cave."

"Cave?" Felicity asked, then realized she should have let Antony do the questioning with his appealing little act.

It didn't matter, though, because Fiona seemed equally ready to display her knowledge to a mixed audience.

"Ninian's Cave. That's where we found the casket. Well, not me personally, you understand, but our team. We were examining the walls of the cave for the crosses carved there by early pilgrims—eighth century they are—and that's when we found the cache. Hidden in a hole behind another rock it was, and very clever, too. Must have been undisturbed for centuries. Which is really amazing when you consider the number of visitors we get there. Pilgrims, tourists, parties of schoolchildren."

"Could you show us?"

Antony had hardly to ask before Fiona was pulling on an anorak. The wind had continued to increase and the morning that started out so bright was now clouding over with a heavy darkness blowing in from the west. Felicity was just wishing for a windcheater over her sweater when Fiona pulled another coat from the peg and handed it to her. "Here you go. The wind out there is fierce." Felicity accepted it gratefully.

Fiona led the way, once again across crunching gravel, to a Land Rover parked behind the museum. "It's three miles across the point," she explained, opening the front passenger door for Antony, "then we walk the last mile and a half. It's private property, but the farmer is very accommodating."

Ninian's Cave. Antony had mentioned that Cuthbert's body may have rested there. And Fiona said they found crosses dating from the eighth century, just when Cuthbert's Folk were fleeing the Vikings. Dominic had spent time in the cave. Were they actually getting somewhere?

Fiona pulled the Land Rover to the side of the road, and they walked through a deeply wooded glen: stands of tall, slim aspens and banks of fern shaded the leafy path. A party of schoolchildren came down the path toward them, their voices ringing in the fresh air, their red cheeks enhanced by their red shirts. Felicity envied their sensible Wellington boots as her shoes were getting caked with sludgy moist foliage.

The path ended at a stone-covered bay washed with wide white waves. They slogged across a treacherously rocky beach to take refuge in Ninian's Cave just as it began to rain. How had those clouds blown in so quickly? It had been brilliant sun only an hour ago. Felicity was more thankful than ever for the jacket Fiona had loaned her.

The cave was an enormous black opening in the side of a sheer rock cliff. From the inky interior of the cavern, Felicity looked out at the white foam washing the pebbled beach. Beyond that, a barren head of land ran into the bay. Here, in dark, damp chill, Ninian, raised in aristocratic comfort, had come for prayer, meditation and renewal when the pressures of job and community became too pressing. Like Cuthbert retreating to his rocky North Sea island.

Fiona and Antony, who had entered the cave first, scrabbled up the rock wall to stand on a narrow projection of stone. Fiona held a torch while Antony groped into a high crevice at least as deep as his forearm. Felicity would dearly have loved to join them, but there was barely room for two on the ledge.

Feeling left out of the action, she perched on a large boulder at the back of the cave and mused. How might the history of this whole area of Scotland have been different had Ninian not obeyed his call? If he had stayed comfortably at his father's court and let the empire crumble around him—or chosen to fight the enveloping evil with sword and spear, rather than with spiritual weapons? For it was in 410, she recalled, at the peak of Ninian's career, that Rome, overrun by barbarian Goths, withdrew from Britain, sending the curt message that they "should look to their own defenses." And so Ninian built the strongest defenses of all.

The schoolchildren had adorned the cave with crosses fashioned from sticks, feathers and stones. Felicity felt a sudden urge to join in this simple act of devotion which pilgrims to this spot had been undertaking for so many centuries. Leaving her rocky perch, she braved the rain and wind which was increasing in fury to scan the beach for appropriate pieces of wood.

She noted with amazement that, incredibly, wildflowers and berry bushes were growing out of the barren rock piles. And everywhere along the rocky beach, people had piled cairns of stone. Marking what? Expressing what? However vaguely, she felt at one with those anonymous modern-day visitors who built cairns and fashioned crosses—a continuum with the etchers of crosses in the cave and the carvers of the stones in the museum—the eternal urge within humanity to pay homage, to express mysteries beyond words.

She found two small, smooth sticks and dug in the pocket of her windcheater, hoping for a piece of string to fashion a cross. The first pocket produced a broken pencil, three crumpled tissues and a glove. The glove's partner was in the next pocket with a mobile phone under it. In the inside breast pocket, however, she found just the thing—a large rubber band. Affixing the crosspiece, she returned to the cave to add her cross to those of thirteen centuries of pilgrims.

Antony and Fiona were still perched high on their rocky shelf, delving into the now-empty niche and, heads bent together, speculating on what it might have held, whose hand placed it there, and when. They didn't even notice Felicity's return. Miffed at being shut out, she turned in a huff toward the crashing surf. The wind whipped her long hair and fine sprays of salt water stung her cheeks. Taking pleasure in the loud crunching, she crossed the shingle-covered beach.

Her steps were just slowing at the edge of the water when the pocket of her coat erupted with a bright, tinny tinkling of "Scotland the Brave." She fumbled, out of practice with mobile phones since they weren't used in the monastery, but at last found the button. "Aye." She startled herself. Less than twenty-four hours in Scotland and she was imitating the speech. Bad habit.

"Fiona, is that you? Terrible connection. It's Laird."

"Aye." She acknowledged that it was a terrible connection.

"Listen, darling, I just got word, we're expecting visitors. A priest and an American woman. They mean trouble. Get rid of them."

Felicity was shocked into silence. She scrunched her feet on the gravel to sound like static on the line.

"Have you got that? Do whatever it takes."

Felicity bent over and rubbed the phone in the raspy gravel. She'd show him a bad connection.

She stood staring at the phone in her hand, the whipping, wet wind sending chills through her. Was that message really as ominous as it sounded? Did "whatever it takes" mean what she thought it meant? Something more direct than crossbows, ground glass and rising tides?

They had to get away. Now.

Chapter 17

"It has to be Bootham. Who else knew we were there?" Felicity huddled against the side of the coach. Maeve had been kind enough to drive them up the peninsula to Newton Stewart, the nearest stop for a National Express coach. It offered them escape, but little warmth.

Antony nodded. "I suppose so. It sounds just too paranoid to think someone else might be watching us. And yet—" He shivered. "I can't seem to stop my skin crawling."

"On the other hand, I wonder where Philomena Johnson has gone off to. If she is connected to the Smith-Johnson professor, I suppose she might be interested in an ancient papyrus." Felicity paused in thought. "It does sound paranoid, but could anyone else have followed us from Kirkthorpe? Or Willibrord could have called his doctor friend—could he have heard us talk about where we were going? Did Nick know?" She sighed. "I don't know. It all seems so far-fetched. And yet, someone knew."

Antony nodded. "Someone who wanted us stopped."

The coach trundled along the narrow, winding road, affording occasional glimpses of the Solway Firth on their right. The earlier rain clouds had blown on and the sky was now a pale, early evening pink. As much as Antony tried to concentrate on the problem at hand, he couldn't quite keep his mind from taking in how the pink and gold glow of the evening highlighted Felicity's skin and hair. He started to reach out to her, then pulled back. What was he thinking—or rather *not* thinking? Even if he hadn't taken vows of celibacy, his monastic lifestyle made no allowances for such urges as lately seemed to be playing around the edges of his mind.

"I suppose we did the right thing in leaving," Felicity mused.

"But I do hate to feel like we gave in to them—whoever they are and whatever they wanted."

Antony shook his head to chase off his wayward thoughts. Felicity was obviously having no trouble focusing on the problem. And she was right. "We were finished anyway," he said. "We found out what Dominic was interested in there, and I don't think they had any more information for us."

"So, if there wasn't anything else to learn, why did that Laird guy want to get rid of us?"

"Yes. You've got a point. I don't think he just meant 'get them out of town.' I keep having visions of being trapped in that cave with the tide rushing in, or a sudden landslide from the top of the cliff sealing off the entrance."

"I'm not sure the tide comes up that high…" Felicity's voice trailed off. "But then, it did at Lindisfarne." She subsided into silence as the seemingly endless road wound up, down and around the fingers of land that made up the coastline of Galloway.

Antony subconsciously ran his fingers up through the thick, dark hair falling across his forehead, then smoothed it down with the palm of his hand, only to repeat the gesture a few moments later. "You're thinking hard." Felicity's words after so many miles of silence startled him.

"I was wishing my notes on that Smith-Johnson book hadn't been stolen."

"We could probably get another copy of the book somewhere."

"I'm sure we could order it, but it would take time—from some small publisher in America. Anyway, I've been going over the theory it put forth—that Cuthbert *did* debate at the Synod of Whitby. It could explain Dominic's interest in the Ninian Papyrus."

"How? If Ninian brought some important manuscript back from Rome with him, and then hid it in that casket in his cave—perhaps for safekeeping when the barbarians were overrunning northern Britain—and then, if Cuthbert's Folk did find it when they were sheltering there with Cuthbert's body, and added it to the other bits and bobs in the sarcophagus—and maybe even carved some of those eighth century crosses… Well, that's all about a century and a half after the Synod of Whitby—if my math's right, which it usually isn't."

"You're close enough this time. But Smith-Johnson was on about some manuscript Benedict Biscop brought back from Rome in the early seventh century. Now, I'm really stretching here, but the manuscripts Ninian had access to and copied from the Vatican library in the fourth century would still have been there for Benedict Biscop to copy in the seventh century—and they're probably still there today."

"So there really *could* be something from that far back that could be of value today—enough value for someone to kill for?" She wrinkled her brow. "I wonder whether the value is in finding it, or in keeping it hidden?"

Antony sighed and scrubbed at his hair again. "It's obviously pretty interesting for a historian, but I'm having a hard time seeing what value it would be to a police detective. I keep trying to find a motive for murder here somewhere, and I just can't."

"So what do we hope to find in Whitby?" She put up a hand. "No, wait, I know. What Dominic did there."

"Precisely. But if Dominic's interest in the Ninian Papyrus is the same as that Smith-Johnson proposed—that Cuthbert's debate at the Synod of Whitby was suppressed—we need to know what that argument was. It must have been pretty persuasive, even though not persuasive enough to carry the day—and where better to find out about it than at the scene of the debate itself?" The fact that Whitby was a charming town and he loved the way Felicity's eyes lit up when he presented a picturesque scene had absolutely nothing to do with it. He pulled himself back forcibly from the thought. He had no right.

Felicity was quiet for a moment, biting her lower lip in concentration. Antony refused to allow his mind to linger on how appealing it made her look with the little crinkle between her eyebrows. "I have two problems with that. First, I simply can't believe that the Venerable Bede—who, according to my church history lecturer," she grinned at him, "besides being a truly holy man, was one of the most careful historians ever to have written; the man who invented the footnote; the first writer to name his sources—could have been involved in what amounts to a political cover-up.

"And secondly, if our idea of Cuthbert's Folk finding the papyrus is at all on the right track—and there are lots of leaps in the just-plausible theory—I simply can't believe that their successors, if the Three still exist—if, if, if... I know, it's all conjecture. But I can't believe any descendants from Cuthbert's Folk would commit murder. They're supposed to be English Benedictines and Dominic was an English Benedictine—one of their own."

"Well done on your first point. If you were arguing that in an essay I'd give you a first. But keep in mind that Bede, careful as he was with his sources, could only work with the sources he had."

"Ah, you're saying the victors write the history books."

"Exactly. Wilfrid, who carried the day for the Roman faction—sainted though he is—strikes me as a fanatic who would do just about anything to promote his cause."

"And does it follow that the Three are fanatics who would do anything—even kill—for their cause?" He caught his breath at the directness of her question, then swallowed twice and made himself breathe slowly, calmly.

"Like you, I have trouble believing that. But I'm trying not to be blinded by my prejudices. The fact remains, though, that Wilfrid and Cuthbert were on opposite sides of the Whitby debate, and the outcome was momentous—we still follow the results of that decision today."

"And Wilfrid was the victor." She paused. "So Cuthbert's followers just might have hidden away any documents they possessed in order to protect them from Wilfrid's lot?"

"Possible. Or Wilfrid's group hid them to keep them suppressed." Antony simply could sit still no longer. He felt cramped, stifled and suffocated. He had pulled off his dog collar hours ago, but he ran his finger around the neck of his shirt as if to make space for more air. He pushed to his feet and made his way to the WC at the back of the coach. Any excuse to stretch his legs. If this had been a train he would have undertaken to walk from one end to the other.

Yes, simply a reason to move about. He tried to convince himself that was all it was. He didn't really need to put distance between himself and Felicity. He was a mature, celibate priest. And that was the end of the story. Being in the close company of a beautiful, charmingly refreshing, if often infuriating, young woman had absolutely no bearing on his restlessness.

Still, questions he thought he had buried deeply enough not to be of consequence any longer seemed to be pushing to the surface most inconveniently, just when he should be concentrating on bringing all his scholarship to bear on the immediate problem. Never since Alice had he allowed himself a female friend, no matter how innocent. Always he hid behind the possibility of a call to celibacy. And the formula had always worked. So why wasn't it working now?

Well, for one thing he hadn't been doing a very good job of keeping the vows he had taken—the sworn duty of every priest to keep the daily office. No matter what he was involved in. No matter if a dear friend had been brutally murdered. No matter if the police threatened arrest. No matter if one's superior sent him on a mission to solve the puzzle that seemed to underlay the murder. No matter if he were required to carry out his work in the company of the most disturbingly delightful young woman he had ever met…

He went back to his seat and pulled his office book from his pocket. The pages were stained and crumpled from the soaking they had received on the Lindisfarne Causeway, the edges of the leaves were dog-eared from being jumbled in his pocket, but the book fitted comfortably in his hand like an old friend and the words were soothing with their familiar rhythm:

> *O God make speed to save us.*
> *O Lord make haste to help us.*

It was better if the responses were given antiphonally. He glanced hopefully at Felicity, longing to ask her to join him. Before he could ask, though, she gave him a fleeting glance, then pulled her jacket more tightly around her and receded into her corner.

He took a deep breath and forced himself to focus:

> *For God alone my soul in silence waits;*
> *He alone is my rock and my salvation,*
> *My stronghold, so that I shall not be greatly shaken...*

It was hours later when the coach came to a stop and the bright lights of a service area wakened Antony. "Forty-five minutes!" the driver called, before opening the door and making his way across the tarmac toward the Little Chef. Antony looked around for a sign to tell him where they were. He had no idea how long he had slept. Chester-le-Street, he read on the side of the petrol station. He leaned over and shook Felicity awake.

"Felicity! Sorry to waken you, but we need to get off here."

"What? Are we at Whitby already?"

"No, but we need to get off." Felicity rubbed her eyes and groaned as she stretched her cramped limbs. Antony began explaining before she could ask. "I just realized. Bootham took us to Maeve's B&B. If he's after us, it will be easy enough for him to check with her and find out we took the coach to Whitby. Besides, Chester-le-Street is an important stop in Cuthbert's sojourn, so it could be important to us, too."

Felicity groped along the overhead rack for her small satchel, and stumbled after him into the dark night. "Oh!" she cried as a blast of chill, damp air hit them in the face, followed closely by her next protest, "I'm starving. Can't we get something to eat?"

Antony shook his head. "Not here. We need to find somewhere less obvious."

She gave one last, longing look at the cheery red sign with the jolly little chef, and drew back into the shadows away from the glare of the well-lit service area. Huddling into their light jackets and bending into the wind, they walked the mile into town from the A1 motorway junction in silence. To the west a faint, cold yellow glow was beginning to show in the sky, making the sharp, wet wind feel all the more penetrating. "Oh, I'm so cold I can't breathe," Felicity gasped.

"Hang on, it shouldn't be much further. Sign said the railway station is this way. There should be a coffee shop open there."

The steamy, orange plastic kiosk on the platform between tracks could hardly be dignified with the name "coffee shop" but Antony and Felicity embraced it's warmth with eager gratitude, and wrapped their hands around the Styrofoam coffee cups to soak in every bit of heat.

"So, is this chronological?" Felicity asked when she had recovered her breath enough to speak.

"In Cuthbert's posthumous journey?" Antony attempted to smile at her over the rim of his cup, but his face still felt stiff. "Approximately. No one knows the itinerary for sure. The Community of St. Cuthbert wandered for some eighty-five years, rather like the Children of Israel bearing their precious ark, spending time as we've seen in southern Scotland, in Carlisle, in Ripon and in Norham on Tweed until the Viking threat cooled down a bit. They found a welcome sanctuary at Chester-le-Street in 883 and remained here until the Vikings returned in 995."

He paused to savor a mouthful of egg bap, the nearest thing to a cooked breakfast the menu offered—apart from sausage rolls which were forbidden to him at the moment, no matter how mouthwatering they looked. "Of course the dates are approximate, but Cuthbert was here at least 112 years. Some say it was even longer. Some historians believe that Cuthbert's wanderings were even more complex than we know."

"And what happened while he was here?"

"Ah, that's what we hope to find out, isn't it?" Warmed and fed, Antony leaned back and sighed. He felt the most relaxed he had for days. He didn't know why he felt suddenly buoyed. They had uncovered far more questions than answers, they were running from an unknown enemy or enemies—not knowing who were their friends or their foes—and now they had to go back out into the furious wet wind. And yet he smiled.

"Right." Felicity wiped her mouth on her napkin, a small square of stiff paper that certainly wasn't worthy of being called a serviette, and jumped to her feet. "Let's get at it!"

Her enthusiasm further boosted Antony's spirits so that they headed down the steep, narrow path from the station toward town with an almost jaunty walk. Until the first blast of wind hit them around the corner. Huddling into their jackets, they passed terraced stone houses with postage stamp-sized front gardens bright with primroses struggling through the gray and, at the end of the street, one desperate-looking palm tree. Felicity waved to the shivering tree and said, "I know just how you feel," then laughed through her chattering teeth.

A query at the newsagent's elicited the fact that there was no tourist information office in town, but that the public library was just up the street. When they had caught their breath enough to explain to the librarian that they were in town researching St. Cuthbert, the librarian's eager look crumpled beneath a furrowed brow. "Ah, yes. I'm afraid you've come at a rather bad time. The schoolchildren are doing a project on him, you see. All the books are out."

She clutched at the edges of her beige cardigan. "But I'll just have a look." She darted off. In a moment she returned triumphant, holding two slim volumes aloft. "You're all right. These have come back."

Antony and Felicity each took one and settled at a table near the window. Antony bent over a battered red volume, *Historia de*

Sancto Cuthberto. He hadn't read this for years. What a delight to see an old friend again! Little wonder the schoolchildren had returned the book. Half of it was in Latin. "You'll be interested in this," he turned it so Felicity could read it as well. "Right in your line, as a classicist."

Heads bent together, they perused the pages silently for some time, Felicity reading the Latin on the left-hand pages, Antony taking the English translation on the right. Felicity was the first to look up. "So, what do you think? Is there anything in all this about land grants to the Community of St. Cuthbert from this Guthred—whoever he was? A grant of all the land between the Tyne and the Tees could be enormous, almost the whole county of Durham—right? So if that grant was still somehow enforceable today, there would be huge motive for murder."

Antony grinned. "Well, I'm impressed. You read the Latin as quickly as I read the translation, and got the import of it. Guthred was the Danish king of York who essentially created a Christian heritage preservation area in this part of Northumbria."

"But Guthred was a Dane. Wasn't he pagan?"

"In the beginning, of course. But Guthred was the Danish king who was defeated by Alfred the Great and accepted Christian baptism from Alfred. There's an interesting legend about that. The story goes that while Alfred was in hiding in Athelnay, in the marshes of the West Country—the last Christian king to hold out against the pagan Danes—St. Cuthbert came to Alfred—"

"But wait—Alfred was 200 years—" Felicity interrupted.

"After Cuthbert. Right. The saint came to the king in a vision, of course."

"Oh, of course." And she didn't even roll her eyes.

"Cuthbert told Alfred to fight again, that God would be with him. Alfred marshaled his scattered troops and defeated Guthred at the battle of Ethendune."

"And baptized Guthred," Felicity interposed.

Antony nodded. "Yes. As was the custom. To submit to a king was to submit to his god as well. So Guthred probably had both political and religious reasons for supporting Cuthbert's community. Eadred, the leader of Cuthbert's Folk at that time, was a strong supporter of Guthred's claims to the Northumbrian throne, so by granting Eadred land, the Dane was solidifying support for his kingship. And also, the pagan Vikings were deeply intrigued by the mysticism and miracles associated with the relics of saints."

"So whatever truth there may or may not be to the legend, Cuthbert did play a part in Alfred's success." Felicity mused for a moment. "Wasn't there something about some great treasure connected with Alfred the Great? Seems I remember something when I was at Oxford."

"You're probably thinking of the Alfred Jewel."

"That's it. I saw it in the Ashmolean. Here we are—treasure again. How valuable is it?"

"The Alfred Jewel? Incalculable. There was an unsuccessful attempt to steal it in 1997—not that anyone could sell such a famous object, of course. But a jewel of lesser quality from the same period was bought for £42,000 and is now in the British Museum. Another one, in the Salisbury Museum, was bought for over £100,000."

"Hmm. If there are any more of those floating around, they would make a start on a children's hospital, wouldn't they? So, what if Alfred gave something of similar value to Cuthbert's shrine in thanksgiving for his victory?"

"And Dominic somehow stumbled across it on his pilgrimage?"

"Someone might kill for that."

"Yes, they might. But, of course, it's all conjecture."

Felicity sighed and leaned back in her chair. "Just when I thought we were getting somewhere. Right. So what about this land grant?"

Antony turned to a map in the front of the book. "It would have included the estate of Chester-le-Street, then called Conecaster, on the north bank of the River Wear, and have included the lands of Monkwearmouth and Jarrow—the Venerable Bede's monastery, you'll remember."

"Yup. That's essentially Newcastle."

"Right. And then, to the west, the grant ran to Dere Street at the foot of the Cheviot Hills."

"So it was enormous. The value today would be incalculable!" Felicity's eyes widened and her voice was urgent.

Antony held up his hands. "Relax. Sorry. To some extent the land grants still do exist. Guthred essentially created the bishopric and county of Durham."

"Oh. So no motive here?"

"I don't see how there could be in the land grants. By the tenth century, Chester-le-Street was included in the Bishop of Durham's holdings, and you can be sure that the ins and outs of church property are well cared for today. It's certainly true, though, that a huge grant of land belonged to the Community of St. Cuthbert throughout the tenth century—the *Haliwerfolkland* they called it, the 'land of the holy man people'."

Felicity turned from the *Historia* to the book the librarian had placed in her hands, *Cronica monasterii Dunelmensis,* and read silently for some time before looking up again. "Well, there's no doubt that there was enough treasure to provide a motive for murder and mayhem once upon a time. Listen to this account of the visit of King Aethelstan to Cuthbert's shrine in 935." Her forefinger traced the Latin as she translated: "The king gave regal gifts in gold and silver, palls and curtains and great bells and many other precious ornaments." She paused. "And twelve vills of land. What's a vill?"

"A unit of land including buildings and their adjacent lands. Our words village and villa come from it."

"Oh, right. Like *villagium.* OK, then." She returned to her translation. "And finally, Aethelstan gave two armlets which he bore on his arms, saying, 'I intend that these be a sign for all who shall come after me that I have established, with most devout heart and under threat of anathema, firm laws and perpetual liberty for the church of my dearest patron, the holy confessor Cuthbert, and of most holy Mary mother of God, as did my predecessors.'" She scanned on down the page. "And in addition, the king filled two cups with 'the best money,' whatever that means, and Aethelstan's army gave more than 96 pounds of silver… and it goes on."

Marking the place with her finger she looked up. "Is there any chance at all that some of that treasure could still be around today? What if Dominic found the hiding place of something like 96 pounds of silver, and was planning to donate it to his African Children's hospital? I don't have any idea what that would be worth in today's terms, but it must be considerable. It seems more of a motive for murder than some manuscript that figured in a theological debate. Although I still like the idea of there being more Alfred Jewels around." She paused for breath and rushed on, "And Dominic did say 'The secrets of your treasure.'"

"Yes, you're absolutely right about the wealth being great and the motive for murder and mayhem being great."

"So—'The treasure of Aethelstan—'" Felicity seemed poised to spring to her feet.

"The only trouble is that you're almost 470 years too late."

Felicity sat back in her chair, her shoulders slumped. "What? Why?"

"Murder and mayhem… That pretty much sums up what happened at the dissolution of the monasteries."

"Yes, I know that. But if some of it could have been hidden away—"

Antony laughed and shook his head. "Fun to think about, isn't it?"

"But?"

"But all the creative speculation in the world about royal jewels and buried treasure is no more than that—speculation. We need facts. Hard evidence."

Felicity nodded dispiritedly. "I know. Something we can take to the police. Something that would convict a murderer."

"Who remains unidentified," Antony reminded her.

Felicity blinked. "Oh, police. We've been concentrating so hard on escaping from that unidentified enemy, I'd almost forgotten about avoiding the police. But you know, there was an officer on the train platform this morning. He didn't give us a second glance. Do you think that means the search hasn't gone beyond Yorkshire? Or maybe the police have realized they were wrong to suspect you."

Antony grinned. "Hopeful thought."

"But that doesn't actually solve anything, does it?" Felicity sighed. "It's just so hard, trying to get a grip on something from so long ago that could have led anyone today to commit murder. Everything has changed so much. It's a different world."

Antony pondered her words, shaking his head. "Yes and no. In some ways, the more things change the more they stay the same."

"But the land grants have been superseded, the manuscripts disappeared, the treasure plundered…"

"Oh, yes, all that. But people and their motives—violence, greed—that doesn't change. We are dealing with raw, primitive evil—the darkness that has always stalked the earth seeking to extinguish the light."

She shuddered. "Always?"

"Well, no, not quite. Good was first. Original sin wasn't quite original. Original righteousness trumps it."

"You're talking about the fall—right?"

He nodded. "I'm talking about the moment when human beings first chose to satisfy their own appetites over doing right, chose self over others. It's at the root of all crime, all wrongdoing. My needs, my desires are more important than anyone else's, so I'll cheat, steal, lie—murder for what I want."

"And that's why Dominic was murdered."

"That's right. He got in the way of someone's selfish desire." *Selfishness. Putting self first. Death.* He dropped his head into his hands.

Chapter 18

Antony sat for several moments, considering the primitive savagery of bare human motive. And its disastrous results. At last he pushed away from the table. "I don't think there's anything more we can do here. Let's go take a look at St. Cuthbert's Church."

"You mean it's still here?"

Antony explained as once more they pushed their way against the chilling wind. It had been such a relief to shelter in the library. "This is the site of the original shrine, built by the Lindisfarne monks more than a thousand years ago. The original building was probably of wood. The stone church was built in the mid-eleventh century. But there has been continuous worship on this site since 883."

Just over Front Street, busy now with shoppers, and around a corner, their gaze suddenly swept upward to the tall, golden stone spire of the Norman church. The embattled sun had managed to struggle through the cloud cover and a few valiant banners of blue sky shone behind the tower. Felicity stopped and stared. "It's beautiful."

"It is. Before Durham was built, this was the cathedral of a huge diocese stretching from east to west across Britain from Edinburgh to Teeside—the spiritual heart of that land grant you were reading about in the library."

As they stepped inside the door a small, bald, elderly man thrust a book into Felicity's hand. "Oh. Is it a service?" She asked.

"In about twenty minutes." He looked at her gravely.

"Noon Eucharist?"

"No, no. Funeral."

Felicity and Antony exchanged glances and moved on up the aisle. Antony chose a pew to the right of the aisle sheltered behind a pillar in the "new" thirteenth-century part of the nave. Golden stone arches soared overhead. Beyond the lacy carving of the dark wooden rood screen, candles flickered on the altar beneath the stained-glass window. The organ began, something Bach-sounding that Antony couldn't identify, to the accompaniment of a buzz of soft chatter. The vicar entered from the vestry in white surplice and black scarf. The church was full of mourners, but it didn't feel mournful.

The congregation rose and sang, "Eternal Father Strong to Save … O Trinity of love and power, thy children shield in danger's hour…"

When the vicar began speaking on Psalm 22: "All they that go down to dust shall bow before him: and none can keep alive his own soul," Antony's gaze went back to the window, Mary on one side, Cuthbert on the other. Peering around the pillar and reveling in the blessed warmth of the church, he looked at the jewel-toned figure of Cuthbert holding the skull of King Oswald. A ray of sun caught fire in the skull, reminding Antony of Cuthbert as "The fire of the North," and bringing to mind yet another story of the saint's life.

On one of his many journeys around his enormous diocese, Cuthbert visited the village where his beloved foster mother Kenswith lived. While he was there, a house caught fire. Wind whipped the blaze, spreading it from roof to roof of the thatched cottages. Kenswith pleaded with Cuthbert to help. He replied, "Don't be afraid, mother. You must not panic. This fire will not harm you or any of your friends." Cuthbert prostrated himself before the cottage and prayed. The wind shifted, blowing the sparks away from the village, even extinguishing some of the kindling blazes. Only the cottage where the fire started was lost.

Now the sun struck bits of red and blue glass in the border of the window, making it dance like flame. With the gentle, comforting words of the funeral service in the background, Antony's thoughts traced images of the fire of Cuthbert's passion to bring holiness to his land, interweaving with the fire of Dominic's passion to save the children of Africa, and even his own fierce longing to see unity in the church. Antony felt unworthy to put his own vision on the same level as that of those two holy men, and yet they all seemed somehow intertwined as the flames bent and swayed with passing clouds—all tongues of flame in the fire in the north. A fleeting flash of rays gathered and shone from Oswald's head, making the empty skull appear full of gold. Could there be a message there?

Surely Aethelstan's treasure was a dead end—vanished in the mists of time like all the wealth amassed by abbeys and shrines—plundered by Vikings, plundered by reformers, plundered by time itself.

Felicity nudged him. The congregation was standing. "Lead, Kindly Light, amid the encircling gloom, lead thou me on…" The hymn over, there was nothing to do but file out behind the others. The vicar met them at the door. "Thank you for coming. So nice."

Antony returned some equally vague phrases.

"Do have a cup of tea. Parish Centre, just over the road."

They passed on out of the building into brilliant sunshine and biting cold. Felicity was several strides ahead of him. "Yes! Tea definitely. I could kill for a cup."

The hall was abuzz with people from the funeral, seniors having their weekly meeting there, and a few schoolchildren wandering in on break for a quick snack. "What a useful place," Antony said. "See if you can snare us a table. I'll see about organizing tea and sandwiches."

The queue moved at a snail's pace and all the salmon sandwiches were gone by the time he got to the counter, so he had to make do with egg salad and cheese and tomato, but the pots of tea were fresh and steaming. By the time he located Felicity at a table tucked away in the far corner, she was deep in conversation with an elderly man in a blue verger's robe. "Antony, guess what! This is Colin Sharpe and he knew Father Dominic!"

Taking care not to slosh the milk in its little white jugs, Antony set the tray on the table. "I'm pleased to meet you, Mr. Sharpe. Can I get you some tea?"

"Oh, no thank ye. Very kind, but no, I'll not have any more. Had me cup already, you see." He indicated an empty cup in front of him.

Antony slid onto a wooden folding chair and leaned forward. "So you knew Father Dominic?"

"I did that. That there monk fellow. Fine old 'un he were, too. Right sorry I am to hear he died. But the lass here tells me you'll be carrying on his work."

"Er, yes, that's right," Antony looked at Felicity who nodded encouragingly. "Yes, we hope to. Actually that's what we're doing—trying to get a feel for what he was about. What can you tell us about his pilgrimage? He died so soon after returning, you see…"

"Oh, aye, so the lassie was saying. And the good monk needing money for his poor brave dying children. Puts you in mind of our blessed St. Cuthbert, doesn't it? And I'm sure St. Cuthbert would be only too glad to share his treasure with him."

Antony swallowed far too large a bite of egg sandwich and was forced to wash it down with a scalding mouthful of tea. "Treasure?"

"Right enough. The treasure of Aethelstan. But of course, you'll be knowing all about that."

"Well, yes. Certainly we know about King Aethelstan's generous donation to the shrine. But surely that's all gone now."

Colin shrugged and gave a little half-shake of his head. "And is that what you're thinking now? And I suppose you may just have the right of it." He looked sideways over each shoulder and leaned forward, tapping the side of his nose with his forefinger. "That may be the truth of it, but there's those as believe that when Cuddy's Folk left here with his body they had to travel mighty light. Keeping just one step ahead of those marauding Vikings, they had enough to do to carry their blessed saint, much less lug along a hundredweight of silver, as it were."

"But surely they wouldn't have just left it there for the Vikings," Felicity protested.

Again Colin tapped the side of his nose in a knowing way. "Not so's the fiends could find it, no."

"You mean they buried it or something?" Felicity asked, leaning closer to Colin.

He raised one thin gray eyebrow. "I'd not be knowing about that. Some of the treasure was stolen, right enough. Some lost. Some of it's on display. You've seen the treasury in Durham Cathedral, I reckon?" Antony nodded while Felicity shook her head. "I've seen that, it's right fine. Lindisfarne Gospels are down in London, of course—good as stolen to my way of thinking."

Felicity poured some tea from her pot into Colin's cup and added milk and a heaping spoon of sugar. She smiled and pushed the cup toward him. "What is it you're not telling us, Colin?"

"Not telling you nothing. All I know is that there's some as believes Aethelstan's treasure is still right where Cuddy's Folk left it—buried beneath the church." He drank noisily.

"Did you discuss this idea with Father Dominic?" Antony asked.

"Course I did. Right interested he were, too." The garrulous verger continued on in his soft northern accent while questions flooded Antony's mind. Had they actually stumbled across the key to the whole mystery? Were caskets of silver, jewels, finely embroidered vestments, waiting to be dug up under the floor of the ancient church—which was still standing and in continuous use on the site of the very church built as a shrine for Cuthbert's relics? If so, how could they find out? Who would they go to for permission to excavate? How would they know where to dig? If they actually found treasure, could it be given to Father Dominic's African children? Who had Dominic approached with his information that they had then taken such drastic action to prevent him?

"Oh, there's a fellow might know something. He was here right after your monk friend, asked a lot of the same questions you're asking." Colin pointed across the crowded room.

Antony looked in the direction indicated. A familiar head-wobble on the long, thin neck of a tall man standing in the shadows in a far corner of the room caught his eye. "What? Willibrord St. John?"

Colin shrugged. "Don't know any Willy-whatsis, but that one there with the mustache, that's some professor-like who digs things up."

"An archeologist? Couldn't be Professor Laird, by any chance, could it?"

Colin nodded. "That's the fellow. Know him?"

"In a way." Antony turned carefully and noted a man of medium height in a tweed jacket with a dark mustache and dark-rimmed glasses locked in deep conversation with Willibrord.

"Laird? But he's supposed to be in Edinburgh." Felicity craned her neck in the same direction.

"No. Don't look. Just get up quietly and follow me." Fortunately, the group at a table next to theirs stood at the same time, providing a shield for them. Antony sketched a small farewell wave to their informant, and grabbed Felicity's hand to pull her to the nearest exit. Where could they go? They needed some place quiet and secure to think. Antony felt the skin on the back of his neck crawl. They had been spotted. They would be followed.

Fighting the urge to turn around, he tugged harder on Felicity's hand and all but dragged her across the street back toward the church. Where could they go? Perhaps the Anker House, a tiny room built onto the side of the church in the Middle Ages to house an enclosed hermit. He started in that direction, then pulled back behind some tall bushes. That would never do. The Anker House had been turned into a museum.

Then he spotted the stairs leading to an exterior entrance along the side of the church. The Lambton Pew—a family pew and vault built as an extension to the church in Victorian times. A vault was exactly what they needed. Signaling Felicity to remain hidden, Antony peered around the edge of their concealing bush. He pulled back with a jerk. Willibrord was just emerging from the Centre. Antony stole another careful look. Their pursuer looked both ways, then set off at a long-legged lope toward town.

"Quick!" Antony whispered, and once again pulled Felicity behind him. They dashed across the open expanse of grass and up the gray stone steps. Antony grasped at the wrought iron railing to pull them faster, praying that the heavy wooden door at the top of the stairs would be open. In desperation, he threw himself against the door. The iron hinges creaked and grated in protest, but under his insistent pressure the door gave just enough to allow them to squeeze through before the hinges stuck. He pushed the door almost shut behind them, the rusty hinges catching to leave a narrow crack that allowed the dimmest sliver of light to enter the room. The stone vault held the cold and damp of a century and a half. With his heightened imagination, Antony felt he could hear the dead around them sighing. Surely just the wind whipping the corner of the church. As their eyes adjusted to the dimness of the room, they were able to grope their way past the Lambton family effigies to the long, wooden bench.

"Willibrord? Willibrord St. John is chasing us?" Felicity gasped to catch her breath. "I can't believe it. I'll never be able to see him as anything but the BFG."

"Whoever killed Dominic might be a big giant, but he's definitely not friendly. I have no idea what Willibrord is doing here. Most likely it has nothing to do with us—how would anyone know we were here?"

"Unless they were following us closely." Felicity's voice was tight and thin.

"Exactly. All I know is Colin identified Professor Laird who was giving out orders to get rid of us, and he and our friend Wills looked awfully cozy. I don't want to confront either one of them until we know more about what's going on."

"What do we do now? Do you think we've found the motive for Dominic's murder? It was in his journal: the treasure of Aethelstan. It has a great ring to it."

Antony rubbed his hair up and down. "I just don't know. But we have to pursue the possibility. The question is, which possibility? Do we go to Whitby to follow the Ninian Papyrus theory, or do we go to Durham to check out the Aethelstan Treasure idea? I need to think, but my brain has about as much light as this room."

"Oh, I'm freezing! How can anyone think in this cold?" Felicity cuddled close to him and he put his arm around her in what he hoped was an avuncular way. The shared body heat did help. "So," Felicity went on, "someone needs to go to Whitby to look for ancient records of the Synod—where—in a library or museum or something?"

"Sneaton Castle. The Order of the Holy Paraclete. A house of nuns. They'll know where the records are."

"Right," Felicity continued in her efficient way. "And someone needs to go to Durham—what—to check ancient diocesan annals to see if there's any record of what became of Aethelstan's Treasure?"

Antony was impressed. "Exactly. I couldn't have put it better myself. Couldn't have put it nearly so well, actually. Your ability to focus is a treasure—" He caught himself just before he said, "my dear."

"Thanks. And the solution is easy-peasy, then. I'll take Whitby and the nunnery. You go to Durham. Is there a monastery there?"

"Actually, there is, Society of the Sacred Mission. But I don't like the idea of sending you off alone."

"You won't be sending me. I'll be going off my own bat. Besides, we'll be safer. He—whoever he is—can't follow us both if we go in separate directions. You know, divide and conquer."

Just so long as they weren't the ones who were conquered.

Antony was quiet for a long time. Thinking hard. What she

said made sense. Was his reluctance merely for her safety, or was his motive more selfish? Did he value Felicity's company for more than solving this mystery? Or would she be safer without him? He clenched his teeth at the thought.

"Can't think of anything better, can you?" Felicity prodded with a note of triumph in her voice.

"Well, no. Matter of fact, I can't. Have you always been so obstinate?"

"I prefer to think of it as independent." She grinned. "One of my grandmother's favorite stories is of trying to help me with something when I was two years old and being told, 'No. Do it by self.'"

"Right then, that's decided." Felicity jumped to her feet. "Back to the train station, then. There are trains to both places, I assume?"

At last, Antony felt his mind was functioning. "Yes. OK. Here's what we do. We both go openly to the train station. I can't see Willibrord or Laird trying anything in public. If we stay in a crowd we'll be OK. Durham is the next stop down the line. We both get off there. I'll go to St. Antony's Priory, it's in Claypath, just down the hill from the station. Actually, we make it look like we're both going there, then you slip around the back side of the hill to the bus station and take a coach to Whitby. It's a hassle to get there on the train anyway. You go to Sister Elspeth at St. Hilda's Priory. I'll ring her from Durham and tell her you're coming. I met her once when she was at the Community for a retreat. I need to let her know about Father Dominic anyway; I seem to remember them being good friends."

"You're a walking directory, aren't you? Do you know every cleric in England?"

"Hardly. Although I suppose we are a rather tight club in some ways. But I told you I've done this pilgrimage route before, albeit piecemeal."

As he spoke, they made their way across the uneven flooring stones of the vault. The cold, sharp sunlight stabbed like icicles when the door groaned open. And then they darted forward into the even sharper wind, with Antony sending up jagged, broken pleas that their course wouldn't end in yet another disaster.

Chapter 19

It had all sounded like a good plan, but in the end, a train going north to Newcastle, from which she could connect on to Whitby, arrived at the cold little Chester-le-Street station long before anything was scheduled to arrive to take them to Durham. As much to escape the cold as anything, Felicity chose to seize the opportunity to speed on her way.

Antony clasped both her hands and held them tightly to wish her Godspeed. "And be careful," he urged, giving her hands an additional squeeze. "I don't like your going off alone."

She had the feeling he was going to abandon the idea of separate missions entirely, so she jumped on the train with a jaunty wave. "I'll ring you at the priory. The nuns will know the number. Don't worry."

She settled in a seat as the train pulled out of the station. She hoped she felt as confident as she sounded. Her argument to herself was where could one possibly be safer than in a convent? But then she remembered that Father Dominic had been murdered in a monastery.

She looked around the car, assuring herself of the innocence of each of her fellow passengers. She really couldn't afford to let herself become neurotic. But now she realized how alone she was, how much she had relied on Antony—his knowledge, his comfort, his inner strength.

She thought of all their days and hours together—the long dash to Lindisfarne in the driving rain, the trek to Whithorn through a pink sunset... How could such desperation seem so idyllic? The companionship, the mutual challenge, facing danger side by side...

But, of course, they would only be apart for a couple of

days. She needed to concentrate on her task so she could have something wonderful to share with Antony when they were together again.

The train to Middlesbrough was being announced in the vast, echoing Newcastle station as she got off the train. Platform fifteen. She raced across the station, thankful for her long legs and that she had only a backpack to lug with her. She leapt on the train seconds before a shrill whistle signaled for it to pull out. At least if she was being followed, it was unlikely anyone else could have made the connection. She walked through three cars before finding an empty seat. What a relief to be able just to sit there and let the world flash by outside her window, with occasional glimpses of the gray North Sea.

At Middlesbrough she was less fortunate with her connection, and had to wait some time before fighting her way onto the tiny two-carriage commuter train with the rush hour passengers. She wasn't lucky enough to get a seat, and a glance at the map told her there were sixteen stops before her destination. The train emptied rapidly, however, as large groups of weary workers departed at each station. Four or five stops down the line, she had not only a seat but half the car to herself as well. A few more stops and she was alone with just one passenger in the car in front of her. Suddenly she chilled. Dark-rimmed glasses; a tweed jacket. How could Laird possibly be on this train?

They were coming into another station. Should she jump off at the last minute and hope he didn't notice? Should she try to attract the conductor's attention for protection? Maybe if she slumped down in the seat he would think she'd got off and leave at the next stop. Her mind whirred with half-formed plans when the man stood and turned to take his briefcase off the overhead shelf. Felicity let out a stream of held breath. Not a threatening pursuer at all, but a tired-looking office worker, anxious to get home to his tea at the end of a long day.

Felicity relaxed in the now-empty train and vowed to be more sensible after this. It was no good seeing shadows around every corner, and suspects in every encounter. She had a spot of research to do, that was all.

As the train sped eastward, the scene outside her window looked bleaker and bleaker, wetter and wetter. She could almost hear the wind whistling above the roar of the train as the vegetation along the track whipped about. Still, an occasional gorse bush gave a spark of gold in the wet, gray world. This was how she had always expected the North Yorkshire coast to look—heavy gray wet sky over rolling green fields, empty save for cows and sheep. And she alone in an empty train. An air of unreality hung over the scene. She could be lost in a twilight zone.

The train crawled along, the empty cars swaying, then rolled to a stop in a siding. A lone white seagull soared and swooped around the field beyond her window. A through train flew by, a streak of red unfurling down its dark blue side. They lurched forward. Felicity saw a sign along the siding, "London 300 miles" with a slim white arrow pointing south.

And then they stopped. The mist thickened in the pale evening light.

At least there was activity from the crew. She wasn't really alone in some time warp between two worlds. The engineer, a small, brisk man with close-cropped brown hair, came out of his cab, stepped off the train, checked the signal, and got back on. The conductor, a huge teddy bear of a man, walked through, muttering something incomprehensible. Then he returned. "Sorry about that. That big train that just whished through, he's broken down. Where were you traveling through to?"

"Whitby."

"Sorry, we can't move until he does. I don't know how long it will be. Do you need to ring anyone?"

"No. Thanks. I'll just wait."

Much backing and forthing by the two uniformed men followed, with intermittent beeps emanating from the cab. The conductor returned. "Sorry. The attempts at repair were a total failure. We can't go forward and we can't go back because there's a train behind us. So we're just stuck. A rescue train will be sent out to help the one in front of us, but I honestly can't tell you how long it will be." He started to walk on, then turned back. "Just let me know if I can do anything for you, or if you want to ring anyone."

Felicity felt her skin crawl ever so slightly. It was a genuine breakdown, wasn't it? She couldn't see how her hidden assailant could have engineered such a thing. And yet, how did she know if what she was told was for real? The conductor seemed to be genuine, but what if he wasn't? How would she know? Maybe the real conductor was tied up somewhere—or had been thrown off the train... No, no—she was letting her imagination run wild. *Just sit back and relax. Breathe. We'll be on our way soon.*

There really was nothing to do but wait. She wasn't sure how long it was until the conductor brought his comforting bulk to her side again. "What we're going to do is take you off the train and walk up to the crossing. Are you all right with heights?"

Act brave, she told herself. "Oh, yes. No problem." She jumped up, glad to be moving, and slung her backpack over her shoulder.

"Bit of an adventure, eh? Something to put on a postcard."

Felicity forced a laugh and tossed her head. If only Antony could see her now. With all his concern for her, he surely hadn't imagined anything like this. The conductor and engineer donned neon orange jackets and white hard hats, extended a ladder down to the rail bed, climbed down themselves, then waited for her to descend.

She hesitated. What were they going to do to her? Should she resist? They seemed so solicitous, and yet... Still, she couldn't see anything else to do, so she stepped onto the top rung of the ladder. The two men proceeded to help her down as if she were fine china. One foot at a time, guided by a warm, broad hand with "Are you all right?" on every rung. It seemed her greatest danger was of stepping on her protectors. She found her footing on the loose shingle which covered a narrow channel along the rail.

One bodyguard on each side, they walked her carefully to the crossing, again inquiring as to her welfare at every step, although they could see she was perfectly fine. She smiled at being so coddled. It was the gentle courtesy of the English, beyond good manners; they truly cared about her comfort. Didn't they?

"Are you all right?"

"Yes. Fine."

And she seemed to be. But where were they taking her? At the crossing, nine men in neon orange jackets converged. The man in charge, whom she dubbed Sir Topham Hatt from her days of playing Thomas the Tank Engine with her cousin's small sons, announced that he had called a taxi for her.

Shooing his two energetic black and white collie dogs into the back seat, Sir Topham Hatt had her sit in his car. "The taxi will be here in five minutes, but you might as well be comfortable. You all right with dogs?" She assured him she was. But did she really want to get into a stranger's car?

Two men set about with repair equipment. Seven stood and talked. Soon another red Network Rail van pulled up and another neon-jacketed man joined the melee. In spite of her fears, Felicity had to bite her tongue to keep from laughing. Especially each time a mobile phone went off—inevitably playing "Rule Britannia" on every ring.

And every five minutes Sir Topham Hatt returned to reassure her, "Taxi's only five minutes away." She had lost count of how many "five minutes" she had been promised, when a silver Vauxhall pulled under the beam of the just-erected, three-globed emergency light which shone out on the hedgerows separating the fields from the roads.

"Anybody need a lift?" Felicity was flabbergasted at the sight of the tall man who stepped out of the car, his curly blond hair illumined by the dazzling light. It couldn't be.

"Jon!" She wanted to fling herself into the arms of her knight errant, but the sheer unlikelihood of his appearance held her back. *If it seems too good to be true, it probably is,* a little voice said in the back of her mind. And yet here he was. "How is this possible? Don't tell me you just happened to be passing?"

"Not at all. I was looking for you. Thought I'd catch up with you at Hilda's Priory, though."

"How did you know where I was going?" This was impossible. She had only known herself a few hours ago.

"Felicity," he put his hands on her shoulders and looked deep into her eyes, "you disappeared! I've been frantic. Been chasing you everywhere. Why don't you carry a cell phone, for goodness' sake?"

She started to answer—monastery rules, habit—but he cut her off. "Never mind that, now I've found you." He started to pull her into his arms, but she resisted.

"Yes, but how did you know I'd be going to Whitby?"

"Wills told me."

"Willibrord?"

"Why didn't you wait for me?" He sounded almost angry. "I left you a note in your room."

She shook her head. She had seen no note. She had never returned to her room.

"You must have known I would come. I told you how I felt about you." He paused as if struggling for control. "Anyway, I knew you were following Cuthbert's trail, but I didn't know in what order. I wasted a lot of time at Durham, then I ran into Wills at Chester-le-Street. Apparently I just missed you there."

How on earth could Willibrord have known? How could he have heard them talking? But before she could voice those questions, she looked at the narrow country lane Jonathan had just driven down. "Do you mean to say this is the most direct road to Whitby?"

"Actually, it is, but you have to give me credit for some pretty good deduction—if I do say so myself. Figured you'd be on the train. Inquired at Newcastle what time you'd be getting in so I could meet you at the station. They told me about the breakdown and where the train was side railed. Voila!" He flung his arms out and grinned in a self-satisfied manner.

She supposed it sounded plausible. Just. Still she hesitated. "I don't think you're giving enough credit to luck. I didn't even know I'd be taking the train until the last minute."

He grinned at her. "Would you consider it cheating if I admitted to praying?" She grinned back, but still didn't move. "Are you getting in or not?" He held the car door open for her.

Felicity looked around at the fields of cows and sheep beyond the hedgerows. No taxi in sight yet. The neon-jacketed men appeared to have made little progress toward getting the train in motion. Her need of a ride was undeniable. She felt herself relaxing under his spell, but she needed to think—if Wills was eavesdropping on her and Antony in the vault, what had they said? She couldn't remember. Had they really said anything that would have made it possible to track her? But the evidence spoke for itself, didn't it? Jonathan was here. And she couldn't deny her pleasure in that fact.

Except—she drew in her breath sharply at the thought—if Willibrord was one of the Three from the sea, why would he send Jonathan to protect her? Maybe to keep her out of the way while he dealt with Antony? She shivered at the thought of an enemy listening at the door of the chapel, spying on them at the train station. What were Willibrord and his cohorts up to? Perhaps she did need protection. "I'd be very glad of a ride. Thanks." She jumped in the car.

"Oh, Jonathan, it is good to see you. I don't know what Wills is up to, but I am thankful he steered you my direction." And then all thoughts of Willibrord St. John or anyone else fled from her mind as Jonathan reached across the seat and took her hand. She hadn't even had time to assume her tongue-between-her-teeth thinking expression.

"I've missed you, Fliss. When Anna told me about the ground glass I was frantic. I felt so guilty that I wasn't there to help. Are you OK?"

"Yes, fine now."

"I wanted to come to you immediately, but I couldn't get off that joy-forsaken island. And then I stayed on to follow up a few leads of my own."

"Oh, did you find anything?"

"I'm not sure. Nothing worth going into right now, at least. Anyway, you're my first concern, and I'll have to admit I'm relieved you aren't with Antony." He gave her hand a warm squeeze.

"Why?"

He let go of her hand to shift gears as the winding, dipping road took a yet sharper turn. "Apart from the obvious pleasure of having you to myself, of course, it's much easier to protect you without your possible poisoner along."

"What?" She gave a cross between a gasp and a laugh that almost choked her. "You can't be serious, Jon. Antony rescued me."

"Yes, *after* serving you ground glass, as I hear it."

"Jon, that's just silly. I'm delighted to see you, too, but don't start making wild accusations." She put her hand in her lap when he reached for her again.

"Right." He returned his hand to the steering wheel. "Sorry. I admire your loyalty, but you'll have to forgive me if I stay watchful on your behalf."

His smile was too much; she touched him lightly on his arm. "Fair enough." But still her mind whirled. Was it possible? Antony was leading the investigation to find the murderer. *Could* it all be an act?

Night was falling as they drove down a lane leading along a green field toward a confused-looking castle/church structure of golden stone—the sort that Felicity recalled is often described in books as "a pile". Jonathan parked and they walked under the stone arch and crossed the courtyard, Felicity trying to make some sense of the buildings. Jonathan had explained that the "castle" was never any such thing, but rather a Victorian residence "got up to look like its betters."

"So is this priory near St. Hilda's?"

Jonathan looked confused. "It *is* St. Hilda's." He paused. "Oh, I see what you mean. The historic Hilda. No, no. The old ruin is up on the cliffs, overlooking the sea. Nice view you get up there, but mighty windy. We can get our exercise if you want to walk up there tomorrow—199 steps up the trod. And we can have a peek around the churchyard. Dracula's buried there, you know?"

"What?" Felicity boggled at Jonathan's seemingly matter-of-fact statement. "Dracula? Buried in the ruins of Whitby Abbey?"

"Oh, no, not there—although it might be appropriate enough, considering the state of the ruin. No, the parish church's up there, too—St. Mary's. Dracula's buried in the churchyard, so they say. Vampire hunters come in droves every Halloween. All got up in black capes and wedding dresses. I've heard it gives the vicar fits, having them trample all over the graves. He's apparently always putting up signs and writing to the newspaper. But let them have a bit of fun, I say. What harm can it do? They're all dead up there anyway. Except the bats. I suppose they enjoy a bit of company."

"But it can't be true?" Felicity shook her head, confused by her scholarly companion's seeming seriousness.

"Of course it can't. Dracula couldn't be buried up there, could he? Stands to reason. Who would bury a vampire in consecrated ground?"

Felicity laughed. "Oh, honestly, I knew you were putting me on."

"Well, yes, just a little. But this is where Bram Stoker wrote *Dracula*, and he has his vampire count buried in St. Mary's churchyard."

Felicity was still smiling and shaking her head when she rang the bell beside a blue door that seemed to be the most likely contender for housing an office behind it.

She heard a light, quick step on the other side, and the door flew open. "You must be Felicity. Come in, my dear. I do hope your journey wasn't too dire. This is a beautiful place, but the north Yorkshire coast is difficult to get to by public transport. I'm Elspeth."

Felicity wasn't sure which implied question to answer first. "Thank you. Yes, I'm Felicity. Antony must have called."

"Yes, indeed. Sounds like you're into something of an adventure. Well, you'll be safe here. Gates are locked tight at sundown." The vigorous, large-boned nun moved rapidly in her long gray habit. "Oh, I didn't realize you had a companion," she said, as Jonathan stepped forward.

Sister Elspeth's brow wrinkled under her long white veil. "Oh, I am so sorry, but we're hosting a meeting of hospital chaplains at the moment. I'm afraid we haven't any more rooms left. You'd be most welcome to join us for prayers, of course. I am sorry."

He held up a hand. "No, no. No problem. I'll get my own accommodation." He turned to Felicity. "So glad I could be of service. I'll see you soon, Fliss. Leads to follow up on," he said in her ear. "Night, Sister." He gave a jaunty wave and walked toward the door.

"Yes. Thank you for the lift." Stunned by his abrupt departure, Felicity wasn't sure whether she was disappointed or relieved to have him go. She always enjoyed his warming presence so much, and yet she found him strangely unsettling. If only she could sort it out—but somehow she couldn't seem to think very clearly in his company.

"Definitely my pleasure." She felt his smile all the way to her toes and decided she was disappointed.

"You've just time to settle in before Vespers." Sister Elspeth returned to business as the door closed. "Dinner in the refectory after that. I should have time before Compline to show you our library. Antony said you want accounts of the Synod of Whitby debate. That's no problem. We have morning prayer at 7:15, midday office at 12:15, mass after that. You're welcome to join us, but not required." She tapped a bell on the desk. A dapper, middle-aged man in a green and white striped shirt and yellow bow tie popped in from the next room. "Reggie, show Miss Howard to the guest house, would you please? Room 6, I think." She turned back to Felicity. "Do you have everything you need, my dear? I'm sure you'll be very comfortable, but let us know if you need anything."

"Yes. No. I'm fine. Thank you."

"Excellent, then." Elspeth's white veil flowed behind her shoulders as she strode to her next task.

On the way across the courtyard to the guest house Reggie explained, "Wealthy tea planter from the West Indies built this place. Can't imagine wanting it for your home, but it's nice for the sisters. They ran a girls' boarding school here until a few years ago. Maybe you know all that."

Felicity shook her head so he continued. "Not enough call for being educated by nuns these days, I suppose, so they converted the whole thing into this conference center. Very busy it is, too. Large groups and small, we get them all year."

The room was cozy, with floral chintz bedspread and ruffly curtains—not at all what one would expect in a convent, but perhaps the sisters' one chance to splash out and indulge in a bit of feminine decorating. Reggie left her with a sweet smile that lit his round features.

There was time before Vespers for a walk in the walled garden where primroses and windflowers bloomed in sheltered spots beneath the round turrets marking each corner. As she matched her breathing to her ambling steps along the green paths, Felicity felt herself relax. It seemed they had been running and searching for weeks on end, and today's misadventure with the train and Jonathan's sudden appearance through the dusk added to the unreality of it all.

In truth, it had only been a few days. Still, it seemed a lifetime ago when she had knelt in the incense-filled chapel at the Community of the Transfiguration and received an ashen cross on her forehead from the man who at that time was simply her church history lecturer. And now?

She reached the back wall and turned along another grassy path past what in a few months would be a glorious display of rose bushes. Now? Was Antony her protector, or her pursuer?

Could Jonathan's accusations actually make sense? Antony was working so intensely to untangle the mystery. She was certain that wasn't an act. Antony truly wanted to know the truth. But what truth? The truth of who killed Dominic? Or did he already know that?

What if she was being used to find out where the treasure was? Assuming there *was* treasure to be found. If that were the case, what would happen to her once they knew the answer?

No, she wouldn't allow herself to think such nonsense. The important thing was simply to settle her emotions. *Simply?* That seemed a worse tangle than the questions of murder and treasure hoards.

At a minimum, Antony was a very disturbing presence in her life. Perhaps besides sorting out the facts of the Synod of Whitby she could sort out some of her own feelings while she was here alone. She was glad Jonathan wasn't staying in the convent. His sudden reappearance in her life and his accusations of Antony added to the turmoil. This really was too much; trying to find a murderer should be more than enough to have to cope with. Trying to understand her own feelings on top of it all amounted to an unreasonable task.

It was hard to remember how sure of herself she had been before Dominic's murder and her flight with Antony changed everything. Her goals had been so clear before her and her confidence of reaching them so high. She would tackle all the male-dominated bastions of the church. Tackle them and conquer them. She could do anything they or any man could do—and do it better.

But now she had seen a new dimension. She had encountered true malevolence. She had always known in a general sense that evil existed in the universe, but she had never faced it personally before. What if she were a priest and a parishioner came to her in pain, demanding how God could let bad things happen to good people? What could she say?

She felt empty, and Antony's serene, steady example of a dedicated priest made her self-serving goals look cheap. She had no qualms about her ability to succeed outwardly. But now she had seen something of the inward qualities the office required—qualities more rare than the brains and determination needed to get through any situation. His gentle, quiet consistency in keeping the daily office, for example. Of course, she had known that was part of the job. But it could always be kept "by intention." One could say a quick, "Good morning, God" and a sleepy, "Goodnight. Thanks."

Suddenly she wasn't so sure her cavalier attitude would get her through. Oh, it might get her past her ordination committee, but would it get her through having to look at herself in the mirror? She could face parishioners, vestry boards, fellow priests and even a bishop or two with bravado. But could she face herself? And facing God was not a subject she even wished to entertain.

She reached the corner of the walled garden and stooped to pick up a handful of dirt. She let it sift through her fingers just as her confidence slipped from her mind. She turned along the south wall where espaliered fruit trees were just beginning to bud and crocuses were showing yellow and purple at their feet. And what about Jonathan Breen—the quickened pulse she experienced every time he made one of his surprise sorties into her life? She hadn't felt anything like that since her college days with Michael. Did that make any difference to her plans?

The pealing of the bell announced Vespers, and she turned toward the chapel. Well, one thing at least, she wouldn't have to face any of that until the present task was accomplished. And no one had questioned her ability with a Latin manuscript since her junior year in college. Even her tutor at Oxford had been impressed. Anything Sister Elspeth could produce she would tackle with a fine-toothed comb. If there were answers to be found here, she would find them. As to the rest of it, like Scarlett O'Hara, she would think about that tomorrow.

Chapter 20

Felicity took a seat in the serene, gray stone chapel filled with gray-habited sisters, their white-veiled heads bowed over their prayer books. The chapel was crowned with a high barrel ceiling that echoed the sisters' angelic plainchant. "Father, look on us, your children. Through the discipline of Lent help us to grow in our desire for you…"

At dinner, under the dark beams of the long, narrow guests' refectory, Felicity joined the hospital chaplains, who were obviously enjoying their annual meeting. Felicity ate in silence, hiding behind the buzz of her companions' camaraderie, trying to eat the delicate baked sole with reasonable manners when her inner urging was to wolf the food in order to be ready for Sister Elspeth. The hidden treasures of the library were calling out to her both for the answers she might find there and for the escape they would provide from her own disturbing thoughts.

Apparently Sister Elspeth was anxious to get on with the task as well, for Felicity's last bite of fruit compote had barely disappeared when a soft swish of a habit announced the nun's presence. The prioress led the way down the corridor, unlocked an arched doorway into the library with a key hanging from a chain at her waist, then progressed to the back of the stacks. Felicity watched each adept movement with admiration.

The prioress selected a second key from her ring and opened another door. "These are our archives and special collections. This shelf is our collection of published works on the Synod of Whitby. Of course, Bede's *Ecclesiastical History* is the standard account. We have Bede's *Life of Cuthbert* here as well." She moved along to another cabinet. "Here are our biographies of St. Hilda, very important to us, of course, and Antony said you'd want the

Latin collection, too."

"Yes. Especially anything unpublished or untranslated." Ironic, that: their best chance of finding some really new information lay in the oldest manuscripts.

A third key unlocked a glass door on an old oak case. "There are a few manuscripts here, but most are on loan to the Bede's World Research Centre in Jarrow. As I told Father Antony when he rang, you would probably have better luck at the British Library or Durham University. Most things of value wind up there eventually. But here we are. I won't deny that I envy you. I've hoped for years to have time to work on the archives myself. The chances of finding something that will really change historical scholarship are so rare—and yet one always hopes. Lost manuscripts do turn up occasionally." She indicated a pair of white cotton gloves atop the case. "Do wear these when you handle the vellum, and I'm sure I don't have to tell you not to work with an ink pen."

Felicity nodded. She had taken in the sister's words with only half her mind. The other half had been on the woman herself: so steady and focused, a brilliant, holy, woman, head of the most vigorous community of nuns in Britain. Felicity realized that here was someone she could talk to—really talk to about her own conflicts and fears.

"Sister?"

Elspeth paused mid-motion from taking the selected keys off her ring to leave them with Felicity. Her hands stilled and she looked Felicity directly in the eyes. "Yes?"

"Could we talk? I mean, would you have time?"

"But of course, my dear." Instantly she was totally *there*. She took a chair on the other side of the table and sat, her hands folded in her lap, completely relaxed, totally listening—even before Felicity said anything.

Felicity hesitated. She had spoken on impulse. Now what would she say? This woman must have a million calls on her time. And yet she was so entirely present to this one who had asked for help. But how could Felicity voice a question she hadn't even formed in her own mind? "My goal, I guess I should say—I don't think I can dignify it with the term 'call'—anyway, my plan to take holy orders—I was so sure…"

Felicity fumbled to a halt and silence filled the room.

Sister Elspeth raised one eyebrow as if willing her to continue, so she stumbled on. "But now… You see, I'm not like Antony. I like *doing* things. Praying all the time is so boring." Felicity gave a small gasp and ducked her head. What a tactless thing to say to a nun. "Oh, I'm sorry. That must sound awful."

Sister Elspeth smiled. "Not at all. Very reasonable, really. Any conversation—and that's what prayer is—is only interesting if you're talking to an interesting person. Someone you care about. Do you find God interesting?"

Felicity gaped. Interesting? God? God was powerful and mighty and somewhere way off out there. Rather like her own father, the provider of all good things. Due enormous respect. Strict. Always right. "Interesting? God is the controlling boss. He doesn't need to be interesting."

Sister Elspeth chuckled. "That's certainly true. God isn't required to be captivating for our amusement. What I meant was, how do you see God? Consider the personality of the person you're talking to. I think you'll find it improves communication. Then let him tell you what he has in mind for your future."

God has a personality? If Felicity had ever heard that in a theology class it hadn't sunk into her consciousness. She sighed. "I don't even know if I should be a priest. Suddenly I don't seem to understand anything. What is a call, exactly? How did you *know*?"

"Actually, I went to university to study finance. My family had very little money and I had won quite a good scholarship. I was the first of my family to go to university. They didn't particularly understand my desire to study when I could have got a perfectly good job. I thought being the CEO of a multinational corporation would be quite the thing. But I found that was what bored me.

I started doing charity work as an escape from the sterility of studying statistics and management theory all day." Elspeth leaned forward, her hands on the table. Again, Felicity noticed how still, how unperturbed this woman was. How centered.

"Interestingly enough, I use those management skills extensively now as head of this community, and I love the work, but when I thought of spending my life in a steel and glass high-rise tower in London or Manchester—" Elspeth shivered. "I couldn't face it.

"Well, that was the push. I think every vocation has a push and a pull. The pull was a growing desire to spend my time working with the poor. I was at Leeds and soon found myself working far harder for the Save the Children foundation than on my university courses. And when I wasn't with the children, I wanted to be in church. Nothing else seemed to matter much.

"Then when it came time to register for my courses the next autumn, I realized that all I wanted to study was theology. Of course, my friends and family thought I was mad—but that was only the tip of the iceberg. I didn't know then I would end up being a nun. It was all just a natural progression. But then, of course, in those days women couldn't be priests, or even deacons."

"Wasn't there ever a boyfriend?" The words were out before Felicity realized how rude the question would sound.

But Sister Elspeth wasn't bothered at all. "Oddly enough, there were far more in theological college than at university. All the young men in the business school were too focused on success to have time for women, or else were interested in an entirely different type of woman.

"My most long-term relationship, though, was with a monk from Kirkthorpe who taught my missions courses before he went out to Africa himself. It was observing his life that showed me I had a vocation for the religious life. Although I could never be as good as he was."

To Felicity's amazement, the prioress's voice caught on a half sob. Then Felicity knew. "Dominic. You and Dominic were—"

"Very dear friends. Yes. He was my role model. Other than our Lord, of course, but it's a great help to have an earthly model as well."

Felicity reached across the table and took Elspeth's hands. "Oh, this must be awful for you. I'm so sorry. I didn't realise…"

"No, my dear, you had no reason to. Yes. It's simply the most awful thing I've ever had to bear. Clement rang me straight away. He knew we were close. That was why I was so glad when Antony asked me to help you. You can be assured I'll do anything for you—to help your investigation, or to help you personally."

Again, Felicity was amazed. In the midst of her grief, this wise, kind, humorous, gentle woman was reaching out to her. "Thank you so much, Sister. You've been a great help. It's just so hard to *know*."

Elspeth gave a small, dry laugh. "No one said it would be easy. Exciting, fulfilling, painful, slogging hard work, fun, excruciating, but never easy. The bottom line is, determine to do the *right* thing. For the right reasons." She paused. "And follow your heart. If it's in the right place, you can simply follow. That's what I did, and I've never regretted it for one moment."

Felicity nodded. "Yes, but how do you stand it—five offices a day—don't you go cross-eyed?"

"On the contrary, the rhythm, the serenity, the beauty are my sanity. How could I possibly face the brutal death of the most important person in my life without my prayer life? The void would be unthinkable." As she spoke, the bell rang for Compline. She laid the keys on the table, rose and glided from the room. Even after she was gone, it seemed her presence lingered as a comforting warmth.

Felicity sat for a long time before she moved to the first shelf of books. She would start with the basic… the Venerable Bede's account of the Synod of Whitby.

She looked over the volumes on offer and decided to start the easy way—with an English translation. The Oxford edition should be reliable and it would certainly save her time. Almost immediately she was grateful for her decision. The story was complicated enough without having to worry about Latin declensions and conjugations. What was all this controversy about the keeping of Easter?

Felicity felt as though she was coming in in the middle of the story. Besides, just knowing the academic issues now seemed less important to her than knowing the people. She set Bede aside and turned to the biographies of St. Hilda. Perhaps it was meeting Elspeth that made her feel drawn to Hilda, but suddenly Felicity wanted to know more about the woman from whom Elspeth and these sisters at St. Hilda's Priory were spiritually descended.

Sister Elspeth had left the outer library door ajar and now the echoing strains of the chanted Compline service reached Felicity:

> *The Lord Almighty grant us a quiet night and a perfect end.*
> *Amen.*
>
> *Our help is in the name of the Lord,*
> *The Maker of heaven and earth.*
> *Glory be to the Father, and to the Son, and to the Holy Spirit…*

It was a perfect background for reading of Hilda's infancy:

> *"Hereric, my husband, where are you? Hereric!" A sob rose in Breguswith's throat and her hands tore at the bedclothes as she ran through blackness in the tunnels of her sleep. Thither and forth she ran, searching, searching, becoming more frantic at each turn. "Hereric, Hereric!" And the more she searched, the fewer traces of him could she find, for it seemed that King Cerdic's poison had removed all vestiges of Hereric's noble life. A nephew of King Edwin of Northumbria, Hereric had been living in exile under the supposed protection of King Cerdic in a nearby kingdom. Each day, Breguswith had longed for her husband's safe return to herself*

and her two tiny daughters. But Hereric would return no more.

And then the dream changed. Breguswith continued searching, but the frenzy lessened. She ceased running and looked instead around her. She felt a warmth at her breast and began examining the folds of her gown. And there she found it. Breguswith drew forth a rare and precious necklace. As she held it up and gazed in amazement, the jewel began to glow. Brighter and brighter it became until it gave such a blaze of light that all Britain was filled with its gracious splendor.

Breguswith awoke, filled with awe. What did it mean? This rare jewel that was to give light to the whole land—it was something in her keeping, something she was to nurture at her breast and cherish, to prepare for the nation. A soft mewling sound rose from the cot next to her bed. Breguswith rose and bent over the tiny bundle. The same warmth she had felt in her dream filled her as she suckled her infant daughter at her breast. Yes, this was to be the fulfillment. Hilda would be the gracious light that would illuminate all Britain.

Felicity shook herself and stretched. The printed words had taken form in her mind as if she had dreamt them herself. She stood and used the table as a ballet barre, going through her favorite stretching routine from days past. Revived, she returned to her study accompanied by the gentle ending of the Compline chant: "In peace, we will lie down and sleep; for you alone, Lord, make us dwell in safety."

Breguswith and her daughters lived at the court of Edwin, pagan king of Northumbria, spending most of their time at his castle of Bamburgh. When Hilda was eleven years old, there was great excitement in the court because Edwin decided to marry Ethelburga, daughter of King Ethelbert of Kent who had been baptized by Augustine. This Christian queen had agreed to marry a pagan king if she would be allowed to bring her priest with her and practice her Christian religion. Edwin even went so far as to promise that he would be willing to become a Christian if "on examination his advisers decided that it appeared more holy and acceptable to God than their own pagan religion."

Paulinus, who had been sent to Britain by Pope Gregory to assist Augustine in converting the heathen English, undertook his duties in the Northumbrian kingdom with vigor. His teachings, urgings and debates had their effect on Edwin and all his court, including the young Hilda. But in the end, the true test of the superiority of Christianity over other religions was to be proven the way all matters were proven—in the field of battle. If Christ sent victory over Edwin's enemy Cwichelm, Edwin would be baptized.

Edwin returned from battle victorious and ordered all the pagan temples in the land destroyed and the idols broken. During his time of instruction preceding his baptism, Edwin built a small church of wood, near the River Ouse. There, on Easter Day, 12 April 627, King Edwin of Northumbria was baptized at York.

Thirteen-year-old Hilda was among those of the king's household to be baptized that day. The church was small and hastily erected, but Paulinus had been trained at Rome under Pope Gregory, so no element of Christian ceremony was omitted: the stately procession, the white robes, the chanted psalms, the devout prayers. And none took it more to heart than the young Hilda.

It was Aidan's teaching that inspired Hilda to become a nun and Aidan who gave her a grant of land to found her first monastery. The land was on the bleak, windswept mouth of the River Wear at a spot that was to become known as Monkwearmouth and where, thirty years later, Benedict Biscop was to found the monastery that would become the first home of the six-year-old boy who was to become the Venerable Bede. A year later, Hilda became abbess of a convent at Hartlepool, a few miles to the south.

Felicity realized she had read the last paragraph three times to make sense of it. Time for more stretches. Her chair grated on the stones of the floor as she rose, and again a few minutes later when she sat down; surely the only sounds in the entire convent as Compline was long over and the Greater Silence reigned. She adjusted her book for better light.

Two years later, King Oswy, Edwin's Iona-trained nephew who now ruled on the throne of Northumberland, returned victorious from battle and, in thanksgiving, granted land for the founding of twelve new monasteries. One grant of land went to Hilda. Her grant was on the site of a former Roman signal station, high atop an exposed, wind-whipped cliff above the swirling North Sea, at Whitby.

It was an immense undertaking, but with her usual energy and efficiency, Hilda set about overseeing the building of timber and thatch living quarters for her monastery that would accommodate both men and women. Two years later, church, dining hall, infirmary, scriptorium, school room and workshops were ready—some forty buildings laid out in an orderly manner along connecting paths. Hilda led her twelve monks and twelve nuns and assorted servants and workmen up the rough, steep, stony track to their new home on the top of the cliff.

Conditions were spare, but not severe. Fasting, of course, was observed, but not self-abuse. Hilda's monastery was a sanctuary where mass was said daily and men and women could give themselves to prayer for the salvation of souls, and engage in learning, study, teaching, and producing manuscripts.

Hilda's energy and organization transformed this desolate hilltop surrounded by foaming seas. In just seven years, the community was so well established that when King Oswy called a meeting of all the church leaders of his kingdom, he chose Whitby as his meeting place, Hilda as his hostess. This tiny dot on the map was destined to change history.

Chapter 21

Felicity's head drooped. She would do more exercises in a moment, another round of *pliés* and *relevés* would wake her up. But first she would just think about what she had read. Perhaps she could think better if she rested her head on her folded arms… As her thoughts drifted, Hilda took the face and form of Sister Elspeth, her habit the gray gown and white veil of the Sisters of the Order of the Holy Paraclete.

Stately and serene in her dove-colored gown, Abbess Hilda strode forward. Of royal lineage, she had spent thirty-three years at the court of Northumbrian kings. With an education that was granted to few, Hilda had felt herself equal to any challenge. After all, it was expressly a tribute to her devotion and organizational skills that King Oswy was to hold his great synod in her abbey—that the greatest question facing church and kingdom should be settled under her care, that the most powerful and learned men of the day from all ends of the kingdom of Northumbria should be gathering under her roof. Hilda had never been unequal to any task in her life. But now she quailed.

She had planned long and carefully. Abbey servants had been sent as far as two days' ride to gather supplies of meat, eggs, milk and vegetables. The abbey bake house and brewery had worked day and night since she had first been informed of the honor—and task—that was to be hers. Temporary huts filled every inch of space inside the abbey enclosure and some stood outside the walls until the high cliff above the huddled seaport village appeared to be by far the larger town. She had thought herself prepared. Thought all in readiness.

But not for so many. Who could have guessed that Oswy's Synod would attract so many? Already she had bishops, entitled to as fine accommodations as a king, sleeping two to a hut. Eyebrows had been raised, but none had refused. What choice was there? There was hardly enough straw left to offer a pallet to a priest, let alone the servants they brought with them. And still they came.

And yet Hilda knew that her greatest challenge would be her greatest triumph. For triumph she would. All would be housed— somewhere. All would be fed—somehow. If only their cause would triumph as well. The issues were clear. The lines drawn. The church was divided. The nation was divided. King Oswy, brought up as a boy on Iona and taught by Aidan, followed the practices of the Celtic church, established at the time of St. Patrick. As did the saintly Colman, leader of the Celtic party, the beloved Cuthbert, and the many Celtic monks in their half-moon tonsures with the front of their heads shaven and their hair worn long.

Oswy's Queen Eanflaed, trained in the tradition brought to England by Augustine of Canterbury, kept the newer Roman tradition which embraced changes implemented by Augustine, as did Agilbert, chief representative of the Roman church; the proud and scholarly Wilfrid; and the vast number of their delegation, with circular tonsures representing the crown of thorns. The two styles of tonsures symbolic of the deep divisions in the church and nation...

For generations, the two traditions had managed to rub along side by side, but now the situation was becoming intolerable. Even in the royal household. Since Oswy followed the Celtic method of calculating Easter, established by the Eastern Church, and the Queen followed the Roman, part of the royal court would still be in Lenten fasting while others celebrated the Easter feast. Such confusion must be settled.

Splendid in scarlet cloak, King Oswy took his place at the head of the hall. Bishop Colman of the Columban party and Agilbert, Bishop of the West Saxons, seated their parties down each side. When there was room for not one more body in the hall, a pounding drum called all to attention, and the king rose. "Those who serve one God should observe one rule of life and not differ in the celebration of the heavenly sacraments. We all hope for one kingdom in heaven. We ought therefore to inquire as to which is the truer tradition and then all follow it together." King Oswy's firm, clear voice that was equally at home ringing across battlefield or council hall, easily reached all those fortunate enough to be seated inside. For those filling the abbey enclosure and straggling down the steep incline, Hilda had ordered translators stationed at the door to relay the message.

The question was a vital one in a day that knew no separation of church and state. The unity of the kingdom was at stake. In a wider sense, the relation of England to the rest of Europe was also in debate that day. Was the church, and therefore the government as well, in this island going to be separate from the universal church and develop along its own lines, or was it going to draw closer to the rest of Europe?

Oswy called first on Colman, third Abbot and Bishop of Lindisfarne, and therefore the direct successor of Aidan. And, like Aidan, Colman was deeply loved and revered for his holiness and long years of devoted service. "Tell us what are the customs you follow and whence they originated." The king resumed his seat and Colman stood.

The old man in his rough brown robe, bowed with the weight of his years of labor, spoke in a soft voice. And yet its very calm added assurance to the words. "The method of keeping Easter which I observe, I received from my superiors who sent me here as bishop; it was in this way that all our fathers, men beloved of God, are known to have celebrated it. This is the method that the blessed evangelist John, the disciple whom our Lord especially loved, is said to have celebrated, together with all the churches over which he presided." Colman expanded on his theme, then folded his robe around him and resumed his seat with an air of quiet confidence.

The king turned to Agilbert, chief representative of the Roman church, to expound the observances, their origin and the authority his church followed. Agilbert, the frailty of his form and the whiteness of the fringe around his tonsure emphasized by the deep

black of his robe, requested in a voice that did not reach the back of
the hall that his disciple, the priest Wilfrid speak on his behalf "for
we are both in agreement with the other followers of our church
tradition who are here present; and he can explain our views in the
English tongue better than I can through an interpreter." When
his words were made clear to the king, Oswy nodded to Wilfrid
to proceed.

Only thirty-one years old, Wilfrid rose with a commanding
confidence beyond his age and launched into his argument with a
vigor that bordered on the supercilious. Although Wilfrid had been
educated at the monastery of Lindisfarne, he disapproved of what he
considered their Celtic insularity. He had journeyed to Canterbury
and then to Rome. After three years at Lyons, he became a monk
and was now serving as abbot of the monastery at Ripon where he
had forcefully established the Benedictine Rule. "The Easter we
keep is the same as we have seen universally celebrated in Rome
where St. Peter and St. Paul themselves lived, taught, suffered and
were buried. We also found it in use everywhere in Italy and Gaul
when we traveled through those countries for the purpose of study
and prayer. We learned, by our own diligent study, in fact, that it
is observed throughout the whole world, wherever the church of
Christ is scattered, amid various nations and languages. The only
exceptions are these men and their accomplices in obstinacy."

He slammed his fist on the table before him and raised his voice
another notch. "I mean the Picts and the Britons, who in these, the
two remotest islands of the ocean, foolishly attempt to fight against
the whole world!" Tossing his head with an imperious gesture,
Wilfrid resumed his seat as if it were a throne.

When the echo of his voice had faded, Colman rose with folded
hands and bowed head as if going to his own devotions. "I wonder
that you are willing to call our efforts foolish, seeing that we follow
the example of that apostle who was reckoned worthy to recline on
the breast of our Lord, and to whom our Lord himself entrusted
the care of his own mother, for all the world acknowledges the great
wisdom of St. John the Beloved."

Colman's gentle rebuke went home. The room was filled with murmurs of assent. Hilda smiled. Surely they would prevail. They must. It was unthinkable that their beloved traditions, the traditions that had been followed here since first the name of Christ was declared in this kingdom, could be swept away at a stroke.

It was apparent that Wilfrid realized he had overplayed his hand. His rigid straightness unbent ever so slightly as if in appeal. "Far be it from me to charge the apostle John with foolishness. He literally observed the many laws that now, when the light of the gospel is spreading throughout the world, we know are not necessary. As such, John, in accordance with the custom of the law, began the celebration of Easter Day in the evening of the fourteenth day of the first month, regardless of whether it fell on the sabbath or any other day. But when Peter preached at Rome, remembering that the Lord rose from the dead and brought to the world the hope of the resurrection on the first day of the week, he realized that Easter ought to be kept according to another formula." He proceeded to explain the calculations at length.

"This, therefore, is the true Easter and in this way alone it must be celebrated by the faithful as was confirmed afresh by the Council of Nicaea." He turned now to address his opponent directly. "So it is plain, Colman, that you neither follow the example of John, as you think, nor of Peter, whose tradition you knowingly contradict. And so, in your observance of Easter, you neither follow the law nor the gospel." And still Wilfrid expounded. Hilda's head was ringing with the barrage of words and mathematical formulae. She could only hope the king was as little drawn to Wilfrid and his arguments as she was.

At length the learned oration ceased. Gently, Colman stepped into the silence. "Must we believe that our most reverend father Columba and his successors, men beloved of God, who celebrated Easter in the same way, judged and acted contrary to the Holy Scriptures, seeing that there were many of them to whose holiness the heavenly signs and the miracles they performed bore witness?" Here Colman paused to draw breath. His final statement bore the ring of personal testimony, "As I have no doubt that they were saints, I shall never cease to follow their way of life, their customs, and their teaching."

Wilfrid again followed with intricate calculations as to phases of the moon before turning to Colman's central argument. "So far as your father Columba and his followers are concerned, whose holiness you claim to imitate and whose rule and precepts you claim to follow, I might perhaps point out that at the judgment, many will say to the Lord that they prophesied in his name and cast out devils and did many wonderful works, but the Lord will answer that he never knew them." The gasp of horror in the room was audible. Only by the greatest act of self-control did Hilda retain her seat. Had Wilfrid actually dared go so far as to imply that the blessed St. Columba, St. Patrick, even, and their own Aidan would be denied a place in heaven?

Wilfrid retrenched. "Far be it from me to say this about your fathers, for it is much fairer to believe good rather than evil about unknown people. So I will not deny that those who in their rude simplicity loved God with pious intent were indeed servants of God, and beloved by him. Nor do I think that this observance of Easter did much harm to them while no one had come to show them a more perfect rule to follow." A sudden smile spread over Wilfrid's sharp features.

He continued in a burst of speed as if his words were oiled. "In fact, I am sure that if anyone knowing the Catholic rule had come to them they would have followed it, as they are known to have followed all the laws of God as soon as they had learned of them. But once having heard the decrees of the universal church, if you refuse to follow them, then without doubt you are committing sin.

"For though your fathers were holy men, do you think that a handful of people in one corner of the remotest islands is to be preferred to the universal church of Christ which is spread throughout the world? And even if that Columba of yours—yes, and ours too, if he belonged to Christ—was a holy man of mighty

works, is he to be preferred to the most blessed chief of the apostles, to whom the Lord said, 'Thou art Peter, and upon this rock I will build my church; and the gates of hell shall not prevail against it. And I will give unto thee the keys of the kingdom of heaven'?"

The words tumbled so easily from Wilfrid's lips it seemed unlikely he had added that last from any thought of strategy, but rather that they flowed from his love of his own oratory. The fact that they hit the room like a flash of lightning shocked him as much as anyone. Hilda held her breath, watching the lines deepen in King Oswy's face, his eyes darken as the implications of the debate worked through his mind. After several long moments of absolute silence in the room, the king turned to the Celtic leader. "Is it true, Colman, that the Lord said these words to Peter?"

Colman met the king's gaze. "It is true, O King."

"Have you anything to show that an equal authority was given to your Columba through St. John?"

"Nothing." The answer hung in the air.

"Do you both agree, without any dispute, that these words were addressed primarily to Peter and that the Lord gave him the keys of the kingdom of heaven?"

Together Colman and Wilfrid answered, "Yes."

The king rose to his feet. "Then I tell you, since he is the doorkeeper, I will not contradict him; but I intend to obey his commands in everything to the best of my knowledge and ability, otherwise when I come to the gates of the kingdom of heaven, there may be no one to open them because the one who on your own showing holds the keys has turned his back on me."

The room was in turmoil. Jubilation. Shock. Glee. Disbelief. Each group celebrated their win or mourned their loss, but all knew that the church in England would never be the same again. Hilda sat in stunned disappointment. She had been so certain the king would decide for his own party. Could this really be the end of their beloved Columban church? She so loved the simple beauty of its worship that allowed even for impromptu prayers; its closeness to nature and the rhythms of the seasons, allowing even for Holy

Communion to be celebrated out of doors in God's great cathedral of creation.

It seemed impossible that all could be at an end. Dear, dear Bishop Colman who had spoken so valiantly for their side, and her most beloved Cuthbert who now sat silent, head bowed in prayer, what must it be like for them? She must not add to the burden of these great men, or of the precious brothers and sisters under her charge here in the monastery, by making a fuss. Hilda had never shirked. She knew her duty to her king and to God. She had prepared priests,even bishops, for the Celtic church—now she would do likewise for the Roman church. This moment of bitter disappointment for her own people was no time to flag in her efforts.

And perhaps in the end it would all be for the best. She must trust the God that in his wisdom knew and guided all. Perhaps it was best for the Kingdom of Northumbria—for all of England, even—to be aligned with the wider world. Would the urban bishopric structure of the Roman church be a better system than the rural monastic structure of the Celtic church for the spread of the civilization and learning that she so valued? Would being aligned with the wider church help bring about more stability and less of the tribal warfare she had seen so much of in her lifetime? The Roman church spoke for the empire from which Britain had been cut off for two and a half centuries. She could only trust and pray that today's pivotal decision would bring about a strengthening of the faith.

And in her heart of hearts, she felt certain that the Celtic church would never die. Oh, of a certainty, the dating of Easter would change, and the style of tonsures would change—she would order it so for her own house—but the beauty at the heart of Celtic worship could never die any more than the beauty at the heart of creation, because it was a reflection of God himself.

Felicity floated back to consciousness slowly as she became aware of pressure on her shoulders. At first she thought the chant wafting gently around the rafters of the room was the closing notes of Compline. Then she realized it was Lauds. She had spent the whole night in the priory library, alternately reading and dreaming. She felt as if she had been actually present at the Synod of Whitby. She felt as if she had known Hilda personally.

She startled fully awake. Strong hands were gripping her shoulders. And moving upward toward her throat. Her incipient scream was cut off by a hand clapped firmly over her mouth.

Chapter 22

She struggled and thrust her body backward, propelled by a strong kick against the table. Her chair teetered back as her assailant released her.

He caught her just before she hit the stone floor. "Let me go!" She flailed with hands and feet.

"Felicity. Felicity, stop! I'm sorry. You'll waken the whole convent."

She slumped with the relief. "Antony! What in the world do you think you're doing? You scared the life out of me!"

"I'm so sorry. Truly I am. I wanted to wake you without startling you. I guess I miscalculated."

"I guess you did."

"Forgive me?"

She sighed. "I suppose so. Stupid." She said the last under her breath as she shook her head. She was determined to go on, but now all her senses were alerted. Had Jonathan's warnings just been proven true? She forced her voice to sound calm. "But what are you doing here?"

"I finished my work yesterday and got a pre-dawn ride this morning with Brother Matthew. He was coming to St. Hilda's for a retreat day."

"Brother Matthew? From Kirkthorpe?"

"Yes, he had been at the priory in Durham on some business."

Felicity thought for a moment. "Oh yes, probably his library renovation project." The last time she had seen the plump, shy brother he was hurrying them out the back door of the monastery with Father Anselm's hushed instructions. She nodded. "So, you finished quickly. Did you learn anything?"

"Yes. I'll tell you all about it. But what's all this?" With a sweep of his arm he indicated the pile of books that had served for her pillow. "Did you really work all night?"

"Sort of. Not quite sure what I read and what I dreamed— like cramming all night before an exam. Think I've got a pretty good picture of it all, though."

"And?"

"Well, I haven't really sorted it all out, but it strikes me as strange that the Celtic party didn't make any defense once St. Peter's keys were mentioned. They had debated the validity of spiritual descent from St. John all the way up to then. And when Wilfrid said the whole world does it this way, why didn't someone mention the Eastern Orthodox world who follow John?"

She sighed. "It's the old division over Apostolic Succession, isn't it? The one that still divides the church today?" She shook her head. "And then another thing that struck me as strange. Bede so valued St. Cuthbert that he wrote a whole book on his life—but never even mentions Cuthbert in the debate. Doesn't such total silence seem out of character for such a strong leader as Cuthbert?"

Antony nodded sadly. "Maybe Cuthbert just felt the same despair over the situation I do today."

His words hung in the air as the closing prayer of Lauds reached them: "Lord, may our observance of Lent help to renew us and prepare us to celebrate the death and resurrection of Christ…"

They were still sitting in silence a few moments later when Sister Elspeth entered in her unhurried, yet direct way. The frown creasing her forehead was new, however. "Felicity, did you spend the night here? Thanks be to God. Reggie just told me—there was an intruder in the guest house last night. One of our visiting chaplains found him in his room and scared him off. I'm so sorry, Felicity, but the lock on your door was broken, your things scattered around the room."

Felicity felt the color drain from her face as the night

Dominic was killed came back to her. The chaos of her disordered flat... Felicity pulled the journal from her pocket. "I think they're looking for this. Dominic gave it to me. I always keep it with me."

Elspeth stared. "May I?" She held out her hand. Felicity placed the slim volume in it and Elspeth turned several pages, reading them slowly. At last she closed the book, and handed it back to Felicity. "Yes, his own dear handwriting." She wiped a single tear from her eye, then raised her chin in a determined gesture and squared her shoulders as if she had just made a difficult decision. "We must talk. But I don't have time just now." She glanced at her watch. "We have a new set of retreatants coming in and I must greet them." She sighed. "It occurs to me that Felicity will want to see Whitby Abbey. The people who are publishing an updated guide book to the abbey ruins want to photograph me on the site of Hilda's priory—a link from the seventh century to modern times, something like that. I'll meet you up there after breakfast. We should have enough time to talk before the photographers arrive."

The sun was streaking the sky pink when Felicity and Antony crossed the courtyard. As they walked down the lane to the bus stop, silver balls of dew hung on the roadside grasses like crystals, and birdsong filled the fresh air as if echoing the sisters' morning chant. The bus took them across town and they alighted at the foot of Caedmon's Trod.

Craning their necks, they looked up—almost straight up. "Are you ready for this?" Antony asked.

Felicity gave a determined nod.

"Right. Deep breath, then." Antony took her hand and led the way.

They toiled their way up 199 steps, every one of them of slick, narrow, uneven stone, to the top of the cliff.

Felicity smiled as she recalled Jonathan mentioning them to her the day before. Perhaps he would meet them here. She had only had a minute to scribble a note to him and leave it with the

Guest Sister in case he returned for her. In his typical fashion, he had been vague about his plans for today. It occurred to her that she should tell Antony about Jonathan's amazing reappearance but somehow, she didn't want to bring the subject up with Antony. She would tell him if he asked about her journey, of course, but otherwise… She smiled inwardly, savoring the memory of Jon's warming smile.

At the top of the climb they were greeted by a ten-foot high red sandstone cross depicting Christ in the act of blessing; David playing the harp; the abbess Hilda; and Caedmon in the stable inspired to sing his great hymn. "To the glory of God and in memory of Caedmon the father of English sacred song fell asleep hard by 680," Felicity read the inscription.

"You know the story?" Antony asked, as they stood gazing upward.

"Oh, yes, my English lit teacher made a big deal of it. And it really is wonderful. Caedmon, the cowherd, who slunk back to his shed every night after supper in his master's hall because he was so tongue-tied when the harp was passed around the table and it would be his turn to sing. Poor fellow, such intense longing to sing to the glory of God, and yet he was struck completely dumb."

"Until one night," Antony prompted.

"Yes," Felicity continued with enthusiasm. This time she got to be the storyteller—what fun. "One night in the cow byre, Caedmon dreamed someone stood by him and said, 'sing me something.'

"And he replied, 'I cannot sing, that is why I left the feast and came here, because I could not sing.' Caedmon must have been heartbroken.

"But his visitor insisted, 'Still, you must sing to me.'

"'What can I sing?'

"'Sing about the beginning of all creation.'"

Felicity smiled and threw out her arms—such a delight to recall the story on the very spot where it all took place. "And

Caedmon sang. A wonderful hymn of praise to God the creator. The first lyric poem in all of English literature. I wish I could quote it."

Antony smiled. "Is that my cue?

> *'Now must we worship the Maker of heaven,*
> *The might of the Maker his purpose of mind,*
> *The work of the Father of glory the Worker of wonders*
> *eternal,*
> *The Author of all marvels first for earth's children*
> *established*
> *The heavens as a roof. Holy Shaper, mankind's almighty*
> *Guardian*
> *Created then the world, making for men*
> *Land whereon to live. Almighty Lord and God!'"*

Felicity choked. The red-streaked sky had turned to blue and gold, and seabirds called in accompaniment to Antony's recitation, like the strokes of a scop's fingers on a harp. Here in the shelter of the cross the sun was warm on her head, and Antony's melodious voice did full justice to the hymn of praise that had echoed across more than thirteen centuries. "I don't remember what happened next, though."

Antony picked up the story, "Our humble cowherd was taken to Hilda for his gift to be nurtured under her careful guidance. Caedmon learned all he could by listening to his instructors, memorizing the stories and ruminating over them 'like some clean animal chewing the cud,' Bede says, and then he turned the stories into melodious verse so that his teachers became, in turn, his audience."

"I'm impressed!" Felicity cried. "I think you've memorized Bede."

"Pretty nearly. I love that passage—such a model for one who would attempt to tell the gospel story." He turned toward the broken walls of the abbey.

"Oh, my!" As she stepped from the shelter of the cross and

turned toward the abbey, a gust of wind slammed Felicity against Antony. Indeed, she would have fallen had he not been so quick to catch her.

"Steady there. Fierce, isn't it? This cliff is still as desolate and windswept as it was in Hilda's day."

Pushing against the wind, Felicity walked rapidly between the graves toward the ocean. "The view is amazing!" She had to yell to be heard as the wind whipped the words from her mouth. She darted forward to get a better view—sun on the white-capped waves, boats tossed in the blue ocean beneath the shining sapphire sky.

"Oh!" She gave a sharp cry as Antony's firm grip on her arm spun her around.

"No closer," he demanded, pointing to the yellow sign with large black letters: "Danger. Crumbling edge."

"I wasn't going over," she protested sharply, rubbing her arm. "There's a wall." She pointed to the low, stone barrier surrounding the churchyard.

"Yes, but even some of that has fallen away. Several graves were destroyed in a landslip a few years ago."

With a last, reluctant look at the exhilarating panorama, Felicity turned and obediently followed Antony toward the magnificent ruin of the medieval abbey that had been built on the site of St. Hilda's original monastery. "Hilda's abbey was destroyed by Vikings in the ninth century and lay in ruins for 200 years," Antony said. "A new abbey was established in the eleventh century, a testimony to Hilda's continuing influence."

Steadied now, Felicity walked ahead across the wide grassy sward of the high clifftop toward the copper-bronze stones of what was once the east end of a magnificent abbey, the triple rows of narrow, pointed lancet windows pointing upward in tiers, flanked by towers, their pointed caps reminiscent of something a medieval princess might wear. Even with the aid of a map from the visitors' center, it was difficult to relate the present structure to the remains of St. Hilda's Abbey, and yet Felicity, the images of her night of reading and dreaming still fresh in her mind, could feel herself walking in the footsteps of Hilda.

Seabirds' cries filled the air. Everywhere the white of soaring wings flashed against the blue sky as joyous cries gave a descant to the deeper roar of the waves beating at the foot of the cliff. It was little wonder that birds played such a part in the legends surrounding Hilda. Wild geese regularly stopped to rest at Whitby on their migratory flights to and from the arctic. Their majestic descent to the green clifftop was said to be for the purpose of paying homage to the well-loved Lady of Whitby. Likewise, it was said that the seagulls that wheeled high overhead always dipped their wings in salute to Mother Hilda when they flew over her abbey.

Felicity caught her breath and blinked as before her eyes a seagull swooped low above a gray-habited figure walking across the flat green clifftop toward them. She all but greeted Elspeth as Hilda. Easy to see why the guide book people wanted to photograph her here. "I hope you haven't been waiting long. It took me longer to get away than I had hoped. And now my plan of an uninterrupted time here is not to be." She indicated a mobile phone clipped to the rope belt of her habit. Felicity found it hard to imagine anything more incongruous.

Elspeth smiled. "The devil's invention, I fear. But there are times when one must make use of them. One of the speakers for the retreat hasn't arrived. I may have to hurry with the photographers to fill in for him. But with luck we'll have time for our talk first." She led the way to what would have been the nave of the medieval church and took a seat on a broken pillar in the north transept, where the walls were well enough preserved to provide shelter from the wind.

"I won't waste time. I have decided—quite on my own authority, as I haven't been able to contact the only other one of us left. I must take full responsibility for breaking my vow, but I can see no other way forward. Desperate times demand desperate measures. And as Dominic gave you his journal—" She seemed to be arguing with herself. She paused, then took a deep breath. "You are familiar with the speculations about a guardianship of St. Cuthbert?" She looked at Antony.

He nodded and leaned forward. "Yes. The Three. Butler suggests it."

"That's right. Three English Benedictines who continue to this day to guard the secret of Cuthbert."

"So it's true?" Felicity almost squealed.

"Quite true. I am such a one. As was Dominic."

Felicity was unable to take in the momentousness of the revelation. She merely jumped to the end. "Do you think that was why he was murdered?"

"I'm certain of it."

"For the treasure?" Felicity could hardly sit still.

Elspeth shook her head sadly and studied her hands, folded as if in prayer. "The secret has remained intact for four and a half centuries, since Henry's destruction of the shrine. But now, when the treasure could be used for such infinite good, the powers of evil gather so strong to prevent it."

"Dominic's notes." Felicity nodded. "He seemed to be saying something like that, but we couldn't really decipher it."

Elspeth smiled. "Yes. Even when he feared a threat, he couldn't bring himself to disclose more than a cryptic warning." Elspeth rose to her feet and began pacing the grassy floor of what was once an elaborate chapel. "I hope I'm doing right to speak. I've never been accused of being weak or hysterical… but the responsibility is so great. If only I could get in touch with—" At that moment, the phone at her belt jangled. "Oh, I do hate these things. I'm sorry…" She left the transept to conduct her conversation.

Felicity turned excitedly to Antony. "So we were right! It's true. The Three do exist." She looked around impatiently. "Oh, hurry up," she said in the direction of the departed figure. "So as soon as she tells us about the treasure, we'll know why Dominic was killed and that will lead us to who… Maybe she even knows."

She jumped to her feet and started in the direction Elspeth had gone. "Why did that ring have to come just then? I was just ready to ask her—"

At first she thought the sharp, piercing cry was the call of a gull. It wasn't until Antony streaked past her, jumping the base of a broken pillar and heading across the lawn toward the cliff edge that Felicity realized that the shriek had been human.

Chapter 23

Antony held the trembling Felicity as she sobbed in his arms. "Don't look down." He pulled her back from the cliff edge.

"But we've got to get to her. Maybe we can still help." She pulled as if she would attempt to descend the cliff to the sea crashing on the rocks below.

"Yes, we'll get help, but not that way." Antony gestured to the other side of the abbey ruins. "The visitors' center. We can phone for help there."

But still Felicity wouldn't move. "It can't be. She was so good. So strong. Like Dominic. How can this happen?" Antony wanted to reassure her that they would find out, but her sobs became wilder. "It's my fault! I shouldn't have let her go. I should have told her to take her call right there and then finish telling us before she left. I should have—"

"Shhh, shhhh, shhhh. It's not your fault. There's nothing we can do here. Come on, we must call the emergency services." Antony all but dragged her away from the precipice.

Felicity was trembling too hard to walk far. "Yes. Call 999. You must. I'll sit here." She staggered toward the abbey. "Warm by the stones. I'll be warm."

Antony was torn. He couldn't leave her. And yet he must. Perhaps, by some miracle, something could still be done for Elspeth. He guided Felicity to a sunny spot beneath a roofless arch. "Don't move. I'll be right back. Five minutes." He tore his coat off and wrapped it around her shoulders. "I'll bring you some tea." He took off at a lope across the grass.

In less than five minutes, with help summoned, he made his way back at an only slightly slower pace, dictated by the need not to slop the strong, well-sugared tea he carried. The sharp cry of a seabird and a muted scrabbling sound overhead made him look up as he approached the abbey. At first he thought he was seeing the shadow of the gull pass over the arch... then he realized.

Time went into slow motion as, petrified as if attempting to run in a dream, Antony tried to leap forward. Tried to scream. Tried to warn her. "Felicity!" At last the cry tore from his throat as the crumbling stones of the arch plummeted toward her.

With a lunge an all-England rugby player would have been proud of, he leapt into the air and propelled himself at her. They landed in a heap just beyond the fall of the largest rocks, Antony's body shielding Felicity from the cascade of smaller stones that fell to the outside.

This second shock brought Felicity out of her inertia. She rolled from under Antony, grabbed his shoulders and rolled him onto his back. "Antony! Antony! Are you all right?" Brushing away the rubble, stroking his cheeks, she sobbed his name. "Antony!"

He came up slowly, showering dust and gravel as he moved his arms and shoulders, exploring the damage. Painful, but not broken.

"Oh, thank God you're all right!" They said it in concert and clung to one another.

Suddenly Antony jumped to his feet, ignoring the pain of his protesting bruised muscles, and pulled Felicity after him. "We've got to get out of here."

"No, we can't. We have to help Elspeth."

"The emergency services are on their way. They'll do whatever they can. We can help her most by finding out who's doing this and why."

Felicity looked around. "You don't think it was an accident? Part of the abbey did crumble in the eighteenth century. Maybe it just..."

A sound of feet running on stone reached him. Antony spun and rushed forward. "There's still someone in the tower!" He headed toward the broken stairway in the turret beside the now-crumbled arch.

"Antony—that way!" Felicity cried and pointed to a distant figure running toward the parking lot.

Antony stopped. "We'll never catch him. Did you get a look at him?"

Felicity shook her head. "Too far away."

Antony went on inside the tower just in case an accomplice remained inside. The tower was empty, but fresh scrabbling marks in the dust showed that someone had been there recently. "Wait here." Without waiting for her to protest, Antony returned to the newly fallen rubble heap and glanced over it.

"Look." He pointed to a large boulder. "That one doesn't match the others. Maybe he carried it up and lofted it at you. Hitting the keystone of the arch must have been pure dumb luck. Or a quick change of plans when he saw where you happened to sit. He can't have known where any of us would sit."

"But he did know we were coming here?"

Antony nodded. "Has to have, I should think. And came prepared to act on any opportunity that presented itself."

"So Elspeth didn't get blown off the cliff, or the ground just happen to crumble under her?"

"Or these rocks just happen to fall on you? What do you think?" As he spoke, Antony retrieved his battered jacked, glad for the shielding it had provided Felicity. He began guiding her across the cow-grazed field back toward St. Mary's and the descent of the cliff. "It won't take the authorities long to figure out the same things we have, and I don't want to be here when they do."

"Oh, no. They'll think you—"

"Precisely. Just as they did at Kirkthorpe. If I'm going to stay on my feet long enough to solve this mess, we have to stay a jump ahead of the police."

"Where next?"

Antony stopped. "I hadn't thought. We need to talk." His hand massaged his aching shoulder as he paused. "Did you discover anything in the manuscripts?"

"I learned a lot, but nothing not already known. The

unpublished things have been sent to Jarrow."

"Right. We follow the trail, then. With luck we can catch a ride back to Durham with Brother Matthew. I'm sure Sister Elspeth's tragedy will cut his retreat short as the convent will be in mourning." He lifted his shoulders in a painful rotation. Best to keep moving before his muscles seized up.

Indeed, word of the tragedy had reached the convent before they did and all the guests were making a silent, stunned departure. Antony located the plump, soft-spoken monk putting his case in the trunk of the little green Mini he had borrowed from the Community. The wind whipped his limp, pale hair across his round forehead. "It's so awful. One c-can't really take it in. D-dead, they said. An accident on the c-cliff."

"Yes. Terrible." Antony had just received Matthew's ready assent to be their chauffeur when Felicity returned from her room with her hastily collected belongings. He would complete his retreat at St. Antony's, Matthew said, so their jaunt wasn't in the least out of his way.

Grateful as he was for a ride to Durham from whence they could catch a train to Jarrow, Antony found the man's presence frustrating. He needed to discuss their work with Felicity. There was so much to sort out.

Perhaps the most important thing they had learned was the fact that, indeed, rumors of the existence of the Three were actually true. If only Elspeth could have told them who the third one was. And now the question still remained—was that third guardian trying to prevent their learning the secret? Or was there another enemy trying to get to it before they did? Elspeth had referred to a treasure. But what was it? *Where* was it? That was the key to everything they needed to know.

They had encountered so many possible candidates for the role of chief actor in all this—Willibrord St. John, Jonathan Breen, the enigmatic Professor Laird, even their birdwatching friend Stephen Bootham, and Philly Johnson with her irritating son. He gave a small shiver. Where were they all now? It seemed any one of them could have been hiding behind one of the broken pillars of the ancient abbey. And who was out there that they *hadn't* met yet? Did the shadow he glimpsed at the top of the turret and the figure disappearing across the expanse of green have a face he would recognize?

The winding roads through spring green fields gave way to the industrial blight of Middlesbrough and Darlington. Then, like a horse heading for the barn, Brother Matthew put his foot down and they sped straight up the A167 to Durham. At the train station at the foot of the rocky promontory, the brother, his gray scapular flapping in the breeze, flung open the doors of his little shoebox of a car. "S-safe arrival at Jarrow." He sent them off with a beatific smile and jaunty wave, promising to ask St. Antony's guest master to have rooms ready for their return.

Antony sank gratefully into the first pair of empty seats the train offered. "Thanks be. We can talk now!" He turned to Felicity. "Are you all right?"

She reached to massage her right shoulder with her left hand. "I am. I'm fine, really. I think. A few sore spots I haven't really focused on yet." Her finger traced a patch of painfully scraped skin on her forehead. "How about you?"

Antony started. He hadn't given it thought. But when he did, he wished he hadn't. He was thankful to have been able to take the brunt of the rubble fall, but he would undoubtedly be bruised and aching for days. He rotated his shoulders to prove he could. "Absolutely fine. A few bruises. We're very lucky."

"Yes. Poor Elspeth. I can't believe it. She was so strong, so focused, so—reliable. Like someone who would always be there, always be able to take charge and tell everyone else the right thing to do. She can't just be gone like that. I don't suppose there's any chance…?"

"Wishful thinking."

She nodded. "I know. Still…" She was quiet for a moment as the train pulled out of the station. "You never told me what you learned at Durham."

"Right. Things happened so fast. Well, the library at the college is excellent and I had no trouble getting a reader's pass. Their collection of Northumbrian history is extensive."

"And?"

"And, the speculations of treasure buried under the floor of the church at Chester-le-Street were correct."

"Oh! I knew it!"

Antony held up his hand. "Wait. Emphasis on *were*. It seems that the threatened Viking attacks left the cathedral church of Mary and Cuthbert alone, and affairs went on rather quietly for half a century. Then in 1050, Bishop Egelric pulled down the old cathedral in order to build a stone church. The hoard was discovered and the bishop managed the plunder the Danes missed."

"You mean, the bishop took the treasure?"

"Yes, indeed. Records state that he found 'a hoard of treasure' and that he kept it for himself. When the church was completed, he resigned his bishopric and retired to Petersborough in order to spend it."

"But that's theft! He can't do that! It's Cuthbert's money."

Antony threw back his head and laughed. "Your principles are 100 per cent correct, but your verb tenses are a millenium out of date." What a delight she was to work with. He had never met anyone so refreshing. She cared so much and would rush headlong at anything she believed to be right. Of course, it led her into danger as often as not, and he felt absolutely sick at the thought of how she needed protecting. Still, her courage was an amazing tonic to his own instinct for caution, his desire to pull back and take cover.

"But it's still wrong," she insisted. Determination to hold on, he added to his list.

"Oh, I agree absolutely. The point is, our robber-bishop Egelric sounds a very thorough man. It's doubtful he would have missed anything buried there."

Felicity folded her arms and sat back in her seat. She was

quiet so long Antony began to fear he had offended her by laughing at her. He started to apologize when she spoke. "Right. So that's a dead end. But the idea is still there, isn't it?"

"What do you mean?"

"Well, the Guardians buried Cuthbert's treasure to protect it from vandals once. They might have done it again, mightn't they—with other treasure? Something acquired later?"

Their arrival at Newcastle's bustling station prevented further speculation. The Metro to Jarrow was waiting on the track. Only a few minutes' ride through an ugly, gray industrial area and they alighted at the stop marked Bede.

"Look at those names." Felicity was almost skipping. Such a transformation from the young woman who a few hours ago was so traumatized she could barely walk, and had then narrowly escaped death herself. This was the real Felicity back again. Antony was more thankful than he could say, and he was amazed and admiring of her powers of restoration. He was feeling far less lively. He needed time to think; time to grieve. This headlong rush allowed for neither. Far more than from the pummeling with stones, he ached with sorrow, with painful memories, with guilt. Elspeth had died for the same cause as Dominic. If he had been quicker, cleverer, more energetic in the task, it needn't have happened. Another failure to add to the list of his ineffective life. Should he tell Felicity? What would she do if she knew?

At least for the moment he could delay and allow his mood to lighten alongside Felicity's heightened spirits. The eponymous names continued as they walked on. "Cuthbert Court!" she cried and pointed. "And, there—Bede Industrial Estate. It sounds like an oxymoron, doesn't it?"

Antony pointed next. "Bede Technology, Ltd." He grinned. "I guess in Bede's day that would have been a scriptorium."

"Isn't it wild to think that for his day Bede was high-tech?" Felicity laughed.

From the road, busy with whizzing traffic, they turned into a wooded haven, walking up a path lined with budding trees toward

St. Paul's church and the site of the ruined monastery. Antony gave Felicity a thumbnail history as they walked. "Bede spent most of his life as a monk here. He left it only a few times for research trips to Lindisfarne and York. The monastery was destroyed and abandoned in the middle of the ninth century, but the memory of its former glory and the fame of Bede ensured its refounding in 1074. St. Paul's is the parish church of Jarrow now. There has been continual worship in this church since the 600s."

"In *this church?* Not just on this site in an earlier building as all the others have been?"

Antony shook his head. "There's a dedication stone inside. I'll show you." They entered the quiet coolness of the ancient stones, and were greeted by a middle-aged volunteer in a bright blue dress.

"Welcome to St. Paul's. One of the oldest churches in England." She paused to push her glasses back up on her nose. "Are you interested in our history?"

Felicity's nod was all she required to launch her tour: "In the year 681, ten monks and a dozen novices from the monastery of St. Peter's Monkwearmouth, just seven miles away, came here to found another monastery on the land given to Benedict Biscop by King Ecgfrith. Among those twelve novices was a boy about ten years old who had already been at St. Peter's for three years. His name was Bede.

"He tells his own story in the introduction to his most famous work." The guide produced a copy of *The Ecclesiastical History of the English People* and proceeded to read at breakneck speed: 'I was born on the lands of this monastery, and on reaching seven years of age, I was entrusted by my family first to the most reverend Abbot for my education. I have spent all the remainder of my life in this monastery and devoted myself entirely to the study of the Scriptures. And while I have observed the regular discipline and sung the choir offices daily in church, my chief delight has always been in study, teaching and writing. I was ordained deacon in my nineteenth year, and priest in my thirtieth... From the time of my receiving the priesthood until my fifty-ninth year, I have worked, both for my own benefit and that of my brethren, to compile short extracts from the works of the venerable Fathers on Holy Scripture and to comment…'"

"Thank you. Very informative, thank you." Antony nodded vigorously, and began backing away before their enthusiastic informant could catch her breath. They really didn't have time for this. Dominic had been murdered. Elspeth had been murdered. Who would be next?

They moved up the aisle. Once out of range, Felicity giggled, "I thought she had started a tape recording."

Antony led the way to the chancel. "This is the original part of the church. It was a freestanding chapel in the monastery."

"So Bede would have actually worshipped here?"

"Absolutely." Antony pointed to a stone slab cemented into the wall.

Felicity looked at the Latin inscription. "The dedication of the basilica of St. Paul on the ninth day before Kalens of May in the fifteenth year of King Ecgfrith in the fourth year of Abbot Ceolfrith founder, by God's guidance, of the same church." She paused to consider. "Ecgfrith. Wasn't he the king that visited Cuthbert on Inner Farne to persuade him to become a bishop?"

"The very same."

"Wow. It makes it all seem so close. As if all those things that happened in the seventh century were still happening today. It's a kind of time travel."

"Yes, I know what you mean. The ages are more closely connected than we busy, high-tech moderns sometimes like to think." He pointed to a small, round window high in the wall comprised of what appeared to be random pieces of colored glass. "That's the oldest stained glass in England—original pieces from the Saxon church."

Felicity looked around. "But where's the scriptorium?"

"The foundations of the ruined monastery are beside the church."

"No, I mean, where are the manuscripts St. Hilda's priory loaned them?"

"Oh, those are at the study centre at Bede's World," he pointed, "up the hill. I wanted you to see the historic site before we go to the modern recreation."

He led the way to the back of the church, where the enthusiastic guide was welcoming a group of ten-year-old boys in blue and gray school uniforms. She ushered them to a rack of small brown monks' robes. "While you're here we want you to really experience the life of a monk, so the first thing is to dress the part." Felicity paused to watch the transformation as twenty little brown-robed figures folded their hands and bowed their heads, polished school shoes sticking out below their robes.

They walked on up the hill through a park with incipient leaves just greening the branches overhead. Antony explained that the interpretative center was established just a few years ago in an attempt to change the modern environment to something nearer the landscape Bede would have known.

"It's beautiful," Felicity gasped, standing in the Roman rotunda. "I hadn't thought of the world being so Roman in Bede's day."

Antony nodded. "Yes, this is the architecture the Anglo-Saxons would have found when they came to Britain—but, of course, this is in much better repair. Remember that much of the passion behind Wilfrid's argument was based on the idea that Britain should be more like the Romans. Rome had withdrawn official rule of Britain some 200 years earlier. But her influence still held in most of the civilized world. Besides, styles changed very slowly then."

Drawn onward by the gentle sound of splashing water, they walked past a colonnaded courtyard with a fountain, and on down a corridor of murals of Roman Britain. Around the corner they were met with the inflected sounds of Anglo-Saxon poetry as a scop would have recited it. "Oh, my goodness, that could be Caedmon, couldn't it?" said Felicity.

They turned again and were greeted with Gregorian chant wafting through the air. "Yes, and this could be Bede," Antony replied.

Antony was thankful that the brothers at the priory in Durham had been able to supply him with some decent, if rather out of date, clothing. A change much needed after the grubbing his wardrobe had undergone on Lindisfarne. That morning's pounding with broken stone and mortar had left a few small tears in the fabric of his borrowed coat, but after a vigorous brushing he looked respectable enough to approach the director with a request to use their study room.

The pale, blond young man tugged at his jumper and fumbled with the papers on his desk. "Oh, yes, certainly, Father. We'd be delighted. That's what the collection is for. We mostly get school groups—most welcome, you understand—but we are delighted to attract serious scholars, too." He cleared his throat. "The thing is, you see, our research director has the keys. And tomorrow *is* Saturday."

"It really is most urgent," Antony insisted. *Would it be too much to say life and death, he wondered?*

"Yes, well." More fumbling with papers followed. "Perhaps he can be persuaded to come in for a few hours in the morning. I'll do my best."

"Thank you. Please tell him—extremely urgent."

The young man blinked. "Yes, of course. So you said." He glanced at his watch. "It is almost closing time now. But do look around for a bit. We open at 9:00 in the morning. You can come back then."

He didn't even make it a question. Antony started to argue, then realized it would be useless. Processes must be followed. Besides, other than a little doze in Brother Matthew's car, Felicity had had almost no sleep in the past twenty-four hours. "Yes, certainly. Thank you, er—Jeremy." He read the name from the plaque on his desk. "In the morning, then."

He swallowed his impatience. Another day. And then would

they find anything useful? The time was ticking. He could almost hear the clock. How soon would the police catch up with him? And how much worse had he made his case by running away? By being present at Sister Elspeth's death? And now, just when they were beginning to find something—and yet had nothing concrete, nothing the police would credit—more delay. St. Cuthbert's Day was only five days away. Would he be a free man then? Would he ever be truly free?

Antony, stop moaning! Aunt Beryl's voice came to him so clearly across the years, he almost jumped. There were times when her no-nonsense approach to life was the only answer. Just pull your socks up and get on with things, whether they were going your way or not.

He squared his shoulders and strode forward to look for Felicity.

Chapter 24

H e found her looking out the French windows toward the reconstructed Anglo-Saxon village where ancient breeds of sheep and goats were raised. She turned with a smile and pointed. "Look at the parallel images: Anglo-Saxon huts below oil storage tanks; an Anglo-Saxon stone cross on a hill ringed with electrical transformer towers."

"It plays with your mind, doesn't it? This clash of cultures."

"It's strange." Felicity ran her fingers through her long hair. "Sometimes I think I almost feel more at home in the older world. I suppose that's why I studied classics." She stopped and looked at the floor. "In spite of my impatience with some aspects of history."

He grinned. "Don't worry. You're absolved." Still smiling, Antony led the way into the museum. "We can't work with the manuscripts until tomorrow. Let's just look around a bit and then get back to the priory. I expect you'll welcome an early night, anyway."

"I will, but I do hate waiting."

"Yes, I know. But let's keep our eyes open. Maybe we'll find something useful."

Their footsteps echoed on the marble floors. "Oh, look. They have adult sized monks' habits, like the ones for children at the church." She pointed to the rack of brown, hooded robes in the corner.

"And here's our friend Benedict Biscop." Antony indicated a vibrant series of red, blue and gold panels portraying the story of Biscop's life.

Felicity sat on the bench before the paintings and read the inscriptions: "'He crosses to Gaul', 'He venerates the apostles in Rome', 'He collects books to equip a new monastery', 'He welcomes a young man called Bede to the monastery'." She turned to Antony with her face alight. "There it is! Collecting books. Do you think the Ninian Papyrus was among them?"

Antony hesitated. "I'd like to think so, but it's an awfully long shot. However, if Ninian thought the document was important enough to copy, I suppose it's possible Benedict Biscop did, too."

Felicity jumped up in her characteristically quick way, and darted around the panel of paintings standing in the middle of the room, then turned back to Antony and whispered, "Look, there's someone wearing one of the monk costumes. Isn't that fun!"

Antony smiled and nodded, not wanting to make Felicity feel uneasy, but the stocky figure with a hood pulled over his face didn't feel like fun to Antony. Was the costumed form lurking in the corner all he appeared to be? Had he been listening to their conversation? Was there something familiar about him? Could that have been the shadow Antony saw at Whitby? Had they been followed this quickly? The peaceful atmosphere of this place was so deceptive. He looked over his shoulder, realizing the next attack could come from any direction.

A voice over the address system made him jump, but the announcement was routine enough. The museum was closing in five minutes. The hooded monk slithered silently on down the hall. With the sense of watching out for pursuing hounds prompting frequent glances over his shoulder, Antony took Felicity's arm to guide her quickly toward the train station.

Back in Durham, bells from the great cathedral on the hill beyond were ringing as they made their way across the priory courtyard to the modern round chapel at St Antony's for evening prayers. Security, security, security they seemed to be saying. And yet, Antony knew it could all be an illusion. No place could be truly secure in the wake of all that had befallen them, certainly not until the mystery was solved and the treasure secure. But even then, how much security was possible in this life? Sometimes one felt secure, then one's parents died in a single blow; one chose a sheltered path for life, then found it led only to a cliff edge. There were landmines everywhere.

He gave himself a mental shake. This was getting him nowhere. And after all, in spite of the impossibility of living up to her demands and the coldness of her comfort, Aunt Beryl had taught him some useful things. Simply getting on with whatever life required of one had definitely been at the top of her list.

Brother Matthew met them just inside the door and handed them a prayer book. "Have a g-good afternoon at J-Jarrow?"

"Very interesting," Felicity replied.

"D-did you learn anything?" Matthew prodded.

Antony shook his head. "Research director off for the day."

"P-p-pity. B-better luck tomorrow." Brother Matthew's pale blue eyes crinkled at the corners. "We have another visitor from Kirkthorpe, arrived this morning." Antony's gaze followed his gesture across the room to a bowed head of blond curly hair. Jonathan Breen. Perhaps not a landmine, but a rug pulled from beneath him at the least. Antony gritted his teeth, stifling his urge to turn from the room.

He was trying to figure out the significance of Breen's reappearance when Felicity spotted him.

"Oh, there's Jonathan. What a nice surprise!" She set out across the room with a smile. "Jon! When you said you had accommodation, I thought you meant in Whitby."

Felicity seated herself by Breen, and whispered in the quiet of the chapel. He returned her greeting with a wide smile that showed off white teeth in a suntanned face.

Antony sat on the bench next to Felicity and turned to his prayer book. He had come to pray; he was not going to let his animosities interfere with that. Discipline had been a strong part of his training for the priesthood. He had resources he could call upon.

After the brief service, he turned toward his room rather than making for the refectory. A long hot shower was what he needed, far more than supper. He refused to admit how little appetite he had for watching Felicity bask in Breen's company. Much easier to blame his withdrawal on aching muscles which, in truth, were making themselves felt more and more fiercely as the cold night air and fatigue settled in. Thank goodness they had caught only the edge of the stone shower. If they had been in the center…

He was almost to his room when Felicity caught up to him. "Antony, aren't you coming to eat?"

He shook his head. "Not hungry."

"OK." She shrugged. "But we have to talk—" She took a deep breath before she plunged. "I should have told you earlier, but so much was happening and I didn't want you to get—well— upset…"

His frown wasn't designed to offer her comfort. "What should I be upset about?" He had little desire to hear anything she needed to confess about herself and Jonathan Breen.

"I know you're displeased that Jonathan is here, but he really was the most amazing help getting me to Whitby."

"He what? He was at Whitby? Why didn't you tell me?"

She tried to explain, her halting explanation becoming more confused as she continued.

"Are you saying that Willibrord heard our whole conversation in the Lambton Pew?" He struggled to recall. "The door wasn't shut quite tight. It's hard to imagine, but I suppose it is possible. Just." And Willibrord sent Jonathan after Felicity? Just like Father Anselm sent him to help them earlier? Antony couldn't think of a less congenial candidate for the role of nursemaid.

"And you just now found it convenient to tell me?" He knew his voice was icily cutting. He meant it to be. He turned and shut the door to his room between them.

Antony plunged under the steaming shower, needing to calm his thoughts even more than he needed to loosen his stiff muscles. Every time the water hit a different bruise it reminded him how lucky he was not to have any broken bones. He breathed in the steam and tried to think. What did Breen's presence mean? Was he there to help them as he kept protesting, or was he trying to prevent their solving the riddle? Or, as seemed most likely, was he merely trying to make time with Felicity?

He was sure Breen hadn't been the robed figure at Bede's World; the American was much taller and slimmer. Nor could he identify him with the shadowy figure he saw crossing the lawn at Whitby. And Brother Matthew had indicated that Breen had been here at St. Antony's all day.

So why was his negative reaction so strong? He hoped it wasn't just jealousy over Felicity's obvious fondness for the man. Although he couldn't deny that was a factor. He certainly couldn't trace it to anything concrete linking Breen to Dominic's death. He had to admit that Jonathan's actions had been nothing but helpful, as Felicity never failed to remind him. Could it be something as simple as Breen reminding him of someone from his past whom he had disliked? Could it be his own guilt confronting him? If so, his response was even more unfair and unreasonable than he thought. And to be fair, perhaps he should give some credence to Felicity's judgment. He sighed as he stepped from the shower and wrapped himself in a thick towel. All right, he would try to give the fellow a chance.

But even such a noble decision failed to bring peaceful rest. Antony tossed and turned a great deal that night, and not all of it due to aching muscles. He dreamed of Bede. Antony was in Bede's small cell watching the scholar move his table closer to the window to catch the rays of morning sun, then glance over the volumes recounting the story he would be chronicling that day in his history of the English church. In his dream, Antony leaned forward, trying to catch the title of the book the scholar held. Was it one Benedict brought from Rome? Was it the same manuscript Ninian had copied and secreted away?

Bede caressed each book on his table—the best library in all England, here, at his fingertips. He breathed a swift prayer of thanksgiving for the care Benedict Biscop had taken to assemble this marvelous collection of books, then placed a clean sheet of parchment on his writing desk, took a freshly trimmed quill and dipped it in the ink pot.

Antony groaned and rolled to his other side as Bede turned to look toward him and the face above the cowl became that of Jonathan Breen. The kind, ascetic features of the scholar monk twisted into a harsh sneer. Antony put out his hand and knocked a book off the monk's table. The crash of a book falling from his own bedside stand woke him. Antony slept no more that night.

Felicity slept through morning prayers, but joined him with shining hair and eyes at breakfast. She looked around the refectory and seemed disappointed that Breen wasn't there. "Was he at prayers?" she asked. Antony shook his head. His night of broken sleep had done nothing to promote the improved attitude he had determined on. And the priory's bitter coffee was doing little to help the situation.

The train back to Jarrow was late. Waiting on the station platform was cold and wet. When the train finally arrived, it was crowded and noisy. It would be just their luck if the director had refused to come in on a Saturday. Or couldn't find the key. Or if the fidgety assistant hadn't even bothered about the message. Or if Jonathan Breen had been there before them and cleaned out the manuscripts. No, he wasn't going to think like that, he reminded himself. And yet, Felicity's chatter about what a nice surprise it was to see Jonathan and how she looked forward to talking to him was a sore test to his resolve.

At least the director, who introduced himself as Kenneth, was at his desk and expecting them. "Yes, yes. Jeremy explained it was urgent. No problem coming in this morning. I had work to catch up on anyway. One always does—I'm sure you know how it is."

He walked as he talked and ushered them up the stairs and into the study room. "Please assure the door is kept closed at all times. Climate control for the collection, you know. Some of them are really quite ancient." He handed them each a pair of white cotton gloves. "Hope these will come close to fitting. Important to keep even the newer documents oil free, you understand. Oh, and here's a supply of pencils. No ink, please."

He unlocked a cabinet. "The papers we borrowed from the sisters at Whitby are on that shelf. These are on loan from the University of Durham and these, as you can see, a much smaller collection, are our own. I apologize that not everything is cataloged yet. We are working on it, but the center is fairly new, you know." Kenneth nodded at the completion of his duty. "There's tea and a kettle just down the hall, but please don't bring drinks in here."

"Oh, yes, we'll be careful. Thank you." Felicity began pulling on her gloves.

Without a word, Antony turned to the volumes from Durham and left the Whitby pile to Felicity. She seemed completely unaffected by his dark mood as she sorted through the papers.

"Oh, these look fascinating. I can't decide where to start. I suppose with whatever looks oldest, if we're on the right track that it's something that would have been available to Ninian in the fifth century."

Antony had the feeling she might burst out whistling or singing at any moment. Frowning, he bent deeper over his volume of Symeon of Durham, a history he was familiar with, but always found worth returning to. Soon Felicity's pencil was scratching rapidly across her notebook page. He glanced over and saw that she was making a sort of chart. In spite of his dour mood he couldn't help asking, "What is it?"

"I can't tell yet. There were two parchments rolled together. This one looks like a letter, and the other seems to be a family tree or something. Royal lineage, perhaps. I thought it might be important because the letter seems to have something to do with the Church Fathers around 155, and the bottom date on the genealogy chart is 597. Wasn't that when Augustine came to England?"

"Mmm, that's right. I'll take a look when you're done."

Without looking up he returned to *Semen of Durham, Libellus de exordio atque procurso istius, hoc est Dunhelmensis, ecclesie*, translating the historian's twelfth-century tract on the church in Durham when the body of St. Cuthbert was still enshrined there in its seventh-century wooden coffin with its engraved images of the Virgin and Child, saints and archangels. One central concern of Symeon's history was to narrate Cuthbert's life and the wanderings of his body from Lindisfarne to its final resting place at Durham. And Symeon was also interested in the gifts which Cuthbert's body attracted—among them the handsome South English manuscript of Bede's life of St. Cuthbert, which was donated to the Cuthbert community by Aethelstan. This included an early witness to the so-called Anglian collection of episcopal lists and genealogies...

"There. That's done. I don't know what it means, though." Felicity pushed her papers across the table to him.

Reluctantly, Antony put Symeon aside and dutifully perused Felicity's work. It was some time before the significance of what he was reading dawned on him. "Felicity, do you realize this is a letter by St. Polycarp?"

"Yes. I thought it was interesting. You don't suppose it's the original, do you?"

"Undoubtedly a copy; they were widely circulated. I've read about this letter. It was highly commended by St. Irenaeus and St. Jerome. In Jerome's day it was widely read, but then most of the copies were lost." Antony ran his fingers up and down his hair twice in excitement. "I've never seen the text before."

"I thought Polycarp's debate with the pope was interesting because it was on some of the same points as the Synod of Whitby," Felicity said.

"Yes, indeed, except it was 500 years earlier." Antony read through the letter with growing excitement, then started over again at the top, forcing himself to go calmly, read carefully. Did this really say what he thought? "This is remarkable! Listen—after Polycarp tells about his journey to Rome and his conference with

Pope Anicetus about the dating of Easter, he says that 'Neither one persuaded the other, so they agreed to each follow their custom without breaking the bonds of charity.'" Antony paused to be very certain of the translation. "Yes. That's amazing. The pope, to testify his respect, asked Polycarp to celebrate the Eucharist in his own papal church."

Felicity leaned forward eagerly. "That's wonderful, isn't it? It's like what you're trying to accomplish in your ecumenical council—getting Christians to take communion together. If Polycarp and the pope could do it, why can't we?"

Antony gave a heartfelt nod, his desire to see that very outcome choking his words. Then he turned to Felicity's second sheet. It did at first appear to be a family lineage. "This is fascinating. It seems to be the genealogy of St. Augustine of Canterbury." But as he studied longer it dawned on him—this wasn't a genealogical pedigree; it was a spiritual pedigree. Here was the ancestry of the ordination of Augustine, the first Archbishop of Canterbury, who came to England in the year 597 to convert the heathen Angli to Christianity under the guidance of Pope Gregory.

"Can you figure out why the two documents were rolled together? Was it just that someone happened to be reading them together?" Felicity asked.

For the first time Antony looked Felicity full in the face, all earlier irritations vanished in the excitement of discovery. "That's what I've been trying to work out. But I don't think it's any accident. I think whoever put these together was trying to tell us something. We need a pointer, though. Something to tell us who or what or when."

"Would this help?" Felicity held out a broken red wax seal. "This held the roll together."

"Felicity! You didn't break the seal on a document, did you?"

"No, of course I didn't. The top piece fell off when I touched it, but it was already broken."

Antony ignored the offended tone in her voice and

concentrated on keeping his hands from trembling as he pushed the pieces of wax together. He felt certain they were onto something important. If he could only figure out what. "*REX TOT BRIT,*" he read the letters stamped in the wax. "King of all Britain." That rang a bell. Yes. He grabbed Felicity's hands in excitement. "Aethelstan! When he defeated the Norse at York, the kings of Scotland and Gwent and the Northumbrian lords swore fealty to Aethelstan. He then had coins minted declaring himself *REX TOT(ius) BRIT(anniae).*"

Felicity squeezed his gloved hands warmly in return, her face alight. "So this must be one of the manuscripts Aethelstan presented to Cuthbert's shrine at Chester-le-Street. Do you have any idea where Aethelstan got them?"

"There's no proof, of course, but I could make a pretty educated guess." Realizing he and Felicity were holding hands across the table, Antony shifted awkwardly to adjust the papers in front of him. "I think there's a very good chance the Polycarp letter was what Ninian had secreted in his cave for safety. Augustine's ordination lineage could easily have been among the documents collected by Benedict Biscop."

"So then the letter would already have been in Cuthbert's shrine with the other treasures the Guardians kept there?"

"That's right. And Aethelstan, who was known for his intellectual accomplishments as well as for his devotion to the church, would have seen the significance and added the second document to make his point."

"That's brilliant! I can't believe you figured all that out."

"Well, there's a lot of guesswork, but it does make sense and follows exactly what we've already uncovered."

"That's great, but—" she paused. "Er—so what was Aethelstan's point, exactly? Aren't you going to explain it to me?"

"Look at Augustine's pedigree." Antony pointed to the name above Augustine's on the chart.

"Aetherius, Bishop of Gaul consecrated Augustine." She obediently pronounced the names as he moved his finger upward.

"Priscus, Nicetus, Sacerdos…" The list went on through thirty-three names. Third from the top was Irenaeus. "Oh, he was one of the Apostolic Fathers, the one who liked Polycarp's letter so much." Antony moved his finger upward. "Pothinus. Polycarp. Oh, Augustine's ordination descended from Polycarp and Irenaeus. That's really cool."

"But look." Antony pointed to the name on the top from which all the ordinations in the list descended.

"'St. John the Evangelist, Holy Apostle'," she read obediently. "Yes, I know. I'm the one who just translated it. That's really amazing to think of the succession going straight back to St. John. But so what?"

"Don't you see? The original English succession descended from John, not from Peter. All ordinations in the Church of England descend from Augustine."

Felicity still looked blank. "Whose ordination descended from St. John, not St. Peter," she said slowly.

"Exactly."

"Oh, that's what this means, then." Felicity indicated a note on the bottom of the original manuscript. "It's sort of a footnote. Obviously added at a different time because the ink and handwriting are different. 'Theodore of Tarsus, first Petrine ABC'," she translated. "Sorry I should have copied that, too."

Antony nodded. "Theodore of Tarsus was Archbishop of Canterbury under Aethelstan. How interesting that he was the first to trace his succession to St. Peter." A huge grin spread across his face. "Do you realize whose handwriting you could be looking at?"

"Whose?"

"Who invented the footnote?"

"The Venerable Bede! I can't believe it. I held that parchment in my own hands." She held out her gloved hands.

"It will all need to be sent to the British Library for authentication, of course. But this find could be earth-shattering."

"How? I agree it's amazing, but how 'earth-shattering'?"

"If the validity of this can be established and is widely accepted, it's the very thing that could bring about unity among churches at communion." Felicity's silence told him he needed to explain further. "It's the concept underlined in Polycarp's letter—those whose apostolic succession is derived from St. Peter could receive communion from those whose apostolic succession is derived from St. John and vice versa. The great schism that has divided the church for centuries could be healed if people could see that more than one lineage is valid—that authentic priesthood is the prerogative of the whole church. That the consecration of the communion elements is valid by Roman Catholic, Anglican, Eastern Orthodox, Lutheran, Methodist, Presbyterian… Who knows how far-reaching this could be?

"Whoever traces their descent from… Thomas, as the Indian church does; James, as the church in Wales does; Philip, Thaddaeus…" In his excitement he stood up and began pacing the floor. At the end he flung his arm out, almost hitting Felicity who was still sitting with a dazed look on her face. He simply couldn't find words for what he felt—elation, relief, profound gratitude. This could be the answer; at least the beginning of the answer for everything he had worked so hard for. A foundation the commission could really build on…

"Antony, I can see this is really wonderful for your church unity work. But do you think it has any bearing at all on Dominic's and Elspeth's murders? Would anyone kill for this?"

He sat down as suddenly as if the wind had shifted course. "Oh, I am a twit, aren't I? Who else would get so excited over such an esoteric point?" He sank back onto his chair.

"No, I didn't mean that. It *is* important. I can see that. It's tremendously important for your unity work. But could it possibly have any bearing on the murders?"

He thought for several moments, then shook his head. "I can't think so. If this became generally accepted practice—complete openness and unity at the Lord's Table—a lot of people would be upset. And a lot of people would lose power and control that they enjoy a great deal. Points scored in the game of ecclesiastical one-upmanship would evaporate. But I can't bring myself to believe that anyone would kill over the prerogatives of apostolic succession in these days. Medieval bishop-princes maybe, but not now."

"Well, there are lots of stories of medieval popes committing murder."

"True. But the days of such power and wealth in the church are long past. This is a very important find. I shall recommend that Kenneth send the manuscripts off to London right away, and I'll take our copies to the Ecumenical Commmission. But I'm afraid it's been a complete waste of time in solving Dominic's murder."

Chapter 25

His excitement drained from him as completely as if he'd fallen down a dark hole. They had worked so hard—following clues all over Northumbria and all the way to Scotland. They had escaped threats and narrowly avoided danger. And what had they accomplished? Perhaps Sister Elspeth would still be alive if they hadn't turned up at her priory. The Ninian Papyrus was an exciting find, if that was what they had found, but it was meaningless for their investigation. Aethelstan's treasure looked promising, but had turned out to be a dead end. Where should they turn next?

He jumped at the touch of Felicity's hand on his arm. He didn't realize he had spoken his question aloud. "Let's take another look at the journal. Maybe we're missing something." Felicity pulled the book from her pocket and handed it to him.

He turned each page slowly, trying to get an overall sense of the jottings as if they had been a continuous writing. At last he sat staring blankly at the faux parchment end paper. "Definitely a theme of treasure and incorruption." He sighed. "As well as an air of peace and confidence—which I wish I could share."

He started to hand the volume back to Felicity when he noticed the lower edge of the end sheet curling away from the back cover. "Oh, I'm afraid this is becoming damaged."

"Little wonder, considering all it's been through." Felicity probed the curl with her thumb. More of the end paper came away. "Wait! There's something under there!" With trembling fingers she pulled out a small triangle of vellum. "Oh, I'm too excited to look. What is it? Is it a treasure map?

Antony took the fragment from her. "It looks very old." He laid it down and pulled on his discarded gloves again before scrutinizing it.

"But what is it? Tell me!"

He turned it over and examined it. Felicity jumped up and ran around the table to stare over his shoulder. "Oh, not a map."

"No, sorry. I'm not sure what it is. It's only a piece of whatever the complete document is."

"It's a kind of triangle, isn't it? What do you call a triangle with no equal sides?"

"Scalene." Antony pointed to the slanted edge where words had been cut through. "Black letter Latin is hard enough to read when it's complete, but we only have half of it."

"Or maybe a third," Felicity suggested.

"I suppose so; why do you say that?"

"Well, a triangle suggests three. There were three Guardians…" She paused, then snatched up the journal. "The triangles! We thought they were just doodles." She turned back through the well-read pages. "See, they're all different. This one is equilateral… This one has two sides equal, but a longer base. Isosceles—right?" A few more pages. "Yes, I knew it! Look. This one is exactly the same shape as the piece we found."

Antony looked carefully, then nodded. "Yes. So whatever this is, each Guardian has—had—one piece of it, and they all have to be together to reveal the secret."

Felicity stared at the piece in front of them. "Well, we're definitely on the right track, but what kind of writing is that? I can't make anything out."

"You're the classicist, but I'd say Gothic script at a glance. Latin, of course."

The words seemed to go every which way on the angled scrap. Words on the longest edge appeared to be upside down until Felicity turned it over. "Oh, I think that's Cursiva. It was often used for writing charters because it was easier to write quickly, especially if the vellum was smooth." She ran her fingers over the back of the fragment. "As this is. Very high quality."

They sat long with their heads together bent over the scrap, turning it one way and then another. At last Antony looked up, stretching his neck. "Circumambient," he pronounced.

"Huh?"

"Writing around. If we had all the pieces together, the words would start in the upper left-hand corner and flow around the outer edge of the paper, working toward the center."

"Why?"

"Isn't it obvious? So that no one piece would make any sense on its own. If the whole point of this brotherhood was to guard a secret, they would hardly want to carry around notes spelling it out."

"It's going to take some time to translate this." Felicity squinted at the left side of the angle, "'Interest in and to... rights and privileges... consecrated in perpetuity...'" She looked up and shook her head. "Oh, it's so exciting and so-o-o frustrating! It's such a fantastic discovery, but we still don't know what it means."

"If there are three of them, I don't expect it's possible to know without recovering the others. And the really dismaying thought is that Sister Elspeth's might have perished with her."

"Or have been found by whoever killed her. This must be what she was killed for." Felicity shivered. "And now we know why our rooms have been searched. I had just assumed they wanted Dominic's journal, but the murderer must have known about this document."

"It's a very scary thought that someone out there is that far ahead of us." The silence in the room seemed to echo the fear.

A fear that Felicity dissipated by jumping to her feet. "I'm starving," she announced. "I simply can't maintain this level of brilliance on an empty stomach."

Antony grinned, more than willing to delay further worry for the moment. "Me too, now that you mention it." He looked at his watch. "Too late to make it back to the priory for lunch. Let's get something next door in Jarrow Hall."

While Felicity tucked the vellum triangle securely back in

its hiding place behind the endsheet, Antony carefully replaced Polycarp's letter and the apostolic succession chart where Kenneth could collect them, then pocketed the copies he had made of them. They crossed the room and Antony locked the door behind them. He turned toward the stairway, but Felicity grabbed his arm. She put her finger to her lips and pointed toward the stairwell.

Was that a shadow of a robed figure on the far wall, or was his imagination playing tricks on him? "Let's take the lift," Felicity said loudly, but continued on toward the stairs.

Antony pulled her back. "Keep talking and go to the lift," he whispered.

Felicity looked as if she was going to argue, then nodded. "I hope they have something good on the menu. Too bad it's Lent. I could go for a thick steak and a slab of chocolate," she babbled her way to the elevator.

Antony darted toward the stairwell. He could hear footsteps descending ahead of him. He all but leapt down the last flight of steps and pushed through the swinging doors with both hands. Across the room, two robed figures sat by the reconstructed wayside well, one of them holding a pilgrim's drinking vessel in both hands. He checked his impulse to accost them when Brother Matthew looked up and greeted him. "Hello, Antony. Have you had a g-good morning? I p-persuaded our guest to extend his retreat to Bede's World."

Breen chuckled and gestured to his attire. "He even managed to get me into costume. Itchy affair. I suppose it's part of the experience, though."

Breen again. Antony bristled. Had he been spying on them all along? Had he escaped Brother Matthew's escort long enough to hold his ear to the door of the manuscript room? Had he heard—Antony opened his mouth to accuse Breen of spying when two other visitors strolled by, wearing the costume robes the museum offered. Was the eavesdropper one of them? Could their enemy possibly have so many innocent-looking faces?

He looked in both directions, wondering where the next ambush might come from. And then he thought—Felicity. He had sent her on alone. If someone had heard their conversation—knew what she was carrying—she was now in far greater danger than before.

He turned and raced toward the elevator, praying he would be in time.

Oh, thank God. The indicator showed the elevator still descending. The bell rang, indicating its arrival. Antony all but threw open his arms to greet her when the door opened and an elderly couple, the gray-haired man leaning on a cane, emerged.

Antony looked each direction frantically. He could see no tall young woman with long golden hair. Where was she? Should he run deeper into the museum? Or to the entry?

Or back upstairs? Had she been seized before she even got in the elevator?

Call the police, that was the thing to do. They couldn't have gotten far, surely. It had only been minutes. But it had taken only seconds to dispatch Elspeth. Praying there were no convenient heights from which Felicity could be pushed, he headed toward the office and a telephone.

And there was Felicity. Chatting with Kenneth. She turned with a smile. "Oh, Antony, Kenneth is so delighted about our find! He'll send—"

"Where have you been? What were you thinking?" Antony grabbed her arm far more roughly than he meant to. "I was frantic. Don't you realize the danger?"

Felicity just looked at him blankly.

"Oh, come on, we need to get back to Durham." So much for their plans for a hot lunch.

And all the way to the station he berated himself. Why had he been so sharp with her? He hadn't even thanked Kenneth. What was the matter with him?

Chapter 26

Felicity opened her mouth to protest, then shrugged and turned obediently toward the train station. She had more important things to think about than her companion's strange moods. Surely this amazing discovery was the key. And yet—and here she could almost understand Antony's sharp temper—they were no closer to the answer.

They knew what their pursuer wanted from them. They knew why Dominic and Elspeth were murdered, didn't they? So why were they no closer to knowing where the treasure was, or who had committed the murders?

Felicity's fingers itched to pull out the vellum and take another crack at the translation, but the train would be pulling into the station in a few minutes, so she simply turned to the journal page marked with the doodle of a scalene triangle. The piece they had found. Did that mean these jottings had particular significance to Dominic?

> *For he did not suffer his Holy One to see corruption.*
> *Even the grave can praise thee, death doth celebrate thee,*
> *Because you will not leave my soul in hell,*
> *Neither will you suffer your beloved saint to see*
> *corruption.*

She read it through three times, then turned to Antony, who hadn't spoken since his outburst at Bede's World. It took her only a second to remind herself that the issues they faced were far greater than any personal tiff. "So, what do you really think—this incorruption stuff—do you *really* believe Cuthbert's body was undecayed?"

He looked at her for a moment. "Um—sorry about that

outburst back there. But I really was so worried when I couldn't find you."

She shrugged. "What outburst?"

"Right. Thanks. Now, I think what you're asking is, do I really believe in miracles? Outside of those recorded in Holy Scripture, that's not always an easy one to answer. But in Cuthbert's case, the evidence is consistent, reported over a period of hundreds of years. The Lindisfarne Gospels exist—executed in thanksgiving for the miracle of Cuthbert's incorruption. His shrine at Durham is intact—and I can't think of any other reason for Henry's thugs to save this one shrine alone. Look at the record: Canterbury, most hallowed pilgrimage site in England—St. Thomas a Becket's bones scattered like a butcher's leavings. The Holy House of Nazareth at Walsingham, second most popular pilgrimage site in Britain—demolished. Glastonbury, hallowed by the very mists of time, some say by the very feet of our Lord—the abbot hung, drawn and quartered, the abbey sold to 'Little Jack Horner'... The list is endless.

"Cuthbert's relics alone were saved. Why? There must have been something very powerful about that body when the coffin was broken open."

"I don't really know that part of the story." And now Felicity was not only ready but anxious for more history.

"Well, then, there's our afternoon's work." Antony got to his feet as the train slowed.

Durham Cathedral and castle riding high on their rocky precipice atop the green wooded hillside came into view. This time it seemed to bring with it a sense of coming to the end of the trail—Durham, the last place on Dominic's pilgrimage and on Cuthbert's. And the last place treasure was amassed around the saint. The answers had to be here if they were to be anywhere.

"Do we need to stop at the priory, or shall we go straight to the cathedral?" Felicity asked as they made their way across the bridge over the River Wear.

Antony paused to look over his shoulder. "I don't want to

sound paranoid, but I really don't feel we can trust anyone. The fewer people who know where we are, the better."

"Right," Felicity said. "So if you can climb this hill and talk at the same time, let's have the history lesson."

"I can do history standing on my head."

"Not going up this hill, you couldn't."

"Too true. So where did we leave Cuthbert—fleeing Chester-le-Street ahead of the Danes?"

"That's it."

"OK," Antony nodded and took a breath.

So for safety, Cuthbert's Folk moved on to the very monastery Cuthbert had once founded at Ripon. After just four months, peace was restored and the monks, now some 500 in number, thought to return to Chester-le-Street. It seemed, however, that Cuthbert disagreed.

At a muddy spot along the River Wear where the river makes a tight U-shaped turn at the base of a high rock plateau, the cart sank in the mud to its axle and would not be budged. One of the monks had a vision of the saint saying that he wanted to be buried at Dunholme. Dunholme? None of them had ever heard of it.

As they pondered, two peasant women passed. "I've lost my cow," one said.

"I just saw it on Dunholme," the other replied.

What a sight it must have been: two peasant women leading, followed by the bishop, the brothers pulling the cart bearing Cuthbert's coffin (which now moved readily), and several hundred robed and tonsured brothers as they crossed the river and wound their way up the steep wooded hill. They found the cow, and at that very spot they laid the body of the saint and built a temporary shelter over it of branches and straw. And so began Durham Cathedral.

The temporary hut was replaced by a wooden building called the White Church.

"Oh, that sounds like Whithorn." Felicity interrupted the

narrative. "Perhaps the monks were commemorating Cuthbert's time there."

"Perhaps." By now they had reached the top of the plateau but instead of heading straight toward the cathedral, Antony turned aside along a narrow road marked Dun Cow Lane. "See, here they are." He pointed to a small carving in the wall: two sturdy women in medieval dress, kerchiefs and aprons, leading a cow between them.

"That's wonderful." Felicity ran her hand over the rough carving and smiled at the squat figures. What would it have been like—standing on that very spot hundreds of years ago with nothing around one but trees and bushes in the company of a single cow and a passel of mud-spattered monks? But so had those simple women made history.

They moved on, and at the top of the winding stone pavement they crossed the bustling market square. "This looks far too medieval not to be a play set." Felicity stopped and watched the hubbub of assorted tourists, students and merchants. "It's just like *Romeo and Juliet*. Don't you just expect Tybalt and Mercutio to spring out and begin dueling in front of us?"

"Well, I hadn't thought of it quite that way, but I'll admit to a certain sense of unreality about the place." Antony looked over his shoulder again. "Don't let that put you off your guard, though. This isn't a play, you know."

He ushered her across the cobbled square to the crowning magnificence of cathedral and castle at opposite ends of the wide green lawn. Behind them the old stone buildings straggled higgledy-piggledy up and down this city of hills.

As they approached the great north door Felicity paused, craning her neck backward, attempting to see to the top of the twin towers. Antony held out his hand. "'The Cathedral church of Christ, Blessed Mary the Virgin, and St. Cuthbert, of Durham.' Quite a mouthful, but as it should be. Cuthbert's name was removed at the Dissolution and restored only a couple of years ago."

"Oh." A pleased smile spread over Felicity's face. "That's wonderful."

"Yes, finally, after 465 years Cuthbert has been given his rightful honor again."

Turning back to the door, they were greeted by the giant lion's head Sanctuary Knocker. Felicity grabbed the heavy iron ring with both hands. "Sanctuary, sanctuary!" She claimed the ancient right of refuge for those fleeing from the law.

"Perhaps it's too bad the custom's no longer in effect. I could use it if the police don't find a more likely suspect." Antony's spoke lightly, but a grim note underneath made Felicity wish she hadn't made the joke.

Inside the cathedral, though, all other thoughts fled from her mind as she caught her breath at the magnificence of the nave. "Those pillars! They're mammoth!" She realized she was whispering; it seemed the appropriate reaction to being so dwarfed by her surroundings.

"It's all the original Norman building. The pillars are eleven feet in diameter. Notice how each pair is carved in a different design, getting progressively more intricate as they come closer to the altar."

Felicity started to move forward, mesmerized by the power of its beauty, but Antony called her back. "We'll go up in a minute, but there's someone you need to meet first."

"What? I thought we were avoiding people?"

"Not this one." Antony turned to the right, away from the great nave and high altar, to a room marked Galilee Chapel. "This is where medieval pilgrims to St. Cuthbert's shrine gathered before making their final way to the saint's tomb."

It was like entering a wood on a winter evening. The slender pillars supporting the zigzag arches of the chapel gave the effect of bare, leafless trees. To the right of the altar was a single tomb. Felicity moved over to look, then gave a small cry that echoed among the low, rounded arches. "Oh. It's Bede!" She read the plaque: "'The father of English learning' died 735."

Felicity moved aside as they were joined in the chapel by a father bringing his two small daughters to the *prie-dieu* and giving them instruction in kneeling. When they moved on, she knelt and read Bede's prayer calligraphied there: "I implore you, good Jesus, that as in your mercy you have given me to drink in with delight the words of your knowledge, so of your loving kindness you will also grant me one day to come to you, the fountain of all wisdom, and to stand for ever before your face. Amen."

Too overcome to speak, she walked slowly to the back of the chapel where Antony stood waiting for her. Looking into his eyes, just crinkled at the corners, she thought, *He has the kindest face I've ever seen.* He reached out and took her hand, and together they walked down the great nave of Durham Cathedral, past the spiral-carved pillars, past the chevron-carved pillars, past the argyle-carved pillars, under the central tower, down the center of the ornate quire with its inlaid marble floor and richly carved pews, around the high altar standing before a delicate screen looking far too fragile to be carved of stone—a sharp contrast to the Herculean strength of the pillars—and up the stairs to Cuthbert's shrine.

They were now behind the delicate stone altar screen which formed a wall separating them from the body of the cathedral. In the center of the small chapel a rectangular slab of green marble was embedded in the floor, engraved with gold letters: CUTHBERTUS. Felicity sank to her knees once more on the red leather cushion of a *prie-dieu* and read the prayer inscribed at the foot of the tomb:

> *Borne by his faithful friends*
> *From his loved home of Lindisfarne*
> *Here, after long wanderings,*
> *Rests the body of St. Cuthbert.*
> *In whose honour William of St. Carileph*
> *Built this cathedral church…*

From the tomb her eyes were drawn upward to the gleaming red, blue and gold tester hanging above the tomb. Christ in glory, youthful, with clean-shaven face, was surrounded by six-winged seraphim and the four Evangelists. "That's Comper," Antony said.

"Oh. I thought it was Christ."

Antony laughed. "It is. Sorry, I meant Sir Ninian Comper. He designed the tester in 1949. He's one of my favorite artists."

"Oh. It's gorgeous." Favorite artists. Suddenly she wondered what else she didn't know about this man. But then her attention was drawn back to the center focus of the room—the polished green stone marking the spot that had been the center of centuries of adoration and conflict. "So Cuthbert finally found a home."

She followed Antony's lead and moved around to the side of the tomb, then made herself comfortable on one of the benches covered with embroidered hassocks as Antony continued the story.

In 1093, the foundation stone of the great cathedral was laid. In August of 1104, Cuthbert's relics were to be translated to the new shrine. It was decided that the prior and nine of the brothers should first open the coffin and examine the body. The brothers were filled with fear and awe. They fasted all night. Then, whilst chanting prayers of devotion, the lid was wrenched off the coffin. Inside was another, wooden coffin, carved with figures of saints and apostles. They hesitated to go further until one of the monks, renown for his piety, told them sharply to get on with it. They lifted the wooden lid. The chapel was filled with a sweet odour like the burning of a rare incense. And there was Cuthbert, lying on his side as if comfortably asleep.

Overcome, the monks prostrated themselves on the floor and recited the seven penitential psalms. "Out of the depths have I cried unto thee, O Lord... I wait for the Lord, my soul doth wait, and in his word do I hope... Let Israel hope in the Lord, for with the Lord there is mercy, and with him is plenteous redemption, And he shall redeem Israel from all his iniquities."

Felicity looked around the room. She felt as if she could see the awestricken monks cowering in the shadows. The air still seemed to vibrate with their ancient chant.

> *They crawled back to the coffin to examine the other marvels it contained, even removing the body so they could see everything properly. When the brothers reported what they saw, however, there was much criticism, particularly from some of the abbots who had come from other parts of the diocese for the Feast of the Translation. In order to placate them, the coffin was opened again. One of the abbots went so far as to shake the saint's head, tweak his ear, tug at all his joints and lift him to a sitting position in the coffin. At length he announced his findings: "The body is definitely dead."*
>
> *And so, Cuthbert was allowed to rest for 433 years. In medieval times, the tomb was made of costly green marble, guilded with gold. There were four seats where pilgrims, especially the sick and lame, could rest to pray. Many of those who received aid left lavish gifts, and this became one of the richest monuments in England. On Cuthbert's Day, 20 March, and other festivals, the cover of the shrine was raised. The heavy oaken cover was lifted by a rope attached to a pulley. The rope was hung with silver bells, and the sound of their ringing drew people in the church to prayer.*

Antony stopped and smiled. "One of my favorite footnotes, though, is the visit of William the Conqueror who made a detour to Durham whilst he was with his troops subduing the North. He came to visit the shrine personally, but not to make obeisance. He began by demanding that the tomb be opened, and threatened to behead all the Durham clergy if the body should prove to have decayed. The community grudgingly began preparations to open the tomb, but William was suddenly stricken with fear. He dashed out of the church, mounted his horse, and galloped without stopping until he had crossed into Yorkshire.

"And so St. Cuthbert continued to be venerated undisturbed and the shrine enriched until 1538 when Henry VIII's commissioners arrived."

"And?" He couldn't stop now. This was the important part.

Antony shook his head. "The records are sketchy, but a document known as the *Rites of Durham*, first published in 1593, includes what purports to be an eyewitness account."

Three commissioners, Dr. Ley, Dr. Henley and Mr. Blythman, brought with them a goldsmith to remove the gold, silver and precious stones from the casket. Under the gold, the smith found a chest strongly bound in iron. The commissioners commanded him to smash it open. The goldsmith took a great hammer and shattered the casket with a mighty swing.

"Alas, I have broken one of his legs," the goldsmith cried. Henley ordered him to throw down the bones, but the goldsmith replied that he could not because they were kept together by skin and tissue.

Dr. Ley went up to see if this was true and reported back to Henley that Cuthbert was "lying whole."

Henley refused to believe him and repeated his order, "Cast down the bones!"

Ley told Henley to come up and see for himself. Henley did so. He handled the body roughly but found it was indeed whole and undecayed. This made a problem for the commissioners. They could hardly scatter the bones of an intact body, so they commanded the monks to take the body into a vestry where it could be kept safe until the king decided what should be done, and they departed for London.

Felicity sat, blinking, trying to make sense of the story. "And the body? The treasure?"

"Ah, that's the rub, isn't it? The conventional line is that the commissioners returned, took the silver, gold and jewels with them and the body was reinterred above the high altar, where it rests today."

"But?" Felicity thought Antony didn't sound convinced.

"But we know the commissioners didn't take all the treasure. Some of it is still on display in the Cathedral Treasury."

"And the body?" Felicity shook her head, her long, blonde hair brushing against her shoulders. "I just can't get my mind around the idea of the body remaining uncorrupted. Are you telling me a man who died more than 1,300 years ago is lying under that marble as whole today as if he died yesterday?"

"Definitely not. No self-respecting Victorian could have been expected to leave something like that unexplored. The marble stone was raised once more on 17 May 1827 by James Raine, the cathedral librarian."

Felicity leaned forward. "And?"

"A coffin, presumably made in 1542, was uncovered; inside was another coffin, probably the one made in 1104. Finally the seventh-century wooden coffin, sadly broken. In the coffin, Raine found a skeleton. The bare bones were clothed in what had been glorious robes. He took out the cache of valuables buried with the body and reburied the bones."

Felicity felt oddly deflated. It was the sensible answer: the body decayed, the treasure in a museum. So why did the sensible answer seem so unsatisfying? "So that's the mystery solved?"

As soon as she asked the question, she understood her disease with it. It solved nothing.

Chapter 27

"It could be left there, certainly. And most people do. But there are those who believe that while the monks were awaiting the king's directive as to what should be done, they hid Cuthbert's body in another part of the cathedral and substituted another corpse."

Felicity thought for several moments. "That is what careful guardians would do, isn't it? For all they knew Henry's henchmen would return with orders to destroy the body. They couldn't take that chance, could they?" Her voice picked up excitement as she spoke, "So they took a body—maybe one of their own who had died recently—and vested it and left some distinctive artifacts in the coffin to make it look good, and—" She lurched to a stop. "And what? What would they have done next?" Then another thought struck her. "You know what I think—I'll bet most of the other monks thought that was the authentic body. I'll bet only the three Guardians knew. The secret would have been too dangerous to share among very many."

"Very good thinking. I tend to agree."

"That still doesn't tell us where the body is, though, does it?"

"I looked at Butler again in the priory library. His exact words are 'There is another tradition, according to which St. Cuthbert's remains still lie interred in another part of the cathedral, known only to three members of the English Benedictine Congregation, who hand on the secret before they die.'"

"So, the remaining Guardian would know. If only we knew who that is." She paused. "But even if we did know, would it solve anything? It's a fascinating question, but would anyone kill for the answer—either to protect it or to learn it?"

Antony shook his head. "Probably not just for the body, but think—if they were able to squirrel away even that little bit of the treasure that's now in the treasury—"

"They might have been able to secrete away more!" Felicity interrupted. Now her mind was racing with possibilities. "And it might still be in the coffin with the real body. And only the one living Guardian would know its whereabouts. And it could be a fortune worth killing for! Gold, jewels, medieval art..." She stopped as a broad grin spread over Antony's face. "What?"

"Got your attention, didn't I?"

"You always had my attention. But I honestly think we could be on to something. I mean, we really do need to follow this lead."

"Yes. I agree. But where?"

"Well, if Butler says 'in another part of the cathedral,' that's a possibility, isn't it? I mean, this is the original building, not like the church at Chester-le-Street that was rebuilt so they found the hidden hoard during construction."

Antony spread out his hands. "All very logical, Miss Howard. It's just an awfully big building. Where do we start?"

She looked around. "Big" didn't begin to describe the oldest and finest Norman cathedral in England: 500 feet in length (was that something like two football fields? She wasn't sure), 200 feet at the widest (more than a football field, right? People always compared things to football fields, but Felicity didn't know the dimensions of a football field.). And then there was the monastery: library, cloisters, deanery, chapter house, kitchen... the list seemed endless. "Well, I suppose the most obvious would be the crypt."

He shook his head. "No crypt under the cathedral, it's built right on the stone. There is an undercroft under some of the monastery, but that part was all so heavily restored in Victorian times that it's hard to imagine old secrets, let alone an uncorrupted body, still lurking there."

Felicity sighed; she wasn't ready to admit defeat. "Restored. But was it excavated?"

"I don't know how extensively, but I recall reading that the refectory, which would be the whole south side, was excavated in the 1960s."

Felicity threw up her hands. "OK. Your turn to suggest something. If you were going to hide a body in Durham Cathedral, where would it be?"

Antony got to his feet and began pacing around the small chapel. After several minutes he spoke. "Well, I'd want a place of easy access, because I wouldn't know if Henry's men might show up at any moment. And I would want a place of great sanctity, a place where special worship took place, even if the faithful didn't know who was among their number, so to speak."

"Under the high altar?"

"Yes, but that might be too obvious. Something more subtle." He continued to pace. Suddenly he stopped, a broad grin on his face. "The Altar of Repose. Now that would be a perfect clue—almost a pun."

Felicity jumped to her feet. "Great. Where is it? *What* is it?"

"On Maundy Thursday a great mass is held to commemorate, almost reenact, the events leading up to Christ's crucifixion. There is a foot washing ceremony, just like he did with his disciples in the Upper Room, and then Holy Communion is celebrated remembering that that is the night on which our Lord instituted his Supper before going out to pray and being arrested. Extra bread is reserved to be served at three o'clock at the Good Friday service the next day because no elements are consecrated on the day when Christ is in the tomb."

"Right. A very ancient practice, I've heard of it."

"Yes, at least as early as the fourth century in Jerusalem, but probably much earlier. It could even be a practice carried on since the first generation of Christians."

"So?"

"So at the end of the Maundy Thursday service, the consecrated bread is carried in stately procession to the Altar of Repose—an altar that has been prepared in another part of the church, usually banked with flowers and candles. The faithful watch and pray before the altar all night until the host is taken to the high altar to be distributed at the Good Friday service."

Felicity nodded. "Yes, like Christ asked his disciples in the Garden of Gethsemane, 'Can't you watch with me one hour?'"

"That's right. So since the Altar of Repose is such a special place, it strikes me that would be a wonderful place to hide a body."

"Yes!" Felicity caught the vision. "Just think of the secret enjoyment the three Guardians would get from preparing the Altar of Repose every year at Holy Week, knowing they were really decking the tomb of their beloved saint. So, where is it?"

Antony led the way down the north quire aisle to a lovely, secluded chapel in the transept. "The Gregory Chapel," he said.

"For Gregory the Great?"

"No, St. Gregory Nazianzus, one of the Fathers of the Church." Antony pointed. "There he is, in the window."

Felicity stood for some time, her neck craning upward, studying the figures in each of the six lights of the window. To the left of the center was the Virgin and Child. To the right—she grabbed Antony's arm and pointed. "Look! That's St. Cuthbert! That must be a clue. What a clever way of marking a tomb!"

Antony looked doubtful and pointed to the brass plaque stating that the window was installed in 1875. For a moment Felicity was silenced. "But no—it still could be a clue. If the Guardians at that time had the window put up."

"Possible. Just possible." Looking around to make sure they were unobserved, Antony lifted the length of Lenten sackcloth covering the altar, and began examining the rectangular carved stone in detail, running his hand over the entire surface. At last he stood. "It appears to be seamless. If there is a body in there—"

"The top," Felicity whispered urgently.

"What?"

"The top of the altar. If this is really a sarcophagus, the lid would lift off."

Antony put both hands on the edge of the thick stone mensa and pushed with all his might. Did it move the slightest fraction?

"May I be of help, Father?" The voice of the tall, blue-robed verger was icily polite.

Antony started, but recovered quickly. "Oh, thank you." He held out his hand. "I lecture in church history, and I was just explaining to my student here the tradition of carving a cross into the mensa and embedding a relic in it. Perhaps you can give us some background on the history of this particular altar?"

"It would be customary to apply to the dean and chapter—"

"Oh, yes, I quite understand. As a matter of fact, I'm sure the dean would want to know that the mensa seems to be unstable." Antony gave it another sharp shove with all his strength. This time it definitely moved a tiny bit.

"What? Surely not. I can assure you, the fabric of this cathedral and all its furnishings are given the best maintenance possible."

"I'm certain they are. That's why I thought this should be reported." Antony started to push again, but the verger rushed forward and grabbed his hands.

"Wait! This must be properly looked into."

In a matter of a few minutes he had summoned another verger and two workmen. The second verger set up a screen to protect the altar from public view and the workmen set about their task. Felicity held her breath, moving into the shadows of a carved pillar to make herself invisible.

"'E's right. Whole top's loose." The burly man at one end rubbed his hands on his overall, then gripped the altar top again. When his partner grasped the other end with equal strength, Felicity had to put her hands over her mouth to keep from crying out in anticipation. Would the uncorrupted body of St. Cuthbert, hidden away since the Reformation, be the next thing they were to see?

The grating of stone scraping across stone echoed in the chapel. Felicity held her breath in anticipation and leaned forward to look. Standing on tiptoes, she held on to Antony's shoulder to keep from overbalancing as the workmen lifted the stone.

Disappointment and frustration choked her at the sight of the empty stone vault.

"Right. We'll get that resealed first thing in the morning. 'Ave no fear. Wouldn't do for some passer-by to knock it about." The workmen were already clearing away their tools, the vergers redressing the altar. Felicity felt as cold and empty as the stone vault before her.

The verger moved away with a backward glance at Antony. "I don't think that fellow trusts me," Antony said as he led the way from the chapel.

They sat in wooden chairs in the nave. "I was so sure we had it," Felicity said. "What do we try next? This is a huge place." As she looked around her, she thought of the church of St. Mary and St. Cuthbert in Chester-le-Street. "Could he be under the floor of the cathedral someplace?" The thought was a daunting one. "Of course, in books the characters would hide themselves in the cathedral and sneak around at night, digging up paving stones. And get hit on the head just as they find a valuable cache."

"Right." Antony chuckled. "That doesn't strike me as being terribly practical. Besides the fact that we have no tools and no clue where to start chiseling, I can't think of a quicker way to wind up in the hands of the very authorities we're trying to avoid." He paused. "But, yes, there are a few burials in the floor—not as many as in most cathedrals, though. Most of the early Saxon and Norman bishops are buried in the Chapter House, with a burial ground of the monks and friars outside behind that. The early bishops chose burial there rather than in the cathedral itself because they did not regard themselves as worthy enough to be interred in close proximity to St. Cuthbert."

Felicity brightened. "Ah, now we're getting somewhere! Besides the fact that the Guardians would have been aware that

Henry's vandals might have left spies behind to watch them, it really isn't very likely the Guardians would have had the time, or even the skill, to move any of the stones of the cathedral floor to hide a body and then replace the intricate tiles and mosaics over them, is it?" She looked around at the beauty of the floor under her feet. Then another thought struck her. "But what about the matter of unconsecrated ground? Is the whole cathedral consecrated for burial? I don't know much about those things…" Her voice trailed off.

"The cathedral would be consecrated, yes. But not necessarily other monastery buildings. And Butler says 'another part of the *cathedral*.' The monastery would have been distinct from the cathedral."

"I suppose it all depends on how literal, or reliable, one can expect the rumor to be. Or even how precise Butler was." Felicity felt the weight of centuries on her shoulders. "It's all so nebulous."

She looked around, daunted by the vastness of the structure. Could a body in a coffin have been hoisted aloft, perhaps with a system of ropes and pulleys, to be hidden even somewhere on the roof?

Or how thick were the walls? Three feet? Maybe even six? Room enough, surely, to secrete a body into the fabric of the building. Maybe she had been wrong to assume the Guardians would have had limited time, skill and tools at their disposal.

Was any repair work being done on the cathedral at the time Henry's men were there? Or a new chapel being added? That would have made their job easy.

"Where do we begin?" It was more an expression of despair than a real question.

As always, Antony had the logical answer. "At the beginning, perhaps? The beginning of our involvement, that is."

Just then a group of schoolchildren, all in glowing purple shirts and black trousers and skirts, following their teacher in an obedient crocodile, stopped at the crossing of the transept just in front of where Felicity and Antony sat, and gazed upward at the central tower. "Now, see, children," the teacher pointed, "that is called a lantern—"

Antony and Felicity exchanged smiles and made their way back to the quiet of Cuthbert's shrine. "Now," Antony said. "Starting at the beginning, we assume Dominic gave you his journal because he feared someone would attempt to steal his piece of the document…"

"I wonder what tipped him off?"

"Perhaps he became aware of someone following him? Or someone asked him a question that was meant to sound casual, but seemed suspicious to him? Or maybe—"

Felicity cut in. "The thing is, whatever the secret is, he entrusted it to me. And I can't let him down. I have to figure this out." She pulled the journal from her pocket, but didn't open it. She placed her hand on it, almost as if feeling for vibrations that could reveal something. "'The secret of Cuthbert.'" She sighed. "*What is* the secret of Cuthbert?

"It could be his burial place, couldn't it? I mean, we've thought all along it was something like treasure or a manuscript, but maybe it's a place."

Antony quoted the now-familiar line from the journal: "'Cuthbert the beloved lies dead and buried… neither did his flesh decay'." He made his characteristic pass through his hair with a ragged motion. "It has to be significant that Dominic insists on Cuthbert's incorruption."

"When he would have known all about the 1827 exhumation," Felicity finished his thought for him.

"Exactly."

They sat in glum silence as two women entered the chapel, perhaps mother and daughter, Felicity guessed. The mother, in a long black coat, stood at the back of the room, making quick jottings in a notebook. The younger woman, about Felicity's own age, knelt at the *prie-dieu*. She knelt for so long, so deep in prayer, back erect, hands folded, eyes closed, that Felicity wondered what she was praying for so earnestly at Cuthbert's tomb. Was she, in the great cathedral built around his relics, repeating the work he had carried out in his hermitage on Inner Farne? Was she wrestling for the soul of her nation—that the powers of darkness would be held back for her generation as they were for Cuthbert's?

When the visitors left, Felicity turned to Antony. "Maybe we're being too literal. Maybe that was the incorruption Dominic means." She pointed to where the young woman had just knelt. "The fresh witness of faith to every generation. It doesn't really matter what's in the tomb, does it? It's what's in the hearts of the people."

"Yes." Antony didn't seem as impressed with her symbolic interpretation as she had hoped. "Maybe. But maybe Dominic means to drive home the point that the body *wasn't* decayed— that those who believe Butler aren't nutters."

"Well, we know he was right about there being three Guardians, so he may be right about the alternate burial, too. Does anyone besides Butler question the authenticity of the bones?"

Antony nodded. "A few. I briefly refreshed my memory on a couple of books after I dug up the dirt on Bishop Egleric and Aethelstan's treasury. The Victorian exhumation was challenged by the nineteenth-century historian John Lingard, who argued there was cause for doubting that the body found was that of St. Cuthbert. Archbishop Eyre, another Victorian, contended that the *coffin* found was undoubtedly that of the saint, but that the body had been removed and other remains substituted."

"Wow, you're giving me shivers. That's just like we speculated. How reliable is this Lingard?"

Antony smiled. "Well, none other than the celebrated historian Lord Acton said: 'Lingard never gets anything wrong.' I guess that's what we're here to find out."

"Where do we start?"

Antony glanced at his watch. "Well, we can start with having a cup of tea in the Undercroft restaurant, then have a careful look around the cathedral and the treasury until closing time."

"And then?"

"The Chapter House is off limits to the public. We could probably get permission to visit it, but that could take days. Maybe those fictional characters of yours had the right idea. I'm thinking it would be most expeditious to secrete ourselves somewhere until after Evensong and have a snoop around on our own."

"After our friendly neighborhood vergers have gone home? Sounds good. Especially the tea." Felicity was on her feet and moving. She hadn't realized she was starving until she confronted the Undercroft Restaurant's abundant selection: scones, flapjack, cherry slices, shortbread, salmon sandwiches, lemon bars… She wanted one of each, but she contented herself with a scone and a sandwich.

While they ate they consulted a floor plan of the cathedral Antony had picked up at the information desk. He traced the vast, intricate pattern with his forefinger. "There are endless nooks and crannies. We should consider each one carefully."

"That will take hours." Felicity swallowed a bite of scone piled high with strawberry jam and clotted cream.

"Well, we'll do what we can. I suppose we can continue tomorrow after morning Eucharist if we need to."

Felicity blinked. Yes, tomorrow was Sunday—how could a whole week have gone so fast since they were at Bamburgh? And how could they still have so many unanswered questions? She counted on her fingers—was it possible? Only three days left until St. Cuthbert's Day, when Antony was scheduled to lead the meeting of the Ecumenical Commission. How dreadful if he were unable to attend and present his stunning new argument for Eucharistic unity because he was still hiding out from the police.

"So, what's the plan?" She tried to sound encouraging.

Antony's excited, little boy grin was her reward. "The tricky bit is trying to figure out where to hide ourselves. The cathedral is undoubtedly alarmed, so our best chance would be to slip into one of the private areas. If we're lucky, the bookshop will be busy just at closing time and we could slip through this door," he pointed to the map, "into the Chapter Library. Then when all is quiet, just make our way around the corner into the Chapter House."

Felicity nodded, amused at his enthusiasm for the cloak-and-dagger drama. "Great, but first—the treasury?" It would be a good way to pass the time until the real work could begin.

They went around the corner from the restaurant and paid the admission to the treasury, making their way quickly to the innermost section which displayed the oldest treasures, those related to St. Cuthbert himself. Antony guided the tour, pointing first to a display of delicately detailed gold and red silk embroidered vestments: stole, maniple and girdle. "These are the vestments King Aethelstan presented when he visited the shrine in Chester-le-Street."

"They're amazing. Such intricate stitches. I can't imagine making tiny pictures of the prophets and apostles in needlework. And to think they've survived more than a millenium."

Antony moved to the next case. "Yes. And this 'Earth and Ocean' silk from Constantinople was probably given to the shrine by King Edmund."

But Felicity was bending over a comb, cut from a single slab of ivory with teeth on both sides. "Look—the card says that this comb is believed to have been used in tending Cuthbert's body! I suppose the Guardians would have combed his hair each time the casket was opened." It was so intimate, so fresh. As personal a detail as the comb and lipstick she left on a shelf at the priory that morning.

They moved on and Antony pointed to a small square of wood encased in silver. In spite of the crumbling of the silver, it was possible to make out most of the engraved crosses decorating it. Felicity bent until her nose was almost touching the glass case. "'*in Honorem s Petrv*,'" she read. "In honor of St. Peter."

Antony nodded. "That is thought to be the portable altar St. Cuthbert used for consecrating the sacrament on his indefatigable journeys around Northumberland as a bishop." Felicity could picture it: the saintly man holding the little altar with the host on it in his left hand, his right raised in blessing, communicants gathered around him with their heads bowed.

"Oh, this is beautiful." Felicity pointed to a small gold cross of extremely delicate work, set with gleaming garnets. "'St. Cuthbert's Pectoral Cross,'" she read. "Amazing. He actually wore this as bishop? It makes me feel so close to him."

"Yes, as does this." Antony indicated another glass case containing wooden fragments reassembled to form a coffin. The oak boards were covered with incised decorations. They walked slowly around the case, identifying the symbols and figures.

"Oh, here's an ox and an eagle and a man and... Yes, the four evangelists surrounding Christ."

Antony nodded. "Yes, and here are the twelve apostles."

"And the Virgin and Child."

"And the seven archangels. At least, there were originally seven, although some are missing now."

"And this is the very coffin the monks of Lindisfarne made for Cuthbert and carried all over the north of England and clear up to Ninian's Cave at Whithorn? The one that rested at Chester-le-Street for more than a century? The one that rode the ox cart and stuck in the mud until Cuthbert's Folk followed the two women looking for their cow at Dunholme? The very one Henry's vandals smashed at the Reformation?" Felicity's voice took on an increasing note of awe with each recounting of the story. They had walked through it all; experienced the journey as completely as was possible, looking for every detail of evidence for the story. And what had they learned?

She felt much closer to Cuthbert's time than her own. The details of past centuries seemed more vivid than those of a few days ago. They knew the names of Henry's malefactors, but not of the perpetrators of the crimes at Kirkthorpe and Whitby. And they were running out of leads. The story was ended, but not completed.

What would she do when this was over? Could she just pick up and go back to sitting in classes? She didn't know where she belonged. Felicity twiddled a loose strand of hair as she thought. How was Antony feeling about the future after all they'd been through? They had shared dreams and nightmares, faced danger, seen death together. How could they ever be the same?

And what had she learned? Not about history or about Dominic, but about life—about the world? She hesitated to admit it, it went counter to all her best modern thoughts, but she had to admit that evil in the world was a real force—far beyond the human injustice she had blamed everything on. But had she learned anything from this up-close and personal experience that could help her explain—much less than deal with—this malign presence?

Chapter 28

Felicity was still questioning when the guard came to tell them that the treasury was closing for Evensong. The first angelic notes floated to the back of the nave from the quire as they entered from the cloister:

> O Lord, Open our lips,
> And our mouth shall show forth thy praise.
> O God, make speed to save us.
> O Lord, make haste to help us.

Felicity's heart repeated the words as a prayer. They were in desperate need of help if they were to complete their quest. They made their way back into the cathedral, but instead of taking a seat they walked, reverently, quietly down the south aisle, past the font, up the north aisle, entering the Gregory Chapel once again—this time not focusing solely on the altar, but noting carefully every monument, every irregularity in the wall or floor, searching for any cranny that could have held a sacred body undiscovered for four and a half centuries.

The words of the chanted psalms carried them forward on every step, marking a pace for their careful inspection. It was like a pilgrimage of its own, as walking a labyrinth can be a mini-pilgrimage. In the corner of the transept, Antony led the way up a flight of curving, stone steps to the crossing where they could look down on the quire. "My soul doth magnify the Lord and my spirit rejoices in God my Saviour," the choir began Mary's great hymn of praise. The dean stepped forward with swinging thurible and censed the altar. Clouds of spicy-scented smoke billowed heavenward. It made Felicity homesick for the peace and security of the services she had attended daily at Kirkthorpe. The daily office had seemed such a routine bore to her, but now she longed for that very order and tranquility.

When the reading of the second lesson began, Antony touched her arm and led the way down the stairs on the other side of the crossing. They came out into a chapel commemorating Durham's Light Infantry as the choir sang, "Lord, now lettest thou thy servant depart in peace…"

At the conclusion of the prayers and anthem, the organ pealed forth with Buxtehude's *Toccata*. "Time to be getting to the book store; they won't stay open long after the service," Antony said.

Once they were in the shop crammed with books and souvenirs, including reproductions of St. Cuthbert's pectoral cross, Felicity could ask in a hushed whisper, while pretending to shop, "So what do you think? Did you see any place likely?"

"No place and every place." Antony's grin was rueful. "Certainly nothing obvious. And yet, who can say what's behind any of these ancient stones?"

"That's the way I felt, too. I guess I'd hoped we might find some secret inscription, or something might give off some sort of emanation." She shook her head. "And then most of the monuments and memorials seemed to be too modern."

"A lot of Victoriana. They were great on restoration. Sir George Gilbert Scott did a lot of work on refurbishing."

Felicity sighed. It seemed the best they could do, to assume that the architect of the Gothic Revival and all those who had worked on the fabric of the cathedral through the centuries would have noticed a hastily dug grave under a quickly replaced stone. And yet…

"Now." Antony nudged her and nodded toward the doorway covered by a rose curtain. Felicity looked around. They were alone in the room. Taking a quick breath, she ducked behind the curtain, praying she wouldn't run smack into a canon of the cathedral, or worse, set off an alarm. *I'll say I'm looking for the ladies room,* she thought. Bumbling Americans were usually treated kindly.

In the library, pale evening light filtered through the tall traceried and leaded windows lining the south wall. Beyond the stacks of books, the room opened out to a pleasant space with work tables. Felicity stopped short when she realized a reading lamp was switched on over a pile of books on one of the tables. She barely missed stepping on Antony's toe as she retreated, pointing to the work space that was undoubtedly to be reoccupied momentarily. Antony nodded and reached for the first volume his hand found. Bending over the dusty tome, he pointed to a random passage and began muttering about how revealing that insight was as he led the way to a table, seated himself and indicated Felicity should do the same, never once lifting his eyes from the book. Felicity nodded gravely, and took a pencil and sheet of paper from her pocket as if making notes.

A few moments later a small, bald man in a black cassock emerged from the stacks at the far end of the room and resumed his study. Still appearing deeply absorbed in his tome, Antony stood and walked the length of the room. The studious monk never looked up. Antony placed the book on a shelf before exiting into the cloisters. Halfway along the east walkway, the door to the Chapter House stood ajar. "Just as I hoped," Antony murmured. "The alarms aren't on in the nonpublic areas—yet."

Felicity let her breath out. It felt like the first time she'd breathed in hours.

"Pity we didn't have more time in that library, though," Antony said. "It's a direct descendant from the medieval Benedictine house. In the unlikely event Cuthbert's Guardians had left a written record of their shenanigans, this is where it would probably be."

"But wouldn't the later guardians have known and taken care to hide that, too?"

Antony nodded. "Most likely. But you never know."

Felicity's eyes adjusted to the gloom and she looked around the Chapter House which served now, as in medieval times, as a meeting place for discussions regarding the day to day running of the cathedral. The ancient glass in the windows forming the curve of the apse let in just enough of the fading eastern light for them to make out the names on the tombs. "Walcher," Antony read. "He was the first Norman bishop. He started the construction of the monastic buildings before being murdered by an angry mob in Gateshead." He pointed to another. "His successor, Bishop Carileph, founded the monastery and built the cathedral."

"In honor of St. Cuthbert. It's on the plaque in his shrine." Felicity nodded and moved on to the next marker. "'Ranulf Flambard,'" she read, tracing the deeply carved letters on the marble slab, then moved on. "'Hugh le Puiset.'" She stopped and gazed around the room. These were the most important men in the cathedral's history. Surely this would be a likely place for Cuthbert to have been buried. She longed to shift the chairs and table, roll up the woven carpet, and examine the paving stones. "Antony—" She stopped as her eyes focused on the engraved brass plaque he was studying. "The original medieval chapter house was partially demolished in 1796. It was rebuilt as a memorial to Bishop Lightfoot in 1895."

"Oh." Her hopes deflated once again. "Another Victorian restoration." She sank into a heavily carved oak chair. "It's hopeless."

Antony put his finger to his lips. Footsteps coming toward them from the cloister. Felicity looked around for a place to hide, but to her amazement, Antony strode to the door and stepped out into the cloister. "Good evening, Father. Reading finished for the night?"

Felicity peered past him and recognized the ancient cleric from the library.

"Never done, Father. Just taking these to my room." He paused with a guilty look. "I left a list on the librarian's desk. I'll have them back first thing in the morning."

"Yes, yes. I'm certain there won't be any problem." Antony beckoned for Felicity. "We'll just walk out with you, Father. Staying at the college, are you?"

Their impromptu escort produced his swipe card and opened the door, much to Felicity's relief. She suddenly realized they had given no thought to getting out without setting off the alarms.

In spite of their fortunate exit, however, her earlier sense of disappointment returned as they made their way back to St. Antony's. She merely shook her head when Antony asked if she wanted to join him for Compline. What was the use? What was the use of anything? What had it all been for? All their running and clever skulking and looking. They had learned nothing beyond a few already well-documented dusty facts.

St. Cuthbert's bare bones were undoubtedly lying snug under their green marble slab as they had for centuries. And if not, the body could be anywhere in the cathedral. Why not in one of the towers? Or cemented into one of the chapel walls? She had read of some Welsh saint whose relics had been set in cement to preserve them; why not Cuthbert, too? Perhaps he was buried in the cloister garden—that could be checked out easily enough. A good team of gardeners could turn that up quickly with stout spades. But what were the chances of the dean and chapter allowing that? And it would take days. Weeks. No, whatever was to be done, they had to do it. And they had to do it now.

In her tiny priory room she lay down on her narrow bed, but didn't even bother to close her eyes. She knew she wouldn't sleep. Her mind raced backward and forward between being sure there was no mystery at all, and devising outlandish schemes for the still-incorrupt body being secreted under an altar somewhere, or perched high on a balcony as part of a railing. On the roof, perhaps, behind a parapet—except the central tower was probably climbed by hundreds of camera-laden tourists every week—exactly the sort of thing the solitude-loving saint would have hated.

When she heard the bells chime two o'clock she decided to abandon any pretense of sleep. Maybe a walk in the priory grounds would clear her head. As she hadn't bothered getting ready for bed, all she had to do was pull on her shoes and jacket before slipping out the back door. A full moon greeted her, highlighting the newly emerging daffodils and spring bulbs in the priory flower beds. Two turns around the garden and she felt ready for anything except her bed, in spite of her damp feet.

The moon provided enough light for unlocking the padlock on the chained gate that St. Antony's monks and guests used as the quickest exit to the street. It was only when the iron gate clanked shut that she realized what had been niggling at the back of her mind for hours. The monks' and friars' burial ground behind the Chapter House that she had seen sketched on the map. That would have been by far the easiest place to bury a body quickly and secretly. All they would have needed was a shovel.

Surely the Victorians hadn't done one of their meddling restorations in the cemetery. She couldn't do a very detailed search by moonlight, but she was too restless to go to bed, and they could go back in the morning if she found anything hopeful.

It wasn't until she was halfway up the hill and fancied she heard steps behind her on the cobbles that she realized what a silly thing she was doing. And yet, except for her cold feet, the pre-dawn air felt so good, and the moonlight gave her a sense of being wrapped in magic. The spotlighted cathedral thrusting up into the sky ahead of her had an almost mesmerizing pull. Glancing over her shoulder to be certain she had only imagined the footsteps, she hurried onward.

The market square was empty except for two cats skittering across the shadows. Inside the cathedral close the castle loomed a dark hulk to her right, but the lights on the cathedral cut bright streamers upward into the night. She made her way along the walk across the front, then plunged into the grass to take her around the side. It was just as well her feet were already wet, because it was as if she were wading now.

The library windows that a few hours ago had seemed so comforting with their soft light now stared at her as coldly as a slate of jet black diamonds. Around the last abutment of what had once comprised the ancient monastery, she recognized the apsidal shape of the exterior of the Chapter House with its sleeping Saxon and Norman bishops inside. And who was sleeping in the graveyard here? A helter-skelter assortment of graves interrupted the smooth green lawn, each of them marked by a triangular "roof" of dark brown wood. It was much like the Community burial ground at Kirkthorpe, except it was less orderly, attesting to its age. Each little roof had a name carved in the wooden marker below it.

Bending close and adjusting her angle of vision to get the most advantage from the cathedral's illumination, Felicity began reading the names on each grave, each followed by the date of the monk's death and a carved cross: Ailred, Alphege, Augustine, Bede, Oswin, Mark, Luke, John. It read like a compendium of apostles and English saints... Peter, Paul, Boniface, Edmund, Benedict... She caught her breath at the next one—Cuthbert. Then looked at the date. A monk named for the saint had died in 1023. Still, she paused, an opportunity for the Guardians? Use a grave already marked with the right name? She would mention the idea to Antony tomorrow.

Felicity moved toward the far side of the ground beyond a row of yew trees, then stopped abruptly. She was plunged into pitch black as simultaneously the cathedral floodlights switched off and a cloud covered the moon. Blinking to speed her eyes adjusting, she moved forward.

Her cry of alarm sounded piercing in her own ears, even though she managed to stifle it almost instantly. She had walked straight into a dense yew tree. Meaning to walk around the hedge, miscalculation had sent her crashing into it. She jumped sideways.

The scream that tore from her throat went unstifled this time. Her own voice frightened her almost more than the sensation of falling. The loose ground she stepped on held only momentarily before caving under her feet as she slid into a freshly dug hole.

She flailed against the dark, desperation closing in on her. *Kick! Fight!* Her instincts screamed. But blackness could not be kicked. *Think,* a voice of reason pierced her panic. Where was she? What had happened? She forced her mind to work. She had landed unhurt on her feet. The top of the hole seemed to be a foot or two above her reach. Deep enough to cut out all light—had there been any light.

She put out her hands to feel the sides. Perhaps four feet across. She inched forward, counting her steps two, three, four... She froze as another cry tore from her, this one catching on a sob.

She was in a grave. And she was not alone.

Chapter 29

Felicity fought down the terror. *Back into the corner. You'll be safer.* She inched backward until she was against the raw earth. She was too frightened to scream—like being frozen in a dream. Tears squeezed out of her eyes and small whimpering sounds came from her throat. Her stomach reacted to the naked fear with a wave of nausea. Then the retching shook her body.

That unlocked her frozenness. Now she was able to scream. But after the first full-voiced shriek she clamped both hands over her mouth to stop herself. Even in her half-hysterical state it crossed her mind to question whether she wanted to advertise her presence. This wasn't a proper burial. Had someone stumbled in like she did only not been so lucky? Or, was a murderer disposing of a body? This was no hastily dug affair. The grave itself must be in readiness for some ancient verger or vicar choral whose service would be tomorrow. And someone was making early use of it.

Her next thought made her grasp the earthen side of her dungeon for support. Could she have stumbled—literally—on St. Cuthbert's burial site? The limb she had nudged felt fresh enough. Could she get up the courage to explore further? Had someone discovered the site, dug up the treasure and left the body exposed to the elements?

She was trying to bring herself to feel the corpse again when she realized—the saint would never have been put straight into the ground without a coffin, he whose body had rested inside triple casketry. Yet surely this was deeper than most graves? Was it possible that it had been dug by someone likewise looking for St. Cuthbert? Someone who had found and removed the saint, then added a victim of his own? Or maybe… With a force of will she quieted her mind. Wild conjectures would get her nowhere.

The smell of damp earth was starting to make her gag again. She raised her head toward the fresh air above her head and inhaled deeply, hoping to draw some of the dewy pre-dawn freshness downward. And it worked—she was greeted with a strong whiff of sweet, perfumed air. A spring flower, something that must be blooming just above her head. She inhaled again, trying to identify the scent. Her next breathful, however, smelled less fresh, and the scent seemed to be coming from below, not from above her head. Had someone thrown a handful of flowers into the grave with the body?

The clouds shifted overhead and a shaft of silver moonlight penetrated the depths of her interment. Commanding her stomach to hold steady, she steeled herself to lean forward and peer at the body. It was too dark for any attempt at identification, but she had the passing impression of white skin in dark clothing. A form not overly tall. Was there something vaguely familiar? Perhaps, but she couldn't manage a second look.

All of her powers of control were required for the simple act of thinking. *First, breathe. Deep, regular breaths. That's it.* She felt the smoothly perpendicular dirt walls for possible hand or footholds, but found none. *Was this what Joseph felt like when his brothers threw him in a pit?* She started once more to scream, but stopped herself. *No. Concentrate.* She could control her voice and her breathing, but she couldn't control the trembling. Her whole body was shaking now. Cold. Fear. Shock.

Bracing her hands against the sides gave her an idea. She only had to gain a couple of feet to reach the lip of the grave. Then she could probably pull herself up. She rejected the idea of standing on her fellow prisoner as quickly as the idea came to her. After all, it would be morning in only a few more hours and someone would find her and help her out. Unless the wrong person found her first.

The thought gave her new energy. Bracing her back against the end of the grave and pushing against the earthen sides with her forearms, she tried bracing her feet likewise on the perpendicular walls. Maybe she could inch her way upward.

She gained three inches, then the earth crumbled and she slid down with a scrape to her elbows that would have been painful had she not been wearing a jacket. *Right. Brace with your knees.* All those hours she had spent at the barre practicing her *pliés.* She could extend her knees at an almost perfect 180 degree angle. Surely such an ability should count for something. Ah, much firmer bracing, yes. But harder to inch upward.

So, use your toes to climb upward. She pulled off her shoes and threw them out. *Now. Brace with your knees to move your hands up. Dig with your toes.* The soil was soft. It was working. *Excellent. One. Two. Three.* Two more and she could reach the rim. If only that didn't crumble under her grasp. If only her fingers and toes weren't so cold.

This time, she didn't even try to stop herself screaming with frustration when she fell.

"Felicity, is that you?" The muffled male voice overhead sounded warm with concern.

"Yes! Help!"

"Where are you?" She could barely hear him over the pounding of blood in her head.

"Over here. In the grave. Be careful! The edge crumbles!" A shower of dirt accompanied her warning. "Stand back, or you'll fall, too!"

A scrabbling and scraping sound indicated her rescuer was assuming a prone position and edging toward the lip of the grave. "Here, can you see my hand?" The voice sounded stifled by the mound of dirt. Something white dangled from a dark sleeve above her. "Can you reach it?"

Her answer was to reach up with both hands. She grasped his hand with her right hand and his wrist with her left. "Pull slowly, I'll try to sort of walk up the side."

It was much harder than it seemed it should have been. Her feet kept scraping the dirt away, making her slip and jerk her arms.

With a little progress, though, her rescuer was able to grasp her with his left hand as well and then pull with all his weight. At last she lay with her entire torso on the grass, her legs still dangling, kicking the air for a toehold. "Here. One more." He heaved her forward and she lay extended on the grass like a beached fish.

One gulp of air and she sprang to her feet. "Oh, Antony. I should have known you would come." She threw herself into his arms. "Oh, thank you. It was—" She backed away as she realized it wasn't Antony. A pale gray dawn was breaking in the east— enough light to highlight the familiar blond curls. "Jonathan!"

"Felicity, forgive me for taking so long. I was so afraid of something like this. But then I got distracted. There were some students in the square—they'd had too much to drink and there was a scuffle. I'm so sorry."

"Oh, Jon, I'm so glad to see you! But what are you doing here?"

"I followed you."

"You what?"

"I was on my way to the chapel to say Lauds when I saw you leave the garden." He reached down to retrieve her shoes and handed them to her.

"Lauds?"

"Not with the monks. I prefer to keep my own office—by the medieval hours. Lauds well before sunrise."

"You followed me?" She still couldn't get her head around that idea. "Why?" Should she be afraid? Antony had made it very clear he didn't trust this man.

"Felicity!" He reached for her hand. His felt warm. "Can't you guess? Why do you think I keep showing up where you are?"

"You said Father Anselm sent you. You said you wanted to help. But then you keep disappearing. Why didn't you—?" She stopped. What was she doing berating him when he had just rescued her? "Oh, sorry, sorry. I don't know what I'm saying. I—" Her words ended in a strangled sob as Jonathan pulled her into his arms.

"Silly girl. Silly, lovely girl. Well, maybe I exaggerated Anselm's directive just a bit."

"But why?"

"Isn't it obvious? Because I'm crazy about you."

Felicity gasped. Was this a joke? "You barely know me."

"I know more than you think. I know you're brilliant and brave, if foolhardy, and gorgeous, and deeply spiritual, and—"

"Whoa—" What was he saying? "Jonathan, I—" She clung to him and ordered her knees to stop shaking. "Thank you, that's lovely, but… Those are all things I would like to be, but most of the time I'm rash and stupid and cynical and a mess."

He laughed. "Yes, those too—that's what I love about you. You're never boring!" He tried to hold her tighter, but she pulled away. She would like to sit down, but was afraid he'd embrace her again. Half of her mind wanted that very much. But the other half knew she needed to think.

"Jonathan, don't use the 'L' word."

He held up his hands and backed up several steps. "Sorry. Terrible timing. I know. What a fool I am. Please. Just put it down to the insanity of the moment. Forget I said anything. No more. I promise. I won't touch you."

"Well, actually, I'm freezing. You could put your arm around me." He obeyed readily. "And now, explain about all that skulking around at Bede's World. Antony said—"

"No skulking. Well, not exactly. Brother Matt really did want me to experience it. Great place, huh?" She nodded. "But I also wanted to keep an eye on you, like I told you. Be sure you were safe."

"Safe? I was with Antony."

"Yes. That's what I mean."

She pulled away from him. "Jonathan! That's nonsense!"

He put his hands firmly on her shoulders and gave her a little shake. "Fliss, I know you're friends. But *think*. He was covered in Dominic's blood. The police are looking for him."

"That's absurd. What possible reason could he have to harm

Dominic?"

Jon shrugged. "Who knows? Maybe someone is blackmailing him for something in his past. Maybe Father Dominic knew something about him. Especially if Antony is thinking of becoming a monk—something that would prevent his being accepted. Something he could be defrocked for—who knows? Little boys, little girls…"

"Jonathan, that's disgusting! You have no right to suggest such things!"

"No, you're right. I don't." He held up his hands. "I apologize. I only meant to make the point that one never knows what lies in another person's past—or their heart." He dropped his voice and ended with a meaningful look at her.

And yet, even as she shook her head against the thought, she had to admit Antony did seem to be hiding something—in spite of the openness of so many of their conversations. There would always come a point when the shutter would drop. She had put it down to shyness, lack of experience of being with a woman, but maybe she was wrong. Maybe he was being furtive.

She could make no reply. *Antony* did *give you the mint cake,* one voice in her head reminded her, while the other argued that his solicitous care for her had been absolutely genuine. He had run to Elspeth at the sound of her scream. She had already gone over the cliff. Hadn't she? Felicity began trembling violently.

Steering her with an arm around her shoulders, Jonathan led her away from the grave to a bench near the edge of the lawn where they had a perfect hilltop view of the nascent sunrise. Birds suddenly sprang into song in the trees that covered the steep hillside below them. Felicity started to relax, her head spinning, but just as the deliciousness of security was beginning to creep over her she jolted upright. "Jonathan, we can't sit here. We need to call the police!"

"Police? Why?"

"That grave. There's a body in it."

"Sounds reasonable to me. There are bodies in most graves."

"Jon, I'm serious. I don't mean a buried body in a coffin. I mean just a body—like somebody dumped one there."

"Are you sure? It couldn't have been a dog or something?"

She shook her head emphatically. "I saw. There was reflected light when the moon came out. A little bit. I—I had the feeling I knew—" She shuddered and her voice caught on a sob.

"Right. My brave girl. You've had enough." His arm still around her, he pulled her to her feet and began walking her around the corner of the cathedral. "Strong tea, a hot bath and bed for you. I'll see to the officialdom." He propelled her across the close.

"But they'll want to question me."

"Maybe. Later. But I don't see why you should be involved."

"Well, because I *am* involved, aren't I?" A thought suddenly struck her. "Jonathan, we need to call an ambulance. Maybe they aren't dead. Maybe someone just fell in and was stunned. I don't know how long I was there—I mean, I don't think it was breathing—but we need to get help."

"Right." By now they were back to the market square. "Can you make it on alone? It's mostly downhill from here. I'll stay here and get everything sorted out."

"Yes. OK." Her steps were unsteady, but she could make it. The visions Jonathan had conjured of a hot bath and bed pulled her like a magnet.

"And Fliss…"

She jerked her head up. In the midst of all this horror, that long unused nickname flooded her with memories of comfort and warmth. Memories of home.

"Hmm?" She turned to Jon as if she were dreaming. If he had opened his arms at that moment she would have walked straight into them.

But he only had a businesslike admonition. "No need to

raise the alarm at the priory. The brothers will be at morning prayers—let them enjoy their peace. I'll deal with whatever is needed here."

She nodded, disappointed, and yet he was being thoughtful. He would take care of things. "And you'll tell the police where I am? I mean, they'll want to know about my footprints and things."

"Yes, of course. After you've had a nap."

She was too tired even to nod. Just keep putting one foot in front of the other and you'll get there. She said it to herself over and over. One foot in front of the other. One foot... The rhythm gave her a focus and helped keep unwanted thoughts at bay—thoughts of being trapped at the bottom of a deep hole with a dead body.

Much nicer to think of Jonathan's arm around her; of his familiar, American voice calling her Fliss, which never failed to take her back to that halcyon summer romance with Kevin. How could life have changed so much?

Kevin, Michael, her brothers, even her distant father... somehow, Jonathan seemed the embodiment of all the men she had known. Men from her safe, secure past. Home, where one was never confronted with lethal hazards and dead bodies.

Chapter 30

The cold iron of the priory gate brought her back to the present. How could she have given into daydreams at such a moment? Even the daydreams of bath and bed. She needed to talk to Antony. She must tell Antony. And then watch his reactions. What he would think of her adventure she couldn't imagine, but in spite of her confused state she was quite focused on the fact that Antony must know every detail. Well, not every detail, of course. But the essentials.

She was almost running by the time she reached the upper hall in the priory. Making no attempt to soften her knock, she hammered on his door. When there was no answer she tried the knob. The room was empty. Was he in the washroom? Where—the ringing of the bell made her smile. Oh. Of course. The chapel. Morning prayers. No. This was Sunday, it would be mass.

She made only the quickest stop in her room to scrub the mud out from under her fingernails and brush her hair. If only she had a pair of clean jeans. Best she could do was brush them off a bit. Then she hurried back along the hall, across the courtyard and into the modern, round chapel. The community sat in silence in their gray robes. Only one head looked up at her entrance—one of the visiting Romanian students she had met briefly at another service. He smiled shyly and indicated an empty seat next to himself. She shook her head, forcing herself to return his smile. It helped push down the panic she felt rising. Antony wasn't there. He would never miss mass on a Sunday. What was he doing? Where could he be?

In the kitchen? Would he allow himself a cup of coffee before mass? She gripped the handrail to keep from stumbling down the steep steps of the priory. *Let him be there. Please.* She prayed. He wasn't.

Out in the garden once more, she sank onto a bench. Should she call the police? No. They must keep Antony out of the police's clutches long enough to find the real perpetrator. But now Jonathan's words came back to her—did she need to be protected from Antony? No, no, no. Ridiculous. He couldn't possibly have been responsible for that body in the grave.

Think, she told herself. But she was so tired; so confused...

Had Antony gone back to the cathedral as she had? Was he still there somewhere? Perhaps he and Jonathan had teamed up by now, both thinking that she was off in dreamland. But what if something quite different had taken place? What if he had gone to the cathedral and... And—

She squeezed her eyes shut to keep out the vague image of the figure prone at her feet in the new-dug grave. It had seemed there was something vaguely familiar. It couldn't possibly have been Antony. Only the dimmest ambient light had penetrated the pit. But still, she would have known Antony. Wouldn't she? Had whoever killed Dominic and Elspeth, whoever had been chasing and threatening them, caught up with Antony?

Closing her eyes caused her to focus on a new sensation— the delicate scent of the spring flowers blooming around her in the garden, enhanced by the morning dew. When she identified the scent of the bed of hyacinth just beyond the bench, she recognized the smell that had come to her deep in the ground. She knew who was in that grave.

Philomena Johnson. Her overpowering hyacinth perfume— or soap or hairspray or whatever—had been a perfect match for her personality. If Felicity hadn't been so terrified at the time, she would have recognized it sooner. The flood of relief left her weak. It wasn't Antony.

She would have to go back. She must tell someone. Surely the authorities would be there by now. They would need an identification. She let herself out the gate and turned her feet once again toward the cathedral. A few people out for an early Sunday stroll brushed by her. She didn't see them. She hardly felt them.

Until she walked smack into one.

"Whoa, Felicity. Where are you going?"

She was so relieved at the sound of the warm, musical voice, her knees buckled. His arms stopped her slipping to the pavement. "Antony! I was so worried. I couldn't find you."

Anger edged his voice. "*You* were worried? How do you think I felt to waken and find you gone? Where were you?"

"I went to the cathedral. I—"

"The *cathedral*? What did you think you were doing? Don't you realize we're dealing with a double murder here?"

"Triple."

"What?"

"That's what I was coming to tell you. Well, tell the police, really. It's Philly Johnson. I found her body. In the cemetery."

Already Antony had turned and was heading back up the hill.

The police had arrived at the cathedral just ahead of them, red and yellow lights flashing atop white cars. Antony started toward the cemetery. "I must see."

Felicity grabbed his arm. "No. Wait. The police. You'll be caught. Let me lead. I know a way."

Fortunately no police lines had been established yet, so they were able to creep up unnoticed. Felicity remained back by the cathedral wall and pointed to the bush she had collided with only a few hours before. "It's just beyond that row of yews."

He had barely moved off when Felicity felt a warm hand on her arm. "What are you doing back here, Fliss? You're supposed to be tucked up in bed."

"I know. But I had to tell Antony. He wanted to see."

Jonathan looked disapproving, but he let it go. "I made some inquiries. I gather the grave was dug to receive the body of a retired prebendry who had given about two lifetimes of service to the cathedral. His funeral is this afternoon."

Behind her double shelter of cathedral wall and Jonathan's comforting presence, Felicity was only barely aware of the police activity. Some time passed before Antony rejoined her.

Jonathan and Antony glared at each other. Then Jon turned to Felicity. "I'd better speak to the police, let them know I called them. I'll make up some story about an early morning prayer vigil to explain my discovery." He squeezed her arm briefly. "I won't involve you, Fliss, unless it's necessary." He started to walk away, then turned back. "But be careful."

She nodded. His words rang in her ears as she and Antony made their silent way back to the priory. Antony suggested they sit on the garden bench, but Felicity shook her head. It was far too cold, and the hyacinth scent was too evocative. She had always been fond of that flower, especially for its scent. But she doubted that she would ever be able to smell it again without returning to the terrors of the grave.

Instead, Felicity led the way to her room. She sat half-reclining on her bed. He took the only chair the room offered. "Felicity, I got a look at the body as they brought it up. Definitely Philly. The side of her head was… Well, she didn't die of a heart attack."

"Like Dominic?"

Antony thought for a moment. "Maybe, but less—um—energetic, I'd say."

"Not so much as if it were something personal?"

Antony nodded slowly. "Much more calculated. It didn't appear frenzied. I would say the killer did his job without rage. Or perhaps it was a different killer."

"Oh, that poor woman. She was pushy and irritating, but what a terrible thing to happen. She certainly didn't deserve this. Antony, do you think—could she possible have been the third Guardian? It seems so unlikely, but if she was—if the secret died with her— we'll never know. Centuries of guarding… It will all be lost."

Antony shook his head. "No, if someone is doing this to get at the treasure, they wouldn't have killed off their last source of information."

"Maybe that means they know the answer."

"Right. Or that the killings are to keep the secret hidden."

Around the same circle again. They looked at one another in silence, thinking through the implications of this new event. Then Felicity gasped. "Antony! You've got to leave. Now! That's the third time you've been on the scene—more or less—at a murder. The police will never accept that as coincidence."

"No, they won't. And I'm not sure it is coincidence. The last two, I mean. I think our presence is making someone violently nervous."

"You think Elspeth and Philomena were killed to keep them from telling us something?"

"Or because someone thinks they told us something."

"But then why not just kill us?" After Felicity asked the question, she wished she hadn't.

Her words echoed in the silence, and for the first time Felicity really realized just how likely that prospect was.

And she realized how much she didn't want to die. She hadn't lived yet. She hadn't even sorted out *how* she wanted to live. She thought she had, but now she saw a whole new range of possibilities—or old possibilities in a whole new light. She had learned so much in the past days—more about herself than about the mystery she was supposed to be solving—but what about once it was over? Would the things she had learned still be with her, or would she sink back into the old certainties? No, she was determined to explore this brave new world she sensed just around the corner. And what did that world look like?

Jonathan. She blinked at the brightness of the blazingly obvious. Jonathan, who always made her heart leap like no one she had ever met before. Jonathan, who had repeatedly rescued her and tried to declare his love for her—if only she had let him. Jonathan was her knight in shining armor.

She sat stunned with the shock of realizing she was in love. And with that realization everything became clear. It was so simple, really: finish up the investigation as fast as possible—they had come to the end of the road anyway, hadn't they? Tell Jonathan she returned his love. And fly off home together. Home. What a beautiful, safe word.

She knew she had a sappy grin on her face, but she couldn't help it. And then, to her utter amazement, a slow tear made its way down her cheek.

"Felicity! What a fool I am." Antony sprang to her side. "You're exhausted and I make you sit up talking about this ghastly murder business. Forgive me."

She shook her head vehemently. "No. It's not you." She took a swipe at her eyes with her sleeve. "Delayed reaction to the shock, I expect." She would have to tell Antony soon. She wanted to tell the whole world. But this was not the moment. "I—well, I guess I'll have to admit I'm a little homesick."

Yes, that would be a good way to approach it with him. She grinned. "I never thought anyone would hear such a thing from me. Ms. Self-sufficient Independence. I—I guess... Well, you remember, I told you about Kevin."

"Kevin?" She could tell by his tone of voice she had hit the right note. Antony had immediately shifted to his counseling role—a cross between priest and uncle. "The fellow back home who wanted you—"

"Wanted me to stay at home and make chocolate chip cookies and sew curtains—*his* cookies and curtains." She gave a little half-smile. "That scenario suddenly sounded good to me." The smile was now a full chuckle. "It scared me, so it made me cry."

Antony threw back his head and laughed. "What a woman! Spends the night in a grave with a corpse, but the thought of making chocolate chip cookies reduces her to tears."

She joined his laughter. "It would you, too. I'm a terrible cook."

The laughter was a wonderful release for both of them. It was some time before he encouraged her to go on. "Tell me about this Kevin who's brave enough to face your chocolate chip cookies?"

She shook her head. "No, it's not Kevin. He was just an example." She took a deep breath. Antony had to know sooner or later. "It's—"

The jangle of the bell at the priory gate sounded as loud as a fire gong. Felicity was off her bed and looking out the window in a single leap. "It's the police." Cold reality flooded in, chasing all thoughts of romance. "Antony, we have to get you away from here."

Her backpack was over her shoulder before Antony had the door open. All the way down the back hall and across the garden her mind worked as her body moved by instinct. Finish the investigation. Then follow your heart. You're doing this for both Antony and Jonathan. At that moment it seemed to make sense.

Chapter 31

Antony strode ahead of Felicity across the dew-damp grass, debate raging in his mind. Was he running from the police or from what Felicity had been about to tell him? All his life he had been running. If he gave in to the safe route this time, he would never break out again. The iniquity of his past would have won. As surely as it seemed to be winning now.

He was determined not to let either one happen. Nor was he going to let Jonathan Breen win. He would sort this out with Felicity when they had time to talk. He would confess all. As soon as the task before him was settled. He squared his shoulders with a physical shake to mirror his internal determination.

Avoiding the main road, he led the way up the hill to the station. Moving quickly and quietly, he avoided conversation until they were settled on the train headed northward. "Look, we've got a lot to talk about here." His voice sounded harsher than he had intended, but it got his companion's attention. "First, I need to explain that we're not doing this because I'm running from the police. I've wanted to tell you this for hours—"

"Antony I need to tell you something, too—"

He held up his hand. "Later. This is important." She settled back. "When I was looking for you, I went back to the library. I found where Lingard was shelved, so I took time to check some ideas I'd been playing with. I remembered that Lingard suggested that Cuthbert was buried somewhere other than his shrine, but I couldn't remember what his conclusions were."

"Oh!" Now Felicity sat upright.

"Yes. His theory is that Cuthbert's Folk would have wanted to carry out his initial request to their community—no matter how belatedly."

"You mean, they took him back to his *desart*?"

Antony nodded. "It makes sense—that instead of hiding his body in some obscure place that would likely be forgotten and lost, they took him back to the piece of earth he loved most in all the world."

"Inner Farne."

"Exactly."

She thought for a moment. "That's brilliant!"

"Actually, it's rather obvious once you accept the idea that it's not the real body in Cuthbert's shrine."

"Antony, that's great. If you're right, that solves the puzzle and will protect the treasure. But how will it solve the murder?" They had been focusing so hard on the historic puzzle it was easy at times to forget this was supposed to have a practical application.

"It won't."

"Well, then—?"

"It won't tell us who, but it will tell us where. Since the point of all this must be to get the treasure that was buried with the body, once we're certain of where it is, we can tell the police and they can stake it out and wait for the murderers who must not be far behind us."

She shivered and involuntarily looked over her shoulder. "Right. That's a relief. Even I'm not so rash as to want to confront murderers myself."

Antony dug in his pocket and pulled out a sketchy map showing the few buildings on Inner Farne. He had penciled in notes of the historic locations they marked and began musing about the most likely location for the Guardians to have chosen for the burial. "I'm not sure. I suppose we'll just have to explore all the possibilities."

When Felicity didn't reply, he realized he really should be thinking more about his companion than just the task at hand. He hadn't even asked where she was going when she barreled into him on the sidewalk in such a dazed state. He turned to ask, but stopped at the sight of her sleeping form, her head cradled between the seat and the train window.

He hated to disturb her when the train pulled into Newcastle, but she woke with eyes as bright as if she'd had a night of sleep. There was a considerable wait for the train to Chathill, the closest station to Seahouses, and since they had come away from the priory without breakfast they settled over veggie pasties and steaming cups of coffee, welcome even if they were only Styrofoam. The coffee shop, situated in the open on the platform, gave the feeling, if not the ambiance, of a sidewalk cafe, but even less privacy as their conversation was constantly interrupted by incomprehensible, echoing announcements of trains over a crackling tannoy. Felicity stared into her cup. "Antony, I need to tell you about last night. I haven't exactly told you what happened. But first, I need to apologize. I know it was stupid of me. I should never have gone out alone. But I just wanted to get a look at the graveyard. I thought—I don't know, in the cold light of day it's hard to know what I thought." She shrugged. "It just seemed like the natural place to hide a body, that's all."

"And apparently that's what someone else thought."

"Philly Johnson. I still can't believe it. If she was the third Guardian... I can't think of anyone who looked less likely to qualify as an English Benedictine."

Antony took a deep, warming drink of coffee, glad for the moment that the conversation had veered once again from what Felicity wanted to tell him about last night. He wasn't at all sure he wanted to hear. "I've been thinking. The 'Three from the See... Three from the sea' line keeps going through my head. Maybe our Philomena was from the sea—one of the 'Vikings'."

Felicity smiled. "That's a role she seemed much better suited for. Brunnhilda or something Nordic, with a horned helmet and a gold breastplate. But wouldn't that mean she was killed by one of her own 'three'?" She was quiet for a moment, then went on again. Something else, I've been wondering—where's Curtis? If she'd been shot with a crossbow, I'd think he just got tired of being pushed around."

"Domestic squabble? I'm sure the police will want to talk to him, of course. But I'm thinking if she was one of the…" He paused. "… shall we say Dark Three—maybe the others just thought, 'Why divide the treasure three ways when we could go halves?'"

"No honor among thieves? So, if that's right, we only have two enemies left." She paused. "Laird and who else?"

"Bootham? Willibrord? Some shadowy figure we don't even know?" They both sat in glum silence for a moment.

Then Felicity brightened. "But that would mean the third Guardian *is* still alive!"

She paused and played nervously with her pasty wrapper, eyes fixed firmly on the table. "Do you think—that is, I suppose it's a silly idea, but I was just thinking…"

Antony wondered why Felicity looked embarrassed to ask her question; it was unlike her to be so hesitant.

She took a breath and the question came out in a rush. "Would being an oblate of an English Benedictine order count? I mean, even if one were an American?"

"Well, I suppose it might. The order was scattered everywhere after the Reformation, especially to France and the continent, of course. But why do you ask? There was never any indication Philomena Johnson had an association—"

"No, not Philly. I was thinking of Jonathan."

"Breen?" He almost spat out the name. "One of the Guardians?" He stopped just short of calling her idea ridiculous. And why was she blushing? "You can't really believe that!" In spite of his best efforts at control, Antony felt his head growing warm, his voice rising and his hands shaking. "That man is the most shallow, irritating, self-centered—" He bit off the expletive that sprang to his mind.

Felicity flung the pasty wrapper she held wadded in her hand to the floor and came halfway out of her chair at him. She looked him full in the face, eyes blazing. "That's unfair! You don't know him at all. He's—he's wonderful." She almost choked on the last word and settled back into her seat, eyes still shooting darts at Antony. "As a matter of fact, I probably owe my life to him."

"What are you talking about?" In contrast to Felicity's heat, Antony's voice was suddenly frigidly controlled. Each word dropped like a separate ice cube.

But the effect of his arctic blast was lost under a blaring, crackling squawk from the loudspeaker just over their heads. "What?" He looked up. "Did that say Chathill?" In total irritation, Antony jerked back his chair and strode to view the monitor beside the platform. "I don't know why they bother with announcements no one can understand. Noise pollution, that's all it is."

The monitor, however, did confirm that their train was at hand.

The little turquoise blue spur line train, just two cars long, had only a handful of passengers. A family of noisy children going to visit their gran, a group of teenagers off to the coast for the day, and a middle-aged man with a pair of serious binoculars around his neck that made Antony wonder where the birdwatching Bootham was, scrambled on ahead of them. Antony flung himself into the nearest seat and resumed his verbal ice storm. "You were saying? About Mr. Wonderful?" He folded his arms and waited.

"Yes, he is, as a matter of fact. But it's obvious there's no getting through to you. And I don't see what difference it makes, anyway." Her blazing anger had hardened into a steely hauteur. "All you really need to know is that I shall see this venture through, then I plan to accept Jonathan's proposal and return to the States with him."

"I don't believe it. That's the most outrageous thing I've ever heard!"

"And just what's so outrageous about that? Is it so impossible someone could be in love with me?"

"No! I—"

"Not everyone is like you English—so reserved no one has

any idea what you're thinking. I don't think *you* even know what you're thinking half of the time!" Before Antony could answer, she rose, as regally as was possible on a swaying train car, and made her way to a seat in the back carriage. Out of the corner of his eye, Antony saw her accept a proffered crisp from the exuberant group of teenagers.

It was some time before the glacier inside Antony could thaw enough to let him think. Was it true—what she said? He thought he had been so blatant about his feelings. But maybe he didn't really know what he felt. The train made a brief stop at Morpeth and the young family en route to Sunday dinner at Granny's jumped off, to be replaced by a young mother with two children. All the while, the questions continued spinning around in Antony's mind.

What had he been about to say? Where would that exchange of verbal fire and ice have gone if Felicity hadn't ended it by marching off? Aside from the issue of his or anyone else's feelings for Felicity, he must consider her idea. *Was* it possible that Jonathan Breen could be the last of the Guardians? Could Antony put aside his instinctive dislike of the man long enough to think through the possibility clearly? Antony hoped he wasn't so unfair as to judge Breen solely in reaction to his smooth charm, good looks and self-possession. But what did the fellow think he was playing at, declaring his love to Felicity at a time like this?

The train lurched to a stop at a station marked Pegswood and the mother and children got off. That left only the birdwatcher in Antony's carriage and the teens and Felicity laughing and chomping crisps in the carriage behind him. What an image of modern life: eating crisps when they were running for their lives.

Bacon-flavoured, cheese, or salt and vinegar? The great questions of life.

And what about his own life? What were the salt and vinegar crisps, and what were the real issues? Finding Dominic's secret? Making reparation? Becoming a monk? Repairing his now-shattered friendship with Felicity? What was he really running for?

Even forming the questions was overwhelming. But one thing was clear. He must take them one issue at a time. In the order given. Rushing things would bring disaster to all.

Chapter 32

Even from the coach station just beyond the war memorial, Seahouses looked more hopeful than when they had been there before. The sun brightened the gray stone buildings. But Felicity shivered when she stepped off the coach. The flowering trees looked cheerful, but the wind that bent them sideways was cold. She and Antony had boarded the same bus at the train station at Chathill, but she had pointedly taken a seat up front next to an elderly woman, forcing Antony to move on further back.

Felicity looked anxiously toward the harbor. The sea didn't look as rough as it had been last time, but she could hardly describe it as smooth. Never mind, she was in no mood to let a few waves stop her. Grace Darling had braved much worse than anything she saw before her now. And she wanted to get this done with. She was sure they had the right answer as to the location of Cuthbert's body—the legendary, uncorrupted body. *And* treasure. So, she smiled as she ticked off the steps: find the treasure, give it to the Children's Fund; throw herself into Jonathan's arms and fly off home. Oh yes, and solve Dominic's murder for the police. That should wrap it up nicely.

Her determination faltered only slightly when she noted the tightly shut boat rental huts along the sea wall. The sun shining on their colorful paint made their shuttered windows seem even more of a rebuff than before. The tight shutters reminded her of the barricade she had so often sensed Antony putting up to shut her out. Had she been wrong to storm off? Should she turn back now to find him? She had half-turned when she noted some movement in the last hut.

The bearded sailor in a dark blue jersey was just shutting

his door when she approached him. "Yep. We sent two boats out this morning. It's safe enow for a sturdy craft. It's the tourists' stomachs I'd worry about. Not many as want to be rocked about this much. But we 'ad two charters."

"But they're gone now?"

He nodded as he shoved his cap firmly on his head. "Birdwatchers, left an hour ago." He pointed to the red hut next door advertising cruises aboard HVM *Cuthbert.* "*Cuthbert* went out before that, won't be back for hours, less they changes their mind."

"You don't have any more to charter?" she asked.

The seaman shook his head. "No, last craft just left." He pointed to the pier. "Archeology, I think they said they do."

She looked toward the pier just in time to see a green and purple boat set off, leaving a spray of foam behind. Two figures, muffled in jackets, at the prow. She had an impulse to run after them—maybe if she waved and shouted they would come back for her. She had made fewer than ten strides, though, before they were around the end of the sea wall.

What now? She surveyed the few scattered cars parked on the wall. One made her heart leap. Could that be Jonathan's? Might he have guessed where she had gone, and followed her? Or asked at the station, even? He seemed to have a sixth sense when it came to finding her. Divine guidance, maybe? If only he were here now. Just imagining his arms around her gave her courage and comfort.

Might he be in the Olde Ship drinking coffee and hoping she would arrive soon? Was he thinking of her as she was thinking of him? She turned toward the inn, then stopped. Antony was heading up the curved path to the gray stone pub. And was that Willibrord beckoning to him from the doorway? She spun on her heel. She would do far better on her own. She would find someone to take her to the island. She could finish this herself and get on with her life. The warmth of the thought brought a smile to her face.

Head up, welcoming the invigorating wind, she strode out onto the sea wall. A longer second pier jutted out at a right angle beyond the one the chartered craft had just deserted. A few boats tethered there bobbed in the shelter. Wild, unformed ideas flitted through her mind. Could she manage to "borrow" one and make her own way to Inner Farne? Even she wasn't that rash. She didn't know anything about sailing.

A sturdy figure stood up in one of the boats so suddenly he startled her. He eyed her almost as if he had been waiting for her. Heavy knitted blue cap pulled down around his deeply weathered face, ancient oilskin coat buttoned up to his neck, the old seaman looked as natural as if he had grown there. "Are you going out?" She approached him.

"Well, now, I don't know about that. Mebbe, mebbe not. Lookin' fer a ride, are ye?" He gazed out to sea. "Rough out there. Rougher 'an it looks."

"I just want to go to Inner Farne. It won't take long."

"Oh, aye?" He pretended to be considering the waves, but Felicity thought he was considering something else. She dug in her backpack.

"Ten pounds? Will you do it for that?" She held it out. "It's all I've got."

He considered. "You got a name, lass?"

She blinked at the *non sequitur*. "Uh, Felicity. Felicity Howard."

He licked his lips and jerked his head. "Come on, then." She thought he was holding out his hand to help her aboard, but he snatched the note and let her make her own way onto the rocking boat. He pointed for her to sit forward, under the small canvas covering. She would have preferred to be able to see where they were going, but had to appreciate the protection the canopy offered.

The engine roared into life under its owner's touch. They putted past the tethered boats and he opened the throttle once they were in open water. Felicity made one attempt at conversation, but either he couldn't hear her over the roar of the motor, or her £10 didn't include dialogue. That was all right. The sea *was* rougher than it looked. It was all Felicity could do to keep hanging on and breathing against the wind and sea spray.

Now that she was on her way, she realized she hadn't thought this through very well. She dug in her backpack for the map Antony had stashed there just before their fight at Newcastle. She wished he had stashed an extra pasty with it. She was getting hungry. But never mind, this wouldn't take long. She pulled out the map and studied it. Yes, Antony had marked it quite clearly.

It was only a matter of minutes until she felt the boat slowing. She peeked around the edge of the canopy and saw the coastline of an island that appeared considerably larger than Inner Farne had looked last week when viewed through the mist from the end of the pier. But to her surprise, they didn't pull into the cove. Instead they continued on eastward. "Inner Farne," Felicity yelled over the noise of motor and sea. "I want to go to Inner Farne. Wasn't that it?"

The seaman was still shaking his head when he cut the engine and pulled up alongside a gentle, sandy beach with a few rocks rising above it. He jerked his head toward shore and held out his hand, presumably willing to help her off his boat if not on.

Felicity sprang onto the beach, glad to have something solid under her feet. "You'll wait here? I won't be long."

Her taciturn chauffeur gave an unpleasant smile revealing yellowed teeth, flicked the throttle open on the motor and spun away, leaving Felicity dripping with spray. "Wait!" she shouted. But he was already gone.

"Well, of all the nerve!" Felicity stomped up the beach, talking aloud in her indignation. "That was the rudest man I've ever met in my life! I'll report him to the Harbor Master when I get back. I—" She came to a sudden stop at the top of the beach. Inner Farne stood high above the water level and had buildings on it: a lighthouse, a ruined monastery, a chapel... This barren rock was not Inner Farne.

The sudden chill that seized Felicity had very little to do with the wind whipping her soaking wet clothing. She had been dumped on a small patch of ground in the North Sea. It looked to be something less than a hundred yards across and— she stood, watching a spot on the beach for a few moments to be sure. Yes, it was shrinking by the minute. The water was rising. And there was no high ground.

She remembered Stephen Bootham explaining between bites of toast that no one was absolutely sure how many Farne islands there were because different ones were covered with water at different times. Covered with water, as this one would be very soon.

She could see neighboring islands. Hundreds of yards away across rough waters. And in the best of times, she could just manage to swim from one end of a pool to another. A heated pool.

Someone had planned this. Someone who had managed to stay one step ahead at every turn. Someone very clever had set a trap and she had leapt into it. It hardly mattered now, but it would give her some satisfaction to know who. At least Philly Johnson's name could be stricken from the list. If that was Willibrord she glimpsed at the Olde Ship, he certainly seemed a prime suspect.

But not the most obvious. She argued with herself even as she thought it, but who had known her movements most clearly? Who had brought her here?

She sat on the highest boulder to think. It was better than standing there watching the water rise. Antony could have killed Dominic. He couldn't have killed Elspeth on his own. But if it was set up with an accomplice—Wills again? And the falling stones he "rescued" her from at Whitby? And Antony could have killed Philly. Wills, Antony and Philly Johnson, the Three from the sea?

Or—She jerked upright as a totally wild, new thought struck her. Antony. Could he be the third Guardian? Could he be that cool, leading her on after she thrust herself on him? And now that she knew the secret, he had to kill her to protect it?

No. No, no. That made no sense at all. Or did it, in a convoluted way? If everything had been an enormous hoax, it certainly would explain his antipathy to Jonathan who kept foiling the plot by rescuing her.

But no, not a Guardian, because then he would have already known Sister Elspeth was one. No, he must be in it for personal greed. She couldn't doubt his sincerity and diligence in searching. But what was he searching for? Was he really searching for Dominic's murderer? Or did he know that identity all too well? Was he searching for the treasure for himself? Could he be that good an actor? Well, his sister was a professional—maybe it ran in the family.

How could you ever really know what was in another's mind?

Antony, one of the "Three from the sea", seeking treasure for his own purposes. As the thought crashed in her mind, she felt the pain in her heart. But she would not turn away. What possible motive could he have? He said the Ecumenical Commission which he cared for so passionately was desperate for funding. So desperate he and Father Dominic had quarreled over the use of the treasure?

But then, what made her think that just because he was a priest Antony would be impervious to the lure of gaining a fortune for himself? Hadn't there been examples of that all through history? The bishop who stole Aethelstan's treasure from Cuthbert's shrine? The monks who sold off the treasures from the Inner Farne monastery? Why should Antony be any different?

Premeditated, cold-blooded murder by this man she had come to know so well was unthinkable, but an accident, an argument gone horribly wrong—that could happen to anybody. Then fear driving one to an elaborate cover-up. Yes. She could believe that. Almost.

Then that would mean their pursuers had been the protectors. Would they have stooped to fighting with crossbows and ground glass? Perhaps, if they saw this as some kind of holy war. But wasn't it more likely that a companion of Antony's—Wills again—was doing those things to scare her off? Antony himself had pointed out that they were fairly lame attempts at murder. So, should she take comfort in the fact that he didn't really want to kill her? She looked around at the rising tide, now only a few yards from her. *This* attempt was lethal enough.

If only she had given credence to Jonathan's warnings earlier so she could have been evaluating everything Antony said more closely. She fought to recall his exact words, but it was futile. They had had hundreds of conversations. Deep conversations when she had felt so close to him. The pain of such falsity in one she had come to admire so much was worse than the fear she felt at the encroaching, swirling tide.

She felt her throat close as the realization of the darkness of such depravity closed in on her. Even when she had been irritated, frustrated, or blazingly angry with him, she had never doubted Antony's devotion. His holiness. He had been such an inspiring role model. All a fraud. Just as well the water was rising. She could never believe in anything again.

But no, that wasn't quite true. She had known all along there was evil in the world. She had just misjudged. That still didn't mean everyone was evil. Dominic had been good. Elspeth had been good. And they had died for it. Jonathan was good. And he was still alive. If she could only stay alive long enough to tell him how much she loved him. Swimming was a hopeless option, but it was her only alternative. And it was better than sitting here and letting the water rise up to her neck like Princess Tiger Lily. After all, she could hardly expect Peter Pan to swoop down and carry her to the *Jolly Roger.*

She stood and started tugging at her wet clothes. She would strip and make a running start. And she would keep her mind firmly focused on Jonathan. Pretend she was swimming toward him. "Jon!" She cried aloud to focus as she dropped her jacket on her backpack.

"Fliss!" The answering call came to her in her imagination.

"Jon, I'm coming!" Down to her shirt and underpants she began running, hardly looking where she was going, seeing only her beloved in her mind.

"Fliss, oh Fliss!" She felt his arms engulf her.

It was the space of three heartbeats before she realized she wasn't dreaming. "Jonathan! It's you! Really you!" Almost hysterical with relief, she collapsed against him. "How did you find me?"

"We saw. Well, we weren't sure, but we saw that Scarcar fellow, a local fisherman, known for getting up to no good, seeming to leave something on the Bush. Matt didn't think it was anything, but I insisted we check it out." He engulfed her in a huge hug. "Oh, I'm so glad we did."

"Scarcar? Matt? Bush? What are you talking about?" Her teeth were chattering so she could hardly get the words out.

Jonathan put his coat on her and, both arms around her, walked her back to her pile of clothes. She was stiff with stinging cold. "Come on, let's get off this place before it floods entirely. I'll explain."

"Just a minute." She shook the sand out of her jeans and pushed her legs awkwardly into them. Jon stood waiting patiently for her, the sun and wind playing in his hair. In the far recesses of her mind, she heard Sister Elspeth saying to her, "Follow your heart."

She held out her hand and he clasped it warmly, leading her to the green and purple boat rocking at the edge of the beach where she had been dumped such a short time ago. "Is that Brother Matt at the helm?" She couldn't believe her eyes.

"Yes, indeed. He's a handy man to have around—comes from a long line of sailors. But you first—how did you get involved with Scarcar? According to Matt, he's a known renegade in these parts. Someone who knew you were coming must have set a trap—paid him to take you to Bush Island."

"Willibrord," she said through chattering teeth. "I saw him at the harbor."

"You were set up."

"And I walked—ran, really—right into it." She was furious as she remembered Antony encouraging the whole idea of getting to the island—giving her a map—bringing her here, even.

They waded the last few feet to the boat. Jonathan boosted her up, Matt grasped her hand, and pulled her unceremoniously aboard. Jon threw her backpack and sodden jacket in after her, and heaved himself aboard over the side of the rocking boat.

Matt handed them an inadequate towel which they shared to dry off the best they could. "Now," Jon turned to her. "Talk."

"It's a long story, Jon. We—I—wanted to go to Inner Farne." She took a deep, trembling breath and plunged. "We believe St. Cuthbert is buried there. We believe that is why Dominic was killed. And Elspeth and Philly. We think a great medieval treasure was buried with him." She held her breath. Would he laugh at her? "We found a piece of a document," she added in desperation to give credence to her case.

Jonathan nodded his head slowly. "Yes. I know." A wide grin spread over his face, revealing his perfect teeth. "So, let's go." The last was an instruction to Matt who stood at the helm, hardly recognizable from the meek lay brother she had known. The wind whipped his usually lank hair and streamed his scapular like a banner. He had exchanged his horn-rimmed spectacles for sunglasses and looked almost dashing.

Jonathan observed her staring at Matt. "Amazing, isn't he? Far more at home with a boat than a prayer book. He has wonderful stories about some great uncle who took part in the Dunkirk rescue—just don't get him s-s-started."

Felicity winced at Jon's unkind humor, but let it pass. Things were happening too fast for her to keep them in order in her mind. "Jon, the Cuthbert mystery—you said you knew?"

"Yes, Matthew and I have studied Cuthbert's life together since my first retreat to CT a few years ago."

"But how did you—"

"Get involved? Uncle Cuthbert. I told you about him."

She nodded. "Surrogate father. Benedictine monk, so you became an oblate—" She gasped and stopped. The boat rose on a swelling wave as they reached the open sea beyond the shore of the little island which was quickly disappearing. Felicity's thoughts mounted like the swelling waters. As they settled into a gentle rocking motion, her jumbled ideas fell into place.

She grabbed Jonathan's arm. "Jon! You are, aren't you? The third Guardian? One of Cuthbert's People—handed on from generation to generation. Your Uncle Cuthbert handed on to you!"

"We're sworn to secrecy— "

"Oh, yes, I know. But I'm so relieved! After I found the third body I was so afraid they were all gone—that the secret would have died with the Guardians." She looked again at Matthew steering them expertly toward the island which now rose clearly just in front of them. Steep basalt cliffs rose straight up from the water, perhaps eighty feet high. Already she could make out birds on the rocks, but how on earth would they ever get ashore there? "And Matthew—how does he fit in?"

"He was helping Dominic. Dominic needed Matthew's fiscal skills as Community treasurer for handling the African Children's Fund."

A new thought struck Felicity. "Oh, it was Matthew, wasn't it? That told you where I was going when you followed me to Whitby? It never did make sense to me that it was Willibrord."

Jonathan grinned and tossed his head. "Clever girl. I wasn't sure I could trust you not to tell Antony—sorry about that. But, yes, Matthew was at the priory and overheard Antony calling Sister Elspeth."

Antony. Oh, no. She had to tell Jonathan the worst of it. "Jon. About Antony. I—I'm very much afraid—" Even now she couldn't believe how hard it was to say it. "I think Antony—"

"Murdered Dominic and hired Scarcar to dump you on a disappearing island?"

She nodded mutely. "It's impossible to believe. But I've

thought it through—I—"

His arm came around her with a comforting squeeze. "Don't think about it. You're safe now. We'll settle this business and you can put it all behind you."

She dabbed at her eyes and settled into the curve of his arm.

Matthew swung the boat expertly around to the back side of Inner Farne into a cove protected from the open sea by a larger island to the east of it, cut the engine, and let the boat idle up to a small landing stage extending into the sea from the rocky coastline. Jonathan jumped ashore and handed Felicity out. She turned to wait for Matthew, but he shook his head. "I'll s-s-stay with my b-boat."

Jonathan leaned back into the boat and picked up a shovel and pickax. Tossing them across his shoulder he led the way up to the bare, grassy field of the island. Then, to Felicity's surprise, he hung back. "After you."

"Oh, I thought you would know where we're going."

He grinned. "I wouldn't want to spoil your fun. You've been following clues and studying this for days and days. Go ahead and show me what you've learned."

"Thank you! That's really cool." She didn't finish her thought out loud: *for once, a man who doesn't insist on exhibiting his knowledge.*

She dug in her now soggy backpack for Antony's map and led the way to Cuthbert's Chapel, the only building on the island in good repair, apart from the modern lighthouse on the other side. Felicity struggled to recall what Antony had told her about the chapel: "Built in the Middle Ages by the monks who lived here when they had grown wealthy on booty from salvaged wrecks and selling seal oil, if I remember the story right." The small stone building had a cross at one end and tiny tower at the other. Felicity led the way inside through a Gothic arched doorway. Light shone through the stained glass of the three arched windows on the south wall.

A plaque beside the door read: "Restored 1827 by Archdeacon Charles Thrope." Another Victorian restoration. She was about to leave, when her heart leapt to her throat. Was it possible? She darted across the room to a small enclosure where a stone coffin was built partly into the wall. Could it be? Something so obvious? And yet—this *was* St. Cuthbert's chapel. She started to turn back to Jonathan when she saw the small engraved plaque: "Thomas Sparowe, Master of Inner Farne, 1423–30." She shrugged and Jonathan grinned back at her.

Why hadn't she paid more attention to Antony's musings on the train? She had been so bone-weary, it was more than she could do to stay awake. But now, she couldn't even make out his doodles on the map. Still amazed and rather flattered at Jonathan's deference, she led the way out of the chapel. To the west were the remains of Castell's Tower, built by the prior of Durham in the fifteenth century for defense. She did remember Antony saying that even though it was built on the site of St. Cuthbert's cell, a defensive fort seemed an unlikely place for a burial.

She stood for a moment, looking around her. Sixteen acres, she recalled, eleven of them bare rock, but five covered with a peaty soil where Cuthbert scratched out his meager living and later monks grew barley. Then she saw it, at the far end of St. Cuthbert's Cove—the reconstructed cross. Cuthbert had erected a cross beside his guest house. Now renewed by each generation of Guardians, perhaps? She looked behind her at the tower marking his cell and recalled the picture of the saint in his final illness, crawling across his beloved island from cell to guest house, dragging his little bag of onions. It was in the guest house that he had begged the Lindisfarne brothers to bury him on his *desart*. It was in the guest house that he breathed his last before one of the brothers ran across the island to the edge of the high cliff on the west, and sent the signal across the waves telling the waiting brotherhood that Cuthbert had departed this life.

She wiped a tear from her eye and grinned at Jonathan. "Sorry, I got carried away for a minute. I'm with you now." She started walking toward the cross. "Thank you for letting me get there on my own. He's buried beneath the cross, isn't he? It's perfect really. It shouldn't have taken me so long to figure it out."

Jonathan dropped his tools at the foot of the cross and looked at Felicity, still waiting for her to take the lead. "Well, he would have been buried facing east, right?' She indicated the direction from the cross that must mark the head of the grave.

Jonathan picked up the pickax and Felicity started to reach for the shovel, then hesitated. "Are you sure this is the right thing to do, Jonathan? Do we really have to disturb him?"

Jonathan stopped mid-swing of the pickax. "No omelets without breaking eggs."

She grinned. "No hospital for AIDS babies without breaking ground?" Surely this must have been what Dominic himself would have done to get to the treasure. If only he were here now.

"You got it. Treasure's no good to anyone left in the ground." His comment was accompanied by the thud of his pick.

They worked in silence for a long time, Jonathan making great, gashing strides with his heavy tool clawing the earth, Felicity turning up only small shovelsful of the peaty soil. She stopped occasionally to catch her breath and survey the view around them. Deep, slate-blue water rippled in every direction, washing the rocky shores of nearby islands. Seabirds whirled overhead, diving into the water, resting on the rocks: black cormorants with long, curved bills; soft gray and white gulls, riding on the breeze as easily as if on water; vivid black and white auks with long orange bills. She was glad she had studied Bootham's bird book even briefly. She wished she knew more. And once her digging was interrupted by a quacking at her feet as a group of black and white eider ducks waddled by. "Oh, look, Jon. Cuddy's ducks! Aren't they sweet?"

He nodded, but did not stop pummeling the earth with his mighty swings. Felicity turned back to the ducks. "Don't worry, we won't disturb him too much." She picked up her shovel, but didn't resume digging for a moment. "Just think, they could be descended from the very ducks that were here with Cuthbert. Oh, Jonathan, isn't this amazing! Just think—what we're doing is truly historic! I only wish Dominic could be here with us. This would mean so much to him." She gazed upward at the clear sky. "But maybe he is with us in a way—Dominic and Cuthbert and Aidan and all who worked and prayed for good on this tiny island... and Elspeth, and—"

Her musings were interrupted by the distinctive thwak of solid iron hitting heavy wood. "Jonathan! That's it! We've done it!" She dropped her shovel and flung her arms around his neck. "We found him! We've solved the secret!"

But Jonathan barely returned her smile before he pushed her away. Abandoning his pickax, he picked up the shovel for more precise clearing away of the soil. In a seemingly short time, the top of a solid oaken box was exposed to the sunshine of a March afternoon for the first time in half a millennium. Such a shallow grave on the rocky island. Felicity fell to her knees. She would barely have to bend over to touch the lid of the casket. This was a truly awesome moment. Surely they should do something to mark it. "Jonathan, I think you should lead in a prayer."

In reply, he lay his shovel aside and bent over. Felicity closed her eyes and folded her hands.

When no prayer was forthcoming she looked up. "No!" She screamed and shoved Jonathan sideways just as he prepared to bring the heavy pickax down on the top of the casket. "You'll damage it!" She shoved at him again. "This is a sacred relic! What are you thinking?"

Jonathan dropped the pick and took a step backward away from her, his hand in his pocket. "The same thing I've been thinking all along. To find the treasure."

It was several moments before Felicity registered the fact that Jonathan was holding a gun leveled at her.

Panic followed the initial shock. Her heart stopped beating. She stopped breathing. Darkness clouded her vision.

She thought she was going to faint.

Then despair, as full realization hit her. How could she have come so far and lost it all at the last moment? The treasure, given for good, guarded for centuries. How could it fall to evil at last? How could she have been so stupid as to swallow Jonathan's line?

The sun glinted coldly off the steel barrel, offering no answers.

Chapter 33

She *hated* feeling foolish. Anger revitalized her. She took a deep, shuddering breath. Her vision cleared. Jonathan's voice cut through the roaring in her head, and she realized he had been talking for several moments.

"Now then, just be a good girl, will you?" Jonathan's words held a mocking edge. "I didn't want it to be this way, you know. Why couldn't you just go along with the program?"

"You aren't a Guardian." Felicity was amazed at the steadiness of her voice. As steady as the gun Jonathan was holding on her. "You're one of the others."

"'Three from the See; three from the sea.' Dear departed Uncle Cuthbert, simple scholar that he was, uncovered all that. 'It's like a mantra to them,' he would say, 'or a secret code.' It all fascinated him. And it was just sheer intellectual pleasure for the old fool.

"Of course, I encouraged him because I saw the possibilities from the first—and I was only twelve years old when he started sharing the really interesting bits. Before that it was just bedtime stories about ancient saints. I never could see the use in that, even if he was named for one of them. But now, treasure—that was a different matter, indeed.

"Our house was just a block away. When my mother had a late night, she sent me to stay in the guest house in the monastery—where I'd be safe."

Abruptly Jonathan's face twisted with pain, hatred, disgust—Felicity wasn't sure. "But that wasn't all he started sharing then. The treasure gave me something to think about while I was enduring what came after the bedtime stories. Other kids would go off to sleep dreaming of fire engines or space ships. I dreamt of royal pilgrims bringing precious gifts— to me. To make up for what I had to endure from my oh-so-saintly uncle.

"Uncle Cuthbert told me about the three Guardians, and when I thought of forming three, ah, more practical counterparts, I had something more than fantasies to get me through those—" His mouth clamped shut and he ground his teeth.

"I lived in the part of my mind that was making plots to avenge myself on the whole lot of them. And I'd do it by reviving their own ancient tradition." A joyless smile spread over his face. "And how sweet it is. I did it! I got even. The old fool—thought he could do anything he wanted with me. I showed him—"

Felicity's mind raced faster than her thumping heart. The malice, the vindictiveness. Now she understood. "But Father Dominic wasn't your uncle. Beating him didn't solve anything."

"Oh, yes it did." His smile bared his teeth and his eyes glinted. "As soon as the blood started, it was Cuthbert's face I saw. And it felt *so* good." He gave a high-pitched laugh. "I wasn't going to kill him at first. I had tried to ferret the information out of him when he returned the night before, but I must have been rather clumsy because he clammed up entirely.

"Next day I saw him go out and thought, aha, I'd just find it myself. Uncle Cuthbert always said there was a map—cut into three pieces. Unfortunately for the old coot, he returned before I'd found it. A couple of good knocks and he'd tell me quick enough, I thought. Certainly didn't mean to kill him until I knew where the treasure was.

"But then, that was all right after all. A—er… friend who was keeping an eye on him for me reported your little tête-à-tête. You provided a charming plan B, my dear. We never could find the map, even with a couple of later visits to your rooms, which I'm sure you noticed. But knowing you had it, all we had to do was follow you."

Keep him talking until help comes, she told herself. There were other tourist boats out there somewhere, cruising the Farne Islands today. Surely one of them would put in at Inner Farne.

Although another part of her mind told her that since it was the island closest to land, the chances were they had already been here.

A flick of his thumb pulled back the safety catch on the pistol he had leveled at her. *Say something*, a distant corner of her mind demanded.

"I don't understand—why didn't you just turn Antony over to the police?'

His mocking laugh returned. "No, you *really* don't understand, do you? The police were never interested in Antony. Anselm didn't send Matt in. *I* did. 'Oh, quick, quick you've got to help him!' Clever of me, wasn't it? Everyone running hither and thither and me in the hall having a good old laugh."

"But why?"

"Because between the two of you, you had all the clues—the map, the journal, all the real knowledge Uncle Cuthbert had just guessed at. All I had to do was set you in motion and follow you to the treasure. Fair division of labor—let you beat your brains out over the details. I'd save mine for the important work."

"As you have done."

"As I have done."

"And yet you tried three times to kill us on Lindisfarne."

"What? Philly's pathetic mintcakes and faked tide chart? Yes—she wanted to get rid of you and do it on our own. I think she was rather jealous of your charms distracting me. She really was the silliest woman. She deserved to die."

"And then you had to decide whether to romance me or get rid of me."

He raised one eyebrow and leered at her. "Not a difficult choice, I can assure you, my dear. You're a very tasty little dish in your puritanical way. Such a shame we couldn't have just stayed with the lovebird scenario. Although, I did rethink the night you had your little adventure on that stalled train. But that rail crew mother-henning you didn't give me a chance. Then you were so trusting and innocent when I showed up, I thought—why not play along? And, of course, as it turned out, it served as rather a practice run for rescuing you from Bush Island—or Bush pond as it is at the moment."

Her anger at herself for being such a fool was greater at that moment than her rage at Jonathan. And she was afraid she couldn't keep him talking for much longer.

"Right. So you formed a consortium of three to find the treasure: you and Philly Johnson and... Oh, what happened there? You got tired of Philly ordering everyone around?"

Jonathan's smile was more of a sneer. "Silly cow. That henpecked husband of hers made her a valuable asset at first. Ansel Smith really is an excellent researcher; he dug out a lot for us—so pleased that his wife was taking an interest in his work. But then she got greedy."

"So you simply bashed her up the side of the head like you did Dominic."

"No, sorry. I can't take credit for that one."

"Who then?"

"You're so clever. Surely you can work that out?"

"Well, we suspected Stephen Bootham for a while, but he doesn't really seem to be very involved. I suppose it's either Willibrord or Laird."

Now his sneer was a taunting laugh. "And to whom do you assign the role of the third Guardian of the Good that I, alas, have been forced to abdicate?"

She thought for a moment. Yes, indeed, who? Who was an English Benedictine that had been involved from the first? "Oh, of course, Brother Matthew!" The thought served to calm her rising terror. She wasn't alone. Brother Matthew was down at the landing station. If they didn't appear soon, he would come looking for them. The promise of nearby help steadied her. "How did you dupe him into working with you? If—"

"Well, Miss Howard, charming as I find this conversation, I'm afraid I need to get on with my work. Lucky you hold our Sainted Cuthbert in such high esteem. You will be able to appreciate the honor of sharing a grave with him."

Jonathan raised his gun a fraction and moved a step toward her. Barely an arm's length away. No hope of his missing his aim.

Felicity looked around her. No launches approached. Matthew, still down at the cove, was beyond shouting distance. She would have to deal with this herself.

Fighting the temptation to close her eyes for greater concentration, and focusing all her attention on the steel-rimmed black hole facing her, she heard in her mind her brother's backyard training. *Focus. Aim. Kick!*

She executed a perfect *grand battment* and kicked the gun from his hand. Miss Lisa would have been so proud of her, if shocked at the Kung Fu adaptation Jeff had added to her classical ballet training all those years ago.

Her recovery was quicker than Jonathan's, so she reached the gun first. *Hold it in both hands. Aim for the body—the widest target.* She could still hear Jeff's instructions in her head. Paintballing had been a great adventure; she always thought she was a lucky little sister to be included. Now she realized just how lucky. "Right. Hands on your head. Walk slowly to the boat."

"With pleasure. Allow me to congratulate you, Fliss. Perfect execution. If very bad deduction." He had taken two strides toward the cove when a familiar pudgy figure in black cassock and gray scapular emerged from the rocky shoreline.

Jonathan raised his voice to carry across the distance. "Ah, Brother Matthew! Well timed. Our Miss Fliss was hankering to meet the person who dispatched the greedy Philly. I think it only fair to grant her last wish, don't you?"

Brother Matt came closer into view and Felicity saw that the timid monk was holding a gun that didn't look the least bit meek. And she realized her mistake. Brother Matthew was indeed one of the Three, but she had assigned him to the wrong set.

"No," Felicity protested. "Not a CT Brother. Not one of our own!" But even as she protested, she realized—Jonathan said he had sent Matt with the faked message from Father Anselm. Matt and Jonathan, plotting the whole thing together from the first. "How *could* you?" She spat the words at him.

"They always l-laughed at me. Not to my face, of course. B-but everyone knew I didn't make it through s-s-selection conference. Th-they all th-thought me inadequate. S-said I'd never amount to anything. I'll sh-show them, I thought."

"What? The Kirkthorpe Fathers laughed at you? That can't be."

"N-not them. S-silly bunch. Too busy p-praying to bother about a mere lay b-brother."

"Then who?"

"My f-family, the whole f-f-f—bunch of them. P-power. That's all that counted. And money. That gave you p-power."

"And so you joined a *monastery* to gain power?"

"It w-worked. T-treasurer, they made me. I held the purse strings. I'll build the library. I'll become s-superior. I'll show them."

Felicity was more alarmed by his frenzied tone than by the gun he held. "And you showed Sister Elspeth at Whitby?"

Jonathan broke in, "No, Matt let me have that particular pleasure. He had the fun of watching from a ringside seat in the tower—just lucky he got to treat you to his little rock show."

"I th-thought it a nice t-touch." But then Matt's gaze turned to the gun Felicity still held. "I think you sh-should d-d-drop that gun." He gestured with the larger weapon in his own hand.

Felicity froze. The gun slipped from her fingers. Matt stepped forward and raised the barrel of his gun. She closed her eyes.

Only the faintest whirring sound preceded the high-pitched scream.

She opened her eyes to see Brother Matt on the ground, clutching his arm as a dark, wet stain spread over his cassock sleeve around the crossbow bolt protruding from it.

Curtis Johnson, silver chains and piercings glinting in the sun, loped across the flat green field from the shelter of the bird-covered boulders of the shoreline. "You killed my mother, you b—!"

Felicity's mind was in too much of a whirl to register the sound of the boat approaching the cove. She was just thankful Curtis had set another bolt into his crossbow and leveled it at Jonathan. She retrieved the gun she had dropped at Matt's demand, but felt she didn't have the strength to aim it.

"Get the monk's gun," Curtis ordered.

She obeyed, as if on heavy medication. This couldn't be happening. "Curtis, what are you doing here?"

"Been following these slime bags. Knew Mom had some business thing going with them. When she turned up murdered I wanted to find out what was going on. Heard them at the pier talking about coming out here." He turned to Matthew, still whimpering on the ground. "Wouldn't talk to me there, would you? You'll talk now!" He raised his crossbow menacingly again.

"Curt! No!" Felicity held out a hand to stop him, but he had already shifted his aim to the weaponless, but far from cowed, Breen.

Summoning every shard of her shattered concentration, she commanded a reasonably steady aim with the pistol she held poised toward Matt before firing another question at Curtis, who managed to maintain his laconic pose in spite of everything. "So it was you who shot at us on Lindisfarne?"

"Yea. Sorry about that. Mom said you were trying to discredit Dad's book so I should scare you off."

"*Scare us?* You almost killed me."

"Nah, I'm a good shot."

A growling sound issued from Jonathan's throat as if he might attempt springing at Curtis.

"Don't even think about it, pal. Like I said—I'm a good shot and this thing's got a hair trigger."

Looking at Matt still on the ground, Felicity had to believe Curtis was right. "But how did you get here? To the island?"

"Came with that bunch of birdwatchers, didn't I? On the

St. Cuthbert, even. Seemed appropriate enough. Just didn't leave with them, that's all."

The sound of running footsteps pounded across the field. "Felicity! Oh, thank God!" Antony stopped short of engulfing her in a hug when he saw she was holding a gun.

She looked at Antony's companions. Willibrord was no surprise, but the other—"What's Stephen Bootham doing here?"

"Wills was waiting for Bootham in the Olde Ship. We saw you get in a boat with that dodgy character and came as fast as we could, but we had to wait a bit for Bootham."

"Sorry about the delay." The muscular bookseller/ birdwatcher, today in a red and white striped jersey that could have come from the costume department of an *HMS Pinafore* production, looked up and grinned when he had completed snapping handcuffs on Jonathan Breen. "Busy day, this. I just sent Laird off with the constabulary."

"Laird?" Felicity asked. "There were Four from the sea?"

Bootham looked confused by her question. Antony answered. "Wills caught Professor Laird in the sacristy at St. Mary's. Seems he'd come back for the last two candlesticks."

"Like the ones in the church at Bamburgh?"

"That's right. He had a lucrative sideline going selling off artifacts from his archeological digs. When the archeology slowed down, he salted the digs with hand-planted valuables."

"So you're a policeman?" Felicity struggled to put it all together.

"Insurance investigator. But I can make do until we get to the authorities." Bootham handcuffed Jonathan before taking the pistols from Felicity and pulling the bleeding, moaning Matthew to his feet. "Right, you lot, that way," Stephen Bootham commanded.

He prodded Breen toward the launch, then looked back at Curtis, still holding his Celtic warrior pose. "Come along, lad. You've done good work. The authorities will be needing a statement from you."

Willibrord turned to follow the group. "I'll just see to helping them get off in Brother Matt's boat. Be back soon to… uh—help clean up here."

Felicity watched them go. The sight of the sun glinting on Breen's wind-tossed curls sent a chilling tremor through her body. She began shaking uncontrollably, her eyes wide with horror as the images of might-have-beens filled her mind. "He—he told me… Father Dominic—he *enjoyed* bludgeoning him. And to think—he could have done the same to me so many times… Why—?" A violent shudder cut off her speculation.

Antony took her into his arms and held her until the spasm passed, leaving only a gentle trembling. "I don't think he ever really wanted to kill you, even though he was willing to at the end."

Felicity felt her head spinning. There was so much to take in. Actions. Motives. Emotions. "It's so hard to believe. So cold-blooded. The calculation makes it all the more horrible." And then it all rushed out in a jumble. Jonathan's troubled story, her feelings, Cuthbert's grave…

But Antony seemed quite capable of making sense of the muddle. "Yes, using you—us—to lead him to the treasure was coldly calculated. But his rage, insanity, even, was fired at the figure he saw as a symbol of his uncle: an older monk, an authority figure, one who refused to divulge the answers Jonathan coveted, felt he had a right to, even."

"Yes." She spoke slowly. "I know the abuse must have been abhorrent to him. He must have truly suffered—not just then, but all his life— carrying that around inside him."

Antony nodded. "The shame magnified everything unimaginably—mixed with hatred and rage toward the one who caused the shame. And then it all turned into feelings of guilt."

She nodded. "Guilt and fear. When I think of the little boy he must have been—angelic-looking with his blond curls—huddled and crying in a dark room. Yes, I can feel sorry for that little boy.

But when I remember what the man that little boy became did to Father Dominic—"

"Of course, the problem was that instead of dealing with the shame, he let it fester and kept it stuffed down with an overglaze of haughtiness and pride. Ultimately, it's selfishness that leads to a calculated murder—the feeling that the murderer's desires and needs have priority over everything else—even over the other person's right to live." He paused. "I'm not a trained psychologist, of course, but it's quite amazing how much a priest gets to understand human nature. Even one who has spent much of his career in a cloister."

Felicity shuddered. "He said he loved me. I don't think he was even capable of love."

"No, probably not, but I think he was truly attracted to you."

Even though he held her tightly, the trembling continued. "He… He said he was. But that makes it worse. The fact that I could attract such a—a monster—" She hiccuped. "And… and—" She paused, not wanting to go on, but knowing the confession had to be made. After all, she was talking to a priest. She took a deep, jagged breath. "And that I could consider returning the affection—" The shaking of her head was more of a convulsion to shake off the revulsion. "It makes me feel so—so dirty. Ashamed. As if I share some of the guilt for his atrocious acts." She paused. "Not to mention stupid."

Easily, almost imperceptibly, Antony slipped into his priestly role, settling into his default position with a comfort that extended its balm to her. He shifted his stance to put just the slightest distance between them, but without withdrawing his comfort. "First you need to understand that guilt is not sin. Neither is stupidity." She smiled at that. A rather wobbly, chagrined smile. "Still, stupidity can be one of the hardest things to forgive ourselves for. And the answer is just the same as for anything else. Forgiveness is the only antidote for guilt and shame, and we can only forgive ourselves, and therefore get rid of the guilt and shame, when we know we've been forgiven by God."

She blinked at that and raised her eyes to his.

"You'd be amazed how often this comes up in pastoral work—probably the most frequent subject we deal with. People carry so much needless guilt and shame around with them—it's a terrible burden. It gets in the way of everything else they try to accomplish in life."

"So what do you do?"

"On a practical level, I try to help them deal with the source of the shame. But on the spiritual side, one of the most helpful prayers I know is the collect for Ash Wednesday. Do you remember it?"

She looked blank. The horrific events that followed so rapidly on the heels of that powerful service had put the memory of any details out of her mind.

"You may recall it came right after the Litany of Penitence. It's a wonderful prayer for forgiveness." His pause indicated that he would not go on without her consent. Felicity bowed her head to indicate her desire for him to continue.

"'Almighty and everlasting God, you hate nothing you have made and forgive the sins of all who are penitent: Create and make in us new and contrite hearts, that we, worthily lamenting our sins and acknowledging our wretchedness, may obtain of you, the God of all mercy, perfect remission and forgiveness; through Jesus Christ our Lord...'"

Felicity joined in on the final "Amen." Even before opening her eyes she felt a lifting of the weight in her chest, a new steadiness to her breathing. She opened her eyes on a brighter, cleaner-looking world.

"Thank you." It was unclear whether she spoke to Antony or to a higher power.

But Antony wasn't finished. He took a deep, unsteady breath. "The sacrament of reconciliation ends with the priest saying, 'Pray for me, also a sinner.' It's time I confessed. I have blood on my hands as surely as you saw in Father Dominic's room."

Felicity was too confused to reply. Surely not. All the deaths had been accounted for, hadn't they?

"When we were recounting our pasts, I glossed over my time as a curate."

"Middle-aged, single women making casseroles and knitting jumpers?"

"That was true enough as far as it went. But I didn't tell you about Alice."

"Alice?"

"Not exactly middle-aged, just a few years older than I was, but even less experienced. Daughter of the widowed incumbent priest. She had kept house for him since her mother died. I thought her cleaning the curate's house was just routine." He paused. "I didn't really think at all."

Felicity thought it sounded positively Victorian, but she said nothing.

"Before God, I had no idea of the strength of her feelings until she quite literally threw herself at me. We were alone at the Maundy Thursday watch…" His silence was filled with the crash of the waves on the rocky shore beyond them. "I rebuffed her. Mercilessly. God forgive me."

This time the silence was even longer. "I found her hours later when I dashed home to freshen up before the Good Friday service. In my bathtub. Wrists slit. So much blood." He shivered and wiped his hands over his eyes as if to erase the image. "Like Dominic. So much blood. If only I had arrived earlier. Just like Dominic. Too late. My fault." He held out his hands and examined them as if still looking for blood.

Felicity took his hands and clasped them tightly. "Antony, listen to me. You couldn't have known. It's not your fault—neither one of them. Not Dominic. Not Alice."

After a moment he nodded slowly and withdrew his hands. "Thank you. I do *know* that. *Believing* it is another matter." He gave a rueful grin. "Ironic how easy it is to assure others of absolution and how hard to accept it for oneself."

"Antony." She touched his arm. "You don't know—your actions might not have made any difference. It's a tragic story, but she was an adult, a troubled one. She made the decision..."

"Oh, yes, I've told myself all that. Still..." He gave himself a little shake. "Point is, I let her down."

"Well, you didn't let me down. Or Dominic. Or yourself." She said it fiercely, then was quiet for a long time, savoring the sudden lightness she felt as her own internal turmoil lifted.

It required only the slightest shift of their bodies for Antony to be holding her once more. As the final tensions drained away, she felt she could have floated like a seagull riding the wind currents above them. Later she wondered how much longer they might have stayed like that, or what might have happened next, had Willibrord not come striding toward them over the hard, flat turf.

Looking toward the shore, Felicity caught sight of the grass-green boat rocking in the wake of Matthew's departing craft with Bootham at the helm. "Oh, that's the boat we saw on the Viking Beach." She turned to Willibrord. "That's why you didn't want us to go there."

He nodded. "I didn't want to tip you off to Bootham's investigation and I was afraid it would raise awkward questions about Dominic's time here."

"You took Dominic out in the boat?"

"I brought him here to Inner Farne. Guardians' role to make regular visits."

Willibrord stood watching Bootham and his charges sailing toward land. He shook his head, looking more like the sea breeze was buffeting him than as if he was performing a volitional act. "So there it is: 'Three from the See and Three from the sea.' I suspected Breen and Johnson, but never Brother Matt."

Antony rubbed his hair up and down, making Felicity almost choke at the dear familiarity of the gesture. "I still can't believe anyone from the Community of the Transfiguration would do such a thing. One of our own—"

Felicity squeezed his arm. "He was a lay brother, not a priest. And he was the treasurer—like Judas." Then she paused and thought. "But if Jonathan wasn't the third Guardian—?" She looked at Willibrord. "Oh! 'Three from the See.' You knew! It's you!"

He gave his head-bobbing nod and smiled. "You recognize our password."

"But Jonathan said he put the sea cohorts together."

"I don't think the original reference was meant to be so specific," Antony said.

"You mean like Vikings, Reformers, and self-serving criminals in general?" Felicity asked, counting each group off on a finger.

"No, more symbolic than that," Willibrord replied. "It's scriptural, really, about laying up your treasure where moth and rust won't corrupt—"

"Or thieves break in and steal!" Felicity finished for him. "They almost did, though, didn't they?" She turned back to the grave. "Oh! The treasure! How could I have forgotten?" She gestured toward the casket pierced by Jonathan's pickax. Even now she could see a glimmer of gold through the broken lid.

Willibrord unzipped an inside pocket in his padded vest and brought out a small envelope encased in a plastic bag. "Antony told me you had discovered Dominic's fragment. Technically we should have Elspeth's as well before we proceed, but it will take some time to have her safe deposit box opened, and we can hardly leave matters as they are now."

Felicity drew the journal from her pocket and prised the endpaper free. Willibrord's isosceles triangle fitted over their scalene perfectly, leaving a hole an equilateral would fill. She squinted at the Latin script, trying to make sense of the archaic wording. "Oh, good. This is the top bit. 'Hugh, by the grace of God, Prior of Durham, sends greetings…' Oh, this circumambient writing is impossible to follow!"

"That is the point of it," Antony reminded her.

"Right. Well, the next line here is something about 'in perpetuity, the mortal remains of St. Cuthbert…' then something about 'this—' er, I think the word is 'conjoined instrument.' Does that make sense?"

Willibrord nodded emphatically. "Exactly right. It means that the validity of the instrument is dependent upon there being all three. When the three pieces are joined, we can present documentation proving that Cuthbert's treasure is and always has been the property of the Guardians, held and guarded in perpetuity on land dedicated to that purpose." He pointed to the center of the document where the points would meet. "That is the signature of Prior Hugh, complete when the three are together."

Felicity still looked blank, so Antony added, "I think what Wills is saying is that under law this would not be deemed treasure trove, which would belong to the Crown, because it hasn't been *found*; it has been *stored*."

"Yes, that's right. That's what we did when Dominic was with us—we took legal advice. Of course it will all have to be sorted out in court, but it was the opinion of the counsel we consulted that the treasure would not escheat to the Crown."

"Of course, if it does, there would still be a reward, which would at least launch the hospital appeal."

"Certainly—"

"Stop!" Both of Felicity's companions jumped at her outcry. "I don't want to discuss legal minutia. I want to see the treasure!"

Wills laughed. "Fair enough." He dropped to his knees and pulled back the splintered wood with his hands. "I don't want to break it any further, and the key is with Sister Elspeth's portion of the charter, but you can have a peep here."

Felicity gazed long at the gleaming objects in the casket. Precious jewels winked at her as rays of sunshine hit them. A wrought gold chalice lay at one end, half buried in coins. Beside it rested an incense boat looking like a miniature Aladdin's lamp, a jeweled pectoral cross next to that.

But with all the dazzling wealth and glitter, one item drew her above all else. She pulled it out from all the opulence and slipped it on her finger. A simple gold ring, the large red stone incised with a distinctive cross.

"His ring. Cuthbert's bishop's ring." Her awe-filled voice was barely above a whisper. And it was tight on her finger. What a tiny man he must have been. And yet the power of his life radiated through the ages.

Felicity raised her head. "That should certainly be enough to build Dominic's Children's Hospital."

"Build it, staff it and endow a research department, I should think. Medieval pilgrims were known to show their gratitude with great generosity. Dominic went over all the plans in detail with Elspeth and me. He was a very careful man. Of course, we gave him our full approval."

Felicity smiled. "Yes. Helping people. Going wherever he was needed. Healing children. Just to think that Cuthbert's legacy still lives. Talk about incorruption."

"And all thanks to those clever Guardians who secreted the pilgrim's treasure from the shrine, under the very nose of Henry's thugs," Antony added with a chuckle.

Felicity, however, wasn't satisfied yet. "But this is just treasure. What about Cuthbert?" Willibrord gestured toward the gaping hole that Felicity, in her innocence, had helped Jonathan dig.

Felicity peered into the grave and saw what she hadn't noticed before—another casket below the one they had unearthed. "So he is there! We were right about the whole thing." She gave a satisfied sigh. "And Cuthbert is buried where he always wanted to be."

Willibrord picked up the shovel and began filling in the open grave.

"What!" Felicity cried. "Aren't we going to open it? Check on the incorruption story?"

Willibrord set his shovel in the soil and stepped back, smiling at her. "Go ahead. You've earned the right."

Trembling, she moved forward, knelt and extended her arm full length. The stone coffin felt warm and smooth to her hand. She caressed the lid, thinking of the mystery it concealed. Cuthbert's ring, still on her finger glowed warmly. She could almost feel them gathered around her: the ancient Lindisfarne brothers who had first discovered the miracle of Cuthbert's incorruption; the medieval monks, translating the saint to his shrine in Durham Cathedral; even Henry's henchmen and the Victorian investigators focusing on the wrong tomb; all those from the See and those from the sea who had been caught up in the incomprehensible.

Still trembling, she turned to pick up Jonathan's ax to pry up the lid, but paused at a gentle quacking sound. A paddling of Eider ducks, four or five mottled brown females and a handsome, white, black and green drake, waddled to the very edge of the open grave as if they, too, would look in. Or defend it.

Felicity sat back on her heels, smiling at Cuddy's Ducks. "You don't think he should be disturbed, do you?" She held out her hand to Antony to help her to her feet. "Nor do I. Some things are best left a mystery."

Antony hugged her. "Quite right. 'Blessed are those who have not seen, but have believed.'"

Felicity turned back to the open grave, wishing she had a bunch of flowers, but nothing grew nearby. Instead she picked up a handful of the earth that Cuthbert loved so well. The peaty, preserving, good earth from his own *desart*. Perhaps the very soil where he had planted barley seeds and so logically argued the birds away from eating his crop. She tossed the dirt onto the casket. It landed with a satisfying, earthy thud.

Willibrord smiled and resumed his shoveling, gently, so as not to frighten the ducks that remained at the edge of the grave.

"We'll need a prayer when this is done, Father Antony. And some holy water."

Antony hesitated, looking around. "I—I don't know. I don't

have a stole or a prayer book or—"

Willibrord laughed. "I'm sure you'll make do. You wouldn't want to fumble your first assignment as the newest Guardian."

"Me?" Antony took a step backward.

"I can't think of anyone who would do a better job. With Father Anselm as the third, don't you think?"

"But I'm not a Benedictine. I…"

Willibrord shrugged between shovels of sod. "Easy enough to become an oblate."

Antony ran both hands through his hair. "Um, would just being a Companion count?" Willibrord laughed. "Why, because oblates are required to be celibate?"

Felicity was sure her blush was redder than Antony's, and her laugh was merrier than either of the others'.

Chapter 34

The peace and beauty of the Community church had never seemed more profound to Felicity. She knelt in the quiet before mass. The St. Cuthbert's Day mass—the opening service of the meeting of the Ecumenical Commission—the service she had so feared Antony would not be free to celebrate. She looked around at the simplicity, purity and strength of the heavy, neo-Norman pillars, the flowing lines of the Early English rounded arches and apse, feeling like a smaller, unornamented Durham Cathedral. Their serenity wrapped around her like a shawl. They had been back in Kirkthorpe for three days now—long enough for Felicity to organize her flat, but not her life.

She had learned so much in the past, frantic, sometimes terrifying days. So much about history—and its influence on today. So much about human nature—the good and the bad. So much about faith—its importance and reality. So much about herself... Or had she? Well, she had learned a lot of questions: learned what she didn't know about herself; learned about faults she didn't know she had; learned how shallow many of her motives had been. Where she was to go from there, she had no idea. But one thing she knew—she wanted to delve deeper into this world that had opened to her. She had glimpsed a new reality and she wanted more of it.

She was a different person from the headstrong, overconfident young woman who was so insistent on her own rights such a short time ago. Would she settle back into her old routines, her old ways, her old self? She was determined not to. She was changed, and she was determined that the change, whatever it was, would be for the better.

The organist began the introit, "Sheep May Safely Graze." Felicity tried to think, but her mind refused to follow a coherent pattern. The only answer she could find was to relax and let the rhythm and beauty of the liturgy carry her.

She heard a soft clink in the north aisle, the unmistakable sound of the thurible reaching the end of its chain as the Thurifer began his gentle swing to distribute the incense. The spicy scent enveloped Felicity further, drawing her into the mystery of being. She looked up to see the procession forming: Crucifer bearing the tall, silver processional cross, flanked by acolytes with flaming pillar candles, her fellow ordinands, angelic-looking in their white albs. Behind them the clergy: Father Clement serving as subdeacon today, Father Anselm as deacon, both with white brocade dalmatics over their albs; and behind them, the celebrant priest—Father Antony in white chasuble with the red and gold cross of St. Cuthbert embroidered on the offray.

She caught her breath. She had hardly seen him at all since their return. Now he stood there, so erect, so solemn, slightly pale beneath his dark hair. Entirely focused on the moment at hand. The consummate priest. Was this really the man with whom she had fled across the length and breadth of northern England? The man with whom she had faced danger and death from multiple enemies? The man to whom she had bared her deepest questions, doubts and fears? The man to whom she had assigned the role of murderer? She blushed at the thought. Already those days seemed like something she had read in a vivid novel. Now they were back to the real world—their chosen world. Would their relationship be anything more than lecturer and student? Did she want it to be?

A holy hush filled the church. Another clink of the thurible followed by a cloud of incense, and the procession began. Down the side, up the center aisle toward the high altar. Her eyes were glued on Antony as he approached, looking straight ahead. He was almost level with her choir stall when he broke his gaze. Only for the briefest moment, he looked straight at her, a hint of a smile on his lips. His small smile was perceptible only to her, but it spoke volumes of shared memories.

They had achieved their goal. They had solved the mystery. They had secured the treasure for Dominic's legacy to the children of Africa. They had found the Ninian Papyrus, offering a new approach for Antony's ecumenical work. They had returned in time for Antony to celebrate the St. Cuthbert Day Mass. But that tiny, half-smile had spoken of something deeper, something more personal. They had achieved their outward goals. But they had also made progress on their inward goals.

She had sensed the change in Antony as each challenge of their journey had been met and overcome. He had confessed his insecurities and sense of inadequacy to her early on. But she could see that it had not been a matter of inadequacy, merely a lack of testing. Before, when a challenge loomed, he had withdrawn from the lists, assuming he would fail. But now, when he had been thrust into a situation for which he truly was inadequate, he had triumphed.

And what about herself? Before her litany of doubts could return, the Old Testament reading began, pushing her thoughts to the background. "Thus says the Lord God: I myself will search for my sheep, and will seek them out... I will bring them out from the peoples and gather them from the countries, and will bring them into their own land... I will feed them with good pasture."

Then Antony led in the collect for the day: "Almighty God, who called your servant Cuthbert from following the flock to follow your Son and to be a shepherd of your people: in your mercy, grant that we, following his example, may bring those who are lost home to your fold..."

As the gradual hymn recounted the triumphs of the saints, Felicity's thoughts became clearer. Yes, spending all that time with Cuthbert, with his story, his legacy, had shown her that it was for real—the idea of personal holiness, prayer—all the sacraments and disciplines that she had chafed at. And it wasn't just St. Cuthbert that had shown her that, it was Antony—the unwavering example he had set before her, even when she had chided him for it. She looked up, hoping to catch his eye, even though he wouldn't be able to see her returning his smile from across the distance of the chancel.

But it wasn't until she knelt at the communion rail and received the sacrament from his hands, as the wafer sat light on her tongue, that she knew these vague understandings weren't enough. Knowledge demanded action. Now she must decide on the direction for the rest of her life. She pictured herself on the edge of the shore facing a shining sea. She wanted to wade in until the sparkling waters of this new life buoyed her up and carried her.

The final strains of the organ voluntary were still echoing high in the vaulted ceiling when she met Antony outside the sacristy. He drew her into a side chapel where the evening sunset was glowing red against the glass. "Felicity, how are you? It's so good to see you. We've hardly spoken—" He ran his hand through his hair. "What I mean is, how are you really, inside yourself?"

"That's exactly what I wanted to talk to you about." She paused. "First things first—Antony, can you ever forgive me for accusing you, even briefly—for thinking you capable of—" She shook her head. "I wouldn't blame you if you never spoke to me again."

"Don't even think of it, Felicity. We were both so confused by events, by the intensity of everything. Of course I forgive you."

She gave him a wavery smile. "Thanks. That's better, then."

She felt she was going through a mental checklist. The things that had been niggling at her mind since she had once again had moments of quiet for reflection. "Another thing is—I mean—we really looked evil in the face. Not some vague power of darkness, but violent, personal evil—the kind I didn't want to believe in. Evil happening to good people…" Even the question was too much to form. How could she hope for an answer?

He shook his head. "Wish I had answers for you. Nice, pat,

easy answers. If there are any, none of the wisest men of the ages has ever come up with them."

Her heart sank. She so needed something.

But he wasn't finished. "I'll tell you what I *do* know, though, and that's where the good, the beauty and the joy in the universe come from. And that's enough for me to be going on with."

A radiant smile split her face.

"And I'll tell you something else. I can't prove it, but I ardently believe that the good far outweighs the evil."

Yes. As he said, no pat answers, but enough to be getting on with.

So then, what about the rest of it? Where did that leave her? "Well... you know how I came here because I loved the atmosphere, the beauty, the peace? I like candles and incense and rich colors and I thought, 'Yeah, I want to be part of this—it's cooler than being a dancer, and *way* cooler than being a teacher. And a new opportunity for women. I could prove—I don't know what I thought I could prove." She paused. "Oh, I'm babbling again, aren't I? I don't know what I'm trying to say."

Antony smiled. "I think I do. And actually, you're doing a very good job. Before, you were just looking at the peripherals, but now you've glimpsed the heart of the matter."

She nodded. "And it scares me silly."

He nodded. "Yes. The holy mysteries. Who *can* explain them? Who can approach them without an element of fear? That's why Cuthbert is such a great example. He just lived it. Just got on with the job and showed others how it was to be done."

"It's such a huge responsibility. Just the thought scares the socks off me. I mean, when I came here, I thought I knew everything. I knew where I was going and why I was going there and how I was going to get there. I thought I knew myself. Now I don't know anything."

He took her hand with a warm, gentle pressure that she felt all the way down to her toes. "I can't think of a better place to start."

Felicity and Antony will return
in

A DARKLY HIDDEN TRUTH

Book 2 in

THE MONASTERY MURDERS

Chapter 1

Friday, Third in Lent

Father Oswin smiled in his slow, thoughtful way, and steepled his
fingers into a Gothic arch. "And how long have you been feeling
this drawing to become a nun?"

Felicity's swallow was more of a gulp. It all sounded so
audacious. Fighting a sudden impulse to run from the room, she
managed to squeak out in a small voice, "Well, for several weeks
now." *Was almost two 'several'?*

Father Oswin nodded slowly and thoughtfully, as he did
everything. At least he didn't burst out laughing. "I see."

"But the thing is," Felicity was quite certain he *didn't* see,
"the thing is, it's so intense. I can't eat. I can't sleep. It's been
growing and growing." She placed her hand over her heart in the
region of the growing feeling—compulsion, she might even say.

"Yes."

Was there ever a more infuriating spiritual director than
Father Oswin? Felicity felt so full of exuberance, of desire
for action, of nervous tension it was all she could do to make
herself stay seated in her chair while the man sitting across from
her in the small confessional room sat so deep in meditation
he could be in danger of drifting off to sleep. *What should I do?*

she wanted to yell at him.

"Yes. I see." At long last the monk opened his hands and raised his head. "Yes." He nodded slowly, giving the word at least three syllables. "Then you must test the Spirit."

"Great! Er—how do I do that?" Ever since she had come to study in the theological college run by the Community of the Transfiguration on its remote hillside in Yorkshire many months ago, Felicity had experienced almost constant friction between their slow, understated pace of life and her out-to-conquer-the-world American energies, but she had never felt the conflict so sharply before. Nor had her urgency for action been so great. "What do I *do*?" She pulled out a notebook to jot down his instructions.

"How much time have you spent in a convent?"

"Um, well, I was at Whitby—Order of the Holy Paraclete—when Father Antony and I were looking for Dominic's murderer… When Sister Elspeth…" Felicity stopped with a shudder.

"Yes, terrible business that. Tragic loss." Father Oswin shook his head. "Hardly a good time for testing a vocation, I would say."

The tiny room fell silent as Felicity's mind replayed those all-too-recent events of chasing and being chased across half of northern England, of how her own rashness had led her so far astray, of the penitence she felt for her guilt in the tragic events. And yet, surely good could come even from that. If she were to become a nun herself, perhaps even in some small way fill up the enormous gap left by Sister Elspeth's energy and scholarship and holiness…

"Perhaps you should revisit the sisters there? Or perhaps look around a bit: Rempstone near Nottingham, All Hallows House in Norwich…" Walsingham, Oxford, Burford, the list went on. Who would have thought there were so many convents in England? "The sisters in Ham Common do a wonderful work among the poor, but London might be a bit far afield." Felicity scribbled as he rattled off the unfamiliar names. "Select two or three for a mini retreat. That should give you some perspective as to what you might be undertaking if you were to pursue a discernment process."

Discernment process? Couldn't she just go off to a convent and take the veil—that's what women did in books. Maid Marian, in *Robin Hood,* for example. Yes, Marian's convent was supposed to be around here somewhere. The Nun, a pub on the main road behind the Community was said to mark the spot.

"Of course, you understand, it can take years to test a vocation." Father Oswin's steady voice brought her back. "It's very important not to rush. Let the Spirit lead you one step at a time. Stay in constant tune with him through prayer."

Felicity sighed. She should have known.

"No snap decisions," he added.

Felicity nodded, even as she argued internally. *But that's how I make all my decisions,* she almost blurted it out. And it was the truth—for better or for worse, that was how she always made her decisions. Fast. Just a year ago, she had been teaching Latin in a C of E school in London. And hating it. When Rebecca, the vicar of the church sponsoring the school, reminded her that the church was one place Latin was still used and told her about the College of the Transfiguration, it immediately fired her imagination, and here she was—just like that—living through the most momentous year of her life.

"I don't know what your class schedule is like just now. Perhaps you have some time off before Easter, if you're thinking of starting right away?"

Felicity nodded. So he did sense her urgency.

"You won't be likely to find vacancies in any of the houses during Holy Week and, of course, you'll want to be here then anyway."

Holy Week. Yes, just over two weeks away. How she looked forward to that. Time to spend immersed in silence, in worship, in holy contemplation. She smiled at herself. If it hadn't been for Father Oswin's presence, she would have laughed out loud.

If she had been told a month ago that she would have felt eager anticipation for a week of prayer and worship, she would have declared that the speaker had taken leave of his senses. Now perhaps she was the one who had gone crazy.

"Yes, thank you, Father. Yes, Holy Week. I am looking forward to that. Everyone says it's an amazing experience." Again she smiled at herself. Fifty-some services in one week, most of it spent in silence. And she was looking forward to it. She truly must have gone round the twist, as the old Felicity would certainly have told her.

"Was there anything else you wanted to talk about?"

The length of her pause was telltale, but Father Oswin wouldn't probe even if he knew she was holding back. How could she discuss something she couldn't even put into words to herself? And what if she was wrong? After all, it wasn't really her problem until—*if*—Antony actually said something. Was it?

"No, nothing else. I've already taken too much of your time. Thank you, Father." She rose and hurried out. Should she have asked him to bless her? Would he have been expecting her to make her confession? She wished she knew more of the forms of this Alice-Through-the-Looking-glass world she had entered almost by accident.

As she made her way through the tangled passageways of the monastery back toward the college, the long skirt of her black cassock, regulation student wear, wrapped itself around her long legs, impeding the speed of her stride, but she still managed to move fast enough to make her almost waist-length golden hair flow behind her. Thoughts tumbled in her mind. She had been so certain Father Oswin could help her. Their little talks always helped. And he had given fairly concrete advice—as concrete as he ever did. So why was she even more confused than when she started?

Perhaps, a little voice niggled at the back of her mind, *because I didn't discuss the whole picture? But how could I? There isn't anything to discuss. And I would look such a fool if I'm wrong.* She shut the door on that train of thought.

So what about Father Oswin's suggestion that she take a sort of mini personal pilgrimage? She had heard others talking about making Lenten retreats. It seemed to be part of the system—the accepted thing. Why shouldn't she? Visit some convents. Get some practical idea of what she was really contemplating for her future. She had vaguely thought that the past seven months she had spent essentially living in a monastery as a student would have been preparation enough, but perhaps she did need to see a wider picture.

It made excellent sense, really. So why did she feel so reluctant to undertake what should be a very pleasant break? A few days in each convent, just getting the feel of the place. Meet a few nuns—the sort of women she would be living with. As Father Oswin said, it wouldn't be a real discernment process, but just enough to get the lay of the land, so to speak.

She would have to get permission to miss two lectures, but if she said it was at the advice of her spiritual director, it would surely be allowed. She had intended to finish her essay on the early sacramentaries and get started on her Old Testament paper, but they weren't really due yet. That wasn't the problem. Why was she who was always so ready to go and to do so reluctant to leave Kirkthorpe?

Still without an answer, she headed toward the common room where her fellow ordinands would be gathering before evening prayers, reading tattered copies of *The Church Times* or *The Church of England Newspaper*, depending upon their churchmanship, and sharing the latest gossip or debating the latest controversy in the church. But first, she would just stop by her cubby and check her mail—or post, as she was becoming accustomed to saying.

The usual notices: cantor tryouts for Holy Week services, workers needed for the weekly youth night at the St. James center in town, sign up for a day out to Rievaulx Abbey… And a letter. A real, written-on-paper, put-in-an-envelope letter. With a stamp bearing an American flag. Must be from her father, Andrew

Howard, a soft-spoken man who worked for the State of Idaho as an employment counselor, but whose main role had always been to keep the family ticking along while his lawyer wife worked an eighty-hour minimum week. Just holding this tangible contact from home gave her a sensation of warmth. She started to rip it open when the bell sounded for evening prayers. She stuck it in her pocket with the wry thought that delaying pleasure was good for the soul, and made her way into the soft, early April evening. Swathes of brilliant daffodils in the grass and birds chirping in the overhanging branches cheered her every step up the hill to the church as the bells continued to peal from the tower.

Oh, yes, yes, yes. Peace and beauty. This was what she loved. This was what she wanted for the rest of her life. She would obey and undertake the obligatory discernment, but there was really no need. She *knew*.

Inside the cool stone arches of the Community church, the ever-lingering scent of incense greeted her and the ancient quiet enfolded her. She turned to the side aisle to make her customary reverence to the icon of Our Lady of the Transfiguration, as did most of the monks of the Community and ordinands from the college.

Her eyes were still adjusting to the dim light as she bowed her head and crossed herself, then raised her eyes to the gentle face she knew so well: the Madonna with her head tilted so gently toward her infant Son, whose hand was raised in blessing and pointing to the background scene of Christ on the mountain top with Moses and Elijah. Felicity always loved the way the candlelight on the glowing gold background seemed to propel the dark-veiled Virgin and Child toward the votary, and the flickering light could seem to make the Transfigured Lord shimmer as he must have to the astounded disciples seeing him in his glory.

But this time, only the bare stone column met her uplifted gaze. The votive candle on the small shelf was cold. Only a smudge of smoke on the stone attested that it had ever been lit. Stifling her disappointment, Felicity turned to her seat in the choir and opened her prayer book. As every Friday in Lent, the evening psalm was 22: "My God, my God, why hast thou forsaken me", the Precentor set the first line of chant. As if taking a deep breath, the entire community paused for the caesura, then Felicity joined the response, "and art so far from my cry?"

But her mind only half-followed the familiar words and rhythms. It was almost three weeks yet until the Maundy Thursday ritual stripping of the church as if preparing a body for burial, followed by the Holy Saturday church cleaning when she had been told every student turned out to clean every dark corner, polish every crucifix and candlestick, dust every carved crevice as an important part of the ancient pattern of Holy Week. And, wasn't it the week before that—the week they called Passiontide—when all statues and images would be removed or veiled? Felicity was new to all this high church ritual she had taken to so suddenly and so wholeheartedly, but she was quite sure she had the information right. So why was the icon gone now? Perhaps they had removed it early to be sent away for professional cleaning? Or perhaps she needed repair, although Felicity hadn't noticed any damage on the vibrant image.

Bowing, kneeling and chanting with the collected college and community, Felicity was soon swept upward with the echoing prayers and wafting incense until, offering a final bow to the altar cross, she left her seat walking beside Neville Mortara, the ordinand who sat next to her. Neville turned aside to reverence the icon, but Felicity stopped him. "Don't bother," she whispered. "She's gone."

"Gone?" Neville's blue eyes startled beneath his gold-rimmed glasses. "Gone where?"

Felicity shrugged, "Cleaning, I suppose."

Neville shook his head. "She didn't need cleaning." He spoke with the authority of one who knew his field. Neville had achieved considerable success as an artist before coming to CT to study for the priesthood, and his dormitory room was so filled with treasures it looked like a miniature museum.

At the door, Neville dipped a long, white finger into the holy water stoop and extended his hand to share it with Felicity. Together they crossed themselves and went out into the late March evening.

Felicity smiled and looked up to continue chatting with Neville as they walked back down the hill to the refectory. It was unusual for Felicity, who stood slightly over five foot ten inches in her stocking feet, to be obliged to crane her neck for a conversation. The breeze whipped at their long black cassocks, and Felicity had the impression of the reed-like Neville swaying with the branches around them.

Neville, who was usually so easy to chat with and whose soft-spoken voice Felicity always found soothing, seemed oddly distracted. "Is something wrong, Neville?"

He gave a little half-startle. "Why do you say that? What should be wrong?" His brow furrowed under his pale fringe.

Before Felicity could answer they were joined by Neville's friend Maurice waving a copy of *the* latest issue of *Inclusive*. "Nev, have you *seen* this? A big rally at Manchester Cathedral—" The stocky redhead bore Felicity's companion away, and she at last had a moment to open her father's letter.

The breeze riffled the page as she pulled it from the envelope. Then she stopped dead in the middle of the stone path. "Oh, sorry," she said to the group behind her, and stepped aside. Blinking, she looked back at the paper in her hand. *Not* from her father. Her *mother* had written her a letter. On paper. By hand. No wonder she hadn't recognized the writing on the envelope. How often had she ever seen her mother's writing? Birthday cards "to our darling Felicity, love, Mother and Dad" had always been written by her father. "Have a happy day, Muffin" notes in her school lunch box had always been from her father. Forms for summer camp to be filled out and signed by a parent were signed in Andrew Howard's neat script. What on earth could have spurred the fast-moving, high-tech Cynthia to put pen to paper? An e-mail would have been shocking, but believable. Just. A letter was frightening.

And Felicity was right to be alarmed. Her stomach tightened and her breathing stopped as she read. Cynthia's law firm had joined one of the new international firms. She had a choice of joining the firm in Los Angeles or in London. "Of course, I could stay in Boise, but there seems little point in that with Jeff's consultancy job taking him to Asia all the time and Charlie and Judy settled in the Silicone Valley and your father and I getting a divorce…"

Felicity gave an audible gasp as she backed into a tree for support. Had she read that right? She smoothed the crumpled paper and looked again. Yes, there was no mistaking. That was what it said.

"Oh, how typical! Can you believe it?" She exploded with disgusted anger to no one in particular.

"Believe what?"

She turned to the rich tenor voice behind her. "Oh, Antony." She thrust the crumpled sheet at Antony with an angry growl as if he had written it. "My mother! How could she? How could she be so—so—oh, I don't know." *Stupid. Uncaring. Pig-headed. Impulsive. Rash. Selfish.* Words whirled through her head too fast to enunciate.

Antony looked up from a quick perusal of the sheet. "Your parents are divorcing?"

"She finally gets around to mentioning it as an aside. A postscript after discussing *her* job and what's a convenient place for *her* to live. I mean, no one pretended it was an ideal marriage. But they're *my parents.* They live together. At home. What is she thinking?"

"And she's coming to see you."

"*What?*" Felicity snatched the paper back. She hadn't read the concluding paragraph. "'… Sunday week after next, so we can have a nice visit before I look over the London office.'" Felicity shook her head. "A 'nice visit.' When did we ever have *a nice visit?* Why should we start now?"

"Um, Felicity," Antony ran his fingers upward through his thick dark hair, then flattened it again with a downward stroke. "Did you see the date on this?" He held out the envelope. "It took this two weeks to get here. She'll be here tomorrow."

Felicity threw her hands in the air. "Fine! She can come whenever she wants to. It's a free country and all that. But I won't be here." If she had had any doubts about leaving, this settled the matter.

When Antony didn't reply, she continued, "I'm going on retreat. Rempstone. To test my vocation. Father Oswin's orders. Oh, and I'll be missing your church history lecture on Monday."

A far corner of Felicity's mind registered the fact that all color drained from Antony's face when she mentioned testing her vocation. She supposed she could have broken it to him more gently, but now it was out. Just as well. She certainly didn't need another complication to her life.

"We need to talk, Felicity." Antony spoke in a tight voice and handed her letter back to her stiffly.

"I don't want to talk about it. Not now." *Maybe never.*

He gave a jerky nod. "All right. But what I meant was that I need to talk to you. I've just come from Father Anselm's office."

Hearing the name of the Father Superior of the Community immediately took Felicity back to that day just a few weeks ago that now seemed like another world, when she had so blithely set out with Antony to solve Father Dominic's murder. Little could she have foreseen what a different person she would be now.

"He's asked me to undertake another investigation," Antony said.

"Not another murder?" Felicity blanched and her voice rose in alarm.

"No, no. Nothing so dramatic. Our Lady of the Transfiguration has disappeared."

"Oh, I noticed she was gone. I thought she'd been sent out for cleaning or something."

"Sadly, nothing so easily explained, I'm afraid."

"So why don't they call the police?"

"Father Anselm suspects—well, shall we say, an inside job? He'd rather have it handled quietly."

"He wouldn't suspect one of the brethren. That must mean a student. I don't believe it. Not even as a prank, surely."

"I suppose a prank is a possibility. But I think he had something more specific in mind. A well-known artist and collector who might have reason to—shall we say, borrow her for closer study?"

Felicity was outraged. "You mean Neville. What an absurd accusation! We were talking about it just a minute ago. I'm the one who told him the icon was missing. I'm certain he didn't know anything about it."

Antony shrugged. "Well, I have to follow up. If it's returned quietly that will be the end of it."

"Why doesn't the superior ask himself?"

"He wants the whole thing kept low-key. The thing is, a representative of the Patriarch of Moscow is coming for the Triduum."

"To Kirkthorpe? For Holy Week? Oh, is that part of your ecumenical thingy?"

"In a way. Our icon was said to have been brought to England by Peter the Great on his Great Embassy. The Russian Orthodox Church has made inquiries about our loaning it for an exhibition they're assembling."

"Oh, I get it. And so this emissary of his holiness shows up here in less than three weeks and we've mislaid the icon. Not good for ecumenical relations, to say the least."

"That's it exactly. And Father Anselm said that I—we—did so well last time, he was hoping…"

Felicity shook her head and took a step backward. "Sorry. My plate's more than full. But good luck and all that." She turned and started walking rapidly toward the dining hall, no matter how little she fancied the Friday night Lenten vegetarian fare that would be awaiting her. Then she paused. "I mean it.

Really. Good luck."

Just before the path curved downhill she hesitated once more. "I'm off for Rempstone on the first train in the morning." She flung it over her shoulder, neither knowing nor caring whether he heard her. But when she allowed herself a brief backward glimpse she was struck by his bruised look.

About the Author

Donna Fletcher Crow is a lifelong Anglophile and history buff. She has written more than thirty books, most of them dealing with the history of British Christianity, including the award-winning *Glastonbury: The Novel of Christian England* and a six-book series, *The Cambridge Chronicles*. *The Monastery Murders* series has grown out of her extensive research trips and pilgrimages to England and Scotland. Donna is a Companion of the Community of the Resurrection in Mirfield, Yorkshire, which serves as a model for her fictional Community of the Transfiguration.

She and her husband live in Boise, Idaho. They are the parents of four adult children and have ten young grandchildren. When not writing or working in her English cottage garden, Donna is kept busy visiting their sons and families who live from coast to coast in the US, and their daughter in Canada who is married to a Church of England priest.

PART I

WELFARE AND
ECONOMIC EFFICIENCY